Gay Dwarves of America

Stories by **Anne Fleming**

PEDLAR PRESS | Toronto

ACKNOWLEDGEMENTS
The publisher wishes to thank the Canada Council
for the Arts and the Ontario Arts Council for their
generous support of our publishing program.

LIBRARY AND ARCHIVES CANADA
CATALOGUING IN PUBLICATION

Fleming, Anne, 1964-
Gay dwarves of America / Anne Fleming.

Short stories.
ISBN 978-1-897141-46-5

I. Title.

PS8561.L44G39 2012   C813'.54   C2012-901453-2

COVER Nancy Beatty (artwork)
Zab Design & Typography (design)

BOOK DESIGN Zab Design & Typography, Toronto

TYPEFACES Gotham Book (body)
Zag Drops Thin (titles)

Printed in Canada

THE CANADA COUNCIL | LE CONSEIL DES ARTS
FOR THE ARTS | DU CANADA
SINCE 1957 | DEPUIS 1957

ONTARIO ARTS COUNCIL
CONSEIL DES ARTS DE L'ONTARIO

Unicycle Boys   8

Gay Dwarves of America   30

Thorn-blossoms   52

Backstock: The Musical   76

Soyez Blessé   100

Peter Who Once Loved Margaret   114

Puke Diary   130

The Pear   158

Thirty-One One Word Stories   174

There is always a boy on a unicycle. It is not the same boy, but if you collected them together, you'd quickly see what they have in common, besides, of course, curly hair and skinny legs and a certain angularity of shoulder, a certain quality to their skin, be it brown or olive or pink, as if beneath the troubled *epi-* lay a clear and radiant *dermis*.

I saw one of them last night on the corner of University Boulevard and the East Mall, balancing on his unicycle as he waited for the light to change, three pedals forward, three pedals back, three forward, three back, wobbling elegantly there in the dark next to other students in jackets and backpacks. And I remembered Curtis.

Curtis didn't yet have a unicycle when I first met him. He was a boy in flood pants and a Bobby Brady haircut and we were both in ecumenical school, a Wednesday-afternoon equivalent to Sunday School, only cooler, since you didn't have to dress up. The leaders were thirtysomething approxi-hippies, the men in beards and corduroys, the women in peasant blouses and loose skirts. They'd probably never been actual hippies, but now that the whole thing was basically over, they could imply they had and no one would know the difference. They all played guitar.

No one I knew went to ecumenical school—no one from my school that is, no one who mattered—so I could hang out with Curtis with impunity. I probably would have anyway at that point, but you never know. He was short then, prepubescent. His flood pants would get floodier before he was done growing.

He bounced when he walked, the full height of his foot from ball to heel—what's that, maybe two to three inches in an eleven-year-old? He waved his hands when he talked. He stood too close or too far away. He was abrupt and overly direct sometimes and elliptical and evasive other times. But he was imaginative and I liked him. I don't know what either of us thought about religion. I imagined myself to be a believer, but looking back from a place of unbelief it's hard to know how sincere I was. Curtis, I think, had a *Jesus Christ Superstar* vision of it all. Fittingly, ecumenical school seemed to involve a lot of playacting. One teacher was big on historical context and motivation, a Stanislavski for the hippy Christian set. Curtis always played Jesus if he could, though he was fond of the Old Testament prophets, too, and he wouldn't turn down John the Baptist. One time when he was Jesus and I was Mary Magdalene, he put his hand on my breast—they were new to me then and not very large—moved it around a bit and said, "We had sex, you know."

I stepped away from him.

"You and me."

"Yeulgh. Curtis."

"Jesus and Mary Magdalene."

"How do you know that?"

"I just do."

"You are so full of it."

His hand on my breast had felt like nothing much, not even like a hand somewhere else, on my back or shoulder, say, like my friends' when they brushed my hair, or my father's when we went for a ramble in the fall colours and he stopped to point out a bird or a fungus or a fox I had overlooked. I don't know if Curtis felt anything either. Nevertheless, another two or three times if we were together fetching something from a remote cupboard or stealing down one of the labyrinthine halls of the church basement, we stopped and pressed our lips together while Curtis kneaded my small and tender new breasts. Then it was June and ecumenical school was over. The following year I took confirmation classes at my regular church and didn't see Curtis again until he was seventeen and had his unicycle.

It was during Caravan, a big multicultural festival in Toronto featuring food and folk dancing: perogies and polka, haggis and highland reels, calamari and calypso. I was working as a clown for the children's pavilion, which was run by a charity. I made a terrible clown. Who talked me into it I don't recall, but there must have been somebody. I hate clowns, always have. I think they appeal more to adults than to children, especially the sad ones. In sad clowns it's no stretch for adults to see themselves, foolish and lonely, boo-hooing in a spotlight. Luckily, my main function at Caravan was to give out balloons that said "Inner City Angels," a function that required me to be neither sad nor entertaining, and most children would run up to me, snag a balloon and run off again without asking more. Some eyed me uncertainly, as if waiting for a wink at the very least. Others, frightened of clowns, hid behind their parents until coaxed. One actually said to me, "You're not a real clown."

"Oh no?" I asked, pretending I didn't mind and thinking I really ought to be talking differently, I really ought to come up with some kind of clown voice. Not to have done, to be speaking in my regular voice, seemed like a failure of courage, of imagination.

"No."

"Have I got a red nose?"

"Yeah."

"Have I got rainbow hair?"

"Yeah."

"Have I got a polka-dot outfit with big pompom buttons?"

"Yeah."

"Have I got big yellow shoes?"

"Yeah."

"Then I'm a clown. Here, have a balloon." When, for the comedy of it, I in later years told friends I'd been a clown, I would say I had said, "Shut up and have a balloon." In truth I was less a mean-ass clown than a dull one.

That night while studying for my Chemistry exam I found an old slide whistle in my desk drawer. I took it with me the next day, foreswearing talk. *Wa-woo-oop, wa-woo-oop*, I whistled. Balloo-ons, balloo-ons. *Toot-toot-toot-wa-woo-oop.* Come get your balloo-ons.

I was extremely bored.

Halfway through the week, Curtis appeared. No nose, no outfit, no makeup. All he did was pedal his unicycle up the path towards me. Children thronged him. They turned their heads from face painting as he wobbled my way. They abandoned the balloon lineup. Boys ran alongside him shouting, Can we try? Can we try? while he grinned.

I recognized him straight off—something about the way he held himself, all straight lines and sharp angles, like a three-dimensional stick man.

He, rolling towards me with the cuffs of his too-short jeans flapping, baby-blue-ringed tube socks flashing and the wallet in his front left pocket outlining itself against the thigh of his jeans with each upswing of his leg, saw only a clown. I saw his almost-the-same hair, I saw his face, unchanged but for a ridge, a Quaker's beard, of acne along the jaw. I saw one of those unfortunate boys whose features puberty barely changes, while around them walk boys inside sudden men.

He balanced before me, pedalling half a revolution forward, half a revolution back, two forward, two back, as the boys, dodging him, were going, Wo-ho. Wo-oh-ho-ho.

I needn't have said anything. I could have just given him a balloon and watched him ride off or play with the children or whatever it was he would have done had I not, in response to his request for a balloon, opted for speech rather than slide whistle and said, "Sure, Curtis. Want two?"

He forgot to pedal. Backward past the point of balance he teetered, boys scattering as unicycle shot out from under him. A long millisecond passed, during which all he had to do was straighten his legs and he'd be standing on them. But no. He landed first on heels, then butt, leaping up immediately, sweaty-faced, plucking his unicycle out from under the covetous gaze of the youngsters.

"Do I know you?"

"Not in the biblical sense." This was a phrase my friends and I had taken to using lately, pleased with our worldliness. "Or wait, actually, yes, in the biblical sense, in a way." He looked off-put, unsure. "Call me Mary. Mary 'Chuckles' Magdalene." There was a clown named Chuckles on the *Mary Tyler Moore Show*.

"Pardon me?"

"Mister, can we try your unicycle?"

"Not right now. Mary 'Chuckles' Magdalene? You're a Christian clown?"

I laughed and sang a vampy few lines of a song we had sung at ecumenical school, *It only takes a spark—va-va-va-va— to get a fire going,* winking and tacking on a whoop-whoo from my slide whistle at the end.

"Jenny?"

"Praise the Lord. I thought this was going to go on all day."

"Can we try your unicycle now?"

"It's too tall for you, your feet won't reach the pedals. Jenny. Wow. I always thought I'd run into you again some day."

"Did you?" I should have let that be a warning. "Well, now you have. Howya been?"

I'd meant it as a joke, but he answered. After ecumenical school, he'd gotten really into religion, reading the Bible in its entirety and having theological debates with his Bible study class, until a few years later he realized that religion was the opiate of the people and he stopped going to church, which was just fine with his lapsed Methodist parents, who'd stopped going to church themselves around the same time in order to explore 'alternate spiritualities,' and who had subsequently invited their Rebirthing coach and her Yogic husband to move in with them, which arrangement had almost driven Curtis back to church, if only for the peaceful banality of it, until at last they had let their pee mellow in the toilet one more time than Curtis's mother could handle and she had asked them to move out. Thankfully, both parents had gone abroad on sabbatical this year, leaving him and his sister in peace, not that it was a literal peace, since his sister broke it playing French horn three hours a day. He'd done five years of school in four and was graduating this year and going to U of T for pre-med.

"Great to catch up. See you in another five," I said.

"But now you have to tell me about you," he said.

Joke, Curtis. Joke.

He stuck around all afternoon, delivering balloons to children on his unicycle, juggling, sucking helium, fetching me lemonade and cookies, and lying on the grass telling me about himself. I knew he'd be back the next day and he was.

I had recently decided to become a femme fatale. I almost had the looks for it, the dark hair, the full figure, the pale face. More to the point, I had discovered I was bored with my last boyfriend, a good-looking and popular boy who couldn't conceive why I might dump him, and who was proving himself all the more stricken since being spurned. I confess I got a kick out of it. I read his letters to my friends and we laughed and laughed. He even wrote poems.

Jennifer, Jennifer, the latest had gone,
The name with the knife in the middle.
Jennifer, Jennifer,
The girl with the knife, the riddle
Of my life.
Knife, life, Jennifer.
You kill me.

Kinda clever, actually, for a jockish seventeen-year-old. He'd improved since his first, which went,

Sweet Jennifer,
I see you in your skirt,
And my insides hurt.
What did I do wrong?
I long
For your kiss.
It's what I miss.
What did I do?
I tell you I'll be true.
Forever, forever,
Sweet Jennifer.

I wasn't thinking of any of this during my clown stint, though. Hanging out with Curtis made me feel like a kid again. He brought a clown nose with him the next day, his face already made up. The same jeans as yesterday were held up by rainbow-coloured suspenders. "You're really into this," I said. He shrugged, but his eyes shone.

In the slow period in the morning, he taught me to juggle, while he himself tried to go from five balls to six. He had a determination about him that had the mark of eternity on it. He would never give up.

Despite having seen the children running after him the

day before, I had had a feeling that Curtis couldn't possibly be a good clown—something to do with his hands, the way he wore them like foreign appendages—but in fact he was. He knew what look to make when he dropped a ball the first time and what look to make the second time and the third. He knew that children like to be teased and he knew that clowns don't laugh at their own jokes, a mistake I made the first time Curtis interpreted my slide whistle utterances.

"I'd like a balloon please," said an appealing little girl.

"One? Or two?" I whistled, which Curtis interpreted to the child as, "Whew! You smell." Which is where I laughed.

"It didn't say that," the kid said, not laughing herself because she feared my laughter meant I was making fun of her. I tried to contain myself.

"Did you say that?" Curtis asked me. I whistled something longer.

"You're right," Curtis said to the kid. "She didn't say, 'Whew, you smell,' she said, 'There's a dreadful odour arising from the general vicinity of this child.'"

Now the girl giggled. "She did not."

"She did. I can tell you, I'm the universally acknowledged expert in clown interpretation, and this clown distinctly said, 'There's a dreadful odour arising from the general vicinity of this child.'"

"Naww, that's too many syllables."

"It takes a lot more syllables to say something in English than it takes in clown." To me: "Say something else."

I whistled *Pop goes the weasel.*

"See? Now what the clown said right there was, 'Tomorrow and tomorrow and tomorrow creeps in this petty pace from day to day to the last syllable of recorded time.'"

"No-ho-ho, it didn't, it said, 'Pop goes the weasel.'"

This could go on for hours, not with the same child, but with different ones. At times, both our clown reserves broke and we would be laughing too hard to even speak, and parents would get impatient and scurry towards us from their place on the path with a look that seemed to ask who'd put these teenagers in charge.

When the last day was done and we were de-clowning

ourselves, I sensed in both of us reluctance to part.

"You want to go to the Ukrainian pavilion for perogies?" Curtis asked.

"Sure," I said. A slab of cold cream on toilet paper wiped away his makeup, revealing the ridge of acne. Faintly disgusted and strangely compassionate, I immediately regretted saying yes.

Awkwardness descended on us, as if the patina of childishness protecting us the last few days had come off with the grease paint. Nonetheless, we tried. We walked up to College Street, or rather I walked and Curtis pedalled, talking of Shakespearean insults, *Star Wars*, epics in general, our best and worst teachers. At the Ukrainian Cultural Centre, a large choir sang dense, beautiful harmonies like I'd never heard before, and Curtis ate my perogies as well as his own.

I recognized a girl from my school in the choir, a solid, large-nosed girl good in sports looking unspeakably beautiful in her traditional costume, blending her voice with her compatriots, the closeness of their harmonies seeming to evoke community and acceptance. I had quit choir that year because I hated the choirmaster, hated the earnestness of choral singing. Now I regretted that, and regretted being dull and Anglo, our culture too dominant to need nurturing like this, to involve togetherness like this. English folk songs were foisted on all general choirs, where they felt less like heritage than smarm. Fa la la la la. Here at the Ukrainian Cultural Centre, I wanted to cry it was so beautiful, the girl, the song, the group of them there, the applause afterwards. Curtis loved it, too. I would have ditched him if he hadn't.

We walked to the subway in the warm June evening talking of our lives, our families: my happily repressed parents, kind to each other, baffled by me, dull as toast right down to their names, John and Mary; his sister, the Human French Horn, his parents, Edwina and Jack, their mid-life crises. I didn't figure on his looking us up in the phone book. I didn't figure on his showing up at my school to—I have no doubt this was his intention—*walk me home*. I didn't want to be a femme fatale with Curtis. I wanted him to stay in his box: Kid known briefly in past, accidentally re-met in one of those Toronto crossings of paths that occur while Christmas shopping at the Eaton Centre or lining up for a movie or riding the subway, those hap meetings in which you catch up, give each other a warm buzz about your former selves, and then don't have to worry about for another three years. Or six. Or seventeen.

My friends and I ridiculed people. It's what we did, what we spent our days and nights doing. We ridiculed the penny-loafered, plaid-ribboned prepsters (who in turn heaped scorn on anyone not them). We ridiculed mall sluts. Scarberians. Welfare moms. White stoner boys in Black Sabbath t-shirts. Black boys with tape decks glued to their shoulders. (We called the tape decks *ghetto blasters* until everyone did, at which point we reverted to *boom box* and pretended we'd never called them anything else.) Browners, geeks, jocks, artsies, burnouts, people with bad shoes, bad hair, big hair, no hair. Men with rugs, men with comb-overs. Men in gabardine slacks. Users of the word *slacks*. Users of the word *youse*. Women in housedresses. Immigrant widows in black. Middle-class WASP housewives in fake-wood-panelled station wagons (our mothers). Middle-class WASP men in suits. Middle-class WASP men in pink golf shirts. Each other. Ourselves.

Who even *were* ourselves? What group did we think we belonged to? Hard to remember. Smart girls with sharp wits, girls who argued with teachers, who questioned authority, who mouthed off but got good marks, girls who thought themselves worldly. Girls who scorned membership in a group.

I could not, as I walked with my friends out of school after a chemistry exam, pretend not to know Curtis, or even not to notice him. It was what snotty preppy girls would have done.

Martha said idly, rhetorically, "Who's the geek on the unicycle?"

"Curtis Myers," I said. Also, it was a good line.

"What? You know him?"

"We went to ecumenical school together."

"Ecumenical school?" Rose asked.

"Ohmygod, *he's* the one who felt you up?" I had known Martha longer than Rose. Most of the stories there were to tell about myself she knew, and vice versa.

"You got felt up at ecumenical school?" asked Rose. "What is ecumenical school?"

"He didn't feel me up, he put his hand on my tits." I had recently started saying *tits* rather than *breasts*. I liked how it was coarser. I liked how it bugged Rose.

"You know I hate that word."

"Tits, tits, tits," I said, and then I shouted, "Curtis!" and waved.

He wobbled over, arms outstretched, pant legs flapping as before, this time revealing one grey sock and one blue. His dismount, with unicycle shooting out the front then snatched in a left-hand grab, was clearly rehearsed.

"Good afternoon, ladies," he said. Oh God. *Ladies*.

"Which do you prefer, Curtis, 'tits' or 'breasts'?"

"Jenny!" Rose swatted me.

Curtis flushed.

"No, I'm doing a survey. Which is it?"

Curtis tapped his chin and looked into the distance.

Martha said, "Are those the only two options? How about hooters?"

"Bosom," Rose said.

"Bazoombas," said Martha. "Jugs. Honkers."

"'Her bosom heaved as he pressed his manhood against her,'" I said. "Who has a bosom, I ask you."

"Dames," said Martha. "Sophisticated dames got bosoms."

"No. No. Swedish farm girls."

"Elderly matrons. Nuns."

"Nuns have bosoms?"

"Sure. You don't think they have tits, do you?"

"Come on, Jenny. You're giving this poor boy conniptions."

"Con*nip*tions. Con*nip*tions. Where does *that* come from? Okay, Curtis, ready? Your answer is?"

"I'm dubious it would be politic of me to answer," he blurted out, as if he'd spent the whole time composing the sentence, as no doubt he had. But we would not let him off. We crossed our arms and tapped our fingers until he gave. "Um...breasts, I guess."

"Survey says? Ding ding ding ding ding! The beautiful Amana radar range is yours!"

"You know," Rose said, "it took me the longest time to figure out what that was."

"It's a stove," said Martha. "Range is American for stove."

"I just always had this idea it couldn't be a regular stove, it had to be some special military stove, you know? Radar range? Like you could watch out for incoming missiles while you baked your meatloaf."

Curtis was standing awkwardly, clutching his unicycle, gawking at each speaker in turn. I thought he looked bowled over. I thought he looked charmed by our banter. I thought he looked nervous. It was out of character for him to say so little. I was relieved he said so little.

"So, Curtis, what brings you to this neck of the woods this fine afternoon?"

"I was wondering if you wanted to go see *The Empire Strikes Back* with me tonight so I can prove to you it's a timeless epic." When I think of it now, how brave. How brave of him to ask me out like that in front of my friends.

"Tonight?"

"It is, it is, it is short notice, but—"

"Il faut étudier."

"What?"

"French exam. Tomorrow."

"Oh. Right. Well. Maybe another night? Can I call you?"

"Uhhhh, sure."

He stuck the unicycle in his crotch, flung himself up on it and rode off with a parting symmetrical to his greeting. "Afternoon, ladies."

"Jen's got an admirer," Rose said, waggling her eyebrows.

"Why does this *happen* to me?"

"Wait," said Martha, trying to figure it out. "You haven't seen him since grade eight and he shows up after your chemistry exam to ask you to *The Empire Strikes Back*?"

"That's right." Ba-da-boom. "No, I ran into him at Caravan. It was fun, actually. He's kind of a neat guy. In a loserish sort of way."

"Did you see his face?" Martha grabbed her tits, raising them one at a time as if in conversation with her and with each other. "Breast? Tit? Breast? Tit? Oh my God."

"When do you think he'll realize he didn't get your number?" Rose asked, pretending to buff her nails.

Oh, how we loved ourselves. Oh, how we raced home and wallowed privately in bouts of self-hatred, of name-calling. Idiot. Stupid. Idiot. How could you have said that, that was so... Maybe nobody noticed. Maybe... No, they noticed. Idiot.

At least, I doubt it was just me.

"Jenny. Telephone."

"If it's Ted, I'm not here," I said loudly enough that if it were Ted he would hear.

"I am not your secretary," my mother said, handing me the phone.

"Hello?"

"Hi, Jenny." It was Curtis, though he didn't say so.

"A little tip, Curtis? It's polite to tell people you're phoning who you are."

"Oh." There was a short pause. "So when can you go see *The Empire Strikes Back*?"

"Uhhh, I don't know if— I'm kind of— No, I'm sorry, forget that, that's an excuse —I'm just, actually, frankly, not that interested in seeing *The Empire Strikes Back*."

"Oh."

"I mean, I thought the first movie was basically just—okay yeah with a few amusing moments—stupid, and I can't see liking this one any better. Basically just, you know, a little boy's fantasy. I mean, 'The Force.' Come on."

I thought he would argue. Instead he said, "Would you come to my grade thirteen formal with me?"

Time. Buy time. "When is it?"

"Next Friday."

Damn. Saturday I could have swiftly said no to. Our own formal was Saturday and I had been keeping it open in case a manly and savagely funny guy I had a crush on invited me, even though the likelihood of his doing so had already decreased past zero. The fact that he'd not invited anyone else either kept me hoping and my friends more convinced than ever he was gay.

"Next Friday. Let me see..." But I was caught. My mental

calendar had clearly shouted *free*. And, too, I had decided that as femme fatale I was not going to lie where these things were concerned. I was going to tell boys I didn't want to go out with that I didn't want to go out with them. Some of them had proved amazingly persistent in the face of such honesty. Witness Ted, the poet.

I riffed through some pages on the telephone table anyway to make it sound like I was checking a calendar and told him my slate was clear. Sure I'd come to his formal.

And so I arrived at Fantasy Farm on the arm of a gawky boy in full eighteenth-century garb—knickers, silk stockings, shirt with puffed sleeves, cravat, plum-coloured jacket. It was an outfit from his summer job at a recreated historic site in Nova Scotia. The only thing he'd left off was the wig. Too itchy.

"If I'd known, I could've worn my Marie Antoinette getup," I said when he picked me up in his father's Lada.

"Seriously?"

"Good God, are you crazy? You'd need a garage just to keep it in." I wore a 50s cocktail dress I'd got from Courage My Love a few days before, midnight blue, raw silk, plenty of décolletage, scalloped neck line, full skirt, little cap sleeves. Bobby-pinned to my head was a matching little saddle-shaped hat with a black half-veil. It was the sort of dress you could be a dame in, a gum-snappin', smart-talkin' full-figured floozy. Curtis looked like Mozart. We were quite the pair.

"Come on, Sugar, aren't you going to tell me I look fabulous?" I said the way I would have to my crush, who would have said, *Darling, of course you look fabulous. It goes without saying.* And I would have said, *You don't say.* And he would have said, *I do say.* My friends were right. He was gay.

Curtis blushed, laughed awkwardly. He ground the gears and avoided looking at me, which I interpreted to mean he did think I looked fabulous, he just didn't know how to say so.

He hadn't brought anything to drink. I had a mickey of rum snugged into a reticule in my purse, rum and Coke, I hasten to explain, being the drink of the day. I confess to not having tried much else except the standard issue: Baby Duck, Southern Comfort, Kahlua. The sweet drinks of teens.

We parked at the far end of the lot. Curtis practically ran around the car to open my door. From the bushes in front of the car came a call.

"Curtis! My man!" A gorgeous smooth-skinned boy with a long pony tail stepped out of the bushes in a tux. "That is some outfit."

Curtis did a double take.

A second boy emerged. Except he wasn't a boy, he was a girl. In a tux. Oh my God, and so was the first one.

"I see you got yourself a date. Sorry I couldn't help you out there, buddy."

He'd asked someone else? He'd asked a lesbian? I wanted to whack him with my purse. Foolish, I know. Why feel insulted he'd asked anyone but me? Before Caravan, I was an unknown star in his dating universe. Plus, he clearly hadn't known until this second that this girl was a lesbian.

"Holy crow," Curtis said. Recovering himself, he introduced me to Karen, who introduced us to her date, Mary. Or, as they called each other, Mare and Kare. They were already a little tipsy.

"Care for another nip, Mare?"

"Kare, another nip would be dandy."

I had never known any lesbians, although come to think of it, there were a couple of my mother's friends, birders both, who seemed a likely pair. These ones were much more exciting.

"Curtis? A nip?"

He hesitated. "Why not?"

"Step into our bushes."

We had several nips from Karen's hip flask.

"Don't think I've seen you around the hallowed halls," Karen said to me.

"I go to Lawrence," I said.

"Ah," she said knowingly.

"Exactly."

"Mare's from Bishop Strachan. Sh."

"What are we drinking?"

"Do you care?"

"Have you done this before?" I asked.

"Gone to the formal with a girl? Can't say as I have. Nope."

"Gonna shock the pants off them, Kare," Mare said.

"Gonna shock the something or other, that's for sure. And you, Curtis, you. You're going to shock the something or other, too, eh?"

"Kare," Curtis said. "There are more than a few who could use some shocking."

Karen held out her arm to her date. "Shall we, Mare?"

"Kare. We shall."

Then Curtis held his arm out to me and I took it, and we strode the length of the parking lot.

In grade two or three, around the time girls and boys are pitting themselves against each other again after a chummy hiatus, my girlfriends and I used to link arms, six or seven of us, and stomp through the schoolyard chanting, *We don't stop for a-ny-body, we don't stop for a-ny-body,* mowing down anyone in our path. Even when the anyone was not a boy, this was one of childhood's great pleasures. To be linked with others. To defy. To overpower.

Arm in arm with Curtis, behind Mare and Kare, I felt that exact feeling as we swept past the rearing cement horses flanking the entrance path and mounted the flagstone steps. My hand clasped the inside of Curtis's bony elbow with solidarity, with new meaning.

Ahead and behind us streamed other, more regularly clad couples, meaning, in 1981, girls in solid-coloured satin dresses with puffed sleeves, sashed waists and pleated skirts and boys in wide-lapelled tuxes or else white disco suits with open-necked, solid-coloured, satin shirts.

At the brow of the hill, the path forked. To the right, the sign directed us, was the Make-believe Ballroom. To the left, Cinderella's Cottage.

Mare stopped dead in front of the sign. "No," she said. "Not possible."

"Possible, Mare," Kare said. People were piling up behind us.

Is that two guys? said a voice ten feet back.

I don't know, said another, *looks like it.*

"Come on, let's go. Maybe Friendly'll be there," Kare said, propelling Mare forward and taking the next set of steps lightly, two at a time.

More voices, stopped, as we had been, in front of the sign.

Oh my God, they can't be serious. Make-believe Ballroom? Gag me with a spoon.

What's with the guy in the—

Pansy outfit? I don't know.

Oh, hey, I know, I know, he's in character. *He dressed for the* Make-believe Ballroom*!*

I wondered if this were true and then felt guilty. Curtis would have worn the outfit no matter where the formal were held. He had almost certainly *not* dressed for the Make-believe Ballroom. And yet it was uncanny that his outfit should so fit. The style of make-believe favoured by Fantasy Farm might have been anything—South Pacific, Arabian Nights, anything— but in fact was firmly European Fairy Tale. The walls, faux stone, were interrupted by cathedral-style arched doorways at one end of the room and at the other faux-doorways backed by mirrors so as to make the ballroom look vast. The windows were faux-leaded glass. Light came from lanternesque wall-lights, glowing orange in the still-bright evening.

We paused just inside the doors, taking in our surroundings.

A girl rustled up to Karen. Lemon-yellow satin. Pinned-up wheat-blonde hair. Fine eyebrows. Scornful mouth. "Excuse me, Karen, just because you think the formal's stupid doesn't mean you have to ruin it for everyone else with your I'm-a-lezzie-freak game."

"Lisa. It's not a game. I really am a lezzie-freak."

"Well, I just want to say, I think it's wrong." In the background, an athletic-looking guy shouted, *Don't listen to her, Mackay, you're cool,* while a guy next to him repeatedly called out his phone number, saying, *Three's company, don't forget.*

"Thank you, Lisa. You know how I value your opinion. I just want to say that I think you are a big bimbo and I'm glad I'm never going to have to see you again." Kare headed for a table in the far corner. "Mare? Remind me why we did this?"

"Shock the pants, Kare, shock the pants."

"Right."

"A pox upon you for a vicious viper," Curtis called over his shoulder to Lisa. His face had broken out in a sweat.

Kare put her hand on his arm. "Curtis. My man. Thank you."

Solidarity.

At our table we managed a few more nips. No one was dancing yet. A scattered few—the ugly, the less popular, the immigrant couples—sat at tables. The greater number stood in clumps in the open space inside the door poised to fall on their newly arriving friends so all could gush and feel watched and admired by the room because, look, they had friends and their friends liked them and were funny, ha ha, yes, they were liked, people liked them, look how people liked them. This was the girls. The boys did the same thing differently, casually rolling away from the girl-talk, hands in pockets, nodding at their buddies, forming their own little clumps. And then a new couple would enter, the process would repeat and the two circles grow. Eventually the couples reunited, moved off, found tables, where no one sat down, but the girls reserved seats with clutch purses.

Everyone seemed more grown up than at my school, and I realized it was because I knew no one, neither their history nor their character. All I had was the external shell of them—tonight, their best, most lacquered shells—and those shells were grown up ones. One couple, it looked like it could have been their wedding. He was a tall, gorgeous black man with loose, elegant posture and the most delicious-looking mustache—broad, thick and short, with a little blank bit in the middle above the lip. She was a tall, gorgeous Chinese girl with high cheekbones and perfect lips and a dress like mine except better. Their hands were entwined. They were the only couple that didn't break into boy and girl upon entering. They glowed. And then I saw that everyone around them glowed. The in-love couples, the out-of-love couples, the couples on first dates clueless with each other, they all glowed. This evening was a culmination for them. They had finished something. They were about to start on something new. They were participants. I was watching. This felt like an epiphany.

Apart from Lisa, some finger pointing and a lot of turned heads, there was remarkably little reaction to Kare and Mare's presence. Curtis got more comments. Whoever had come up with the idea he'd dressed expressly for the Make-believe Ballroom had to be a talker. On one trip to the bar for Cokes, every second person he passed called him Prince Charming. He bore this good-humouredly.

And then a group of rowdy white kids entered, five or six couples that seemed completely familiar to me, and I realized that if it were my own formal, that is the group I would have been with. I didn't like them. I didn't like the way they burst into the room as if we had all been waiting for them, as if they wanted everyone to know they'd had a fancy, grown up dinner party ahead of time, where the liquor flowed freely and the spirits were high. One boy immediately got up on a chair and yelled, "Class of '81, I salute you," while his friends made like they were embarrassed and ineffectually tugged at his sleeves when really they were already rehearsing how they were going to talk about it afterwards. And then I realized, with a sick feeling, that Ted was one of them. My ex-boyfriend. The poet.

At the same time, Curtis bounced back across the floor with his usual goofy gait, bowing floridly as people called him Prince Charming, almost spilling the Coke I planned to pour rum into.

I turned my head away. Was it possible to avoid Ted for the entire evening or should I approach him right off and get it out of the way? I was just thinking the latter when Curtis returned with our drinks, the lights went down, the DJ began to fade in the first song, and the student council president— the beautiful Chinese girl, natch—welcomed everybody, gave a slide show of a dozen-odd shots that included Curtis in school colours on his unicycle at a football game—"Ride 'em, Prince Charming!" someone shouted—waxed eloquent about endings and beginnings—"Please. Please. I'm getting all choked up here," Karen said—and enjoined us to have a good time as "Betty Davis Eyes" came up and the mirror ball turned.

Inevitably I did run into him, you know that already.

There was only so long I could keep Curtis from dancing. It was his formal, not mine. I owed it to him. Mare and Kare had been cutting a rug since the get-go. After forty minutes or so, I finally gave up the winsome chatter I'd been entertaining Curtis with and let him ask me to dance. Two songs later I had to pee and left Curtis dancing with Mare and Kare. And on the way to the washroom, there was Ted.

"Jenny." He was completely taken aback. "You look... You look fantastic."

"Thank you."

"Who are you here with?"

"Ted—"

"Innocent question."

"Ted, I really have to pee."

He stood in front of me. Not threateningly, I should point out. Joke-threateningly. He was in no way scary.

I turned and pointed then pushed past Ted toward the washroom.

"Hang on. Who?" Ted squinted at the dance floor.

"The one with the lesbians in tuxes."

"No, really, show me the guy. I'm not going to hurt him, I just want to know."

"I'm not joking, Ted. That's Curtis. That's who I came with."

Ted let go of my arm. His hand went up to his mouth and he burst into the high-pitched, eye-shutting laughter of shock, disbelief, ridicule. He pointed, laughter-limp, at Curtis, then at me, then at Curtis, then at himself. He hooted. He bent over. He slapped his leg.

"Shut up, Ted, it's a mercy date."

I went to the bathroom and peed. Coming out of the cubicle, I glimpsed myself in the mirror. Before fully knowing it was me, I thought, "Wow." And then I looked closer. Femme fatale? Or femme comique? Or comique femme fatale ironique? I felt suddenly sad and uncertain. I wouldn't get back with Ted, I didn't want to. I didn't like his friends, I didn't like his type. But I liked his looks, and I didn't like Curtis's, and what I thought as I looked into my own eyes was, I'll never meet anyone, I'll never meet anyone exactly my equal to love.

And then I took out my lipstick and fell all over again for its crimson plushness. Reapplying strongly-coloured lipstick, I've discovered, is a fail-safe curative.

Some feelings are unrecreatable. Happiness, for instance. Pain. But not shame. Shame you can feel over and over again. It's what the sight of unicycle boys does to me.

I got drunk. Ted, the boob, told Curtis that I'd called him

a mercy date. Came up to him where he stood talking *Empire Strikes Back* with a bespectacled friend while I had my feet up, draped his beefy arm over Curtis's skinny shoulder and said, "Hey, Prince Charming. How's it feel to be a mercy date?"

"Pardon me?"

"Jen here, she called you a mercy date."

"What?"

"He's full of shit, Curtis. I dumped him, he's jealous."

Ted undraped his arm. "You can call me anything you want, Jenny, but you can't call me a liar."

"He writes me poems, Curtis. 'I see you in your...*skirt*...'"

"Who're you here with, I ask her—"

"'...and my insides...*hurt*...'"

"—and she points at you—"

"'...what did I do *wrong*...'"

"—and what can I do, I laugh, and she goes—"

"'...I *long*...'"

"She goes, 'Shut up, Ted, it's a mercy date.'"

"'...for your *kiss*, it's what I *miss*...'"

Clearly cottoning on to the fact of this total stranger and I once being an item, Curtis looked from Ted to me to Ted to me. His face went a startling colour of red. Then he waved his awkward hand. "You belong together," he said in disgust, and walked off.

Ted smirked. "Listen to your date, Jen."

I ran after Curtis. "Look, you needed a date, I said I'd go, that's all I meant, I didn't mean it like— Come on, Curtis, don't—" I had no idea what I was saying. I was babbling. I only knew that as soon as Curtis walked away, two things had happened. Possibly two contradictory things, I've never quite sorted it out. One, I dropped all notions of being a femme fatale; all I wanted was that Curtis not be hurt beyond repair. And two, he stopped being a mercy date. Not because I suddenly wanted him, but because I couldn't stand to *not be wanted*. I had to have that again. "Look, Ted's an asshole, he's a complete asshole, you're ten times the man he is." Shameless, completely shameless. But it began to work. "Seriously. It might have started off like a mercy date, but I'm glad I said yes, I'm glad I'm your date. I've been glad of it all night." This was true. "I like you, Curtis. I mean it." Also true. So much more effective than flattery, the truth. I took his hand, spun him around and planted a big kiss on his lips. So much more effective than truth, lust.

We left. In the car I sensed that he was again uncertain. I put my hand on top of his as it worked the gearshift. "Let's go to your place."

Little about the sex lodged in my memory, but I remember his face, wonderstruck after all, rapturous. I remember his arm about me afterwards, his awkward hand patting my shoulder.

At five in the morning, his sister started to play the French horn in the basement. Just scales, but it was beautiful. Used to it, Curtis slept on. I rose, put on my dress, my shoes, tucked my nylons into my purse, my hat into my palm, called a cab. Felt the French horn arpeggios like an elegy as I closed the door.

He didn't call. Not calling meant another two things. Either that he knew I'd betrayed him once at the dance and again when I convinced him I hadn't the first time, or that he'd never cared much in the first place. I will never know.

And I haven't, actually, found anyone exactly my equal to love, or equal to my love, or whatever I'd meant in my maudlin state. It's always been him loving me too much or me loving him too much, and sometimes I think I should have snapped up Curtis while I had the chance. But seventeen. How could I have known?

He's a doctor now. His wife is a semi-famous character actor. They show up in *People* every now and then with their two daughters and their Bichon Frise. His skin's as clear as day.

He ran his finger up and down slight snake of King Street: King Street South, bend, King Street North, slither, King Street West, bend-slither, King Street East. The only main street in the country that went four ways. Back to King Street South. Which was his problem. How to make it work. How to revitalize it. Every idea he had was trite, unoriginal.

He turned his eraser on its side.

—Rmmm-rmmm, he said. He ran the eraser over to Fairway Mall and plowed into its walls.

—Bring out the wrecking ball, he said, stabbing the eraser with the unfolded paper clip he'd been using to pick his teeth, and swinging it.

—*Eeeeer-pqhhhh,* went the wrecking ball-eraser.

His mechanical pencil was aghast. —There goes Big Steel Man!

—*Pqhhhh.*

—Oh no, and Randy River!

—*Pqhhhh.*

—Ack, Tip Top Tailors, Stitches, Northern Reflections, Cotton Ginny. They're all going down, down, down. Where am I going to shop?

—*Pqhhhh. Pqhhhh.*

The eraser bounced happily over the chaos and destruction. —Onto Zellers! The big finale! Ready? *Eeeeer-doing-oing-oing.* Oh no, Zellers has metal walls. Bring out the battering rams. *Boouf. Boouf. Boouf. Boouf.*

—"Attention shoppers, we are being demolished—and you

know what that means—once-in-a-lifetime prices! Catastrophic savings! Buy now, before there's nothing left but rubble! Buy! Buy! Buy! Cashiers, stay at your tills until further notice."
—*Boouf. Boouf. Boouf.*
—Ahhhhh! Screams and confusion. Hordes of running terror.

He spun his pencil around his thumb and back. "Okay, King Street. Okay." He wrote down:

Mixed income housing
Business incentives
Sidewalk repaving failed—other sidewalk initiatives? public art?
Move market outside

He spun his pencil again. He leaned back in his chair. He put an arrow next to mixed income housing. He spun his pencil. He thought:

INT   STUDENT APARTMENT   NIGHT

JOHN, 20, a tousled, half-handsome urban planning student, sits at his drafting table deftly flipping a pencil around his thumb. Suddenly, John drops his pencil, takes fistfuls of hair, throws his head back and says

JOHN
Oh, God! Why me? Why now? Is it my destiny to save King Street? Or is it only a lame assignment that will do no good anyway, even if I can think of something interesting?

He buries his face in his hands, then turns it back up to the ceiling.

JOHN (CONT'D)
And how will I know the difference?

John closes his eyes.

SFX - A CIRCLE OPENS IN THE CEILING, LETTING IN A BEAM OF BRIGHT LIGHT.

SOUND of ANGEL CHOIRS.

John opens his eyes astonished. He drops to his knees and grasps his palms together, holding them up. ANGEL CHOIRS trail off like a RECORD BEING TURNED OFF.

GOD (O/S)
(in nasal, whiny voice)
Destiny, shmestiny, just do your work.

Abruptly the circle of light closes, the room is as it was. John has tears of joy streaming down his face. He begins his work with renewed vigour.

He twirled his pencil. He wrote down:

Buskers?
Arcade By-Law?
Theatre/Cabaret
Liquor licensing
Alien invasion

—Johnny!
—Penguin, thank god. I'm going nuts here. Nuts I say. Nuts!
—Johnny, Johnny, Johnny, you work too hard.
—Incorrect. I don't work hard enough.
—King Street?
—Affirmative.
—King Street is a snap. Mixed income housing. Bench or two on the sidewalk. Incentives, tax breaks. Swanky jazz/hip hop/blues bar naturally, of its own course, takes place of stinky windowless bar for alcoholic men. Coupla trees. Bingo: you've got a sunny, friendly neighbourhood during the day,

lively atmosphere at night, safe, interesting, perfect.

—It's all so, so...

—Exactly what the prof would do? Liable to get you an A, A minus? What?

—Boring.

—This? This is exciting compared to most of what planners do.

—I know, I know. I'm doomed.

—You'll get over it. Take a break. Come on down to a surfin' safari.

—Can't. Must plan.

—Johnny.

—No whining.

—Johnny.

—No pleading.

—Whoops Johnny, whoops Johnny, Johnny, Johnny, Johnny.

—All right. If we're going to drink, let's drink.

—Whoops, Johnny!

Back at the drawing board. Mixed-income housing, two park benches and a street mosaic created by street youth in consultation with a local artist it was. He spun his pencil. But, oh! blowing up the mall was a hard option to give up. Why didn't people come to King Street anymore? Because they went to the mall. *Pqhhhh.*

What you needed was a good stock of people nearby. People on foot, not people with cars. Students. Artists. Old people. All people who needed low-income housing. Co-ops. Converted warehouses. Were there any empty warehouses down there? There were abandoned houses, that was for sure. But who owned them? Could the city buy them for cheap? Or CMHC? Turn 'em into co-ops? He had zoning maps and service maps. They were supposed to have gone on their own mapping expedition for that extra level of detail, but he'd gone with Penguin and they'd never got past the bar.

—Ha! You gotta see this, yelled Pen from his desk.

—What?

—Hamster-breeding web site.

—Hamsters banging each other in cyberspace?

—They're serious! They got like hamster shows and everything!

—What, like hamster obedience? Hamster retriever trials?

—Conformation. Best of breed. All that.

—Is it going to be your pick of the week?

—Don't know yet.

—Hmm.

Skateboard park. What about a skateboard park. Next to the converted warehouse, which may or may not exist. There had to be an abandoned warehouse down there somewhere. Damn. He'd have to go with the three abandoned houses in a row on Queen Street. Make their conversion into a student competition. Student architects are cheap.

—*I* want to start a web site, Pen whined.

—We could put a camera in the toilet, John said without lifting his head from the blank page in front of him. Like those net-cams on Hockey Night in Canada. Kybo-cam.

—Too scatological, John. You'd get too many weirdos.

—You're one to talk.

—There's also the pure disgust factor. No, it's gotta be, like, totally specific and obscure.

—Breeding habits of the lock-spittle beetle.

—Now you're onto something.

—There's no such thing as a lock-spittle beetle.

—And you're going to let that stop you? Come on, brainstorm, brainstorm.

—I'm already brainstorming King Street. Leave me alone.

Co-op housing. Co-op artists' studio and gallery. Like in Guelph, all those potters. That worked. Skateboard park. Mosaic. Busking festival. He needed some yuppies, though. How would he get yuppies? He wouldn't. They were unplannable. If everything worked, they would just come once it was hip. Insta-yuppie, there was no such thing. They didn't work that way. They waited till the neighbourhood tide had already turned, and then they swarmed up the beach like crabs.

B-minus. Pure B-minus. John swivelled on his stool.

—Lithuanian dadaists, he called out to Pen.

—Lesbians who swim with the whales, said Pen.

John got up and padded to the door of Pen's room.

—Soft cheeses north and south, he said.

—Opera lovers of Kansas.

—Gay dwarves of America.

Penguin's eyes went wide.

Welcome to the Gay Dwarves of America Web Site!

Sick of giving head just cause you're the right height for it? Sick of Snow White jokes? Interested in dating other dwarves or just making new friends? Check out our bulletin board. Try our chatline. Or e-mail us. Right now we're just a few gay dwarves, but oh what a mighty force we could become if only we banded together.

▪ Famous Gay Dwarves

▪ Dwarf-on-Dwarf Sex

▪ Health Issues for Gay Dwarves

▪ Our Fabulous Founders

Click.

Our Fabulous Founders

(photo)

OSBORNE. I was just another lonely gay dwarf going from one one-night stand to the next until I met Izzy. Finally I feel understood in every way. Finally someone looks into my eyes instead of onto my bald spot and sees my hurting soul. I knew I was gay by the time I was twelve—around the time when other boys' sweet, sweet butts were at eye height. Sometimes I wondered if that was the reason I was gay. But twats were at that height too, so it had to be something more than that.

I was the only dwarf I knew. The only dwarf in my school. The only dwarf on my basketball team. The only dwarf in Scouts. The only dwarf at the Y. Like all dwarves, I thought of running away to the circus. Then I got a scholarship: fashion design, what else? I already designed and sewed all my own clothes. It was a natural step. Karmically not so good though. I mean, there's the hard work, the glamour, the creativity, all that's fine, but really, what's fashion all about? Height! All those models towering over slavering, autocratic designers with Napoleon complexes. Not the place to work out your issues around stature, let me tell you.

Since giving it up and going back to school I am so much more at peace with the world and myself and I want to share that peace and self-love that I've learned with my brothers the world over.

(photo)

IZZY. Hi. I'm Izzy. The web site was Ozzy's idea. Crazy, huh? But he takes it serious. He's so cute when he's serious. And he's right, too. I never dated another dwarf before him either, I didn't have any dwarf friends. I stayed away from them. We all had our own little place in our group, right? We were the dwarves, they were the norms, we were dwarves. Mascots. Pets, almost. Doing tricks. (Ha, ha.) And now? Thanks to Ozzy and Gay Dwarves of America, I'm not just my own dwarf among dwarves, I'm my own man among men.

---

to: gda
from: mel
re: what the?
Are you guys kidding or what? I have ten dollars riding on this.

to: mel
from: gda
re: what?
What.

to: gda
from: mizzd
re: tsk, tsk
scuse me? twats? not a very woman-friendly site, is it, boys?

to: gda
from: anon
re:
Suck my dick, short boy!

to: gda
from: Viola
re: hello out there
Found your web site a couple of weeks ago. Figured you had to be a couple of college kids joking around. Then thought maybe not. Then thought definitely. I mean, Ozzy and Izzy? Come on! But you never know—truth stranger than fiction and all that. And what the heck. I'm not sleeping, I might as well be typing in the deep of the night. You see, my son is a gay dwarf. Well, he's a dwarf. A Little Person. And I think he's gay, though he hasn't told me yet. And I'm worried about him. At first I thought the problem was girls. Tried to tell him things get better after high school, that the silly ideas there about who can date whom (regardless of how they actually feel) evaporate later on, and people regret that they didn't date the people they liked instead of the people they matched. If I could go back and say yes to Haji Khan instead of mooning over Vince Gerrard, I'd do it in a flash. Wonder if Vince would do the same with me? (Oh, get over it, honey!) Then I found a copy of Playgirl in his bedroom. (My son's. Not Vince's. Who knows what's in Vince's bedroom.)

So what exactly is it that I'm after? I don't know. Should I tell him that I know? And about your web site? He's not the only one and all that? Has as much a chance at happiness as anyone? (He does, doesn't he? You're happy, aren't you? You seem happy in your pictures.)

—Did you answer this? John asked Pen.
—What?
—Mom of gay dwarf e-mail. Viola.
—Yup.
—What did you say?
—By all means.
—By all means what?
—Just by all means.
—That's it? That's all you wrote?
—I thought it kind of summed things up. Don't you? Izzy's a man of few words.

—You're Ozzy! I'm Izzy.

—Okay.

—Should've told her we were joking.

—Aren't we sensitive all of a sudden?

—Did you sign it Izzy or Ozzy?

Shrug. Penguin pointed the remote and unmuted the television.

—You're useless, did you know that? Useless.

No reaction.

—What is the Geneva Convention, Penguin said to the TV.

to: Viola

from: Izzy

re: hello out there

Whatever Ozzy wrote you, forget it. He's... um, unpredictable. I love that about him, except when I hate it. It's never boring around here, I'll tell you that. My advice is: give him an opening. Your son. Like, rent a gay movie or something (*Philadelphia* is one my ma loved), and then say how terrible you think people who discriminate are. Something like that. And then if he wants to, he can come out. What do you think? Is it a plan or what?

(p.s. sometimes it *is* boring around here. I can't figure out what's wrong with Ozzy. He doesn't seem to care about anything. He watches TV. He goes to the bar. He eats cereal.)

—You got a D? I don't get it. You're the one who gave me the B- spiel.

—They just don't understand genius.

—What did you do?

—Took what was already there and intensified it. Teenage Wasteland, that's the concept. You zone the whole thing for arcades, head shops and cheap pizza outlets, nothing else, except for a hardware store that sells only discount spray paint, so the kids have easy access to the basic graffiti-making materials. Then, cut the street lighting by half so there's lots of dark corners and doorways for smoking up and making out and destroying property.

—You're fucked.

—The world is fucked, my friend. I'm just along for the ride.

to: gda
from: king
re: howdy

hey, you all. glad to see another dwarf-positive site on the web. are you all members of the LPA? you should have a link to it. i have told the webmaster about it and he's going to check you out and maybe put a link to yours. you may want to reconsider your word choice in your introductions (i.e. t**ts) if you want a wider audience.

—What did you say to Mom about me? Penguin said.

—*Penfield, darling*, John said, imitating Pen's mother the way they did every time she was mentioned. She didn't call. Why?

—Not Penfield-darling. Pay attention, John. When have I ever called Penfield-darling "Mom"? Penfield-darling, when it's necessary to speak of her at all, is my mother. I mean the other Mom. Dwarf-Mom.

—Oh, her. I don't know, why?

—She's very concerned about me. Wonders if I'm taking vitamins. If I'm going to counselling. Whether I'm having a mid-life crisis. Don't laugh, she's serious.

He snapped his fingers and yelled over the next table at Sal, who was swinging a beer-laden tray from shoulder to table. —Garçon! 'Nother pitcher.

—Fuck your garçon shit, Pen. Ask me nice.

—Oh, Salvatore, please may we have another pitcher of beer?

—That's better.

—Kay, Johnny. What'd you write?

—I told her Ozzy was depressed.

—You think Ozzy is depressed?

—Who knows what's wrong with Ozzy.

—What's wrong with Ozzy, John?

—Nothing. Nothing.

—What's wrong with Ozzy, John?

41

—I don't have a fucking clue, Pen, I really don't.

—What's wrong with Ozzy, John?

—Just: does he care? About anything?

—Fuck off. Why should he? He's a useless puke who eats and shits and drinks and watches TV like all the other useless pukes on the planet.

—Ozzy. Not you.

—Why, I oughta...

—No, but seriously, *are* you okay? John asked.

—Who are you, Dr. Phil? I'm fine.

—Fine, then. Who's Dr. Phil?

Pen's name came up for the pool table. They won it from two girls who were killing themselves over how bad they were. Their hilarity made John smile inwardly.

—Check this backspin, said the cuter one as she aimed a bank shot at the middle pocket, then undershot the cue ball so badly it jumped before jostling the ball it was aimed at.

—Contact, the one with the chopsticks in her hair said. You made contact, that's what's important. They busted up over this.

—Think we should get ourselves some a what they had, John?

Maybe the girls weren't supposed to laugh at that, but they were supposed to notice. They didn't. They were an impermeable set. They were encased in a bubble.

—I don't know, Pen. Looks kinda dangerous.

Pen's next turn he laid a series of loud, vigorous shots that made the balls rattle in the cups as they went down.

Chopstick-Hair crouched so her eye was at table level while the other leaned her face to the same height. Cheek to cheek.

The Bubble of Love, that's what it was. The Bubble of Love. Longing for Angela surged through him, making all John's organs ache, skin included. After the girls flubbed their next shot, he cleared the table and they hung up their cues and doubled away laughing.

—What else did Viola say, John asked as Pen racked the balls.

—Who? said Penguin, chalking his pool cue.

—Viola.

—Who?

—Dwarf-Mom. Did she ask her son if he was gay?

—Ha! How's this for circumlocution? She goes and rents *Philadelphia* and waits for him to say it. Classic, eh?

—And? Does he?

Penguin shook his head. —Falls asleep on the couch. Poor fuck.

—What do you mean?

—You want your mother prying into your sex life? Penguin sank his last ball, then missed the eight.

—Yeah, but it's not just about sex, John said, missing his shot.

—How do *you* know?

—I read. I watch TV.

Pen rolled his eyes. —Joke, John. Joke.

John blushed. He watched Penguin lean on the table to line up his shot. His t-shirt pulled out of the back of his black jeans. John wondered what it would be like to be attracted to that. If it was Angela instead of Pen leaning over a pool table, he'd be in a drool induced by those hips of hers, he'd be in danger of moaning out loud. Come home, Angela, he thought to himself, looking at Penguin's back that was just his back.

John made himself think of the next step if there were to be one, of putting his hand under Pen's shirt on that piece of skin, of putting his lips on muscle. And then for the length of time between eye-blinks, he felt it. Pen's skin would feel thin, almost not there, and everything underneath his skin, muscle and anger and bitterness would be right there under his hand singing like a hydro line, and

INT   CAMPUS BAR   NIGHT

> Penguin, a tightly wound, skinny guy in black
> t-shirt and jeans stiffens at the touch of his
> roommate, John, a tousled, half-handsome
> urban planning student. Then he swiftly twists
> around, takes John's jaw in his hand, and with

eyes hot as, hot as...something hot, he draws
John's lips to his own. The two guys' lips mash
together as if, as if they were starved for it, as if
nothing else existed in the world. And then...

Then the feeling, the knowledge was gone and John felt a
weird combination of pride that he could have gone that far,
and smugness that no one knew what he'd just been thinking,
and shame that his whole life he'd let himself be limited by a
word. What are ya, a homo? Fuck off, ya homo. In high school
he and his friends had run a whole campaign based on it. "Vote
for Timbo, he's no homo." Ironically intentioned, sure, but still.
     —I'm going home. In his head he heard Homo.
     —You do that, said Penguin. He bellowed out the name of
the next person on the chalkboard for pool.
     Penguin wasn't depressed. He was too wired to be
depressed.

John flipped on his computer and checked his e-mail account.
One from his brother, one from a friend at Western, a cutesy
forwarded message from the same friend's girlfriend. Nothing
from Angela. Maybe the phone lines were down in Guatemala.
Maybe she was out for a stint in a village with no running water,
much less a working computer. Maybe she didn't love him
anymore.
     He checked the GDA account. There were eight pranks
along the usual lines, including one that said, "Gay fags must
die." He wrote back, "Only gay fags? Not sad ones?" Then he
opened the last message.

     to: gda
     from: king
     re: re: re: howdy
     >
     >Why the fuck would we want a wider audience?
     >love, Ozzie
     >
     Fuck you too, asshole. You guys are so full of shit. You say
     you got a chatline and you got no chatline, you say famous

gay dwarves and then you got pictures of yourselves stuck up there. you're so full of shit. damn right i'm stick of the stupid jokes, every fuckin day another stupid dwarf joke, including you. fuck you, pardon my french.

John wrote:

> **to:** king
> **from:** gda
> **re:** Ozzie's last missive
> Sorry.

He was about to queue it. Then he added:

> love, Izzy
> (p.s. de rien about yr French)

Then he checked the web site. King was right. If you clicked on "Famous Gay Dwarves" there were the same pictures they'd used for Ozzy and Izzy, one of which they'd got from Pen's yearbook, the other from a magazine. He tried clicking on "Dwarf-on-Dwarf Sex." Ooh la la, Pen had been busy. Fun with Photoshop.

John stared at the computer for a long while. Then he opened a new file and wrote:

> **to**: viola
> **from**: izzy
> **re**: mea culpa
> Listen, you were right the first time. We are just a couple of college students. We're not gay and we're not dwarves and it was a joke and I'm sorry and I hope things work out for you and your son.

Then he trashed it without sending it. He checked the mail again. There were two new prank e-mails, and one from Viola. She must have been writing right then, at the exact same time he was writing her. Where? Where was she? Somewhere in the

States—*college* students, she said, not *university* students—but other than that? Was it later or earlier there? Colder or hotter? Did she have a cup of hot chocolate by her computer? A glass of scotch? Did she have some little personalizing thing on top of her computer? Gumby and Pokey? Mickey Mouse? An Etch-a-Sketch frame for the screen? A picture of her kid? Maybe a picture of the two of them on her screen saver. He wished he knew all of it. He wished she would feel it if he mentally kissed her palm, pulling her hand gently away from where her fingers twisted a strand of hair, opening it with both of his hands and putting his lips gently to the hollow cup of flesh.

Jesus, he was mentally kissing everyone tonight. Angela had to come home soon.

to: gda
from: viola
re: you two
Boy, you two are really something! My advice is you should talk to each other and not me. You remind me of my grandparents when they used to fight. "Tell your grandfather the light in the refrigerator needs changing." "Tell your grandmother the light bulbs are where they've always been." Ozzy's depressed, Izzy's obsessive-compulsive...

Nothing new on this end. I keep giving Peter these big openings, he keeps not taking them, and I don't want to force him to say anything if he doesn't want to. Besides, maybe there's a perfectly good explanation for the Playgirl, maybe it's Dolly's (his best friend) and she doesn't want to keep it at her house. Her parents are Baptist and very strict. She spends a lot of time here. Her parents are a little suspicious of me, being a single mother and all, but she told them my husband died, so now they're sympathetic.

I think I should just let things be for a while. As long as Peter knows I love him no matter what, well, what else can I do?

John wrote:

to: viola
from: izzy
re:
Dear Viola. I will miss you. Peter will be fine.

He sent it, turned off his own computer and then went into the living room and bent down in front of the computer, one of Pen's three, that acted as the GDA server. Index finger hovering over the on-off switch, he blinked several times slowly, then jabbed the button and listened to the machine's waning hum as it powered down. He took a seat and waited for Pen to come home.

—They don't like being called dwarves. They prefer Little People, John was explaining to Pen the next morning after waking up with couch print on his face upon Pen's arrival at quarter to seven. Now they were in the kitchen, John watching a small pot on the stove, waiting for it to boil.

—Like that's a whole lot better. 'I'd like to thank all the Little People.'

—Or person with dwarfism.

—Mr. Fucking PC, Pen said. 'We're talking about real people, Pen, real people.' Come on, John. They're not real, they're virtual. If they were real, they wouldn't have to rely on the fucking Internet to fill up their dull, empty lives.

—So you're virtual, too.

Pen stopped his pacing around the kitchen. He stared at John. —Basically. Yeah. He sat down and breathed out a long, boozy stream of air. John decanted boiling water from the pot into a tall glass beaker where it tossed up coffee grinds into a chaotic swirl.

—Your life doesn't have to be dull and empty, Pen.

—God, John. You are just so sickeningly well intentioned, aren't you? You want me to find God? You want me to find love? You want me to find fulfillment and meaning in my work?

—Yeah. I hope you do. Well, God you can take or leave, I don't care.

—I love that dwarf site, John. It makes me laugh. I crave laughter. Without it I'll die. He laughed. Please let me keep it.

—That's up to you, Pen.

—Now you sound like my grade three teacher. You never sound like yourself, you know that? I don't know if there even is a self in there. It's like you've unconsciously sampled the voices of everybody you've met in your life, and I just like push a button and out comes Dr. Phil or Angela or my grade three teacher—how'd you get her voice, by the way—or Elmer the Safety Elephant or Gloria Steinem or your dad.

—Shut up, Pen.

—Ooo, argument's getting good, now, he's hauling out the big guns. Shut up: the battering ram of the inarticulate. Face it, you have no self. You're selfless. You are. I mean it. You're even trying to help me, you think you're helping me, right? You can't help me, John. I'm an emotional dwarf. I deserve that site. It's mine. I'll move out to keep it if I have to. Maybe I'll move out anyway.

—Aw, Pen, don't...

—No, seriously. This situation is fucked. Dwarf-Mom is right, we're like a bickering old couple. We used to have fun and now we're a bickering old couple and you're the wife. You're the wife, John, you're the wife.

Pen's face was all screwed up. Water came out the corners of his eyes. John palmed down the coffee plunger.

—You make no sense, man. You make zero sense.

Now Pen had his head down on the table and John did what he'd been thinking of doing at the bar. He put his hand on Pen's back.

—Bed, Pen said, rising and slouching off. John leaned back against the counter, ran one hand over his face with its rasp of morning beard, and folded his arms across his chest, inside which his heart thumpa-thumped. He heard Pen brushing his teeth and spitting. He heard Pen's door close. He leaned some more.

And then he tiptoed up to Pen's door and put his hand on the handle, listening. Nothing. He turned the door handle. Pen was curled on his side on his futon, facing the wall.

—Pen! John whispered. Four steps and he was by the bed. He crouched. Pen!

No response. John couldn't tell if he was really asleep or not. And then he didn't care. For as long as it took to spoon behind Penfield, he didn't care. He put his arm across Pen's waist so his hand rested against Pen's chest and still didn't know if Pen was asleep or awake.

Oh, fuck, what if he was asleep? And woke up, going, What the fuckin' fuck?

What if he was awake?

—John.

Ohfuck. Awake. Fuck.

—What are you doing?

John cleared his throat. —I'm, uh, lying with you.

Pen said nothing.

—You seemed upset.

—Never made you climb into my bed before.

—That's true.

—You could go now.

—Okay. John sproinged to his feet like a jack-in-the-box.

He put on his running shoes and wind jacket and gloves and ran down to King Street. It was Saturday morning on the busiest street in town and there were only handfuls of pedestrians in each block. He ran all the way downtown and then back along the railroad track, through the park with the deer behind their fence, up to the university and then past it, out into the beginnings of the countryside. Fifty kilometres up the road, more or less, and fifty years ago, his father had been born and lived until he was about the age John was now. He stood there looking up the road, hands on his hips, until he'd stopped panting. Then he turned around, walked home, went to bed and slept. He and Pen never talked about it again, not the web site, not anything that had happened that morning.

A month and a half later, John went to work as the co-op student at the Goderich Town Planning Department, Pen went to work for the City of Mount Royal, and Angela came home from Guatemala. John and Pen e-mailed each other sporadically, reporting on pickle-butt bosses and sorry-ass co-workers. Originally they had arranged to take the apartment back from the off-stream co-op students currently in it, but there was a room available in a house down the street from Angela's, and John wanted to take it. He was relieved when Pen wrote to say he'd had it with Planning, he didn't know what he wanted to be when he grew up, but a planner wasn't it, and he was taking some time off.

Six months later, John got a postcard from Atlanta, Georgia with a picture of what looked like an old circus promotion photo, a very tall black man beside a white man of average height in a top hat. In large capital letters, the message said, "I'D." Pen, he thought, though the handwriting could have been anybody's. Who else would send a postcard with a single contraction on it? Who else would write to his parents' address? Over the next month, circus pictures from around the States followed, each with one word on them. Postmark Tuscaloosa, Alabama: 'Leopard Boy' (unhappy-looking black boy with patches of white skin), message: LIKE. Postmark Amarillo, Texas: Bearded Lady Triplets, message: TO. Postmark Wichita, Kansas: Strong Man: THANK. Postmark Las Vegas, New Mexico: 'The Marvellous Mexican Midget' (drooping mustache, crossed bandoliers, twirling six-guns): ALL. Postmark Trinidad, Colorado: Dapper Dan & His Dancing Dogs (cowboy holding a long pole with a dog balanced on either end): THE. Postmark Cheyenne, Wyoming: Fat Lady: LITTLE.

PEOPLE never came. John had thought maybe it would make sense, finally, of the lot of them, that the postcard saying PEOPLE would have some image, gay dwarves maybe, that would tip him off as to what Pen was up to, what the hell he *meant*. He put them all up on the fridge, flipping them over a couple of times a day, sometimes arranging them with the fronts showing, sometimes with the backs. He thought of photocopying the backs and pasting them onto pieces of postcard-sized cardboard so he could see both fronts and backs at the same time, but he never got around to it.

After another three moves from work term apartments to Waterloo apartments and back, Angela finally asked if they really had to keep them on the fridge anymore, and John said, Yes. Yes. I'm still waiting for PEOPLE. I'll always wait for PEOPLE.

Thorn-blossoms

"Who are we going to be today, Mommy?" Willa asked as they got out of the van.

Hélène, Hélène, today I am Hélène.

"Nobody," said Heather. They had dropped Ben off at the arena's front door, they were late, the coach was going to be pissed. Ben was supposed to get his chance to play forward today and would no doubt get bumped back onto defense. His stalwart little back in its coach-mandated blazer shouldering the awkward hockey bag made Heather almost weep.

"We're here, Mom," Heather said to Lois.

"Here?" said Lois.

"Ben's hockey game," said Willa.

"Ben?" said Lois.

"Your grandson," said Willa.

"Oh," said Lois. As they walked to the arena, she whispered behind her hand to Heather, "How many children do you *have*?"

"Three, Mom. I have three children. Taylor is fourteen, Ben is almost eleven, and Willa is six."

"Four years between them!"

"Hyep."

What her mother meant, or had meant before her response had become formulaic, was, What a long time away from your career! What a lot of years of early childhood! Why didn't you do it all at once and get it over with? Way to string out the time at home!

I don't have a career. I like early childhood.

Luckily—sort of—her mother now mostly thought Heather

was twenty-six, Heather-with-new-baby. One baby. "What's the baby's name again?" she would ask. "A boy's name." And "Why don't you bring the baby over more?"

"Taylor." Heather had given up explaining that Taylor was no longer a boy's name at all. "She's not a baby anymore."

When Taylor really had been a baby, Heather would have loved to bring her over to her mother's house. Loved to. Steve was working, her friends were working, they were articling or doing their MBAs, they came for quick visits and went back to their busy (free) lives. They didn't really get it, having a baby, being a mother. They gooed and squealed and then made a beeline out of there. Her mom would get it—how the baby's sharp, delicate fingernails felt between your teeth, what a weird animal reminder the whole experience was. Breastfeeding! So cool. So weird. So actually not-weird.

Heather would call her mother to suggest tea or lunch, she'd call just to talk. What she got was her father's voice on the answering machine and she would want to hang up, she would want to cry, but instead she would leave a jaunty message. "It's me, with a very intellectual question, a poo question, in fact. I've got a poo question. Her poo was always, you know, baby-shit brown, and suddenly, today, it's goose-shit green. What's going on? Any tips from one who's been there? Bye." She would hang up and take the baby out for a walk, let old ladies coo over her on the street, strike up one-off conversations with people in coffee shops over headlines or weather. When Steve came home, smelling of paper and office, pencils and mucilage (no one used mucilage anymore, apparently, but she swore she could smell it—"You just like saying 'mucilage,'" he said, kissing the side of her head, and it was true, mucilage mucilage), nothing seemed wrong at all. Her day was suddenly recast in the light of the three of them as a family. They would coo over Taylor together. Steve would run a bath, wash her little head, croon to her, hold her in the sling while they ate the takeout he'd picked up on the way home. He would be interested in the poo. Together they'd go back over what they had eaten the last three days. When the phone rang at eight or eight-thirty, they wouldn't even bother to answer it. It would be Lois saying she was just finishing dinner, she'd been out all day doing interviews, and about the poo question she had no idea.

"Here's your coat, Mom."

"It's gorgeous out."

"Yes, and lucky us, we're going into a cold, dank arena." Heather held the coat behind her mother as if to help her on with it but Lois bent her shoulders away like a sulky child.

In the lobby, they milled about with the other parents ("Hey, Heather," "Hi, Lonnie," "Hi, Lois," "I'm sorry, I've forgotten your name") while on the ice a group of twelve-year-old girls played ringette. When Lois caught sight of them she grabbed Heather's arm. "Look at their sticks. What's happened to their sticks?" she hissed.

Evil stick fairies have chopped them off. "It's a game called Ringette." *Next they're going after rakes and shovels. All the tools of the world! Oh no!* "I think they sort of stab a ring with a stick instead of pushing a puck around. More efficient, if you think about it."

Lois had already moved on. "You might have mentioned I'd need a coat. It's frigid in here."

"Mom," Heather said. "Would you like your coat?'"

"Ha ha," she said. "Like fun." But she let Heather put the coat on her. She caught sight of the ice again. "Now, this is an innovation I haven't seen before. They've got a stick and a ring."

Simon's dad came in and pointed at Heather with two finger-guns. "Hildie?"

Hildie had been the first person Heather had turned into at hockey arenas. Hildie was Swiss and made her own cheese. Hildie brought a cowbell to hockey games and shouted *Hut hut hut hut* in the stands like she was on a ski hill. Hildie did not distinguish between one team and another when it came to cheering. "Bright display of skill!" she shouted.

"You're hilarious," said her friend, Lonnie, who was fiercely partisan.

Willa loved when Heather was Hildie. She braided her hair, called Heather Müttie, called herself Vilhelmina.

Hélène had appeared one day when Willa was at a birthday party. Heather had nipped over to the Mac's in the strip mall next to the arena to pick up some dish soap (they'd been using shampoo the last two days), and found herself buying cigarettes. Hélène was French, sullen, divorced, completely uninterested in hockey. Hélène smoked and brooded outside the arena or read novels in the lobby or lounge or wherever it was warm. (Heather carried unread book club novels with her wherever she went in case of spare time—then read magazines.)

"You smell like smoke, Mom," said Ben as he got into the van after his game.

"Simon's dad," she said. "Smokes like a chimney." What the fah. She was lying to her children just like she'd lied to her parents when she was Taylor's age.

"Hartley?" said Simon's dad now. Hartley was British and stroppy, Hartley had asked the coach when he'd said Ben had 'some talent' but not much of a work ethic, "Why should he have a work ethic? It's a game." ("I thought she was French," Heather heard the coach say as they walked away. "Isn't she French?")

"Not this week."

"Ce n'est pas Hélène?"

"Bain-oui. No. Just Heather today." Lois was smiling and positioning herself for introductions. "Simon's dad, Lois Small."

"Pleasure to meet you." Simon's dad shook her hand and inclined himself forward in a shadow of a bow as if he had never met Lois before.

"Sorry," Lois was saying. "I didn't catch your name."

"Ray Kavanagh, but most people call me Simon's dad."

"How do you do, Simon's dad. Have you seen this before, this new hockey with a stick and an o?"

"Ringette," said Simon's dad. "My daughter plays."

It was amazing to see Lois rise to social occasions. Left alone, she was a vacant, grumpy person, disturbed (so Heather surmised) at the contradictions between her mind and le monde. Introduced to someone new, she pulled it out her ass (as Heather's friend Shelly used to say), she was bright and lively, her old self. Almost. Look at her with the man who had pulled over on Woodbine. Look at her with Simon's dad. Her social technique held up just fine: ask questions, listen, add, ask questions. Probe, joke, befriend. *How fake, how mercenary,*

Heather had thought as a teen when she'd recognized this technique as technique. *You can't live by formula.* But the thing was, ninety-nine times out of one hundred, Lois was sincere. Even if there was a Machiavellian tint to it—she was a journalist, after all, she was going to use the stuff people told her when she probed, joked and befriended—she was genuinely interested, even, as with dull, ordinary people, when she was primarily interested in them as specimen.

"Tell me about, what's it called?"

"Ringette."

"Ringette. Tell me about ringette."

Simon's dad told her about ringette. She listened and nodded, repeated and questioned. She was making sense. You would not know she typed long essays of nonsense, that she called up people in her Rolodex and asked them mad questions. That she could not read what she had written, that Dad would find her in tears at the typewriter.

"Have you seen this before," Lois said to Simon's dad as the ringette players cheered at the end of their game, "this new hockey with a round thingy and a straight thingy?"

* * *

Nothing looked right but if she got the paper, she would know. Every week they read the lists. "Mum, Lois is reading!" "The girl's hardly four." "She is, she's reading." "Hm." "Go on, Lois. Read." "Caldwell, Carl-e-ton Ernest." "Carleton." "Killed on active service. Hutchinson, Gordon James, missing, believed killed." "Is that today's?" "Last week's." "Have we seen today's?" "Phillip, run out and get the paper, would you." Today it was Lois's turn to get the paper. They wouldn't always give her her turn, sometimes she had to take it. They went right from the house, then right again. She knew left and right, this was her left and this was her right. You went right and then right again. Then things were not as familiar, they were half familiar, oh, now here was a tennis court. There was a big water. She had taken a wrong turn. She ought to have gone right. Frank would be waiting, he would be checking his watch, shaking his head, he would have a little smile the way she was always late.

He'd try to be mad. Now where had they said? There, at the little where they sold cold? She was really very late, she had better hurry. Frank was always on time, he was always waiting for her. His face when he saw her, that was the thing she liked best. Maybe really she made herself late on purpose just to see it go from repose to animation, from anyone's to hers. Where *was* he? The day felt all wrong. They'd missed each other. He'd think she didn't care. He'd think she liked that smarmy Hugh, who wouldn't leave her alone. The sun made her squint. The boardwalk was bumpy. What had happened to their walk on the boardwalk? Her feet needed roughening up. At the end of a summer, they'd hardly notice this. No one said it but it was Dad's name they were looking for. Each week, Mum would sit still as a stone until the list was read. You didn't even notice how still she was until the [Ss] were past and her shoulders dropped and her face softened. At the end, she was in full motion again, and cheery through her tears. She always knew a few names, she knew their mothers and wives and sisters. She editorialized, "Oh, that's Jane Bean's cousin from out Fergus way." "I wonder if that's Ian Smockler's boy or the Rog Smockler's?" "Oh, not Benny, too. Oh, their poor mother." It was her turn to get the paper if only she could find the darn store. This street. They thought she was too little for everything, but she'd show them, oh boy, wouldn't she just. Maybe she could ask someone. Hello. Hello. Can you tell me can you tell me where the can you tell me where the store is?

* * *

"Time to go," Heather called out to Ben and Willa. Lois was napping in the living room. Willa's feet pummelled the stairs but there was no response from Ben, oh, wait, except for that thud, Ben had been in the driveway taking shots against the garage door for the last ten minutes. His hockey bag in the van, his jacket and tie on. Mr. Keen.

"Don't forget your coat," Heather said to Willa, picking up her mother's coat and poking her head into the living room. Lois was not there. The blanket Heather had covered her with for her afternoon nap was scuttled at the end of the couch. Her shoes sat neatly on the floor. "Mom?" Heather ran downstairs to the rec room hoping to find Lois watching TV. Lois liked TV now. She liked Sesame Street. But Lois was not watching TV. How could she have got out? Heather had been in the kitchen the whole time, she would have heard the door open (she hadn't heard Ben open the door), the music hadn't been on that loud. She ran upstairs. "Mom?"

Taylor emerged from her bedroom with a look on her face Heather had not seen in a long time, a plain, serious look. "Have you seen Grandma?" They checked each room. They checked the bathrooms. They went outside. She was more comforted than she could say that Taylor was acting like a grown-up. If Steve had to be away, at least she was not alone.

"Ben, have you seen Grandma?"

"Nope."

"Are you sure?"

"Isn't an old lady in the world that could get past me." He stickhandled back and forth.

"Damn. Damn. Damn. Damn."

"Have you checked the back?" Taylor asked.

It was too simple. Heather was afraid to get hopeful. But it had to be the answer. Because otherwise Lois had a ten-minute start on them and a ten-minute start meant a mile-wide radius. She could be on Queen Street, she could be on the beach. She could be in the park. She could be anywhere.

No. Lois was not in the back.

"Oh." Heather slumped in the doorway.

"What?" said Taylor.

"Her shoes."

"What about them?"

"They're in the living room. They're not on her feet."

"Maybe it'll slow her down," said Taylor. They laughed.

"All right. Willa, get in the van. Taylor and Ben, get the walkie-talkies and go out on your bikes. Taylor, take the cell, call me if you find her."

This was why Heather's father had put in an alarm system with a door chime. This is why he had key locks on the inside of doors. This was why he dropped Lois off Saturday mornings looking bleary-eyed and old and near breaking.

* * *

Taylor had been smoking. Steve talked to her. "What do you think about smoking, Taylor?"

"I think smoking's addictive, I think smoke smells nice, I think smoking causes cancer, I think smoking's expensive but anti-bourgeois."

"Are you smoking, Taylor?"

"Do I look like I'm smoking? Ah, put me out, put me out." She slapped her arms idiotically.

"Thigh-slapper, Tay. Hoo."

"Sometimes."

"Do you think that's a good idea?"

"Good in what sense? Good for organic tobacco growers, good for—"

"You, Taylor. Good for you."

"Well, yes and no." Heather listened and it made her crazy. Steve thought he was some kind of superior uber-parent because he treated Taylor like an adult. But she was not an adult, she was fourteen. "Obviously if I get addicted, that's, you know, bad, but who's to say, I mean, it's better than other kinds of addiction, in terms of self-destructive behaviour, there's no immediate result, right? I mean, committing suicide by cigarette takes a long time..."

"You are not allowed." Heather could not help breaking in. "You are fourteen. The law does not allow it. The law is well founded. The law is good."

"Oh, come on, *Hélène.*"

"Hélène does not exist, she is a made-up character, number two, I am a grown-up, I can make bad decisions for myself."

"Hélène the made-up character buys duMauriers. Hélène the made-up character's actions have effect in the material world. Hélène the made-up character draws smoke into your lungs."

"So should you be like me?"

"The answer is obviously not. A loser who has so little in her life she has to make up fake personalities at hockey arenas to keep herself from shooting herself? I don't think so. But since I'm genetically related to said loser, what choice do I have?"

"Oh my God, could you be more snide and obnoxious?"

"If I tried, maybe, I don't know."

Heather was reduced to inarticulate Hrrrarrrghs and arm waving. She got up close into Taylor's face. "Smoke and your internet connection's gone, baby. Thing a the past."

Later Steve said, "You know that's exactly the wrong way to talk to Taylor, right?"

"Oh, and you know the right way?"

"Well—"

"Teenagers need boundaries. They don't need their parents to be their friends. They've got friends. They need someone to hate. They need someone to blame. Someone they can say to their friends, 'Yeah, I would, I would totally do it, but my Mom'll kill me.' I'll be it, I don't mind. You can keep your little illusory friendship with Taylor."

"You're in a good mood."

"Oh, fuck off."

"I just want to keep her talking to me."

"Sooner or later she'll sniff the fakeness and it'll be game over for you, too."

"It's not fake."

Heather put three fingers of each hand across her face in front of her eyes. "Fake fake fake."

The phone rang. Steve and Heather made Who can that be? faces at one another. Eleven o'clock at night. Heather snatched the phone up.

"I'm wondering if you could possibly come over," her father said.

"What? What is it?"

There was a silence and then a funny noise. It took some time for Heather to realize it might be a sort of man crying sound. "I don't think she can read anymore."

"I'll be right over." It was a joke. Her mother would have laughed.

"Thanks," he said.

"What is it?" asked Steve.

"Big crisis. Mom can't read anymore."

"What?"

"I'm sure there's more to it. That's all he said."

At her parents' house, Heather almost smacked into the locked front door. She wasn't used to it yet. She was used to walking right in. By the time she found her key, her father had opened the door. He had his glasses on his nose and a sheaf of papers in his hand—pretty much the abstract image she had of him in her head when the word "Dad" was used: open collar, grey pants, glasses on nose, papers in hand. She leaned up and kissed him on his stubbly cheek. "Mom asleep?"

"Finally."

"So what's going on?"

"She's written it. The Last Thing."

He was referring to Lois's column in *Chatelaine*, Plaques and Tangles, which she had started soon after being diagnosed. She had been, at the time and shortly before, well into her research for a book on aging. She had spent weeks with Alzheimer's patients—and Parkinson's patients and hip-replacement patients and macular degeneration patients and arthritis patients and diabetes patients—in their homes, in institutions, in hospitals. She'd gone to caregiver support groups and day programs, she'd gone to research labs. She'd talked to sociologists, geriatricians, seniors' advocates, seniors themselves. And she had started losing words. Really losing them, not just casting around for them, knowing they were there. Losing them. The word "fridge," gone for days at a time. Alzheimer's, she'd thought, and then dismissed it as too ironic. More likely she was having sympathetic symptoms. More likely it was plain old brain atrophy. Plain old aging. She was sixty-three.

Six months later she was riding her bike home from lunch with a friend when suddenly College and McCaul could have been Lima, Peru. She did. Not. Know. Where. She. Was. She could feel her own eyes grow wide. Terror bloomed in her stomach. Her heart rioted. Science fiction was real. There were alternate worlds. Danger surrounded her. The people were robots, they couldn't be trusted.

At sixty-five, the book was out, and the diagnosis was as firm as it would ever be: probable Alzheimer's. Because you never knew until the brain autopsy.

"I start this column," she wrote, "with the knowledge that

one day soon, I will write The Last Thing. The last coherent sentence. After fifty years putting ideas into words and sentences with the purpose of giving people information they didn't have before (and maybe entertaining them in the process), I will between one day and the next, go from being able to not being able. This is aging. This is Alzheimer's. In all likelihood, I won't even know I've written The Last Thing," she went on. "I'll go on writing gobbledygook."

Her father sighed. He looked at the sheaf of papers and at Heather. He handed them to her and walked into the dining room. The workroom. Lois's office.

At my desk the back of the oven.

I forget the children while becoming a child.
Summer evenings cloud low reds. Is it the rain
or is it the fear of what strikes? All winter we
had roots. Again a snow snow beyond, now
round

Mother never lived to be old. My old dream,
I forget the children

At the desk all the children's bash

If I never eat another root I' p often we don't
know a tiny flapper will launch. Fly (fall Fly fall
In the end for the most part and then

liver arm-joints

We don't know now about the rain not at all

I forget the children while becoming a child.

"That's a good first line," Heather said. "'I forget the children while becoming a child.'"

"It's about the only coherent sentence in the whole thing."

"'Mother never lived to be old' is not bad."

"She won't stop," he said. "She's obsessed. She types and types. For about three days, it's almost all she's done. She gets up in the middle of the night and types. Only then she talks to people, too, it's like she's in the newsroom at *The Record*. She thinks I'm the editor.

"At first I was sort of relieved. It gave me some time to myself. She wasn't pestering me every five minutes. She wasn't following me around. We'd been doing the last few columns together. She'd make some notes about things she wanted to write, she'd make an outline. Then she'd write a sentence. She wanted me right there to read it out to her so she could write the next one. It took us about a week, what would normally take her a day." Heather had no idea her father had been doing this. "But this time she was doing it all on her own. She wouldn't come for lunch. I came in and she was typing away quite happily. You know how she types, you know that smile when it's going well.

"'Lunchtime,' I said. She put her finger up as if to say wait, so I waited, but then she seemed to forget about me. Well, it can't hurt to eat a bit late, I thought, and I left her alone. At around three, I thought, she really does need to eat, it's not good. But I was so happy for the break, I let it go. Finally, there was a silence. She was getting up from the desk, pulling the paper from the typewriter and putting it facedown on a stack.

'All done?' I said.

'All done,' she said.

'Great. I'll put it on the computer tonight and send it off.'

"We had a late lunch, early dinner, soup and sandwiches. I suggested we go for a walk since we'd missed our walk that morning. But she said no, she had to work on the column.

"'You finished the column just before dinner,' I said. She didn't believe me. 'Here, I'll show you.' And I went to get it. Just before I handed it to her, I looked at it. It wasn't like this, it wasn't fragmentary, it was pure nonsense, much of it was not even words. But I couldn't take it back now. So I passed it over. She looked at it and said, 'Stop playing tricks on me. This is not what I wrote.'

"So she went back to the typewriter. This time it didn't go so well. This time she knew she wasn't making sense. She blamed the typewriter, 'the machine,' she called it. 'Frank, something's wrong with the machine, I think someone's switched the letters on me. They've coded it, they've turned it into an encoder, we've got to decode it again.' So we went back to how we did it before, only now I did the typing. That seemed to go well. She was writing about recurring dreams and about vivid dreams and how many Alzheimer's patients wake from these vivid dreams and believe them to be true. She has this recurring dream that she is out somewhere and she has forgotten you and Joel and then she tries to get back to you and she can't. She wakes quite desperate. She'll leap out of bed and try to leave the house."

Poor Dad. Heather hadn't known it was this bad, that her father had to manage this day after day and night after night. Mom had seemed so well. They had whiteboards all through the house with the things she needed to remember written on them. Jokes, even: "Socks first, then shoes" in Frank's handwriting in the bedroom, after a Far Side cartoon he liked.

"She screams at me. 'Let me out, let me out, I've got to find them.' It tears your heart out. The compassionate thing to do, it seems to me, would be to let her look. But would that fuel the delusion or defuse it? I just don't know." Heather's father did not usually talk this much all at once. His voice was steady, his eyes were clear. There was nothing neurotic about it but it was clear it was a *need*, this telling the story. "Anyway, she talks, I type, I read back to her what she's said, she adds more, it all goes fine. Then she wants to see it on paper. And I lean away from the typewriter so she can read over my shoulder and she sort of slaps my shoulder and says I'm in on it. The encoding. I've been typing nonsense. But I haven't been. It's regular old words and sentences. I can show you. Well, that was the end of me doing the typing. Ever since it's been type type type. And it's all this." He tapped the sheaf of papers.

"Dad, why didn't you call the magazine and tell them she wouldn't be able to do it?"

Suddenly his calm broke. He covered his eyes with his hands and wept. "She's never missed a deadline," he said. "Never."

Calling the magazine was admitting she'd turned a corner.

That she was worse. That she really did need care now.

"Do you want me to stay, Dad? Do you want someone here if she's up again tonight."

"No, it's okay, I'll deal with it. But if you could write something..." His eyes pled.

The pages reminded Heather of Gertrude Stein, a minor hero of hers in high school. She contemplated forwarding the column just as it was. There was a certain beauty to it. There was a truth to it that was beautiful, too. Do you really want to see Alzheimer's? Here it is. But her father would be embarrassed and appalled.

So Heather took the pages home and stayed up all night, wrote the column in something that approximated her mother's voice, sent it in. The series won a National Magazine Award. At the awards dinner, Lois got a standing ovation. She smiled and blinked and tried to make a speech, though Joel and Heather and Frank had all tried to avert one. "Thank you," she said. "Like training pink...thorn-blossoms," (she meant roses), "like... Of course...Mother never learned to....drive....or any of the... Well, women and men, women and men, you know..." They surrounded her like a pack of sheepdogs, Frank took her arm, they herded her from the mic.

* * *

Ben took the beach. Taylor took Kew Gardens. Heather drove up to Queen Street and east as far as she thought her mother might have had time to go (would she go farther than the Waterworks? in knee-highs? what if she'd gone farther?) and then systematically drove round each block back towards home. (No shoes. Wouldn't someone stop a woman with no shoes? But what could they do if they did stop her? Lois might or might not remember her address but that was far across the city and no one was home. She might give her childhood address, in Kitchener.) The day was bright and sharp. People were out raking their lawns. Children jumped in leaves. Women her mother's age in sunhats bent over their spent flowers. People walked dogs. Dads pushed strollers or pulled wagons.

None of the people on the streets was a spry seventy-year-old in tan skirt, knee-highs and an orange sweater.

Taylor called. "She's not in the park. Ben's checked the beach all the way to the Waterworks. We're going to do the streets round here." Heather had every confidence in Taylor. Taylor was fine. Taylor was going to be okay.

A few minutes later, Taylor called back. "She's standing out on Woodbine trying to flag down cars." Heather drove as fast as she could and pulled over behind a BMW with its flashers going. Taylor and Lois were standing with a slender, expensively dressed black man. Ben stood a bit back of them, astride his bike.

"Mom," said Heather. "Mom."

"Hello, dear," said Lois. "Have you come to pick me up? This is...what did you say your name was?"

"Tyrone."

"This is Tyrone. Thank you so much for your help, Tyrone," she said to the man. She had a newspaper tucked under her arm.

"No problem," he said. "Only next time, don't run out into the road. I nearly hit you." A car honked at them as it sat behind them, trying to get into the left lane.

"Thanks," said Taylor to Tyrone, as though they had a separate relationship from the rest of them—as, in fact, they must have, as the two sane people with a crazy person.

"Mom?" said Ben, hesitantly. "We're going to be late for hockey?"

"Hockey, shit, I totally forgot. Cover your ears, Willa. Sorry, we've got to go. Ben, put your bike in the car. Taylor, are you okay?"

"Fine, Mom."

"You have keys?"

"I'm fine, Mom."

"You want to come with us?" *Please come with us.*

"I'll be fine, Mom." She shook her head, had that you're a moron look. She turned back into a teen. And the Good Samaritan, Tyrone, in his turn, turned into a threat—he'd won Taylor's trust, he knew she was alone, he knew she had a key to her house. *Don't think this way. Do not think this way. Taylor is fine, Tyrone is kind. He will drive off, she will ride home. Taylor is fine.*

* * *

The stands were right behind the players' bench. You could lean forward and place your hands on the glass if you wanted. Willa pointed out Ben to Lois in the warm-up. "Oh, what a lovely skater," she said, then went on, as she always did, to talk about what a lovely skater Frank had been, how they had met skating. Lois had been trying to show off and she had fallen and he had helped her up.

Lois appreciated people who did things well: she came alive for them. For all the ways her mother had changed, Heather was struck today by the things that had not changed: rising to social occasions, judging Heather for "staying at home," being a sucker for the innately talented. She adored Heather's husband, Steve, who was so innately talented he was almost always out of the country.

"I had brand new skates," Lois was telling Willa. "Practically the first thing I bought with my paycheque. We'd never had new skates, they either swam on us or pinched, but somehow it never mattered." What you knew from this was that it had mattered, quite a lot, but less and less as she worked her way out of poverty. "I had new skates, a new job, and all I needed was a new fella. Well, I found one, all right. Good-looking, a fine skater, and a Rhodes scholar, no less!" She was very proud of that, she, the high-school dropout, married a Rhodes scholar. She had no insecurity at all about not having a degree.

Heather found it both disconcerting and comforting when her mother seemed to reappear from the recesses of her Alzheimer's. She had always been enthralled by the mystery of her mother's life before she had entered it. It was so much more exciting and important than her own life. She did not tire of hearing the stories, in fact, she wanted to hear them again and again. There was the story of the day Lois's father came home from the war ("I was out on the swing Orme had put up on the maple out front, when a soldier walked up our street with a bag over his shoulder. He was a big, friendly fellow, a bit like a

Newfoundland dog but with red hair, and I liked him right away. 'Would you like a push?' he asked. I think that's when I knew he was my dad. Then a sort of shriek from my mother and she flew out the door into his arms."). The story of the day her father disappeared. ("Just before Christmas, 1948. Dad had been home not much more than a year. He'd had a couple of jobs, but right then he was driving a milk truck. He had to get up in the middle of the night, three-thirty or four in the morning. Well, he got up that morning, went off to work, delivered the milk and never came back.") There was the story of applying to the newspaper at sixteen and getting the job, the story of the lecherous editor, the women's page editor with the drinking problem. The story of how she got herself assigned to cover a Mafia trial in Guelph. The story of her mother's death and the discovery of the letter from her father with the absolutely fantastical news that where he had gone when he disappeared was back to Italy, where he had a wife and children they knew nothing about. The story of tracking her father down after all those years, of finding him in Italy and meeting her half-siblings. The story of falling in front of Heather's father while skating. Of marrying in secret so she would not lose her job at the paper. Lois's life was a movie. Heather's life was a post-it note. A whiny one. How I couldn't get my mother's attention. How I disappointed my parents. How I failed to use my potential.

What stories would her children tell? How my mom pretended to be Swiss. The day Grandma ran out onto Woodbine.

The game began. Ben was on the bench. On defense. "I'm no good at defense," he would say after each game. "So I can skate backwards. Big whoop." Every time the other team scored, he took it personally. In house league he and Eric tried out the elaborate plays they made up after school. In Select, Heather watched the droop of Ben's shoulders at each goal scored against them, at each goal they scored that he wasn't a part of. He loved putting the puck in the net. He spent hours practising putting the puck in the net. He loved passing the puck to someone else who put it in the net. When Heather watched Ben and Eric playing in the driveway at home or Ben and Steve at the Moss Park outdoor rink, she sort of got why people played sports: joy. But here, Ben was miserable. She did not get why he wanted to play here. Prestige? How far did that go?

Now he was on the ice, backing up as the other team skated towards him. Now he was making a move and the other player skated past him. He turned, churned his legs to catch up. The coach was yelling, "Ya let him get past you, stay with him, stay with him." Ben dove to knock the puck away from the other player's stick and took his feet out and got a tripping penalty. The coach hollered at the ref for calling the penalty. To the players on the bench, he said, "No more stupid penalties. You take the man, you don't take the puck." The other team scored while Ben was in the penalty box. He skated back to the bench with his head down and his skates biting the ice. As he stepped onto the bench, she saw the coach bend down to him and say something that kept his gaze on the floor. He gave a sullen (hurt) nod, a sullen (hurt) half-shrug. Man, the coach was a bastard. You don't motivate kids by telling them they screwed up.

The next time he was on the ice, Ben totally smoked one of the other team's players, a quick little guy who was beetling up the ice with his head down. (Steve and Ben had tried to explain body checking to Heather. Steve used words like holistic and beautiful and satisfying and clean. *Ow*, she thought. *Meanie*, she thought. But Ben loved it. He was good at it. The coach patted him on the back when he went off. And that would make Ben happy, the approval of an a-hole.) The other team's fans hollered at the ref in outrage. "Nice, clean hit," said Simon's dad, clapping his hands. Now the teams were mad at each other, now the teams' fans were mad at the other team and the other teams' fans. It was a rising tide of antagonism. It made Heather feel like she was suffocating. It was why she turned into Hildie. Ben passed to Eric, who passed to Damien, who dropped a pass to Eric, who put a neat wrist shot in the top left corner of the net. "Offside!" shouted a parent from the other team. "That was offside!"

Lois had followed all this with a series of Ohs of different pitches—a medium Oh of sympathy with the hit, a series of ascending Oh oh ohs leading up to the shot, cheering when it went in. Then, with the puck drop of the next face-off, she was doing the same thing for the other team. Oh oh oh of expectation, an oooooh of disappointment as the promising play was broken up. For a big disappointment, she threw in a "Crumb." "Oh, Crumb." She was doing Hildie's job, rooting for both teams. Heather cheered up for a moment. Her mother's craziness was a thing of beauty. And then it felt like Heather's heart was going to come out her nose. *Her mother's craziness was a thing of beauty*. Her mother could not follow a hockey game. She could not recognize a joke. Her mother was gone. All that was left was a shell. Not only that, they were all shells, every single person, shells made up of pat phrases and set stories. Everything they built up about themselves that said otherwise was just filler. They were small and ridiculous and the fact that they cared about things so passionately—who won a stupid game, how a person was treated unfairly—was sad and pathetic and *all they had*. Heather began to weep, right then and there. "Mom?" said Willa. "Are you all right?"

Lois put her arm around Heather, put her hand on the side of Heather's head and drew it to her shoulder. "There, there, dear," she said. "There, there."

"Heather?" said Lonnie.

Heather waved her hand in front of her face and tried to contain herself.

Heather remained on the brink of tears, but she recovered. The game went on. The antagonism continued. Each team blamed the referee for bad calls, missed calls. Each team seemed to think the other was uniquely mean-spirited and unsportsmanlike. Damien took spectacular dives that resulted in penalties for the other team. Eric, good-natured Eric, was roused to such anger that he had a chest-pushing match with somebody in front of the net. Ben skated in protectively and did some shoving of his own. All three got penalties. Ben's team scored short-handed, which made them instant heroes— they triumph even when unfairly penalized! But to the other team, Ben was a now a bad guy. The parents yelled at the ref, "Watch Number 10. Kid's a goon." When Ben came off after his next shift after the penalty, Heather saw the coach pat him on the back. Like that was a 'good penalty' versus his earlier attempt to salvage a mistake, which was a 'stupid penalty.' He was turning her son into a thug.

The coach of the other team yelled at Ben's coach, accused him—fairly, Heather thought—of encouraging fighting. Ben's coach yelled at the other coach, "You wanna take it outside after the game? Huh?"

Was he kidding? He had to be kidding.

"You and me, buddy."

"This is GTHL, it's not Junior A. You should be out on your ass for encouraging fighting. Out on your ass."

The ref gave them both bench penalties. Ben served the penalty.

Heather zoned out. She saw her father's face from when he'd dropped Lois off that morning, the fatigue in his smile. She wondered how much longer they could do this. She thought, This is it: hockey idiots, loss, what to make for dinner. When she was little and her parents had people over for dinner, life seemed to be about government policy, nationhood (would Quebec separate, should Quebec separate?), wise use of resources, justice, equity, civility. Neighbourhoods not highways! Important things. Heather had not cared at the time. She and Joel preferred to play Princess. She had a princess costume from Halloween. Joel had his paint smock, a white shirt of his dad's turned backwards, tied just under the chest with a blue ribbon from the gift-wrap drawer and a construction paper cone hat. A bear was the king, Barbie was the queen and Ken was a series of idiot suitors they sent on impossible quests while they stayed in their castle on their feather beds and sipped lemonade with maraschino cherries on swizzle sticks. When Heather was five and Joel was three, this was deemed cute. But when she was eight and Joel was six, her mother and father had a talk with her. Joel would not stop playing princess unless she stopped playing princess. And Joel needed to stop playing princess. They took away the costumes. They bought them new games. And Joel and Heather kept playing it anyway. Fun, Heather was certain, frivolity, Heather was convinced, was much more important than whatever it was the parents were on about. She'd thought there was a big divide between childhood and adulthood, that she'd pass a point and change, that she'd turn into the kind of serious grown up person her parents were, but she had not, she had stayed the same. And now it turned out that there was much less to life than those dinner parties had suggested. Oh, yes, Steve was making a difference with his green buildings, but there were more self-interested people in the world than not (she included herself in this), they all had to make money and then dinner, they all chose convenience over conscience three-fifths of the time, they all got sick and needed looking after, they all diminished, they all died. Why, why, why did she still care about any of it? Why did she feel like she wanted to strangle somebody?

* * *

Oh oh oh.

Oh.

Oh. Oh. Yes, lovely, oh. Go go go. Yes. Yes. Hooray. Super.

Around her a clatter of voices. *Your mom's like you, eh? Cheers for both teams. That's all right, we'll get it back. No problem. Come on, Tornados.* WHERE WERE YOU? WHERE WERE YOU? WHERE WERE YOU? YOU GOTTA GET BACK. That man there, what a yeller, he's a story. *Watch. He'll bench Ally now. Yup. I don't know what to do, Heather. She's always the first one to sit. Same for Ben. He takes it so hard. I'm thinking of switching her to a girls' league, but she says the hockey's just not as good, she's got her eye on the Olympics, she's like, Hayley Wickenheiser played with the boys, I'm playing with the boys. She wants to push herself and all she does is sit. It sucks.* CHUCK IT INTO HIGH GEAR, TORNADOS. YOU'RE PLAYING LIKE A BUNCH A GIRLS. *I want to see some disciplined hockey out there. Discipline, you know what that is? Let's GO, let's GO, let's GO.*

The yelling man, he's the, I need to. Where's my thing, my that thing with things in it

Reverse it, reverse it, reverse it.

Mom, where are you going? YES. FINALLY. NO, NO, NO, THAT'S A GIVEAWAY PASS. *Mom? Up the boards, up the boards, up the boards. Mom, the game's not over yet.*

"I need my—"

"What do you need, Mom? I'll help you get it. What do you need?"

"My thing, you know, my that I hold in my hand, that I—"

"Your purse? Your purse is here, Mom. Let's see, we've got Kleenex, sunglasses, ID, what do you need, Kleenex?"

"I need the story. Excuse me, sir, I need to Excuse me, could I Excuse me—"

"Mom? Leave him alone. That's the coach, he's coaching, if you want to call it that. I prefer to call it bullying, I prefer to call it intimidation, but we'll call it 'coaching' if he wants, we'll let him browbeat our children in the name of 'coaching'. Mom, don't lean on the glass."

"Excuse me, sir, if you could answer a few quick questions."

"Get down, Mom."

"Back off, Passive-Aggressive Lady. You're not doing your kid any favours."

"Are you talking to me?"

"'Are you talking to me?'"

"You're sure not doing my kid any favours."

"Kids earn their ice time on my team. You're lucky I'm not going to hold you against him."

"Excuse me, sir—"

* * *

The coach went back to yelling at the players. Lois was leaning forward from the stands, thin hands gripping the top of the plexiglass behind the bench, still trying to get his attention.

"Could you get your hands off the glass, please?' said the coach.

"If you'll just—"

"Man, I hate this arena. If I could ban parents..."

"Mom, get down."

"Excuse me—"

Lois refused to get down. The coach, to make her move, took his elbow and bashed it back against the glass not far from her face. It worked. She let go of the plexiglass and pitched cheek first into it while the rest of her body dropped to the concrete floor. There was an audible snapping of bones, a wailing sucking in of breath, a deep full-chest whimper. Before Heather knew what she was doing, she had jumped onto the back of the bench with her hands over the plexiglass and around the coach's throat, squeezing as if she could squeeze his head right off the neck. She squeezed for about two seconds and then let go and dropped down beside her frightened, bewildered mother. It was probably the most athletic act she'd performed in her life.

Willa stared down with giant eyes, almost as frightened as Lois. "It's okay, sweetie," Heather called up to her, thinking what a ludicrous thing that was to say, thinking of the number of people around the world at accident sites at this moment saying, "It's okay. It's okay," when it wasn't. Land mines, trains, collapsed bridges, dog bites, cross-checking.

Lonnie was on the phone, she was crouching down and hugging Willa, she was on the phone with 911.

The coach was saying, "She strangled me. You saw it. You saw it. She tried to strangle me. I've been assaulted. "

Two peanuts were walking down the street, Heather thought.

"You intimidated an old lady," shouted Simon's dad and then there was more shouting and more and a whistle and Lois whimpering like a hurt child. It looked like Lois's ankle was broken, and possibly her wrist as well, maybe her hip. She would go to hospital. She would not recognize the hospital as a hospital. She would not recognize her need to be in a hospital even if she recognized it as such. She would wake up and want to get away, she would try to get up and injure herself in the process and they would put on restraints, Heather's mother would be strapped to a bed, howling in incomprehension and rage and it would be Heather's fault. She had to call her father. She could not imagine calling her father. It would be Heather's fault. She would excuse herself, she would find a way to live with it, *it would be okay. It would be okay.*

Backstock: The Musical

A man, tall, bald, wearing metal safety toes over his shoes and a Crimson-Eggplant Cornice Jacket, clicks around a cavernous stock room, coffee in hand, clipboard under arm. *"Here it is,"* he sings as his toes snick, *"my dominion, my domain. My pallet jack. My fleece racks. My triple racks of backpacks. My employees*—morning, Clara, morning, Chuck—*my coffee. My gain. So why does it give me such sorrow and pain?"*

Employees trickle in. They whip box knives out of back pockets, they whssht shrink-wrap off pallets, they phht box-tape down boxes. *"Because I'm all alone,"* the big guy sings to an absent somebody. *"Because I don't have you. Because you're true to someone who doesn't deserve you. Because you're you."*

"Hey, Gord," says Clara. "What do I do with this back order?"

"Give it to Jim," the big guy says, nodding to a man with biker-length hair and beard clad in Navy Men's Medium Rad Pants and a plaid shirt. *"Because I'm all alone. Because—"*

"Hey, Gord," says a thirtyish lesbian in a Steel Blue Men's Medium Beefy-T. "Anyone doing Extremities?"

"Anne," says Gord. "Hats, socks and mitts are all yours." Gord consults his clipboard, sips his coffee. *"Remember the slide show, the Nechako slide show. The projector broke down, we told jokes like two clowns deep in love."*

"Hey, Gord-o. I need the afternoon off."

"Sure, Jim. What is it?"

"Heather has a doctor's appointment, wants me to be there."

"You bet," says Gord. He contemplates the clipboard,

goes to take a sip of coffee but then forgets and his MEC Insulated Mug hangs in the air halfway to his lips. "*And after the slide show you got on your bike. You zipped up your raincoat. You rode off with Mike, and I cried.*

"*Now every yellow raincoat is you. Every yellow raincoat I see in the mist, every yellow raincoat is someone I'd kiss in the rain.*

"*Remember the day hike, the Black Tusk day hike. It poured from the start, we poured out our hearts on the trail. We picked ourselves up—*"

"Hey, Gord," says a skater dude in a Black Watchman's Cap.

"Yeah, Jack."

"You're—"

"What?"

"Never mind." Jack watches Gord as he goes back to singing. "Singing," Jack says to himself.

"*—the others caught up and we laughed it off but my heart was caught from then on.*

"*Now every yellow raincoat I see on the street, every yellow raincoat I race over to meet in the rain.*"

"Hey, Gord," says a guy in a Men's Large White Beefy-T under an unbuttoned plaid short-sleeved shirt.

"Yeah, Matt?"

"Is it true we're getting a new general manager?"

"It's true," Gord says, with a funny look on his face.

"I heard she's from Head Office," says Matt.

"I heard she's Mike's girlfriend," says Jack.

"Who's Mike?" says Clara.

"Mike's the man, as in, 'Stick it to the.'"

"I don't get it," says Clara.

"He's the general manager."

"Oh, the one who's brain dead."

"He's not brain dead," says Gord, "He's in a coma."

"So I guess it can't be nepotism if he's in a coma while his girlfriend is hired," says Matt.

"I thought 'nepotism' was for, like, hiring your nephew," says Anne.

"She's been at Head Office longer than he has," says Gord. "She used to work here. We used to work together."

"You know, like, 'nep'? *nep-ph*-ew?" Anne says. Everyone gives her a polite head-cocked glance before ignoring her.

Phhht. Whsshht. Wheel. Stack. "*It's true, it's you,*" sings Gord. "*Remember that bike trip. We went to Deep Cove.*" Unbeknownst to Gord, Karen enters. She's wearing a Women's Medium Yellow Downpour Jacket. She watches Gord as he sings, "*My God, how my heart skipped. We met Mike. He drove. We had lunch at the diner, the one with the doughnuts. Mike kissed you hello. I thought I'd go nuts. Then he rode his bike home and left us the car. We didn't know then he'd not get very far. I had to say something. I told you I loved you. You had to say, 'Yes, Gord, I feel something, too.' But who knew, who knew, that right at that moment, Mike's head met cement.*

"*Now every yellow raincoat is you. Every yellow raincoat I see at the beach, every yellow raincoat is someone I'd reach for in the rain.*"

Karen approaches Gord. "Oh," he says. "Hi."

"Hi."

"How's Mike?"

"The same. I tell him about my day. He says nothing."

"He's in a coma."

"Oh, and that's any excuse?" Karen bursts into tears and falls forward onto the chest of Gord's Cornice Jacket. Just as he goes to pat the back of her Downpour Jacket, she pulls away, wiping her tears. "Sorry. Bad joke. It's going to be okay, right? Working together again?"

"It's going to be great."

Karen sniffs. "Why don't you introduce me to your staff?"

"Karen, meet Clara, aspiring potter, Anne, aspiring writer, Dave, aspiring screenwriter, Matt, aspiring photographer, Herman, aspiring revolutionary, Choi Ping, aspiring social activist, Jill, aspiring video artist, Jack, skateboarder, Dave, aspiring anti-intellectual intellectual, Chuck, one-time painter, Jim, aspiring union organizer, Big Bad Barry, well, you know Big Bad Barry—"

"No aspirations whatsoever," says Big Bad Barry. The employees wave or nod in turn from the spots where they toil.

Herman jumps on an empty dolly and skims across the middle of the stock room as if on a skateboard. Clara drops the last two handfuls of Waterproof Breathable jacket hanger hooks onto a rolling rack, grips the end standard of the rack, takes a running jump, hops onto the back and rolls. She lowers her weight so the far end tips up and spins the whole rack in a circle. To the left, Choi Ping runs up a ladder to the third tier of clothing racks holding Rainwear. To the right, Dave runs up a ladder to the third tier of clothing racks holding Fleece. In the back middle, Big Bad Barry climbs at half speed up and down a ladder fetching Dry Goods and Camping Gear from top shelves like he's climbing to a bass line. Chuck hoists himself up on the end of a large wooden bin on wheels filled with backpacks and surfs it across the floor. Wow. Synchronicity. Jack looks on, bemused.

"*We work backstock, backstock, backstock, backstock, we work in the back,*" Jack's co-workers sing. "*We take fleece pants out of the box and put them on the rack. We unload trucks, we break down flats, we stock the store—*"

"*With sleeping bags!*"

"*Inflatable pads!*"

"*PFDs—*"

"*—and cotton Ts.*"

"*Climbing ropes!*"

"*Degradable soaps!*"

"*Cycling tights!*"

"*Mini mag-lites!*"

"*Mitts and gloves—*"

"*and butane stoves!*"

"*Gore-Tex socks!*"

"*Kryptonite locks!*"

"*Gore-Tex jackets.*"

"*Freeze-dried packets.*"

"*Gore-Tex pants and—*"

"*Bootie rands!*"

"*Silk long johns.*"

"*Short pitons!*"

"*Fanny packs.*"

"*Mesh stuff sacks.*"

"*Skis and poles—*"

"*and skin of moles!*"

"*Sunglasses.*"

"Night ski passes."

"Calendars."

"Nalgene jars!"

"And fleece, fleece, fleece, fleece, fleece, fleece, fleece, fleece, FLEEEEEECE!" They link arms, they form a chorus line and surge forward. *"We work backstock, backstock, backstock, backstock, we work in the back."* Jack has to jump out of the way. *"They wouldn't hire us in the front and so we work in back."*

The workers now rock climb shelves, rappel down them from ropes affixed to the ceiling, they nip up and tip down ladders like so many Donald O'Connors on so many couches, they toss down garments, they Stomp with safety toes, they Carbonne-14 rolling bins, errrr, errrr, errrr, in giant circles. They cohere back into a chorus line, march forward, march back.

"We work backstock, backstock, backstock, backstock, we work in the back. They wouldn't hire us in the front and so we work in back."

Abruptly, the workers resume work. Jack stands idle for a good five seconds until he resumes work, too. A truck's horn sounds in the loading bay. Karen and Gord exchange looks of longing and helplessness before Karen turns to go. *"Now every yellow raincoat is you. Every yellow raincoat I see at my...work..."* Gord chokes up. The horn sounds again, mournful. Gord clicks sadly up the ramp to the loading bay.

Standing on a ladder by a two-level rolling rack, Anne leans forward to stab Trek Jackets with a giant beige thumbtack, whose pointy end she then caps with a magnet encased in plastic that will set off an alarm if someone tries to take it through the sensors at the front door. Dave does the same to the rail of clothing below. On the other side of the rack Matt and Clara lean, poke, snap, lean, poke, snap. Behind them, Chuck is up and down a ladder, loading packs into a big wooden rolling bin. Big Bad Barry does the same thing with miscellaneous camping gear.

"I love my job. It's so stimulating," says Dave.

"It pays the rent," says Matt.

"Seriously?" says Anne.

"It pays half the rent."

"How long have you been working here?" asks Clara.

"Four years," says Matt.

"Three years," says Anne.

"Two years," says Dave.

"I'm only here until I get a grant, though," says Anne.

"I'm only here until I sell my script," says Dave.

"I'm only here until my first solo show," says Matt.

"No way," says Clara. "I'm only here until I start making a living as a potter."

Anne sings, *"I'm only here until I get a nice fat advance."*

(Chuck has a lovely baritone voice. *"I'm here for life."*)

"I'm only here till the gallery calls."

(*"I'm here for life."*)

"I'm only here till Chris Haddock takes my script."

(*"I'm here for life."*)

"I'm only here until my pottery sells."

"There's nothing wrong," Chuck sings, *"with being a lifer. There's nothing wrong with that. It pays the bills, there's no stress or strife or an ego that needs to be fat. What's the use in imagining fame? Who needs one more painter? Colours on canvas, a teeming brain—is one so much better than the other? Hiking's my art now. No one gives a fart now if I paint except my mother. Give me a map and a compass. I'll take off and there's one less whiny artist whining away: why me, woe, woe, ah me, no no. Recognize me! Idolize me! Love me! Buy me! Buy me! Bye me. No. There's nothing wrong with being a lifer."*

"I'm only here until my novel's out."

Barry leans against the shelves and sings, *"I'm here for life."*

"I'm only here until the gallery begs."

"I'm here for life."

"I'm only here until I sell my script."

"I'm here for life. Work on the workdays, fish on the weekends, visit my kid once a year. Work on the workdays, phone up my good friends, maybe crack open a beer. Work on the workdays, fish on the weekends, visit my kid once a year. Work on the workdays, phone up my good friends, maybe crack open a beer."

ANNE:	**CHUCK:**	**BARRY:**
I'm only here until	There's nothing wrong	Work on the workdays,
my agent calls.	with being a lifer	fish on the weekends.
MATT:		
I'm only here until	there's nothing wrong	work on the workdays,
my show goes up.	with that.	fish on the weekends,
DAVE:		
I'm only here until	The novels in my head	visit my kid once a year.
I'm the Sundance Kid.	don't need to be written	
CLARA:		
I'm only here until	they keep me amused	Wrap up the workdays,
I sell my bowls.	while I'm stocking mittens.	phone up my good friends.
ANNE:		
I'm only here until	I can paint and	There's nothing wrong
the GG's mine.	I can box	with being a lifer,
MATT:		
I'm only here until	I can hop from	there's nothing wrong
my Guggenheim.	rock to rock	with that.
DAVE:		
I'm only here until the	I can live	It pays the bills
red carpet at Cannes.	inside my head	there's no stress or strife or
CLARA:		
I'm only here until	I can hike	ego all bloated
I buy a kiln.	until I'm dead.	and fat.
ANNE:		
I'm only here	You'll die too	Work work workdays
until I	one cold cold day.	fish fish weekend
MATT:		
I'm only here	Let me die up	work work workdays
until I	on a peak	fish fish weekend

DAVE:

| I'm only here | A heart attack | call up my friends |
| until I | while I take a leak. | visit my kid |

CLARA:

| I'm only here | Who cares what I've done? | call up my friends |
| until I | Who cares what I've done? | visit my kid |

ANNE, MATT, DAVE,

CLARA:	CHUCK & BILL
I'm only	Here
I'm only	Here
I'm only	Here
I'm only	

ALL: Here.

"I don't need art, I need to walk," says Chuck. They go back to work in silence.

Lunchtime. The backstock area is empty but for Jim at the backorder shelf. Atop a tall stool he peers at a green-letters-on-black computer screen, poking intermittently at a keyboard. Heather enters and stands beside him. You'd be hard-pressed, seeing them from behind, to tell who is who. Their hair is the same length, the same shape, just the same blend of dark and grey.

And then they spin. Jim has a long half-grey beard. Heather does not. "*We gotta get out of here,*" they belt. "*Hunh! We gotta get out of here. Hunh! We gotta get out of here. Oh, yeah.*" Funk it up, Jim and Heather. Heather spins Jim on the stool. Woo.

Then a last spin and Jim's got a banjo on his lap, Heather's got a mic on a mic stand, which they both lean into. They croon in 4/4, they harmonize in thirds and fifths, "*Our dream house is a cabin. We're building it up north and when the roof is finished, we'll up and sally forth.*

"Our cabin is old-fashioned; it's fashioned out of logs. We're going to keep some chickens, we're going to keep some dogs.

"The chickens will give eggs; the dogs will give us fur. Our coats will hang on pegs. Our cats will purr and purr."

"I'll spin the dog hair into yarn," sings Heather, *"knit it into mittens. I'll keep some goats in our rude barn. The cats will have more kittens."*

"We'll be happy. We'll be together."

"I'll hunt."

"I'll gather."

"We'll be together in Bella Coola. We need each other, we don't need much moolah. We'll be sustainable, untwixtanduntwainable, our love unexplainable. We'll be we—

"Gotta get out of here. Hunh! We gotta get out of here. Un-hunh. We gotta get out of here. Oh yeah."

Their arms drop. Their posture relaxes. "Did she say what it's about? asks Jim.

"I think it's the results of my pap smear."

"What?"

Heather shakes her head. They exit.

At the greeny, woody front of the store, seven cashiers serve seven customers. Behind the seven customers are seven lineups. Beside the end cashier, Helga sits on a stool, training a new cashier who's doing just fine. Helga calls out to Karen passing by. "Well?"

"Well what?"

"You know what I'm talking about. You saw him?"

"I saw him."

"And?"

Karen, now past Helga, retraces her steps. "And I can't help it. I love him."

"I knew it," shouts Helga.

"But what about Mike?"

"Ah, Mike's in a coma. What he doesn't know won't hurt him."

"What if he wakes up?"

Helga shrugs. "He wakes up."

"What if he wakes up when I'm with Gord? I'd never forgive myself." Karen looks down. "You know, when he had the accident, Gord and I... Gord and I..."

"I know, I know, you'd just declared yourselves. Listen. There is no cosmic connection between you and Gord and Mike's accident."

"How do you know? There might be. There must be. There is. It feels like there is."

"There isn't. You're being a martyr. Tell you what you've got to do. You've got to break up with Mike."

The cashiers turn their heads in shock, and say in unison with Karen, "Break up with Mike?"

"Leave him."

Karen and cashiers, still shocked, now with orchestral backing: "Leave him?"

"Leave him."

"I can't do that," says Karen.

"Why not?" says Helga.

"Why not?" say Karen and the cashiers. Violins scurry up the scale, flutes take up the chase, wood blocks hop, hop, hop.

"*Oh you can't leave a man in a coma,*" Karen and the cashiers sing brightly. "*That just wouldn't be fair.*"

Karen: "*If he conked out thinking that you love him, he can't wake up to find you just don't caaaaaare.*"

"*Oh, you can't leave a man in a coma,*" sing the cashiers.

The customers weigh in: "*That is callous, that is shallow, that is cruuuuuuel.*"

Cashier 1: "*If you were in a coma—*"

Cashier 2: "*Would you like it if he left you?*"

"*That's the test, you use the golden rule.*"

"But," says Helga.

"*What if he never wakes?*" Karen muses. "*What if he's lost? I'd have been true, but true at what cost? Still...*"

Cashiers: "*You can't leave a man in a coma.*"

Karen by herself: "*You can't leave a man in a coma.*"

Karen and cashiers together: "*You can't leave a man in a coma.*"

Customers, in a key change: "*You can't leave a man in a coma.*"

Karen and cashiers: *"You can't leave a man in a coma. No, you can't leave a man who's just not there."*

In the quiet after the last chord, the store sounds are murmury and uncertain before settling into an easy, bustling groundnote. Karen continues crossing the store as before she was interrupted. A voice over the public address system calls, "Karen, line one. New boss-lady, line one."

Karen picks up the nearest extension. "Hello? Yes? Really? Wow. Give me ten minutes. I'll be right there." Karen hangs up. "Hold the fort, Helga," she shouts, already running out the door.

Through the door Karen's just run out, Jim walks in, dejected. He slouches, abstracted, to the backstock area, where Gord brings skids down from the truck bay and workers break them down. Jim sits on the spinny office chair by his backorder desk that he sat on while playing the banjo before.

"Heather, my Heather," sings Jim, *"my heart is tethered to you. Heather, my Heather, I don't think I can weather loss of you."*

"Everything okay, Jim?" Gord asks.

"Fine," says Jim. "Fine." Pause. *"Heather, my Heather..."*

Heather appears, spot lit, ghostly, sitting on top of a ladder. *"Our dream house is a cabin. We're building it up north, and when the roof is finished, we'll up and sally forth."*

"Our dream house is a dream," sings Jim. *"Our dream is nearly over. We thought we'd move up north. We thought we'd be in clover."*

Jim and Heather together: *"Our cabin is old-fashioned. It's fashioned out of dreams. The dreams are made of vapour, with moonbeams at the seams. Moonbeams vanish with the sun, vapour shifts and drifts away, and we are left with nothing, oh, we are left with nothing, but the love we gave away."*

Poof. Gone is the spotlight. When the lights come up again, there's no Heather on the ladder, no magic in the room.

Karen runs into Mike's hospital room, where he is one in a line of five patients in comas. At the end of Mike's bed stands a doctor with a large nose. A nurse, who's been holding Mike's hand, passes the hand to Karen and stands aside.

"He's awake?" Karen asks, breathlessly. "He's awake?"

"I prefer to say 'semi-conscious,'" says the doctor. "We're seeing eye movement. We're hearing vocalizing."

"He's awake," confirms the nurse.

"Mike!" says Karen.

Mike's eyelids flutter. Flutter flutter. Flutter flutter flutter. Flutter. Then open wide.

"Mike, it's me, Karen. I'm here."

"Total," says Mike.

"Total, yes, I'm totally here for you, Mike," says Karen.

"Total quality."

"Mike, Mike, you're too good for me. I'm not total quality. I'm not what you think. I almost— Oh, Mike, I almost—"

"Total quality management."

Karen stands up straight. "What?"

Mike repeats it. "Total quality management."

"You've been in a coma a long time. You're bound to— "

"Yes! Total quality management."

Karen can't help herself. She falls in with Mike's delighted state of wonder and revelation. "Well, total quality management to you, too, Mike."

Mike leaps out of bed. He goes to grab Karen as if to dance with her but he's yanked back by his nose tube, at least until it pops out of its attachment so that as he waltzes Karen, he trails rubber tubing as well as IV pole. Doctor and nurse tail him, trying to detach all the trailing paraphernalia, but he's unstoppable.

"*T-Q-M, T-Q-M, T-Q-M, T-Q-M,*" he shouts gleefully, like Oliver waking up in the rich man's house and throwing open the window sash.

"Mike! Oh, Mike! Whoa, watch out."

"*The total quality management waltz: it came to me in a dream. The total quality management waltz: the thing we need is a...team! Yes, teams! No more managers, we'll call them team leaders. (Is that a tanager out there in the cedars?)*

"*The total quality management waltz: the teams will all brainstorm, continuous improvement, a productivity maelstrom.*" Mike drops into excited speech, "I see it all now, Karen. The whole organization, a team of teams, a wonder of wonders, a winning combination. No more Out-of-Equipment

Co-op! We'll turn it all around. No more disgruntled workers. They'll be involved! Their voices will be heard!"

In the backstock office, workers grumble. "I'm so disgruntled," says Jill. They're all crammed into the tiny backstock office, propped on desks and filing cabinets and shelves and the floor. Gord's not there yet.

"If you can be disgruntled," says Anne, "can you be gruntled? If you're gruntled, does that mean you're happy?"

"No one listens to us," says Jack.

"Union," Jim mutters.

"You can't live on this wage," says Matt.

"You can't live alone on this wage," says Dave.

"You can live on noodles on this wage," says Clara.

"You can live with your parents on this wage," says Choi Ping.

"Union," says Jim.

"I've been working here ten years and I'll never make more than what I'm making right now. If I did, maybe I could afford to have my kid live with me instead of in California with his mother," says Big Bad Barry.

"Union."

"Don't they want to keep good workers?"

"Is 'gruntled' sort of like 'chuffed'? I mean, 'chuffed.' It sounds like you're pissed, but you're not, you're happy. Man, am I chuffed. Man, am I gruntled."

"Union."

"Hey, Jim," says Matt. "Do you think we should unionize?"

"That's what I'm saying. That's what I've been saying for years. Union."

"*Union?*"

"Union."

"That starts to sound weird after a while, eh?" says Anne. "'Union.' 'Union.'"

"*Un-ioooooooon,*" everybody sings, drowning her out. "*Un-ioooooooon. Un-ioooooooon. Un-ioooooooon.*"

Jack rolls his eyes, peels away from the meeting, goes back to work while Dave works up some beats and Dave starts rapping, "*We're working for a co-op, we should make a living wage,"* and Jill steps in, *"or else why not start a grow-op, fuck society, fuel some rage."*

"Yeah, the workers on the floor can take courses and make more," complains the other Dave, *"while we're stuck here in the back, making peanuts, taking flak."*

"'Making peanuts'? 'Taking flak'?" says Herman. "Man. You white people can't MC worth shit. *Yo, workers of the world."* Herman puts his hand out to them as if it held a mic and turns his face away as if for them to shout.

"Unite, unite," they oblige.

"Yo, workers of the world,"

"Unite, unite."

"We're working, we're not shirking, but they're always at our backs—"

"Is it really that bad?" says Carly. "I mean, we've got showers. We've got a really nice lunchroom. We've even got okay benefits."

"Yo, workers of the world,"

"Unite, unite."

"Yo, workers of the world,"

"Unite, unite."

Gord walks in, doing a little popping. "Yo, workers of the world. What's up?"

Jack trails in behind and leans in the doorway, while the rest of the workers look down, toe the ground, don't answer.

Now dressed in khakis, a shirt and tie and a Men's Medium Forest Trek Jacket, Mike addresses five or six other top-level head-office types in a boardroom. "A continuous feedback loop! Continuous improvement! Employee involvement!" Mike begins to waltz. The others exchange wary or amazed looks. "T-Q-M, T-Q-M, T-Q-M, T-Q-M."

"This came to you while you were in a coma?"

"Yes-Q-M," says Mike, still waltzing.

"How did a Japanese management style based on the thinking of U.S. statistician W. Edwards Deming get into your coma?"

"Good question. I don't know. *I don't know, I don't know, T-Q-M, T-Q-M. The Total Quality Management Waltz has taken me by the gonads. The Total Quality Management Waltz. It's the answer. Come on. Let's go, lads."*

He grabs his cohorts by the hands, pulls them to their feet, gets them waltzing! *"One-two-three, team-two-three, brain-two-three, storm-two-three, em-ploy-ee in-volve-ment, contin-u-ous fee-eed-back, im-prove-ment, in-volve-ment, contin-u-ous fee-eed-back, wooooo."*

ALL: *T-Q-M, T-Q-M, T-Q-M, T-Q-M...*

"Yo, workers of the world," Herman prompts as he pushes a handcart of cycling gear through the staging area.

From their various perches and stations comes *"U-nite, u-nite. U-nite, u-nite. U-nite, u-nite."*

Intermission.

It's the end of the day in Backstock. Workers ride out on their bikes. Gord loads empty pallets onto the electronic pallet jack.

"Bye, Jack."

"Bye, Gord."

"Bye, Gord."

"Bye, Carly."

Karen enters. Gord gazes at her.

"I need the week off, Gord," says Jim.

"Okay. Why?" Eyes on Karen.

"Heather's having chemo."

"Kay. Have a great week."

Jim exits.

Gord takes the pallets up the ramp to the loading bay, drops them off, then rides down the ramp atop the pallet jack like a charioteer, one foot on either prong. He glides over to Karen, jumps down and gestures to her to step on, then stops her. "Safety first," he says, handing Karen a pair of protective steel overtoes. She dons them and steps onto one arm of the pallet jack. Gord, on the floor, spins Karen gently, gracefully around. It's a pas de deux, part ballet, part foxtrot, with a big electronic beast between the two dancers. Karen's part is to keep her balance, to anticipate Gord's moves, which she does, admirably, so that it looks almost as if she is the one driving the pallet jack, her feet directing it as if it were a skateboard. The moves become more intricate, more difficult as they go. The dance is a joyful game, a contest between them, a test of each person's skill and ingenuity. Gord's safety-toe clad feet clatter on the concrete floor like hooves or cowbells. After the most dramatic maneuvre yet, there's a pause. Gord and Karen lock eyes as if they've completely forgotten the game, the dance.

After a long moment, Karen speaks. "Gord..."

Gord jerks the pallet jack for the first time. Karen has to jump off. Her safety toes clatter.

"He's..."

"I know," says Gord.

She looks down. She takes off the toes and hands them to Gord. She runs off. Gord sings. "*Because I'm all alone. Because I don't have you.* Heather's having chemo?"

"Any news from HarperCollins?" Dave asks.

"Nope," says Anne. "Any news from Chris Haddock?"

"Unh-unh."

"Any news from the gallery?" they ask Matt. Matt shakes his head.

"*No news,*" they bluesify, "*no news. No news, no news. It's no news we got the no-news blues.*"

"*I check my mailbox,*" wails Anne.

"*No news.*"

"*I check my inbox,*" says Dave.

"*No news.*"

Matt: "*I check my voicemail.*"

"*No news. No news we've got the no-news blues.*"

ANNE:	*No news Monday*
DAVE:	*No news Friday*
MATT:	*No news on the weekend, no news coming my way*
ALL:	*No news we got the no-news blues*
ANNE:	*One day I hope. Next day I mope.*
DAVE:	*One day I'm fine. Next day I pine.*
ALL:	*No news we got the no-news blues.*
	No news, no news. No news, no news.
	Got to get some good news soon.

The workers set up a chain to backstock the fleece, passing it hand to hand, and sing their chorus again.

In a boardroom with frosted glass walls, the backstock workers gather for a meeting. Gord's not there yet. Jim is conspicuously absent. A shadow appears behind the frosted glass—somebody listening to them. No one sees.

"So what does it take to unionize?" Carly asks. "You just say, Hey, we're a union, give us more money and better benefits?"

"Jim would know."

"Where are you people from?" asks Dave. "You join a union that already exists. The first unionized McDonald's joined the Canadian Auto Workers Union."

"That is somehow very fitting."

"I want to be a Teamster," says Choi Ping. "Teamstah."

"I read a script once about a teamster," says Anne. "The Diane Something Story. Her son died in a car crash. She fought corruption."

"Yo, we're teamstahs, teamstahs. Don't mess with the teamstahs, teamstahs."

"I looked them up," Matt says. "I've got a list. There's the International Brotherhood of Boilermakers, Iron Ship Builders, Blacksmiths, Forgers and Helpers."

"I am not joining a brotherhood," says Clara.

"The Bakery, Confectionary and Tobacco Workers—"

"The convenience store workers union," says Chuck. Blank looks. "That was a joke. Why does nobody laugh at my jokes?"

Gord enters. "Hey, team."

"Teamstahs," says Choi Ping.

"So I guess you've heard by now we're adopting a new management system."

Mike pops his head round the door. "Did someone say 'New Management System?'" Karen follows him, looking embarrassed.

"Actually, I said 'new management system.' No capitals."

"Naaaah, you said New Management System. I heard ya. Listen, it's not just new, it's totally new. It's not just quality, it's total quality. Come on, everybody, up, up on your feet. Up. Ready? TQM, TQM, TQM, TQM. Waltz with me. Come on."

Mike grabs Karen and waltzes with her. A few people rise uncertainly. Mike lets go of Karen and grabs Carly. Carly waltzes enthusiastically. Meantime, Karen has snagged Gord to waltz with. Mike takes Karen back from Gord. Carly waltzes with Clara.

"TQM, TQM. We're going to waltz this co-op into the stratosphere. TQM, TQM, TQM, TQM. Come on, everybody. Loosen up. Have some fun. TQM, TQM, TQM, TQM."

Matt and Chuck waltz half-heartedly.

Herman crosses his arms and says, "We reserve our right not to waltz."

Everyone stops.

"Okay, you no-funs. Do it the boring way. But let me tell you, I'll knock you right out of your comas as soon as you get the amazing importance of all that I'm saying. The basic idea is you, the employees, have thoughts and ideas that never get used in traditional management."

As Mike goes on in this vein, Gord and Karen exchange glances. Dancer Gord stands up from Gord's body and walks over to Karen, holding his hand out. Dancer Karen takes his hand, stands. The two begin to waltz, while Mike keeps time. "The big guys decide without input from you. Nothing gets better and nothing improves and all start to grumble, morale starts to worsen and no one's productive and profits go tumbling and everything crumbles till we're out of business. But—"

Suddenly Gord and Karen tango. Mike keeps up his old waltz "—with this model, there are no employees and supervisors, there are teams and team leaders, working together to brainstorm ways to do what we do even better. Teams give their input, it's participative management—"

Real Gord and Karen do very slight shadow versions of the same moves their dancer-selves are doing. Whenever this movement gets carried away, drawing Mike's attention to them, they stop and the dancers disappear in darkness. Then he warms to his topic and they start again. Finally, the tango becomes quite heated. Real Gord and Karen are quite noticeably tango-ing. Mike's head snaps from the whiteboard to Gord and Karen, who freeze. Again the dancers disappear.

"So," Herman says, "you want to use our brains as well as

our bodies, but you're not going to pay us any more money?"

"Well, yes, but your job satisfaction will be much higher."

"So is that it?"

"Well," says Mike, "I guess so." He checks his watch.

En masse, the backstock "team" rises and tangoes out of the room, leaving Mike and Karen.

At the same moment, Mike and Karen say, "Were you always like this?"

"What do you mean?" asks Karen.

"Dreamy and goofy and—" He mimics some of the movements she made during the tango. "What do you mean?"

"Corporate. Jargon-y. 'Team'-y. *You used to be sweet, you used to be shy. You used to be alternative, Mr. Off-the-grid, now you're a corporate guy.*"

Mike returns, "*You used to be sweet. You used to be fun—*"

"I'm still fun," says Karen.

Mike shakes his head. "*You used to be game for anything, up for anything, now you're* a wet blanket."

"I'm not a wet blanket. *You used to want to watch the birds not botch the words of the language.*"

"I'm not botching anything."

"'Participative management'?"

"*You used to want to climb the ranks, fill your bankbook with poundage.*"

"No, I didn't. I was never about that. *You used to be sweet. You used to be kind. You used to be clear-sighted and true, now it's clear you are just plain blind.*"

"*You used to be sweet. You used to be supportive. You used to be a wonderful friend, now you're all bent and abortive.*"

"Bent and abortive, Mike, that's awful."

"I wouldn't know, being as how I'm blind."

"*You used to be sweet,*" Karen sings with regret.

"*You used to be sweet,*" Mike echoes.

"*You used to be fine,*" she goes on.

"*You used to be fine,*" he echoes again.

In unison: "*You used to be loving and hot, but now you're just not. You used to be mine.*"

Karen's turn to echo. "*You used to be mine.*"

Mike's turn. "*You used to be mine.*"

Together: *"You used to be,"* harmonizing, *"mine."*

"So is that it, then?" Mike says. "We're done?"

Karen nods.

"I'll crush your little union."

Mike exits.

"What little union?"

"Jim, how's it going?"

"What do you want, Mike?"

"Me? Nothing. Just checking in, catching up. How you been?"

"You asked me that already."

"You didn't answer."

"I'm fine."

"You've been missing a lot of work."

"My boss knows all about that."

"Your team leader, you mean."

"Gord. You know, tall guy. Decent. In love with your wife."

"Ouch. You know what they call you round here?"

"What."

"Mr. Union."

"And?"

"Well, say you were to miss a lot more work, I'd have to call it a case of absenteeism. We'd have to look at warnings, we'd have to look at disciplinary measures."

"Have you heard of compassionate leave, Mike? Have you heard of leave without pay? Have you heard of union busting, Mike? Have you heard of the Canadian Labour Code?"

Mike leaves. Heather enters from the office where she's been lying down. She is wearing a floppy hat because her hair is falling out.

"Why didn't you just tell him?"

"He'd organize some sort of soppy fundraiser. I don't want everybody on the sympathy wagon, it'd make me barf. You've got cancer. That's life."

"I've got cancer. That's life."

"I didn't mean it that way."

"We've gotta get out of here, Jim. When chemo's finished, let's go up north, let's go finish the house. I hate this place, Jim. "

"The co-op? It's not that bad. Even Mike's not really that bad."

"You know what I mean. The city. *We gotta get out of...* Hunh."

Heather can't funk it up anymore. She sits. Heavily.

As the team tags fleece, Chuck is up a ladder in the background painting a "Goodbye Jim and Heather" banner, but his work is screened by darkness.

"Any word from HarperCollins?"

"Uh, yeah, they, uh, said no. But guess what? Polestar's going to take it."

"Polestar, what's that?"

"A very small, very reputable, very excellent small press."

"That's great. Congratulations."

"So how about you? Heard anything?"

"Yeah, yeah—"

"Really? Diane Ferris?"

"No, no, it's this, um, café in my neighbourhood, they'll, uh, let me put the photos up on the walls for, like, a month, as long as I fill the holes and repaint when I'm done."

"That's great, that's great, congratulations."

"Dave?"

"Uh, I'm doing a corporate video for head office."

"Way to go."

"Clar?"

"I got into the Womyn's Solstice Craft Collective. We're having a show at the Ukrainian Hall next Saturday."

"*Congratulations!*" sing Matt and Anne to Dave and Clara.

"*Felicitations!*" sing Dave and Clara to Matt to Anne.

"*Our creations have found their homes. Our expectations may be reduced, but at least we have produced and our creations have found good homes.*"

"*Congratulations! Felicitations! Our creations—*" As their song repeats itself, Chuck comes down his ladder, backs up, finds a light switch to illuminate his painting and flips it on. Everyone stops. Awe. He has painted a giant mural of co-op workers, reminiscent of Diego Rivera but in a more west coast style. Their fists are raised. Jim is in front, leading them. It's a stunning work of art.

"Almost time for Jim's going-away party, everyone," says Gord, coming out of the backstock office. "Wow."

Karen enters from the floor. "Wow."

In the painting, she and Gord tango in the background, while the workers unite in the foreground.

And now they take up the same pose. The workers march in place and hum Solidarity Forever, while Karen and Gord tango, and then Jim lurches in, drunk as hell.

"Fuck the union," Jim shouts. "Fuck it all."

Everyone stops, freezes in place.

"Jim," says Gord.

"Fuck it all," he repeats and weeps. Everyone else is in tableau, exactly as they are in the painting, which lowers behind them. Jim falls to his knees, still weeping, the only figure in motion.

Curtain.

Soyez Blessé

Myrna McIlroy strode up Charles Street, thinking, "Why *shouldn't* I get married? Why *shouldn't* I?" It was 1995, she was twenty-seven. She'd been reading Virginia Woolf's *Night and Day*. Why shouldn't she? No reason at all. Katharine Hilbery would marry Ralph Denham, or else the other guy, the one with the bulgy eyes, and Mary Datchet would marry someone or other—Ralph, Myrna hoped as she read the Mary sections, though her allegiances switched with the point of view, so in the Ralph sections she felt for Mary but stopped rooting for her, hoping instead along with Ralph that Katharine would notice him. The point was: they had to marry. The point was: it mattered that they end up with the right person, or if they didn't, that it be a tragedy. Or so it seemed when Myrna was on page ninety-nine.

In real life, it didn't matter in the same way, or if it did, there was no way of knowing who the right person was, there was no narrator making it clear one person was a better choice than another. So people married and were unhappy or people parted and it was no tragedy at all, just too bad, just hard. Or even not too bad. A relief. Better for everyone concerned. Myrna knew all this and still muttered "Why *shouldn't* I?" as she crossed through the park, where pods of ratty young men played drums and hacky sack while a toddler belonging to one of them ate dirt nearby. If one couldn't marry at the end, how did one know one's story mattered? How did one know who the right person was? The answer was that one's story didn't matter. One's passion was fleeting with no end to secure it. It was like a ribbon fluttering in the wind, swept up into bare November trees. A book about it would never be truly satisfying.

Myrna put the crook of her elbow to her eyes and let one sob into it as she walked. Her brother Gary could get married as many times as he liked, but she could not marry even once.

Even if somebody did love her enough to ask.

Why did everyone leave her? Why did no one love her enough? What was wrong with her?

"Oh, Myrna Jayne, get ahold of yourself," she said out loud.

There was her mother on Commercial Drive, waiting outside the store, looking like someone in an ad for early retirement. Tanned, fit. Well adjusted. The kind who went for bicycle trips in the San Juan Islands with her equally fit, financially secure significant other. It made Myrna feel tired. She had not told her mother yet about Jude. Beth waved.

"Hello, Darling," Beth said when Myrna was close enough.

"Hi, Mom. How was the trip?"

The trip was wonderful. She'd show her the pictures at lunch. How was Myrna? How was Jude?

"Yeah." Jude was impossibly handsome and fucking someone who did not know yet how neurotic she was. Myrna would take her back in a flash.

"Jude is 'yeah'?"

"Fine." Probably.

"Are you okay?"

"How come Gary gets to marry twice, and we can't even marry once?"

"I did marry once. Remember?"

"You know what I mean."

Myrna's mother had dropped out of school to marry Myrna's father, not thinking of it in the conventional drop-out-of-school-to-marry sense but in an anti-establishment sense, university being the establishment (Beth's parents expected her to become a lawyer), and "homemaking" a radical act. Her mother had a speech. "I am a Home Maker." Equal emphasis on Home and Maker. Naturally, everything in their house was homemade: curtains, place mats, tablecloths, napkins, kitchen table, garden chairs, spice rack, lamps, lampshades, futons, duvet covers, sheets, pyjamas, afghans, towels, soap, cleanser, shelves, towel racks, bedside tables, writing paper. Beth had had about seven small businesses. She had made soaps and lotions, she had knitted hats and mittens, she had felted hats, she had woven rugs. She had sold cards with nature photography. She had been busy, she had seemed happy. A store on West Broadway bought pretty much anything she made.

Myrna's father went off to work whistling, he made beer on weekends, he went orienteering and cross-country skiing, he was always going off to loppets.

On Myrna's seventeenth birthday, which coincided, as it so often did, with Thanksgiving, when they were all sitting around after pumpkin pie moaning about their full tummies, Myrna's father had said, "I'll be moving out later this month."

They all—Myrna, who was called Jayne then, her brother Gary, Laura, his girlfriend, later-to-be first wife, and Jayne's girlfriend, Val—turned to stare at him.

"Your father and I have had an open marriage," said Jayne's mother.

"A what?" said Laura.

A look passed between Jayne and Gary. Their parents had surpassed themselves.

"I've been seeing Dorrie Graham," said Jayne's father. Dorrie Graham was a colleague of her father's. She worked for the World Health Organization.

"We didn't want to tell you, because, well—"

"—it just didn't seem like any of your business."

"For, um, how long?" said Gary.

"Six years," said their father.

"Six years that you've been seeing Dorrie or..."

"I've been seeing Dorrie for, oh, what is it now—"

"Four years," said Beth.

Jayne pictured Dorrie at the cottage—she had been a frequent guest, both with and without her husband—homemade beer in hand, hand in pocket. There was something kind of dykey about her, actually. And her father went for that. Jayne shivered. Who had slept where? What were they thinking?

"I had a fling with Michael Greenberg," Jayne's mother said. Her arms were folded across her chest.

Now, in Dr. Vigari's, Beth said, "I don't think it's the legal aspect of marriage that matters, do you? I think it's the ceremonial aspect."

"This is nice," said Myrna, pointing to a handcrafted box made of barnwood, infixed with a modern blond glass-topped box enclosing old photos. "Look, you can customize it."

Myrna's mother knew the artist, of course. "I didn't know he was still doing these," she said. "Do you like them?"

"Don't you?"

"I loved them when I first saw them. Now I think they're kind of..."

"Kitschy."

"No, not kitschy..."

"Nostalgic."

"I was going to say 'overt.' But if you like it, you should get it."

"I can't afford it. I can't afford anything in this store."

"I'll give you something to give them. Come on, let's go for lunch."

"No, Mom. I want to get them something from me."

Myrna's mom had a hard time seeing anyone paying prices she asked for her own work. *I could do that,* her tone was always saying. *Don't pay that. I'll make one for you.* "What does Jude think you should get?"

"Oh, Jude's hopeless at this sort of thing. She would have no idea." Boy, Myrna would feel silly later, but she couldn't seem to help herself. "What's wrong with overt?"

She bought a raku tea set and they strolled down the street for lunch. Beth talked about her trip, she talked about couples, about Gary and Monique, herself and Fern, Myrna and Jude, Gary and Laura, she talked about her marriage to Myrna's father. "Your father is the restless type," she said. "Gary is steady." Her voice had affection for them both. Myrna had heard it all before. "Restless" was a synonym for "he always wanted to sleep with other people." Whether or not that was true, he was still with Dorrie. "He always wanted to sleep with other people" was something Beth could say to herself to explain why he'd wanted that 'open marriage.' Another thing Beth could say to herself was: I'm a lesbian! See? It wasn't my fault. Or, on other days, I'm a lesbian! It was all my fault! Although, to her credit, she never disavowed the marriage altogether, or her love for Doug. She just shifted the point from which it was viewed.

Myrna phased out, watching a couple close to her age say nothing to one another, just look off into the distance, tap the table with idle fingers. They were bored. They knew each other too well. Then someone passing by the patio greeted one of them, who came alive while the other, clearly listening, looked down with a half-smile and then up, alive also, as if this third person, or any third person, was what made their relationship tick. Myrna watched a dog lying in the sun. She watched an old woman in a turban shuffle down the street.

After splitting up with Jayne's father, Jayne's mother had been depressed and pretending not to be. Jayne liked her most, then. Jayne would come home and find her in pyjamas, eating healthy snacks in front of the small black and white television they had had since Jayne was born. As they took off coats in the vestibule, Jayne and Val would hear sniffling in the living room, nose-blowing, a shift in breathing, and the sudden clack of snatched up knitting.

"Hi, Mom. I'm home," Jayne would shout, to give Beth more time, while she and Val half rolled their eyes.

Jayne and Val made dinners for Beth. They put candles on the table. They played checkers and crokinole and dictionary. They wrote their essays on the homemade kitchen table. It was homey and familial and it made Jayne feel pleasingly grown up to care for her mother in this way.

"You want to talk about it, Mom?" Jayne asked one day early on. "About Dad?"

She shook her head and cried openly for the first time. "Oh, no. Good riddance, I say." She didn't mean it. "I don't mean it. I don't know what it is," she went on. "Maybe it's menopause. Maybe it's empty nest syndrome."

"I still live here."

"You don't need me, Jayne. You haven't needed me since you were twelve."

That's true, Jayne thought. She had a flash of being twelve, of the sensation of very long legs and bony knees. She had a flash of her happy parents, who had been faking it.

"What do you know about llamas?" Beth said.

"I know absolutely nothing about llamas."

"I was reading about llama farms. I need a project."

"Why don't you start with something, um, simpler. Like yoga."

"Oh, God, I hate yoga."

"I never knew that. How could I not know that?"

"I tried it years ago. It made me insane. All these people moving like molasses, pretending to be spiritual. Go do something, I wanted to shout at them." She gestured at herself as if to point out her current lethargy and burst into a fresh batch of tears.

"Great. I'll sign us both up, then."

"Do," said Beth, in a suddenly sincere voice.

"You just told me you hated it."

"Maybe I'll like it now. Maybe it'll be good for me. Besides, we never do anything together anymore." Excuse me. What did she call what they were doing right now?

Jayne signed them up. The teacher's name was Fern.

"That wasn't so bad," Beth said afterwards. "I almost sort of liked it."

Jayne had felt clumsy. Bony. Taut as elastic. Not to be flexible was apparently a personality flaw.

Myrna admired the pictures of the San Juan Islands. She plied her mother with enough questions to keep her talking until their food came. The next moment. That would be a good time to say something. Like *Jude dumped me. Jude met someone else. Jude's been having an affair the last three months.* Spinach when you chewed it felt sort of squeakish. Along chalkboard/fingernail lines, only milder. *Jude's moved out.*

Doug had moved out the day after Thanksgiving. Beth stopped working. She wouldn't call her friends. When they called her, she brushed them off. She lied. Jayne kept bugging her. "Mom, you should call Beverly. Call Joan. They're your friends. They love you." But she didn't call. So when Beth proposed they host a New Year's Eve party, Jayne said, "Sure."

"You invite your friends, too," Beth said. "Not a big gathering. Just a few friends. We'll have beer and wine and appetizers. I'll make your friends play charades. They'll love it. They'll pretend to hate it but really they'll love it."

Jayne was envisioning Beth's friends upstairs and hers down in the basement. Adults and teens. But no adults showed up. The teens were upstairs with beers in their hands, a dozen people from band in Jayne's living room, a bunch of girls from Val's soccer team in the kitchen, a couple of friends from other classes hovering at the dining room table, trying not to hoover the food too badly.

Jayne pulled Beth aside in the hall. "Mom. Where are your friends?"

"Oh, they'd just put a damper on things," she said.

"You didn't invite them?"

"I was going to. I just. Every time I picked up the phone to do it, I put it back down again."

"Mom. That was the whole point! You need to see your friends. This is not good for you."

"Forget about me, Jaynie. It's New Year's Eve. Have some fun."

"I don't want to have fun, Mom."

"Listen to yourself, honey."

"Augh."

Beth went off and filled her wine glass. Jayne went and found Val. "Oh, my God," she whispered. "She didn't invite anyone."

"So?" Val shrugged.

"That was the whole point!"

Val drank her beer and shrugged again. "Nothing we can do about it now," she said.

"Time for charades!" Beth went through the house announcing. She got loud when she was drinking. Exuberant. "Come on, everybody, into the living room!"

"Oh, my God," said Jayne.

But Beth was right. Everyone had fun. She got the band people and the soccer people mixing. There was enough alcohol that it felt like a party and not so much that anyone was out of control. People came up and told Jayne how great her mother was. Beth came up and told Jayne how great her friends were. Jayne relaxed. It was okay. She was in grade twelve. These were people she'd known for years. They were good people. They were fun. They were funny. Her mom was okay, too. Drunk, sure, and still drinking, but okay. It was all all right.

They counted down to midnight, went out to bang pots and pans on the porch, and heard the neighbourhood's pots and pans ring from down the street and across the way. Steve Alto and Steve Tenor played Auld Lang Syne on their saxophones and everyone else put their arms around each other's shoulders and swayed back and forth as they sang. Beth was between Jayne and Val.

"These two are my saviours," she said, in the lull after the song. "You know my husband left me? We had an open marriage. Ha. Open for him. These two are my saviours. I love 'em. Aren't they cute? They're such a cute couple!"

"Ha ha," said Jayne. She and Val were not out to anyone at school. "Couple a cards, eh, Mom?" They were only out to Jayne's parents because Beth had cornered Jayne about it last spring: "Okay, which is it? You're either stoned or in love." "Mom." "I knew it!" "I toke up every day." "It's 'toke' or 'smoke up,' my dear, not 'toke up.' You're in love. Who is—." She had been about to say "he," but then had stopped. "It's Val, isn't it?" A look of wonder came over Beth's face. "You're in love with Val." Jayne blushed. "Wow," said Beth. "Okay. I can get used to that." And she had.

Now, in a stage whisper, she said, "Oh. Sh. Forgot. Nobody knows they're a couple!"

"Okay, Mrs. M.," Val said. "Time for bed."

"Mom, you're so drunk," Jayne said.

"I am. I am so drunk," said Beth.

"Sorry for my drunk mother, everyone," Jayne said. Beth allowed herself to be led off to bed.

"Oh, my God, Jayne," said Val in the upstairs hall outside Beth's bedroom. "What are we going to do?"

"Nothing?" said Jayne. "What does it matter? The people who are going to be mean will be mean, and the people who won't won't."

"No, but listen. I don't want people to think I'm a lesbian."

"Yeah, but you are."

"Not like that. I'm not."

Oh, come on, Jayne wanted to say. *You totally are. We both are.* But Jayne didn't look like a lesbo and Val did, meaning that Jayne was not sporty or masculine and Val was.

"I just love you," said Val.

In retrospect, Jayne could see that Val had already been pulling away. Protecting herself. Deluding herself. Beth's blunder only accelerated things. Early in January, Val went on a date with a boy on the basketball team. Then on another date with a different boy. She started wearing mini-skirts. In March, she started dating Steve Tenor. She still came over to Jayne's house. She still made out with her. She still loved her. She wouldn't break up with her. In the end, Jayne had to do it.

Beth and Myrna finished lunch. They hugged in parting on the street. Beth asked about Myrna and Jude's plans for getting to Mayne Island for the wedding. *Jude's not coming.* Or, *Oh, yeah. Forgot to mention. Jude's mom has a blastoma.*

"Yeah, we'll probably catch the last ferry Friday," said Myrna. "Jude's got to work. I probably don't, but she does." She went home, cried a while, then read more *Night and Day.*

"Oh, for Pete's sake, Jayne," her mother had said a few years later. "You have nothing to do with it."

First Jayne had moved out. Then Beth had gone back to school. At SFU. The same school as Jayne. She had crashed Jayne's coffee dates, she had yoo-hooed down halls, she had dropped by to pick her up and give her rides. Then she had confessed to having a crush on her yoga instructor. Now she was going to every single event during Lesbian Week: Lesbian Bingo, the Dyke March, the Butch Bake-Off. At first Jayne just thought, Oh, she's coming as a friend of Fern. Fern's partner was having chemo and didn't go out on bad days. When she did, there would be a group of them, six or eight women in their forties and fifties. They'd wear hats in solidarity, but you could tell by the pallor who the sick one was. Then Beth started coming without Fern. And Jayne thought Oh my God, she's pathetic, she's lonely, she's living through me.

"Mom. What are you doing at all these Lesbian Week events?" Jayne asked her finally at the dance on Friday. Jayne had had too much to drink. Jayne's new girlfriend, Sarah, was in Borneo with God, also known as the orangutan lady.

Jayne had come with a group of friends. They had dragged her onto the dance floor, she'd been having fun until she spied her mother dancing in a dated fashion across from a grey-haired woman with large hips Jayne recognized as one of Fern and Ariel's friends. Her mother waved and danced her way over to Jayne. That was when Jayne asked her what she was doing there.

"I'm having fun," Beth said, as if Jayne, too, were having fun.

"I mean at Lesbian Week. You're not a lesbian."

"Says who?"

"Says who? Says you for the last forty-five years."

Her mother shrugged. "Well, I am one now. Ask Doreen." She gestured to the woman with the large hips. Doreen couldn't hear them. The music was too loud. Doreen waved. Doreen, it seemed to Jayne, leered. Jayne felt sick.

"You can't be a lesbian. I'm a lesbian." As she said it she realized how ridiculous it sounded. It was then her mother said for Pete's sake, it had nothing to do with her.

Jayne said, "No. No. You can't be a lesbian. If you were a lesbian, you would have made muffins, you would have invited me over, sat me down, fed me muffins, and said, Jayne, I have something to tell you." Jayne was on a roll, she shifted gears. "You're not a lesbian. You're lonely."

A look appeared on her mother's face that Jayne had never seen before. Beth turned to Doreen, took her arm, said something into her ear and scurried off.

Gary's wedding, thankfully, was small, just Monique's mother and sister and small nephew from France, four couples who were Monique and Gary's friends, then Doug and Dorrie, Beth and Fern, and Myrna. The ceremony was in the Anglican Church on Mayne Island, a building Myrna had always loved. The summer she was eleven, she had gone every Sunday. Vaguely baffled by the goings-on, she had liked nonetheless going up to the front of the church in the middle of the ceremony and kneeling on the velvet cushion. The first time, she held her hands up in the shape of a little bowl as the dozen other souls did, expecting a little white whatchamacally, but instead the minister whispered, "Have you been confirmed?" and she shook her head and he put his hand on her head and blessed her. Although she was embarrassed about having been discovered to be faking, the hand on the head, the blessing, felt surprisingly good. Nobody did that. Nobody blessed you in the ordinary course of events. Myrna almost cried, thinking about it now. Bless you, she wanted to say to everyone in the church. May you be blessed. She imagined herself doing it, saying it to everyone, and when she came to Monique's relatives, she imagined herself speaking French, saying, "Soyez blessé," and then realized she would be saying, "Be wounded." Which of course was about as likely.

Fern had picked Myrna up from the ferry the night before. "Where's Jude?"

"I don't know," said Myrna.

"Oh," said Fern. Fern was very tactful.

"Where's Jude?" said Beth, when they got out of the car. All the wedding guests sat beneath patio lanterns strung over the lawn, a fire burning in the firepit.

"She couldn't make it," said Myrna. "She sends her regrets." She took her bag inside the cabin. Beth followed.

"What's up?" she asked.

"She left me," Myrna said. "She's gone." She wept into her mother's shoulder for a long time and then dried her eyes. "People get over this, don't they?" she said. "It's hard to believe."

Fern's partner, Ariel, had died. Myrna had not been to a sadder funeral. "Celebration of life." People had pooled money to rent the Heritage Hall. There'd been a slide show—Ariel as a baby climbing out of a crib, Ariel as a little girl on a stick pony, Ariel with her brothers and sisters, Ariel on the rowing team, Ariel with her arm around a series of women, Ariel with her arm around Fern in the mountains, Fern on the beach, Fern in front of Christmas trees—which had rendered Myrna a puddle.

Fern had spoken about Ariel's strength and resolve and sense of humour. Ariel's friends had followed. They had told stories. They had held hands and sung songs, Doreen and Myrna's mother among them. Myrna had wept continuously.

Now the lights were up and people were mingling. Myrna

was still wiping her eyes. She could hear Sarah telling someone about Borneo. "They're harvesting the forest like there's no tomorrow. You can't blame them, really, what else is there, but orangs have a huge range, they're like moose or bear or wolves, they need miles—"

She and Sarah would break up soon. Myrna could feel it. She didn't know yet who would do it, but she could feel that it would happen.

She went to find her mother. Doreen was, uncannily like Sarah, expounding in a loud voice. Her topic was the Y2K bug that was going to screw all computers in five years. Beth stood beside her, but stared off into the distance. No. Not into the distance. At Fern, across the room. Fern's hand was on Ariel's brother's shoulder. Then they were hugging. On Beth's face was pure love.

As soon as she had got home from the Lesbian Week dance, Myrna had left a sloppy apology on her mother's answering machine and fallen asleep with her clothes on. She called again in the morning, apologized again, and Beth had accepted her apology, but they had still been uneasy with one another. Now Myrna walked up to her mother, took her hand, entwining her fingers with Beth's. Beth smiled, squeezed Myrna's hand and didn't let go. Myrna looked at their hands together and forgave her mother everything, for all time.

Now that it was happening, she did not grudge Gary his second wedding. It was a bit strange, but no less beautiful than his first wedding, allowing for the fact he was giving the same vows a second time. The love was beautiful, as it had been the first time. That was the problem. Love was beautiful.

Even if she never met another person she wanted to marry, she should be able to. She should. Commitment ceremony schmemitment ceremony. She should be able to *marry*.

The reception was held on the patch of lawn between the three cabins on their property, the original cabin, which housed the kitchen and was the place Myrna and Gary stayed when they came now, and the two smaller sleeping cabins they had built for Doug and Dorrie and Beth and Fern. Inexplicably, they all got on. They played bridge together. They downed bottles of wine. Perhaps that was the secret. Lots of wine.

It was late August. The rain held off. A First Nations caterer from a neighbouring island, with whom she had been in love for the past forty minutes, barbecued salmon over a half barrel, while his partner made bannock. A giant bowl of local greens tossed with Salt Spring Island goat cheese took up practically a whole card table.

Myrna floated through the day like a ghost observer. She could not seem to sustain a conversation. She wished she could go do the dishes or help with the barbecuing. She realized how often she used these things as an escape.

"There are only going to be two speeches and mine is very short," said Gary. "I love my family. I love my friends. And I love Monique. You're all here, and I am blessed. Thanks." He raised a glass.

Ga-ry!

Myrna blubbered, helplessly. Her mother pulled her chair up close to Myrna's, put her arm around her, drew her head to her shoulder. They blubbered together.

She got home from the wedding about three in the afternoon, dropped her bag and went to make a cup of coffee to drink while reading *Night and Day*, which she was only halfway through and starting to tire of. Why didn't Katharine and Mary just get together? There was definitely something there. Virginia Woolf might not know it yet, but there was. Mary was always touching Katharine's clothes. Katharine was always showing up at Mary's apartment late at night. In the ghost book, that's what would happen. Mary would invite Katharine in. They would talk about politics. Katharine would stay.

Peter who once loved Margaret

I saw my Aunt Margaret, who died in China the year I was born, on West Hastings one morning last fall.

"Margaret," I called. She turned her head, but seeing no one she recognized resumed her course through the doors to SFU Harbour Centre. I had a powerful feeling she would be waiting for me inside by the elevators.

There were no elevators.

My feet found the escalator, and I rose, mindless, like shoppers everywhere, until served up to the second floor into a world of green: walls, floor, ceiling, all green.

I did not see my aunt. I did not see much of anybody. Down a hall I wandered, past the Alan and Margaret Eyre Boardroom, the Royal Bank Instructional Computing Centre and Hime Koshevoy Publishing Lab to a dead end with a washroom, which is as good a place as any to look for a long-lost relative if your bladder is more than half full.

Of three stalls only one was occupied, by the owner of size seven-and-a-half shoes whose heels beggared the imagination. It took me right back to last season's *Canadian Idol* and the mesmerizing drama of whether the poor young women with toes stuffed down a ski hill of a shoe into vicious little leather arrowheads would possibly make it through the three or four steps they were required to make so as not to incur the criticism of being Celine Dionesque comme Martha Joy, in my opinion the most talented of the year's crop, MOR taste in music notwithstanding. I waited a breath or two to let my heart slow, then cautiously ventured, "Margaret?" knowing full well it was not she—when has a female Fleming gone higher than a half-inch?—but feeling I must leave no stone unturned.

"Norma," said she.

"Norma Fleming?" Could my father's cousin possibly be in Vancouver, too?

"Norma none-of-your-business," said the owner of the shoes, straightening her skirt, or so I surmised from the angle of leg and the light swish of material.

I fled hot-faced into the handicapped stall and then hesitated to do my business there as someone with a handicap might enter to find the stall occupied and, not being able to hold it, soil herself while waiting for able-bodied me to void my bladder. I had heard a disabled person tell just this story. Norma was now washing her hands, and taking her time about it, I might add. When she left, I would come out and use a different stall. But in this I was thwarted by the door opening and two new women entering mid-chat.

"And then when I got there, they weren't on sale after all," said one voice.

"After you'd gone all that way?"

"Yeah, I know."

Now I had to either wait for them to leave or just take a chance and pee as quick as I could and get out of there.

"So did you get them?"

"No way, I wasn't going to pay that price. Are you kidding?"

I decided to take a chance.

"How much were they?"

"You don't want to know."

"I do."

"No, you don't."

"Come on."

I was mid-stream at this point, no longer paying attention to entrances and exits, just wanting to know what the woman had wanted to buy that was so expensive. Then there was a thump on my door. Someone's crutch. The other crutch, silver, with brown rubber stoppie on the end, was on the floor by the orthopedic shoes. Oh my God, I had done it, I had prevented a disabled person from using the disabled washroom.

"Sorry," I shouted, missing the price the other woman

had not wanted to pay. "Almost done." My urethra trickled interminably. Time expanded. At last I was done. Zipped. Belted. "Sorry," I said again, but the woman with the crutches was by now in a regular stall. I would have preferred not to wash my hands and just put distance between the bathroom and myself, the land of my embarrassment and the self who caused it, but told myself instead that embarrassment is not the worst thing and that my obligation to hygiene was greater.

With the high traffic in the washroom, you would have thought there would be corresponding traffic in the halls, but there was not. They were just as deserted as before. I did a complete circuit without seeing a soul and then actually jumped when the double-doors I'd just passed clunked, opened, and spilled name-tagged American Sign Language speakers out into the hallway. At the School for the Deaf my great-aunt May was sent to around 1910, they taught lip-reading only, no sign language. "Hard of hearing." That's the term we used to refer to Aunt May, which for the first time strikes me as strange. You don't say "hard of sight" or "hard of locomotion." "Hard of heart," however. The ASL speakers divided into two streams around my island, tumbling downstream to the atrium, the down escalator, out of view, leaving me, once again, alone.

I traversed a hallway of offices all with closed doors, off lights. Then, past a jog in the corridor, a light, an open office door. "Margaret Fleming?" I asked a seated figure before I saw it was a tall man with a blond beard. He wore shorts, though it was fall. His leg hairs were blond. Beside him, a grey and white oval raised its head, becoming a dog.

"Carl Arnold," he said with good humour.

"Do you know, is there a Margaret Fleming around here at all?"

"Not that I know of."

"She's my aunt."

"Ah."

"I saw her just now ducking into the building but I can't find her."

"Great. Well. Good luck."

"She's been dead since I was a baby."

"Oh. Well, then." Movement caught my eye. Small, quick

movement a distance behind Carl's head. "The ghosts' offices, they're—" It was a mouse, running along the top of a corkboard above Carl Arnold's desk. He rose, held his hand poised above the mouse as if it were a fly and then whacked it. Barehanded. It fell to his desk, stunned or kaput I couldn't say for sure. "—a little—" He pinched the tail near the body and tossed it to his dog, who chewed it waggishly three or four times before spitting it out, sniffing it, taking it back into its mouth and gulping. "— harder to get to." Carl finished, settling back into his chair.

"I don't think my aunt really is dead." The word *dead*, suddenly, had special significance on account of the mouse. "Apparently she isn't. Sorry. Sorry. Never mind. Sorry."

"Hang on," Carl Arnold said. He typed her name into a field on a search screen. There were no returns. "Well, she doesn't work here."

"Thank you," I said. Carl Arnold smiled. His front tooth was chipped. I wanted to ask how. I wanted to run my finger down his bearded cheek. This was unsettling, given the mouse killing. I gave a weak wave and began to walk down the hall.

"Unless she's using an alias," he called out. It was his turn not to be able to shut up, apparently.

"Unless," I said without turning. Then it was like there was an invisible line between us, I mean connecting us, like telephone wire strung between poles, that stretched as I walked and got thinner like a piece of claymation rolled Play-Doh until it disappeared with a poof and I forgot all about Carl Arnold.

Aunt Margaret was my father's sister, the middle child of five. In my father's den was a picture of her and when I was very young, I thought she and my mother looked like twins, but it was a superficial resemblance conveyed by hairstyle, black and white photography and the white fur of the academic gown in a patch on the chest. They'd been friends at university, she and my mother. That was how my parents met, through Margaret. All my mother's friends looked like one another in photos. I did not realize that the same would be true of me and my friends some time in the future. There was really only one thing I knew about Aunt Margaret other than the date and place of her death (and obviously I was wrong about that), and that was that she had been in love with a young man named Peter, who was a schoolteacher, and that she had wanted to marry him, but her father had forbidden it, a schoolteacher being too lowly for his liking. Not only would she be cut off from the family were she to marry him, said my grandfather, any of her siblings who talked to her would be cut off, too. She, feeling that she could not put her siblings in the position of having to make that choice, had broken the engagement off. She joined a religious organization and went to China and died.

Aunt Margaret was not on the second floor. I went down to the first.

I have this feeling sometimes that all I have to do to find Aunt Margaret's Peter is to Google him.

Peter.

Of course, it returns a zillion results.

"Peter who once loved Margaret" gives nothing, though if you search without the quotation marks, you get an obit of Princess Margaret ("Margaret further defied convention when she fell in love with Group Captain Peter Townsend, once equerry to her father and comptroller to her mother") and an interview with comedian Margaret Cho saying the kind of person she'd really like to marry is an FTM.

Finally I found a lecture hall. To my surprise and wonder, it was filled with old women. Jackpot. The instructor was telling us to break into small groups to discuss our personal and cultural definitions of greatness and as everyone's attention shifted from the front of the room to their immediate surroundings, I scanned the class, but it was happening right before my eyes. I lost the ability to distinguish between people. Forty-five heads in variations on the bowl cut in a colour scale of sweatshirt-grey to cloud-white. A hand tugged at the hem of my sweater.

"We need a fourth," said a woman with kitchen-sink-coloured hair. With an effort, I discerned that her face was long and thin, with a nose rather like a foreshortened rose thorn. Beside her was a plumpish woman with a mushroom-cap-shaped nose and sheepskin-coloured hair and next to her was a woman with bright red rectangular glasses and a spray of diner-teapot-coloured hair. They were becoming distinct again. I breathed out. The first woman had not relinquished her hold on my sweater-hem. She tugged me into a waiting chair. "What is greatness?" she asked.

"Can we introduce ourselves first?" asked the second.

"I think thinking of introductions is a sign of greatness," I said. They laughed, but I was serious.

Maryam was the woman with the long face. She looked Middle Eastern, Lebanese, maybe. Estelle had the round nose and looked exactly like a woman I'd seen in an NFB film on Cowichan knitters. Daisy, of the red glasses, was Chinese and very chic. I had never met anyone less Daisy-like. They were all staring at me.

"Oh. Me. Hi. Anne. Do you know, is there a Margaret in this class?"

They did not.

"Well?" said Estelle.

"I think greatness, I think the great are innovators," said Maryam. "I think that's what sets them apart. They did something new. Something grand."

"I don't think greatness can be defined," said Daisy.

"But you know it when you see it," said Estelle.

"Well, yes, perhaps, perhaps, but don't you think if you named all the people you think are great you would see they had something in common?"

Daisy thought not but listed Aung San Suu Kyi, Camille Claudel. Colette. Frida Kahlo. A mother in the neighbourhood she grew up in in Singapore who took in foster children. The teacher who died in the Virginia school shooting. Ella Fitzgerald.

Maryam thought Shirin Ebadi, Edith Piaf, Benazir Bhutto and Beryl Bainbridge were great. She had tears in her eyes.

Estelle picked Corazon Aquino and three people whose names I didn't know and I thought with embarrassment how little I knew about First Nations history and politics and culture, and then she said, "Peggy Fleming" and the use of my surname made me feel for a moment like she had seen into my heart. "I loved Peggy Fleming," she said with a smile like the sun.

I wondered if Aunt Margaret had ever been called Peggy. I wondered how "Margaret" could be shortened to "Peggy" and also how "Dick" made sense from "Richard."

They were looking at me again. "Great women? Do they

have to be women? Didn't she just say 'greatness'?"

Maryam: "The course is on great women."

Daisy: "Great women writers."

"Oh. Well. Aphra Behn? I've never been able to read more than about eight pages, but that's probably just me. I've never been able to read more than eight pages of Milton, either. Virginia Woolf? Toni Morrison?"

"Now you are talking about writers only. We are supposed to talk about greatness, what comprises greatness."

"Um, that mathematician, Somebody Somerville? Queen Elizabeth? The first? Though maybe Helen Mirren, she was great in *The Queen*. Helen Merrell? Very cool voice, like ice, like, I don't know, something cool and smooth. Everyone named Helen?"

Daisy: "I think that the intent of the discussion was to see how our definitions of greatness exclude women and exclude writers."

Maryam: "But, oh, they don't. We've been talking about all women."

Daisy: "Not the teacher in Virginia."

Estelle: "Well, are those the private or public ones?"

Maryam: "What do these people have in common?"

Me: "They put themselves in the public eye?"

Estelle: "Oh no, no, they—"

Daisy: "Not the foster mother."

Maryam: "They are leaders."

"They took chances," said Estelle. Her voice was soft and very firm. "They put themselves on the line."

"Not the writers," said I.

"Oh, not those ones," said Maryam.

Then we had to report back to the large group.

"Pointless," said Daisy under her breath. I could see not liking Maryam or myself, but how could she not like Estelle?

And then I saw my aunt again. She was near the front of the room. Her hair was the colour of clouds. Her group had identified three different kinds of greatness: greatness of mind, greatness of body, greatness of spirit. There were subcategories, too, greatness of giving, greatness of endurance, and so on, but they had realized that each subcategory could be fitted into one of the three, e.g., endurance into body and spirit, giving into mind and spirit. They had agreed that the greatest of the great had all three, but many greats had only one. The instructor seemed very pleased with them. They seemed pleased with each other.

The other groups echoed the first. Maryam said that we had thought that innovators and leaders and those who gave themselves to greater causes were great. While they were all looking back at us, I looked right at Aunt Margaret and waved. "It's me. Anne," I mouthed but she showed no sign of understanding. I guess she had never learned from Aunt May to lip-read.

The discussion moved on to what makes a great writer. Aunt Margaret was wearing a grey felted wool jacket. She looked young for her seventy-seven years. I wondered if she had been involved with any men since Peter or if she had been more or less virginal. She might have married. I wondered if Peter had married. I thought I remembered my mother saying he had but very often I am wrong. Peter might have followed her to China. They might have staged the death. But her father was dead by then himself, not so long after giving the edict, six or seven years only. With her father dead, there would be no need to fake her own death. Therefore, her death was real. But if so, what was she doing in front of me?

"You seemed to be trying to get my attention," she was saying, but my eyes were full of tears.

"You're alive," I managed, at last.

"Oh, I wouldn't count on that," she said.

"How are you?"

"Very well, thank you, how are you?"

"I'm overwhelmed."

"Look, I think you think I'm someone I'm not."

"You're Margaret Fleming. Aunt Margaret. I'm named for you."

"But your name's Anne."

"You did learn to lip-read."

"It's not hard."

"Who taught you?"

"Who taught me what?"

Why was she being so evasive? "Oh, come on. Aunt May. Who else?"

"Why would Aunt May teach me to lip-read? Whoever she was."

"People like to teach other people the things they've been taught."

"It let her spy, did you know that? It made her very uncomfortable, morally. She made herself look away. When she was overhearing something she wasn't meant to hear. Or rather seeing something she wasn't meant to hear."

"Does anyone else know you're alive?"

"Several people, I'm sure."

"I mean Jenny or Carol? Uncle Bob? Aunt Joan?"

"I don't know who you think I am."

"When did you come back from China? Do you want to go out for lunch?"

"You really think I'm your Aunt Margaret, don't you?" she said. I loved her voice. A fruity alto, an apple wine.

"I have so many questions to ask you. For instance, I'm totally curious about MRA, like what was that all about? 'Moral Re-armament.' I mean, whew." I stopped, conversationally catching up to her. "Who do *you* think you are?"

"Oh, I'm not sure that matters. You seem very convinced."

"No, I'd really like to know."

"I seem to remember a little sushi place on a corner."

At the restaurant, she shrugged off her neat, navy London Fog, loosened her scarf and told me she was Margaret Murdoch (what a terrible urge I had to stop her right there with the weak pseudonym—surely she knew I knew Murdoch was her mother's maiden name?), born in Vancouver in 1941 (sheering a whole twelve years off her real age! I had not thought she would go that far). Her father was a doctor whom she never knew (another transparent fiction: her grandfather was the doctor). He, the fictional father, died during the war. Her mother taught school, leaving Margaret and her older sister and brother at home with their grandmother each day. She was a remarkably adept liar. She offered the information with no hesitation at all and only modest elaboration—not so much detail that you thought she was laying it on thick, not so little that you thought, Ah, she's only got the bare bones of the story. One afternoon mixing sourdough, her grandmother sat down suddenly, said, "Oh," and died, right there in front of Margaret's eyes. If she closed her eyes, she could still see the pattern of the housedress her grandmother wore. She closed her eyes. A curious expression crossed her face, a child's expression, puzzled, or possibly filled with wonder. "White, with deep red flowers." I wondered if she had heard this story from someone, her own mother, even, whose mother had died suddenly, leaving the doctor, Bill, adrift and bereft (or was it Bill's death that left Harriet adrift and bereft?).

She went on with her story, her growing up, her mother's endurance, courage, her mother's late remarriage, her own summer as a mother's helper in Hawaii, the wealthy young Americans who vied to take her out in their convertible cars. She hadn't wanted to go. Ever since her grandmother died, she'd been afraid her mother would also sit down suddenly and cease to be. But her mother said she was far too serious. She needed to be young. She needed to be carefree. She needed to do something out of the ordinary. So she went off to Hawaii and there she met—

"Peter!"

"Yes," she said, with a passable, even superlative, stab at surprise. "Peter." She stared at me for so long I began to be uncomfortable.

"I suppose there are many men named Peter," I mumbled into my tea. "What happened?" She had killed off her father, so it could not be that he objected to the match.

Peter was a student at the University of Hawaii. He had grown up there. His father was a high school teacher, and—

"He intended to be one, too," I said.

"Yes," said she. "He idolized his father. They loved to have long, impassioned arguments about historical and current events and so on."

"And?"

"His father didn't like me."

"Why not? What was there to object to?"

"Really, I think it was just that he could not stand losing Peter to anyone. But in part it was because I was not Japanese.

He had been in the army, Peter's father, the U.S. Army. There was a detachment of Japanese-Americans who fought in a unit together. He himself had impulsively married a white girl from Mississippi who he met during his training, and she had left him when Peter was four for a white Navy man. After that, it was just Peter and him. He thought Peter's and my romance was just as impulsive and misguided as his own had been."

"Was it?"

"Oh, I don't know. I suppose. Isn't any romance impulsive? But I don't think it was misguided, no."

"So?"

"It was 1963."

"The year before I was born."

"I spent my days with the children, a boy and a girl, four and two, and when they were in bed and their parents were not out for the evening, I went out with Peter. To a movie, to a beach, to a beach party. Wonderful nights. They make me ache to think of them now. His father hardly saw him. He was very jealous and he told the family, my employers, that I was neglecting their children in order to see his son, which I assure you I had not been doing. Often, they had me babysit in the evenings, when by rights I should have been off. One time, they came home early on purpose, and found me with Peter, slightly, shall we say, dishabille, and when I say slightly, I do mean slightly. My shirt was untucked. That was all. They were outraged. They fired me on the spot—and rehired me an hour of shouting later when they realized that losing me would curtail their social life—they spouted abuse at Peter, called him all sorts of names, oh, they treated him horribly, and me, too. I was a slut, a dirty low girl. They thought they'd hired better quality than that but they were sadly mistaken and so on and so forth." You could hear her hearing it. "To betray their trust by inviting a man to their house was bad enough, but to put out for a Jap just showed what kind of a person I really was. They implied quite thoroughly that it could not possibly be that I was in love with Peter, that a white girl could not possibly love a—." She waved her hand instead of saying the word "Jap" again, for which I was grateful, Japanese restaurant and all. "Therefore, I must just want to put out for whatever man came along. When

Peter got home that night, his father was sitting there, waiting for him. Smiling. Smiling and smiling. He could not keep the smile off his face. Peter knew, right then, what his father had done. "How was your evening?" his father said. Peter knew then that the Morrisons had not come home early because Cherry was not feeling well. They had come home early because someone had telephoned them to tell them to check up on their mother's helper. Peter could not believe it. He knew it, but he could not believe it. I could believe it. I had not been an adored only son for twenty-two years. I could believe it. I was the girl who loved the adored only son. Peter's father never did admit to his action. He never denied it, either. He acted gleeful every time the topic came up. Gradually, Peter questioned that his father had had a role in the whole affair. He blamed only the Morrisons.

"I did not think I could forgive Peter's father. Peter, of course, was angry, but not as angry as I would have liked him to be.

"We could not see each other the next day. I was convinced I was not going to stay with the Morrisons after what they had said to me, but I needed them to pay me before I could go anywhere else. They, for their part, refused to pay me until the end of the month. I could not see Peter the next day. I was miserable. I despised the Morrisons. For the children's sake, I had to pretend I did not loathe their parents for the few minutes of the day we were in the same room. It was tremendously difficult. That evening they had me come with them to a party children had been invited to as well as adults. In the first few weeks I'd been there, they would have said they didn't need me, they would have happily sent me off in a convertible with three white boys to have a swell time. They would have sent me to Lover's Lane, with a wink.

"Rainy days, I took the children to the aquarium, and there Peter found me on the third day. We did not have much time—he was on a break from work and had to rush back to the hotel—only enough to fill each other in—*it was my father*, it was your father! *if you had seen the look on his face*, oh, the things they said to me, Peter, they were vile. That sort of thing.

Only enough time to say with all our looks, 'I love you.'

"The end of the month was five days away. I made it another two, then left them a note. 'Sorry about your tennis game, Cherry. Please mail a cheque care of Mrs. S. Katharine Murdoch, 3795 West 47th Ave, Vancouver, BC, Canada or be prepared to face legal action.'"

That threw me. The name. My grandmother's name. I had almost forgotten she was my Aunt Margaret.

She went on, still quoting the note. "'You are wrong about me and Peter. Margaret.' I wasn't sorry about her tennis game at all. I went and checked in at the YWCA. I left a note with the doorman at Peter's hotel.

"I thought we would marry. I was certain we would marry. There was not one snippet of doubt in my mind. Peter had brought me to his father's house. He had invited me in, into their duo. Their dinners. Their debates. He had insisted on it. He had explained to me why his father hadn't seemed to like me, he had explained the history with his mother (who wrote, every year, on his birthday). He had said it would change. His father would get to know me. His father would like me. Of course he would. 'Anyone I love this much my father must love, too.'

"Then when I saw him again, I saw it on his face, like a label:—"

I knew what she was going to say before she said it. My lips made the shapes of the same words:

"Peter who once loved Margaret."

I felt very very strange. She was assuredly not my aunt. She assuredly was. Both possibilities were simultaneously true.

She had tried to get work at a department store (she had worked at Eaton's at home) but lacked a work visa, and ended up a waitress in a Chinese restaurant until she had enough for a flight home. In 1964, she joined MRA and went to China,

"Where you died."

"No, no. I didn't," she said. "You've got to concede the evidence." She made a gesture, two cupped hands opened towards me. "Ask your father," she said, "or your mother, or whoever's sister you think I am." She was putting on her coat, knotting her scarf. "Someone might have died. It wasn't me."

'Ask your father,' she'd said first. I thought it was a clue.

I called my dad, adopting a bluff, breezy tone. "I saw a woman downtown who looked exactly like Aunt Margaret," I said.

"Really," said he, breezy also.

"How funny, I thought, if she'd faked her own death."

"I saw her," my father said, breezy no more. "When they sent the body back from China. There's no question she was dead."

How sad he must have been. She was thirty-four.

**The Private
Puke Diary
of
Sarah
the
cat**

Saturday, August 3
While sniffing intruder's shoes: blup. Into shoes. Felt better.

Monday, August 5
Sat on fridge. Blup. Felt better.

Tuesday, August 6
Intruder clearly noseless. Shoe-blup gone, fridge-blup remains. Dozed on couch. Woke. Blup. Kak. Kak. Blup. Felt better.

Thursday, August 8
FRIDGE-BLUP UNTOUCHED!!! Kneaded intruder's bed pillow. Blup. Felt better.

Friday, August 9
Finally, fridge-blup gone. Ditto pillow-blup. Sat on fridge. Jumped to counter. Licked spills. Spied open broom closet. Investigated. Hurled. Felt so-so.

Sunday, August 11

Toyed with small white mouse substitute from intruder's purse. "Tail" quite convincing! "Body" stubby and unlifelike. Snoozed on change table. Woke. Blup. Still felt queasy. Settled in corner of crib. Kak. Kak. Blup. Felt like a million bucks.

Monday, August 12

Crib-blup untouched! Investigated laundry basket. Burped. Felt better.

Wednesday, August 14

Perched on intruder's chest, early a.m. Purred. Ears split by shriek. Unceremoniously tipped to floor. Sulked under bed. Puked. Felt better.

**The
Puke Diary
of
Douglas "Collie" Collins
reconstructed from memory**

December 25, 1973, 1:23 a.m.
Awake. Must barf, must barf. Ran to bathroom. Barfed Christmas
cake into tub. Felt hot, hot. Feverish.

Christmas cake!

Christmas!

Christmas Day!

Accompanying this astonishing thought sequence was a thud
and a tinkle from downstairs. I almost peed myself. Santa,
downstairs. I would get to see him. I, Doug "Collie" Collins,
would be THE kid to verify the existence of the guy in red. My
name would go down in history. There'd be a movie. Collie's
Christmas.

We'd had this debate at school. Large. Divisive. I was pro-
Santa. The losing side. But I knew for a fact there were people
who let themselves be thought to be anti-Santa when they
were really pro-Santa. My friend John Guildford, for instance.
My friend Brett Kiley. Crossing their arms. Looking at their feet.
While Brian Maitland tried to do math ("Midnight to six, that's
six hours. Six hours is...how many minutes?") and tried to shame
me. "Awww, little baby Collie believes in Santy Claus. Int that

cute." Don't you know, Brian Maitland, that time slows? Theory of relativity, Brian. The reindeer go so fast that time slows.

Anyway, I needed evidence. I tiptoed back into the bedroom, slung my Brownie camera over my shoulder and onto my back, crawled hands and knees to landing. A thump and a shout and laughter. Woman's laughter.

Mrs. Claus? Could it be?

I crawled down the stairs on my belly, using my elbows for propulsion until I was two stairs above where the living room was visible. I thrust my camera down, pointed it at the living room and snapped. Only then did I look.

Mrs. Claus? Not even close. I almost wept. Okay. I did weep. My "parents" were on the floor. The round table from Grandma —on which me and my little sister had left our eggnog and homemade cookies for the man who gave us hope each year—was knocked over. My mother, up on her elbow, fed my stepfather a broken cookie.

"A-rum-rum-rum," he said, gobbling it up.

"Those are Santa's cookies," I shouted. They had drunk Santa's eggnog, too, before knocking over the table. The glass was beside my mother.

"God, Dougie. Go to bed."

I sat there, burning.

"You're making Santa get behind. There he is, he's up there in the sky, he's waiting, he was about to come, but then you had to go and get up and now he has to wait. Keep him waiting and he may skip over our house altogether. Go on, go to bed."

I went back up the stairs. I was beginning to get a headache, the kind where your mind goes on trips, where it soars off like a flying carpet, swirling you through unknown worlds of purple cloud. If my parents—*my* parents, Betty and Jim—were Santa, like Brian Maitland said, life was a slow, evil thing, not soon enough over.

June 30, 1978

For John G's twelfth birthday, his dad let him invite five guys to a Canadians game at Nat Bailey. We all agreed to fill the hip flasks we had bought at the army surplus the week before with filched liquor. Vodka, we had heard, was odourless. Every time John's Dad's back was turned, five flasks came out. Glug, glug, glug. He bought us hotdogs and fries. Our parents agreed when the puking started later it had to be food poisoning. They blamed the stadium.

October 12, 1979

Football in the nuts. Enough said.

March 11, 1981

Birthday.

"I think he's old enough for a glass of wine on special occasions, don't you?" my mother says to my stepfather.

They are pretending to be festive. They are pretending we don't all hate one another. This makes me hate them more.

"Fifteen?" says Jim-Dad, raising his eyebrows, but Mom's already poured the wine. And then strangely, as she passes me the glass—"Can I have some?" says my sister—and they toast me—I recognize their profound inner weakness and almost fall apart. My sister has made a cake. She brings it in proudly after the "okay, everyone pretend the cake's a surprise" hush and quietly starts Happy Birthday. Her eyelashes flap rapidly over her blue blue eyes. My mother and father and godfather join, they harmonize. It is excessively corny and brings tears to my eyes.

My friends and I are going to go get wasted later. Brett has hash. Gordie has a two-four. We will do stupid things of one kind or another until one of us pukes. Me, as it turns out. They will bring me home in a toy wagon, rain alighting on my face.

"Dougie, is that you? Dougie, you're drunk." "So are you, Mom." "I'm not fifteen." "Which makes it sadder, in a way." Oops. "Aw, Mom, don't cry. I didn't mean it. Come on. Please." "Just go to bed, Dougie." "You too, Mom."

August 31, 1982
Into bushes outside Police concert. Be slightly less of an idiot, Collie. Let G. be the one who pukes every time.

June 24, 1983
Five in the morning after our grad party. I've been asleep for maybe fifteen minutes when suddenly my stomach's going wrench wrench lurch.

Severe, violent food poisoning.

Crab salad.

Horrible.

Much worse than vodka.

September 12, 1990
Wedding day. Woke up, looked at each other, laughed. Ha. Our private bliss was going to be public knowledge. How great was that.

We could hear voices downstairs. Dishes clattering. I was

still getting used to Leanne's family, how they *liked* one another, how they got together and laughed versus our bitter, pinched half hour once a year. I wanted her right then, first thing in the morning as we looked into one another's faces and laughed at what we were pulling off. I kissed her. I put my hand on her ass, I shifted my weight. She slapped me on the chest with the back of her hand and said, "Uh-uh-uh, " and then she deep-tongued me and thrust me back on the bed. Hoo. How was I going to last the day? How was I not going to pass out from lust?

Her mother was making us a frittata, her sister Sarah was making fruit salad, her sister Kate was opening champagne, her brother Max was mixing up orange juice, Max's wife Janet was setting the table.

After breakfast, Max and Pete and I went to a barber's to get shaved. We met John and Brett and Gordie there. I had never had someone else shave me before. It was strange and exquisite. I felt like Mussolini, I don't know why. I guess he's the only public figure I associate with being shaved. I must have seen a movie.

We strolled back to the house, hands in our pockets, laughing. Brett alluded to toy wagon stories that would be in his speech. John, what a fuck-up, he'd get wasted way too soon. I loved him. I loved all of us.

The day passed. We were happy. We got into our wedding clothes.

Suddenly, in the limo on the way to church, my stomach had a spaz-out. Stop, stop, stop, stop, I shouted to the driver. I opened the door and threw myself onto Fir Street. Not wanting to puke right on the sidewalk, I ran twenty feet to a sewer grate, bent over and heaved. I thought about Leanne, her fishing trip, her lost fall. Guy walking by said, "You're in for it now, b'y. Today's just the beginning." Obviously, I was getting married—the tux, the decorated limo.

I didn't get it, didn't get it at all. Why was I puking? It's not like I was scared or nervous or freaked out. Seriously, not at all, I don't care if no one believes me.

What I think now is I just really really really fucking loved Leanne.

**Baby Hal's
regurgitation record,
lovingly recounted by his mother,
Leanne Macintosh-Collins**

January 14

Ha-ah. A-aa. Floor. Light. Laundry basket. Wiggle. A little burp, a little...WHOA. A FOUNTAIN OF SPIT-UP, THREE FEET INTO THE AIR. WHEEE. Back down on my face. WAAAUGH.

All clean. New sleeper. Nice jiggling. Ah. Nap. Nap, nap. Wake. Hungry, hungry, hungry, hungr—ah. Slurp, slurp, slurp. Up on the shoulder. Smells nice. Open mouth. Spray-paint couch with vomit.

Up, up, up. Hee. Mom says to Dad, "Don't say I didn't warn you." "Who's my little projectile vomiter?" Dad says. "Hey? Who's my little—Holy Christ!" Mom bent over laughing. "Okay. That's it. We're going to Emerge. Emma, look after David."

January 15

I've got pyloric stenosis. I'm going to have an operation. They are going to take a knife and cut me open and fix the muscles around the valve between my stomach and my intestine. My mother is not sure she can handle it. The mere idea makes her woozy, but then insane anxiety snaps her out of it. This skin is not meant to be cut. It is not. This skin is perfection. This skin is intact. "I can't stand it, I can't stand it," she walks around saying. "I can't. I can't stand it." She is like an I-Can't-Stand-It robot. There is nothing else she can do but walk back and forth and say "I can't stand it." She is useless to all until the operation is over, I am in recovery, awake and hungry again. I am so hungry I am going to eat and eat and eat and eat.

January 16
Cry. Eat eat eat eat. Cry. Sleep. Eat. Oh, erp, burble, plup. Spit up. Plain old, regular spit-up. I cry, my mom cries, she cradles me against her chest.

The Private
Private
Extremely Private
Private Diary
of
Emma Macintosh-Collins

(Mom, Dad, David: I will NEVER trust you AGAIN in my ENTIRE LIFE if you so much as peek at these pages. Not only that, I will TORMENT your every living breath. I will WAKE you when you want to sleep. I will slip laxatives into your coffee (or chocolate milk, DAVID). I will make you THINK I slipped laxatives when I actually didn't, so you will worry all day, and stay close to bathrooms when you don't need to. I will disturb you when you are working, I will whine when you are not.

Trust me. You don't want to take the chance of finding out what might happen.

Put the book down.

Now.

That's right. Put it down.

Thank you. I love you and trust you always.)

August 31

I am sorry. I am not writing a puke diary.

We came home from Gambier (which was weird, more later) and my aunt Sarah who was cat-sitting our cat who I called Sarah when I was three because I loved Aunt Sarah so much had left a little book on the counter that said "The Private Puke Diary of Sarah-the-cat." We laughed. Sarah-the-cat has this condition that means she throws up a lot, like basically every day. It's gross but not that gross, you get used to it, you just pick it up in a Kleenex and then spritz the spot with the environmental stain remover and wipe and there you go.

Dad said, "Wouldn't it be funny if we all wrote our own puke diaries? It'd be, like, our lives, through puking."

My father is a radio producer. This is the kind of thing he would do on the radio if he could, if "puke" on the radio was okay, which it's not, which makes sense, because think about it: some people, all they have to do is hear the word puke and they feel like puking, so you have all these people talking about puking on the radio, you have people all across the country feeling like puke and then turning their radios off. Anyway, doesn't matter, Dad has his own little radio show. Us. We are his own little radio show. He will record stuff and then edit it and send it to all the relatives. "Summer with the Macintosh-Collinses," "Thanksgiving with the Macintosh-Collinses," "Christmas with the Macintosh-Collinses." Needless to say, there is some eye-rolling. Like, "Dad, can we just live and not record ourselves living?" I will play piano for him. That's all I will do.

He loves us a little too much. Back off, Dad.

But a diary is not a bad idea. A regular diary. If I throw up, I am not writing it down. You cannot tell my life history from the times that I threw up, okay? But writing things down generally? Okay.

Gambier was weird because Tory was not there and I had nobody to hang out with except Aaron, who is only eleven and who used to be annoying, a fly, swat, swat, but when you have no one else, it's funny how you'll come to like even people you didn't like before. You get to know them differently. Plus, people act differently around different people. Anyway, he'd show up in the morning, and we'd go off and do things, berry-picking then making a fire and making bannock on a stick, or beach-combing, or working on the fort, or just going to the fort and drawing and reading. And then about a week before we were coming home, he said he loved me and he wanted to kiss me, and what's weird is, I let him. It was kind of exciting and nice, but weird and embarrassing also. Like, what is Tory going to think? Not that Tory is ever going to find out, unless Aaron says something—he said he wouldn't, but you never know, he can be a turd, especially when Tory is also being a turd—what would she think if she found out her best (summer) friend was actually kissing her little brother. And liking it! I mean, I wouldn't have to tell her that part, I could say I didn't like it, but then, why was I doing it? Maybe because I wanted to practice or something, for real boys. But then is that fair to Aaron? Because I do like him. Oh. You know what? I just had a realization right this minute. I think I might like him even more than I like Tory. Oo. That is something I think I don't even want to know.

September 1
Being back in the city is boring. I can't wait till school starts.

September 2
Oh my God. Tory phoned to see if I wanted to go to the PNE. She didn't say Aaron was going to be there with his friend Aidyn. It was extremely weird. I was meeting Tory at the gates. Aaron and Aidyn were running up the side of the statue of the runners but I only saw them as generic boys, I didn't register who it was until I waved at Tory and she said Hi, and Aaron turned his head and I saw him. I didn't even know how to look at him. I wanted to turn and run. Luckily, he went back to doing what he was doing as if I was any of his sister's friends. Tory

said, "Sorry. I had to bring my stupid brother and his stupid friend," and I said, "That's okay." "But we don't have to stay together," Tory went on. "I want to see the SuperDogs." So we went in together and then the boys went straight to the rides and we went to see the SuperDogs. Just once when we were standing in line to get in Aaron and I looked up at the same time and caught each other's eyes, one clear look. Dark lashes, blue eyes, I love that, but I had no idea what it meant, the look. I am a human who is true? That's what it seemed like at the time, but maybe it was just, you know, blankness. I want to tell you that the SuperDogs are genuinely amazing. The commentary, however, is inane.

Tory is dog- and horse-obsessed. This is not new but I saw it with new eyes. She dragged me around to all the animal exhibits and told me all about the finer points of this horse and that horse, like I could even see the difference. It was kind of cute. What was weird was I felt no need to impress her whatsoever. I felt very separate from her, very unlinked. I felt like her equal. The whole time she was talking about I don't know, hocks and hoof-care and whatnot, I was thinking about Aaron and the summer and how my heart felt when the actual lip-touch moment happened. Well, actually, the like fourth or fifth lip-touch moment. The first few were too what-do-we-do-with-our-noses, what-do-we-do-with-our-hands.

Finally we went to the rides. After the Wild Mouse we met Aaron and Aidyn and we went on a bunch of rides together. Tory and I were fairly well matched in terms of ride-tolerance. The Wild Mouse was about our speed. The pirate ship freaked us in a way that was gratifying only once we were back on terra firma. The corkscrew roller coaster was not as bad as I thought it was going to be because it went so fast and it was so smooth.

Aaron and Aidyn were on a quest to go on every single ride. We picked rides based on how short the lineup was so they could cross more off their list. We went on the kiddy rides. It was hilarious, I really liked that part. Bumper cars were excellent.

After a few days, we tried Aaron lying on top of me. Through his shorts and underwear and my shorts and underwear I could feel his penis against me. It felt incredibly good. Then we would move a bit, sort of a, I guess it was a humpy motion, which sounds quite icky to say, but which felt amazing. And then he was lurching and moaning. I liked his voice a lot right then, a light unh, it was so boy. Afterwards we pretended not to notice the wet spot on his shorts while we walked down the pebbly beach, looking for good driftwood.

Aaron and Aidyn went on the Hellevator. Aidyn was all go go go beforehand, but afterwards he was like NOT. EVER. AGAIN. We laughed at how serious he was. He kept leaning over with his hands on his hips and going Fuck. Fuck. Then Aaron said, "So I guess you're not up for Revelation, eh?" Revelation is the extreme of all extreme rides. Aidyn said, "No way. No. I am staying on the ground." "So you are giving up on our quest?" Of going on every ride, he meant. "Hey, if I go on every ride except Revelation, that's good enough for me." "I'll go," I said. "What?!?!" they all said together. Aaron smiled. "Okay. Let's go." We had to buy separate tickets, you couldn't go on Revelation with just regular tickets, that's the kind of ride it is. There was a medium line. Not that many people could go on at a time. The ride is like a giant giant giant Zipper: a long arm with pods at either end. The arm spins around an axis. The pods spin around another axis. When there were people behind us in line so Aidyn and Tory couldn't see, I held his hand. I said I was scared. "You don't have to do this, you know," he said. "I know," I said. "Don't do it for me," he said. "I'll go by myself." I just sort of giggled or something, I don't know. I think, quite possibly, I am a complete idiot.

When we got in the little pod and they strapped us in and closed the door, I don't know what possessed me, I put my hand on his crotch. His eyes bugged at me and he grinned. And then we were flung up into the air. Way way way up into the air. It was insane. It was stupid. Suddenly we were like five storeys in the air. Upside down. And then we were beaning for pavement, then we were whipped away from earth and flung heavenward. My heart wanted to kill me but it didn't want to die. It was full of pure fear. Nightmare fear. The killer's coming, aaaugh, move your foot, run, run, what are you doing, run, but you can't. That kind of pure razored fear.

Off the ride, my legs carried me just past range of the people in the lineup and then they collapsed and I puked my mini-doughnuts. Aaron was laughing. He was laughing his guts out. "I hate myself," I croaked. "What?" he said. "Nothing," I said. "King of Playland!" he said, throwing himself in the air behind his raised fist. I was never surer of anything in that moment than that I meant nothing to him and never had.

God, I can't wait for school to start.

**The Private
Vomitacious Volume of
Leanne Macintosh-Collins**

July 1972

Family trip to the Rockies. Stuck in middle seat of station wagon. Dad wouldn't pull over because we were in a rockfall zone. Threw up on Sarah's favourite pants.

July 1973

Family trip to California. Moved to door seat. Barfed saltwater taffy down outside of station wagon. Barfed again at foot of the largest trees in the world.

July 1974

Family trip to Alaska. Barfed four times on windy dirt roads out car door. Finally got to sit in front seat.

July 1975

Family trip to Bella Coola. Barfed over side of freighter going up coast.

July 1976

Family trip to Montreal Olympics. Meditated on the genius of barf bags after filling two.

October 31, 1978

I was Kermit the Frog and Sarah was Miss Piggy and Katy was too old to go trick-or-treating, so she went to a party. Max was, what was he that year? A bunny, probably. I love my Kermit costume. I didn't want to take it off when we came home. We went to a party at Emily's and then we all went trick-or-treating together, Emily, Jessica, Michelle, Robin, Alisha and Vashti. I got 24 Rockets, 11 Mars bars, 9 Crispy Crunches, 4 Nibs, 8 Smarties, 4 M&Ms, 9 Caramilks, 6 Crunch bars, 2 Eatmores, 7 Tootsie Pops, 4 Tootsie Rolls, 5 Oh Henrys, 6 Reeses Peanut Butter Cups, 2 Mr. Bigs, 7 Chiclets, 1 bag of popcorn, 1 bag of chips, 1 C-Plus can of pop, and a whole bunch of caramels and cheap orange Halloween candies (Sarah likes them, I gave all mine to her). We spread it all out on the floor and counted, obviously. Mom let us have 5 things and then we had to put the rest away. I chose a Mars bar and 4 caramels, which I said should only count for 2 more things because a caramel is like half of one of the mini-chocolate bars, and Mom said okay, that was fair, so then I had a Caramilk and a thing of Rockets. After tonight we're only supposed to have two a day until they are gone. This year Mom let us keep the candy in our closet instead of her closet, which was obviously a mistake on her part because Sarah and I couldn't get to sleep and we were talking and then we decided to have just one more thing, and after that we had one more thing and after that one more thing, and this was on top of the hot dogs we had at Emily's and the apples we bobbed for and the candy apples we made and the candy we ate when we were out, and finally we both ate so much we felt sick and I threw up, though Sarah didn't, and now I don't want any candy at all, ever.

August 23, 1980

Dad decided we should all learn what it's like to go on a fishing boat, so he sent us out two at a time with his friends, Nick and Sue, and actually, I was kind of interested, it was Katy who didn't want to go (she had a boyfriend, she was always going to his soccer games), but it was me who got sick. I was fine on the way out, but when the Fraser River hit the ocean and things got bumpy, I got queasy and it only got worse after that. Katie rubbed my back and tried to distract me. Sue gave me Gravol and after a while I fell asleep on the bench in the cabin. So much for learning about fishing.

Fall 1980

Sigh. My lost fall.

Nope. Forget it. I don't want to do this. Sorry, Collie.

Okay.

The day after the fishing boat disaster, I still felt sick. For the next week I had low-level nausea. Then blinding headaches. The doctor diagnosed migraine.

Then, the first week of grade eight, coming home from the corner store, I fell off my bike. I couldn't believe it, I couldn't figure out what had happened. I'm on my bike, I'm on the sidewalk. Nothing in between. For, like, a couple of minutes, I couldn't walk in a straight line. Then I could again.

In Strings, I fell off my chair. How do you fall off a chair with a cello between your legs? My friend, Andrea, could not stop laughing. She said it was the funniest thing she had seen in her life. She couldn't describe it. People started calling me Spaz. Of course they felt like crap when they heard the diagnosis. They tried to make it up to me, but the damage was done. The hurt had hurt. Here I was completely unanchored, psychically adrift, I can't tell you how terrifying it was that my body was acting like a poltergeist. And all people could do was be mean. Anyway.

CAT scan. Tumour. Biopsy. Bad news.

My sisters and I had played a game before—what would you do if you had six months to live. Sarah said shop. Katy said climb Mount Everest. See the world, I think I said. Well, I wrote that list over again. Tell my friends why I love them. Record the unaccompanied cello suites. Learn to fly a plane. I think I still have it somewhere, the list. The only thing I did do was record the unaccompanied cello suites. We did it on Sarah's tape recorder. No, I wrote my friends letters, too. Every now and then Norma or Kirsten will bring them up again. But what I really wanted to have done before I died was to have children, which I could not do at age fourteen, though I contemplated trying. I would get Michael Nagossian to sleep with me at Brian Falconer's party, went the plan. I would get pregnant, gestate, give birth, cradle the baby, then die. The baby would remind everyone of me, would keep me alive. In some versions, the baby would literally keep me alive. My love for her melted the brain tumour and I recovered. As it turned out, Michael locked himself in the closet with Sandra Turner. It was broken, the lock, and Brian's dad had to take the door off to get them out.

They operated. A success. Got all the tumour. More tests for cancerous cells. Negative. No chemo, no radiation. My head was shaved, of course. I hated that. I swore never to cut my hair again. And I never have.

May 16, 1986

My nineteenth birthday. My sisters take me out to Luv Affair. You can guess the rest. Drinking, dancing, gross guys, a cute one, laughter. Barfing.

October 8, 1989

There's nothing worse than throwing up in a tent.

Okay. There are worse things. Throwing up in space I imagine is not very pleasant. Bastinado I've heard is not nice. Cancerous brain tumour? Not the best.

This guy I'd met had the idea we should go up to Long Beach for the weekend, it'd be great. There'd be no one there because it would be the off-season. It was supposed to be a group of us, but people dropped out for various reasons—Tim had to have emergency dental surgery; Faro's father died; I don't know what happened to the others—and then it was just Collie and me. I've wondered since if he actually engineered it. But Faro did go to the funeral, Tim had had a run-in with an olive pit. Anyway, he was cute, this guy with the Volkswagen Rabbit and the Cowichan sweater and the curly hair. "Do you still want to go?" I remember him asking in the kitchen of the Vine Street house where I lived with Faro and Janet. "Yes," I said, feeling shy and bold at the same time. Feeling like I was saying yes to much more.

On the long drive, we told each other our life stories. I heard about his mother and his sister and his stepfather, his friend who died, his other friends, his girlfriend who dumped him. I told him about my parents and my sisters and brother and my time in New York. After a time, I found myself recounting the fishing trip, the nausea and headaches and weird head trip of having your motor functions go wacky. The diagnosis. My "lost fall." I never told people this because, let's face it, when you tell people you had a brain tumour, well, it's something of a conversation stopper. It changes things. People feel sorry for you. They don't know what to say. But I think I knew when I told him, I think on some level I knew even then that something was beginning that would not end.

I thought it was just the long drive, but about an hour after our dinner of soup and bread under the tarp, after retiring from the cold into Collie's small backpacking tent, as we were holding hands for the first time, our legs covered with our sleeping bags, and playing travel backgammon, and smiling at one another stupidly, he leaned towards me for a kiss and I suddenly couldn't hold it in. I deked like we were playing one on one basketball and dove for the zipper, hurled myself into the cold rainy night and threw up on a giant fern. I began to shake. Collie was out there with me. "What is it? What is it?"

I shook my head. "Just the flu."

He led me back to the tent, zipped me into his best sleeping bag, got me a pot to puke in and held me all night. Every day for weeks he phoned to see how I was feeling. Not sick? Not dizzy? Handwriting okay? Want to go for a bike ride?

I'm fine, Collie. I'm fine.

But I do it, too. Can't help it. Every time I feel sick, I wonder, Is it back? I can almost feel it at the back of my head: a thing that shouldn't be there. And then a few days pass, and I feel better, and nothing else happens, and I live in moment after moment, happily.

October 20, 1990

We've been married a month, and I've been feeling sick for a week and a half. Today, I race to the toilet and empty the contents of my stomach. I've either got a brain tumour or I'm pregnant. I buy a home pregnancy test. Pregnant. Then, the whole first trimester, I worry I'm pregnant *and* have a brain tumour. Then the nausea stops and I go back to being a regular human being.

April 1994

This time, it feels like pregnancy, not a tumour. And of course it is. Pregnancy.

April 12, 2003

Couldn't be pregnant this time. I'm too old. I'm on the pill. Must be the flu.

April 13, 2003

Held it together all through rehearsal, then dashed as fast as decorum would allow to bathroom, where my coffee and biscotti popped back up to say hello, as David would say. No, wait. That's for burping. Well, anyway, big breath in. Big breath out. Big breath in. Big breath out. "Leanne? That you? You okay?" Sharon asked me.

"Fine," I said. "Fine. Just a little upset stommy."

April 14, 2003

Damn. Should have bought the test on the way home yesterday. I have two students in the morning and one in the afternoon. Do I have time to nip down to London Drugs at lunch? Yes, I do.

I wait till Donelly is gone, then I take the test not because I really think I'm pregnant but because it's a simple, concrete thing I can do to put my mind at ease, and there it is: the blue line. Well, I'll be. We're going to have another baby. To my surprise, this makes me blissfully happy.

Puke Diary

David Allan Macintosh-Collins

I don't remember the first time I threw up. I'm sure I did when I was a baby. Baby Hal pukes a lot. Well, not so much anymore. You should have seen it when he was projectile vomiting, though. Holy man, it was unbelievable. Baby Hal is very cute. He does this thing where if you blow on his tummy he claps his hands. I can't help it, I have to do it over and over. The projectile vomiting was gross and funny, but when he had to go to the hospital and have an operation, I was very worried. He was only one week old. He was a tiny baby. I couldn't believe that a tiny baby might die, even though I know they do. It makes me appreciate him more.

Okay. When is a time I remember throwing up. I was sick last year. When was that. A couple of times. I got to stay home from school. Oh, yeah, Thanksgiving, it was just before Thanksgiving, so I got almost a whole week off. Apparently, a long time ago when I started kindergarten, I was so nervous, I threw up and they sent me home. Thing that was weird was, I wanted to go, I didn't want to get sent home. I was excited. But I guess I was nervous too. Or maybe you can throw up just from excitement. Dad said that's what he did on the day he got married to Mom. His stomach just couldn't handle. I think I inherited the stomach from him. Then I was sick in January. I remember because it had snowed out and I really wanted to go out but I couldn't because I had a fever. Oh, yeah, and then that time with the neighbour's dog that finally got smoked by a truck. That was this summer. I was watching it. It's the Urys' dog, they always just let it out and it runs up and down the street and poops all over, it drives Mom crazy. Well, I was doing chalk pictures on the front walk, I was trying to imitate the style of Toulouse-Lautrec like we did in my class at the art gallery, and this truck drove up the street, it had its windows open and this guy, the driver was on a cellphone and he was shouting, he was really mad, and Peppy, that's the Urys' dog, started chasing the truck like he does with every vehicle that comes up the street. He chases it on the road, it always makes me nervous, but he hadn't got killed so far so I wasn't paying that much attention, then all of a sudden I was, because the truck was going way too fast and the guy was yelling, Sea urchins, you ordered f***ing sea urchins? which I thought was pretty funny, as in strange and ha ha. Our street is too narrow for two cars to pass, so if there's a car coming the other way, one of the cars has to pull over or else schmook, or if they're going slow, deadlock, one of them has to back up. But this guy's going too fast, and a Hummer is coming the other way, and *it's* going too fast, and the guy's yelling, and the dog's barking and it looks like they're playing chicken, it looks like they're going to crash, and then whssht, the guy in the truck whips over into this spot where there's no parked car and the Hummer zooms by and gives the other guy the finger and there's this sound, it's almost like a car alarm, it goes up in pitch from like a high C to a high E. Peppy. People start coming out of their houses. Dad, Dad, I shout, and Dad comes out, and Mom and her student, who were having their lesson in the basement, and we run over there. Peppy, he's a Sheltie, he's lying weirdly. His head's half bashed-in, the bone in his snout is broken, his teeth are broken. Mrs. Ury comes out and Nick, whose supposedly dog it is, and Nick is going, "Peppy? Peppy?" in this voice like he's four and innocent when he's actually nine, like me, and mean, unlike me. I always said Nick only pretended to like that dog, but maybe he really did have some attachment to it. Anyway, my Dad was the one who picked up the dog and took him howling to our car and took Nick and Mrs. Ury to the vet's. I kept seeing Peppy's bashed in head even after they were gone, and then I threw up. I heard Dad throwing up later, after he got home. Peppy died. The vet put him down. There was nothing they could do.

Then, when else?

Three times in the summer, once when I was spying on Emma and Aaron through the binoculars and I saw their mouths open and their tongues, like, meeting before their lips covered up the tongues. I put the binoculars down because it grossed me out, the thought of someone else's spit in my mouth, the ew-barfness of feeling, like, the slimy lump of someone else's tongue? The more I thought about it the sicker I felt until I gagged, but didn't really throw up, and then I had to distract myself so I pretended I was a broken man on a Halifax pier.

Once when I looked down the outhouse hole, which I shouldn't have done.

Once when Mom had a migraine and Emma and I were looking after Baby Hal and I went into the yurt to see if she wanted me to get her some Ginger Ale, and she'd thrown up in a bowl, and I said I'd clean it up and she said, "No, David, that's not your job," and I said, "No, really, it's fine," and I took it and I put it down the grey water drain, and then I had to run outside and barf myself from the smell.

Don't tell Dad, Mom said, so I didn't. That was about two weeks ago. And that's about it. All the times I puked in my whole life.

One way to begin is to describe the pear, grapefruit-shaped and golden, rough to the touch, hefty in the palm, its weight surprising for its size, promising succulence. Liquid is heavy. I am mostly liquid, too, and also heavy. There are one hundred and fifty-six pounds of me in this world. Is that not a strange thought? Not that we weigh a certain amount, but that we contain mass, a more or less fixed supply of matter, and this mass, particularly arranged as it is, is us. Nothing beyond that mass is us; everything beyond it is not-us; and yet, that's not the way it feels. It feels as if...well, there is no good way to describe it, but it feels as if my consciousness is as large as all I can see and hear and taste and smell—not that I need to go through all of the senses, although, duh, there's only one more, so okay: touch —but if my consciousness is as large as all that, and contained within myself, a mere one hundred and fifty-six pounds on the planet's surface, well, there's clearly a disjunction there, isn't there? Everything in one person's purview; a body maybe a tenth of a cubic metre in volume and one hundred and fifty-six pounds in mass. It doesn't fit.

I will eat the pear she gave me. Its mass will join my mass. I will encompass it, though I will not become it; it will be gone, and I will persist. I will try to live the life the pear would have wanted for itself.

No. Wait. Scratch that.

What life would a pear want? To ripen and fall to earth, to be nibbled by ants, pecked by crows, phaged by phages, to rot nicely in the soil around its life-encasing pips, osmosing its best organic wishes to its small, nutty hopes for propagation?

Hey.

Maybe I *will* try to live the life the pear would have wanted for itself.

I will eat the pear. With each bite, I will tell you how it was, our meeting, our time together, our parting. That's how to tell stories like ours, isn't it? Though that order is not necessary, I suppose.

All right. Bite one: my teeth slide bluntly over the flat curve of finely pebbled skin, denting and bruising it to a darker brown before catching and slicing through to the pearly flesh. After stopping suddenly in mid-conversation on Keefer, she darted into a store, leaving me jawing to blank-faced shoppers rifling the produce stalls. We were talking about extreme sports and then I asked her a question about something else, but she had already taken two pears cashierward and I never got my answer.

Befuddled, abandoned on the sidewalk, I wanted to explain myself. This has always been my fault, to want to explain myself. Here I am, explaining myself to you and I have done nothing wrong.

A woman squeezed in front of me to examine the lychees, giving my badly placed self a clucking look. Sara emerged from the store. She had heard my question.

Here. Have a pear, she said.

What she meant was, Sometimes it's better to eat fruit than to talk about things we mean. I had become expert at that point at deciphering what she meant. We had known one another precisely one week.

Bite two: the pear fills its promise of succulence with a surge of juice bursting forth from the broken walls of its cells. We met on the train. She didn't know where she would stay, buoyed with confidence the world would take care of her. I was tempted to let some other soul offer to share a room, but I did think I'd like to see her face again with its quick eyes and faint freckles, its red, red lips. She liked to think she was a free spirit. I liked to think she was a free spirit. I'm not sure she was. Reader, I invited her to share my room.

Bite three: My intentions were chaste.

Can you say that? That intentions are chaste or unchaste?

You are chaste or you are unchaste. Intentions be damned.

No, my intentions *were* chaste. My intentions have ever been chaste. It's the intentions of others that have kept me from a life of chastity. Oren, the hired hand. Helmut, the greenhouse supervisor. Gwendy, in that strange arrangement that worked so secretly and so long.

The night before I left home when we talked the whole night through, my sister told me she and Rona Friesen had agreed I was asexual. Until Gwendy, I thought they were right. It was a comfort to think so. Afterwards, I reverted best I could.

With Sara, I did not wish for some sort of barter arrangement, that was never my plan. I imagined she'd, in the lingo of youth, *crash* here only, that I'd give her a key and she'd come and go on her own schedule. I imagined she'd be out day and night, a bebackpacked youth meeting other bebackpacked youth. And so she did.

Bite four: time is getting out of whack here. On the same day that she gave me the pear I savour, she took sixty dollars from my pockets and caught a ferry, caught a VW van full of lean young bodies full of love, leaned her full young body into all of theirs. They spoke a vague, wistful language.

From a Gulf Island farm, she writes: Your rooms were too small and there were no geese. I want to live as if timelessly. I know you loved me and I'm sorry.

She *knows I loved her?*

I held the postcard as if to rip it in half, then did not.

Did I love her? There was no reason to love her. No, that's not true, I don't know why I said that. You could love her just for those freckles, just for those green eyes, just for the green apple she was eating when I got on the train at Winnipeg after visiting my sister and her new baby, my first niece, the continuation of our family that had for so long seemed threatened with extinction after the two of us. (Pear juice drips down my chin.) She said hi first, giving me a glance then going back to the window and digging her incisors into the fruit. After a cool greeting, I dug my book out of my bag, not just because I wanted to read, though I did, but because I wanted to demonstrate I was not going to be a hassling seat-mate, nor did I want to be seated next to same.

We pulled out of Winnipeg again into prairie—what else?—and she nibbled her apple down to thread and cartilage, peeling the flesh off the translucent carapace with her small teeth.

She folded the seeds up in her hand and asked what I was reading. I showed her the cover of the book. Is it any good? she asked.

Yes. I think so.

It's about cod?

Yes. Codfish.

That never made sense to me, she said. Codfish. Tuna fish. We don't say robin bird, we don't say chicken bird. Why tuna fish?

Bluebird? I said. Mockingbird, mynah bird, hummingbird. I knew there were more but I was running out of them, those were all I could think of. Even as I spoke, the rebuttal to my argument was obvious and I blushed with embarrassment. Except for mynah, perhaps, which I would have to look up, they were all adjective-birds, whereas tunaness was not a particular attribute of a fish. Or was it? From whence did "tuna" stem? This, too, I would have to look up. (And now I do: Latin, thunnus. Mynah is from Hindu. No meaning given. They are just names.)

If she noticed my shoddy logic she certainly didn't care. She had made her point. She had moved on. So tell me about codfish, she said. Are you from Newfoundland?

No.

Okay. Tell me about codfish.

Would it make a difference if I were?

I'm just wondering why you'd be interested in codfish.

Isn't everyone? Aren't you?

I am now, she said.

So I told her what the book had told me, about cod wars and ghost nets, nets separated from their ships that rise with their bloated, useless catch and fall, rise and fall.

Have you ever caught a codfish? she asked. I shook my head.

We should go cod fishing when we get to the coast.

My first thought was that Pacific cod are a garbage fish, that you wouldn't want to catch one, but I didn't say that. I said, Okay.

How did she know I was going to the coast? I might have been going to Medicine Hat.

In the observation car, she befriended others, introduced me to them. She got us to play Murder, a card game in which the person who gets the Queen of Spades must kill the other players by winking at them. It was the unlikeliest thing, this crowd of fat American tourists and well-heeled Japanese tourists and a bright, white-haired Saskatchewan farm wife whose husband had died and who was going to visit her daughter in Vancouver, and two young white dudes from rich Ontario families going out tree planting. They kept trying to hit on my friend. To my pleasure, she quite obviously preferred the white-haired farm lady to the two boys, and quite possibly me to the white-haired farm lady.

Back in our seats trying to settle down for the night, I read more about cod and she read a novel. Then she asked me what I'd been doing in Winnipeg and I told her. She asked if I got along with my sister and I said yes, anyone would get along with my sister, she was wonderful. I asked if she had any siblings, and she said yes, three sisters and two half-brothers. Their allegiances were constantly shifting; lately they were all off her, but that was all right because she didn't really like any of them either. She guessed she was running away.

I couldn't tell what kind of family she might come from. She might be the child of a carpenter and a nurse in a small Ottawa Valley town, of a wealthy Anglo banker with a French-Canadian wife from Montréal, or a wealthy Francophone banker with an Anglophone wife. She might be an orphan from Nova Scotia, a dental hygienist's daughter from Fredericton, a professor's daughter from Guelph, a mill worker's daughter from Sudbury. When I asked where she was from, she said she'd lived a lot of places. Military, I thought.

As we rode the train together, I was—I realize in retrospect—careful where my arm rested, which way my head flopped as I dozed in the rocking of the train. You're too old for her, intimated the furtive wordless homunculus lodged in the crypt of my inner mind. You're the wrong sex. I think. (The homunculus and I have ever been foggy on such matters.)

I assumed, as I am wont to do, that she couldn't possibly

be interested in me. This had so often happened to be true that I had long given up its ever being otherwise. I was like Jack Lemmon in *Some Like it Hot*. I was very like Jack Lemmon in *Some Like it Hot*.

And so I took the sympathetic looks, the seeking out of my eyes, my understanding, the resting of her forearm next to mine, of her cheek on my shoulder, as carelessness.

The pear, actually, to tell the truth, is a bit mealy. I don't know how to tell a love story. There is so very little to it. Two days on a train. Five days in Vancouver. We were supposed to go fishing the next day. I had us booked. I put it on my credit card.

I've let it sit too long, the pear.

We arrived in Vancouver late Friday afternoon and took a taxi to my house. It was early summer and my horticulturally inclined downstairs neighbours Burt and Val were out putting in new grasses in their ever-evolving garden.

They asked how the baby was, how my sister was. They pretended to take the presence of my companion in stride.

You must be Val and Burt, she said, before I could answer. Nice to meet you.

I blushed. This is Sara, I said. Sara's going to stay with me a few days.

Great, said Val, raising her eyebrows at me.

Hey, said Burt to Sara, raising his eyebrows at Val.

The baby's marvellous, I said. A wonder. Her little hands, her little eyebrows. You could count the hairs. Verna is over the moon.

Sara clutched my arm. Your sister's name is Verna? she said. Why didn't you say something? Why didn't you punch me?

Burt and Val raised their eyebrows at each other. I knew what they meant. There was a falseness to this intimacy. Sara didn't know me but was acting like she did. Despite being embarrassing, this gave me pleasure.

Inside, she examined my apartment, peering at the bookshelves, the CDs, the pictures on the wall, the pictures on the fridge (exhausted-looking sister with newborn; Gwendy at the bird sanctuary, holding Bob's arm and smiling), the contents of the fridge (scant). She was finding out all about me in the way that two kinds of people do—people who are curious about everyone and want to know everything about how other people live (she *was* one of these people) and people who wouldn't normally do this but want to eat everything up about this person they've just met. She might have been one of those people, too.

On the train she'd asked what I worked at.

I am a parasitologist.

I didn't ask what you are, I asked what you work at.

There is not really any difference. I work at studying parasites.

Why do you have to have an *-ologist* to define yourself? If you lost your job, say, and no longer worked at that thing, what would the "I am" mean then? You are more than your job, the wholeness of you.

I would be an unemployed parasitologist.

She was quiet and I thought she was sulking, but after a moment she said, You just like saying the word, don't you? Parasitologist.

No.

I lifted my book to my face and read for what in conversational terms was a long time, twenty seconds maybe. Then I said, wrapping my tongue lovingly around the word, Parasitologist. Parasitologist.

It was our first big laugh together. My first big laugh in a long time. She took it up, too, *parasitologist*, and for the next few days we'd say it out loud, reverently, as if to ourselves, when the other was not expecting it.

Do you study parasites in cod? Codfish?

No. Fish, fish aren't my thing.

What is your thing?

Animal parasites, domestic animals, farm animals. These days, poultry.

Poultry? Chickens?

Turkeys. Ducks. Geese.

I want to keep a flock of geese.

Okay, I said.

And what sort of parasites do poultry have?

The usual sort. Worms. Bugs.

We were quiet. We fell asleep. When I awoke I felt her eyes on me. Her accusing eyes.

You work for the poultry industry, don't you?

I work for the university.

But who funds you?

There is some poultry money, yes.

Do you eat chicken?

I do.

You know how they are treated.

Free-range. I eat free-range chicken.

You'll take their money, but won't eat their chickens?

I shrugged. I grew up on a farm. After a pause, I went on. Actually, free-range chickens are more apt to have parasites than wire-grown chickens. It's the contact with the ground. That's one of the things I've been studying: how do you control parasites in organic flocks?

Really? Her face just beamed. And? How do you?

I think she was genuinely interested. I really do.

Why don't you live on a farm now? she asked.

I wouldn't be doing what I'm doing.

Oh, come on. You could live on a farm somewhere, couldn't you?

I'd rather not.

Why not? I'd love to live on a farm. You grow food, you eat it. What could be more beautiful than that?

Many answers ran through my head: A painting? A symphony? A good book? That is the most simplistic thing I've ever heard. You have no idea, do you?

Nothing. Nothing, I said. That's the thing. But she was not interested in subtleties.

Why don't you want to live on a farm?

And the next string ran through my head. The responsibility. The bank. The stress. Rats. The hired man. (When Dad had his stroke and had to move into the nursing home, I fired him.) The way it never stopped. Failure. I couldn't save the farm. I tried. It burns me to this day, the memory of selling it, the thought of who I sold it to.

I've never found anyone to live on a farm with, I heard

myself saying.

I'll live on a farm with you, she said.

Of course, she was being glib. I knew that. She was joking. *Parasitologist*. We had only just met. But if I am to be truthful in my recollection, I must register that her words caused a sensation in my abdomen, a tightening, a shimmering, noted not so much by my conscious mind as by the part of my brain that dealt with low-level daily idiocies of feeling that as a foolish and unloved person I experienced. (Not the homunculus. A blob next to it.) Down, Rover, down, that part of the brain would have been saying if it could ever rouse itself to speech.

Okay, I said. Next stop, let's get off, buy us a farm.

I'll need a farm name, she said.

Not me, I've already got one. I laughed, but this kind of joking was like a knife. Elmers and Velmas, the town kids called us. *Oh, Jesus, would you look at the Velmas.*

Call me Verna, she said.

My eyes stung. But I laughed. I did. I laughed. Already she had me. Already I'd given up part of myself.

I want you to show me hidden Vancouver, she said that night. I didn't know hidden Vancouver. When my sister or cousins came to visit, I took them to an assortment of: the aquarium, Stanley Park, the Museum of Anthropology, the Cypress lookout, a sushi restaurant on Cambie, Granville Island, the Endowment Lands, Second Beach, Denman Street, Robson Street, Van Dusen Gardens, Gastown. In short, all the tourist places.

So she said, all right, we'll find it together. We clinked glasses and I got her sheets and blankets for the chesterfield and both of us made up the bed she would lie in.

Thanks, she said. You're a sweetheart. The universe will repay you for your kindness.

Sure.

It will. Her eyes were green and clear as a tropical lagoon.

I place all my faith in the universe, I said. Good night.

It's just the weekend, I thought. She knows I won't be working on the weekend and wants to use her tour guide while she has one.

You've got a beard, she said the next morning as I poured coffee. She reached out to stroke it where it had grown since the day before. I tilted my head away. Do you shave it every day?

I nodded.

You're a bearded lady.

Yes. Thank you.

Sorry.

There are more of us than you'd think. Seriously. Start looking. You'd be surprised. This is true. Bearded ladies—and mustachioed ladies, let's not forget them—are everywhere. We are successful. We are down at heel. We have boyfriends, girlfriends, husbands. We are tall and short, fat and thin, Italian and Greek. Sorry, bad joke and not true either. Look at me, German by descent. Look at the other bearded women I know: Scandinavian, Punjabi, Iranian, Welsh. My bad joke endangers my point, which is that we are—as members of minority groups often say—just like everyone else.

Have you ever thought of growing it?

Ask me next if I've thought of joining the circus.

Have you?

I gave her a look.

You asked me to ask you.

Though what bearded lady hadn't? There were times I longed for the old days when I could've made a living at it instead of being a freak in no ways but one and having no talent for it.

A woman I worked with wanted me to grow it, I said. In the eighties. She had just come out—one of those come-out-screaming lesbian-feminists. She was convinced it was only a matter of time before I did too. How I would screw the patriarchy by growing a beard was beyond me. I went for electrolysis instead.

Was it?

Was it what?

Just a matter of time.

No.

Her green eyes focused on me like an owl's on its prey.

Later, on the skytrain out to Surrey (her idea —"Nobody ever shows you the suburbs, why is that?"), she asked, If you went for electrolysis, how come you still have— and instead of saying *beard* again, she reached out and stroked that stretch of jawline. A ludicrous pounding erupted in my chest.

Infection, I said with a rush of shame at not only having a beard, but not being able to get rid of it properly. I pulled my face away, though I longed to do the opposite, lean it into her long, tree-froggy hand.

In the afternoon, I showed her the farm, introduced her to Chris, my grad student, showed her our chickens.

This, she said, looking around, this is hidden Vancouver. I could live here. She wanted to stay all afternoon. She wanted to help with the chores.

Awesome, said Chris, taking her to meet the other enthusiastic scrubbed young things who ran the market garden. She said she'd make her own way home.

That's it, I thought, she's gone. Youth has won her. This struck me as beautiful, the idea of youth winning youth, the idea of me as a conduit, delivering her to them, them to her. Tears of recognition of the sublime ran down my face as I walked to my office, where I stayed until nine.

My home was dark as I approached. Yes. Gone, I thought, opening the door. Then my nostrils twitched: a baked something with garlic and cheese. I flicked on the lights.

Where've you been? Sara squinted from the chesterfield. I made eggplant parmigiana for us.

At dinner she told me she'd decided to stay and volunteer at the farm for a while. I don't have to stay here. I could move to the youth hostel if—

No, no, no—unless you'd—

No, I'd—

'Cause if you—

I'd rather stay with you. She grinned in a particular way then that made me hop up and clear the table.

Every day for the next week, we rode the bus together to UBC, she spending her days at the farm, I starting off there, then going to my office and crunching data.

Late Wednesday afternoon, I went back to the farm under the pretense of straightening out data discrepancies with Chris only to discover that he and Sara had gone to Wreck Beach. Knowing he'd have to be back to coop the chickens for the night, I left a message. He called at eight. Sara was not with him. Nor was she, as on eggplant parmigiana night, at home.

At 3:45, I heard the door click. Although I relaxed, I could not fall back to sleep. Once I realized I wouldn't sleep, I wanted to read, but was afraid if I turned my light on, Sara would interpret it as a) a veiled admonition for coming home late and waking me, or b) evidence I'd been worried about her like a waiting-up parent. I lay in the dark, telling myself she was acting exactly as I had thought she would initially, and that this was as it should be.

In the morning she was up at seven as usual. What was I doing that night? she asked. Someone she'd met was doing a fire dance for the summer solstice on Granville Island. We went. The dancers were beautiful, as naked as they could get, with their skin painted. Both men and women muscular and graceful, like panthers or snakes. Sara danced with leaping, long-skirted, dyed-haired, nose-pierced types while the drummers drummed and the rest of us bobbed in place and the fire dancers swung fire around their heads and behind their backs and around their fronts and under their feet, and the jugglers juggled fire and ate fire and we all felt the beat of the drums and the heat of the fire and knew instinctively that this was what civilization was all about, that primitivism and civilization were the same thing, and this was it: sun, earth, humans, drums, fire.

As we were leaving, we passed a VW van with the side door open and three people playing hacky sack outside it, two girls with army shorts and spaghetti-strap t-shirts, scarves wound through their hair, and a boy in India cotton drawstring pants. They blew kisses at Sara and called out some goddess greeting or other, Kali, Inanna, I don't know.

The next morning, before she had a chance to allude to plans she might have had, I suggested breakfast at the Ovaltine.

What's the Ovaltine?

A diner. I wonder if they serve Ovaltine. My mother used to drink Ovaltine.

Ovaltine?

Kind of a cross between hot chocolate and coffee and malted milk.

Ovaltine.

Parasitologist.

Can we get a newspaper? I love going out for breakfast with a newspaper.

I grabbed a fold of *The Vancouver Sun* and draped it over my head. Off we go, I said.

How come nobody's snapped you up?

My heart stopped. I don't know, I said. They just haven't. Ugly, is what I thought. Big teeth, big jaw, eyebrows like old toothbrushes used to clean silver. Beard.

Off we went to the Ovaltine. A drunk with a husky on a rope stopped us to ask for a light and oh yeah, how bout a loonie, how bout your life savings, what the hell, come on, how about yer ar-ar-ess-peeees, how bout you leave me in yer will and die tomorrow, har har har, coughing fit, no, no, I'm kiddin' ya, no, I'm unna die first I'll bet you that, you're all right, you two, you're all right, thanks, me and my cur we thank you, you have a nice day now.

After breakfast we walked down to Crabbe Park, another place I'd never been, though I knew it was there, don't know how. My stomach felt all loopy. We stopped by the stone for the women who'd died in the Downtown Eastside and she leaned against my shoulder, folding herself into my side. Such a beautiful place and then this, she said, hushed, clinging to me. My hands hung at the ends of my arms, my arms hung out of my shoulders. What was going on here? What was going on?

She changed topics. Doesn't it make you want to go for a swim, just seeing the water?

No.

Come on. She took my hand. Let's strip off all our clothes and go for a swim.

She was touching me. She was touching me a lot. She was holding my hand. She was taking my arm. She was taking me back to Chinatown and we were talking about extreme sports because we didn't want to talk about prostitution and drugs and poverty and cultural genocide. I thought extreme sports were evidence of a decadent culture and she thought they were the perfect expression of human nature, the urge to test ourselves, the urge to go beyond, the urge to be in our bodies, the urge to compete, the urge to folly. And I said, Sara? What's going on? It was the bravest thing I'd said in about eight years, but she didn't answer and instead bought me the pear, a Japanese pear shaped like an apple, flecked and golden-russet-coloured and now half-eaten, discarded. I spit the last bite out; close to the core it's like eating a still-wet but drying sponge.

I'll save it for later, I said about the pear, putting it in my pocket.

Come on, let's go home, she said, grabbing my hand.

Home. That was the word she used.

At the bus stop she stood in front of me, right in front, her back touched my front. She drew my arms around her waist. On the bus she leaned her elbow on my shoulder to look out the window.

You tell me. Was this a romance or wasn't it?

We got home and played Scrabble. I booked the fishing charter. In the late afternoon, I had a bath. I thought... I thought she might join me. Instead, I was leaning back with a washcloth over my eyes when she called my name and said she was going out. I became aware of a rumbling from the street, a characteristic rumbling. A Volkswagen rumbling. I waited for and heard what came next, a low zhoosh as the van door opened, zhoosh, shut. The shift from idle into gear.

That night I did wait up.

The next day I heard from Chris that the van people knew about a farm on Salt Spring where you could stay as long as you liked provided you helped out.

And today I got a postcard: Dear Edna, Your rooms were too small and there were no geese. I want to live as if timelessly. I know you loved me and I'm sorry.

This is to say: Sara, don't flatter yourself. I would have loved anybody.

Thirty-One One Word Stories

Thief.

Martyr.

"Evening."

Egg.

Rifle.

Magazine.

Acrobat.

Martha.

Longboat.

Scale.

Salamander.

Parade.

Spoonbill.

Grit.

Fine.

"Fine."

Malinger.

Cheat.

Evening.

Respite.

Sashay.

Chesterfield.

Steer.

Coke.

Louse.

Louise.

Motorhome.

Plague.

Stacked.

Had.

Maroon.

Acknowledgements

I'd like to thank all the people, little and big, who helped this book become book. That'd be the bedrock-y arts councils of Canada and BC, the bulwarkish Creative Studies department at UBC's Okanagan campus, the discerning/honoured/very nice editors of the books and magazines that first published the stories (*The Journey Prize Stories 15*, *No Margins*, *Toronto Life Magazine*, *The Malahat Review*, *Drunken Boat*, and especially *The New Quarterly*, which published three, including the title story, and has been something of a literary home for me), the equally discerning National Magazine Award juries of 2003, 2005 and 2009, esteemed editor Beth Follett, fine readers and friends Marlo Edwards, Jake Kennedy and Cindy Holmes, forebearing parents Pat and Ross Fleming, and beloved wee family, Cindy Holmes and Kate Fleming-Holmes, who are so interesting to live with.

About the Author

Anne Fleming is the author of *Pool-Hopping and Other Stories*, which was shortlisted for the Governor General's Award for Fiction, the Ethel Wilson Fiction Prize and the Danuta Gleed Award, as well as the critically acclaimed novel, *Anomaly*. She divides her time between Vancouver and Kelowna, where she teaches creative writing at UBC's Okanagan campus.

"This is Jodi Picoult at her best: tackling an emotional hot-button issue and putting a human face on it."
—*People*

"The author presents the white-knuckled narrative in reverse chronological order. The effect is mesmerizing, as Picoult establishes moments in the overarching event before revealing how they came to be."
—*Houston Chronicle*

"An important and thoughtful read that is perfect for book clubs looking for deep conversations."
—*PopSugar*

"Once again, Picoult shows her bestselling knack for lacing her page-turning tales with topical themes."
—*The Philadelphia Inquirer*

"Picoult has achieved what politicians across the spectrum have not been able to: humanized a hot-button issue. Excellent for book clubs, this should also be considered for discussions in critical thinking and political debate."
—*Library Journal* (starred review)

Praise for *A Spark of Light*

"[A] nail-biting thriller." — *O: The Oprah Magazine*

"Drama abounds in [Jodi] Picoult's latest issue-driven novel. . . . Picoult's extensive research shines throughout. . . . This is a powerful story that brings clarity to the history of abortion and investigates the voices on both sides of the issue." — *Publishers Weekly*

Praise for *Small Great Things*

"*Small Great Things* is the most important novel Jodi Picoult has ever written. . . . It will challenge her readers . . . [and] expand our cultural conversation about race and prejudice." — *The Washington Post*

"A gripping courtroom drama . . . Given the current political climate it is quite prescient and worthwhile. . . . This is a writer who understands her characters inside and out." — Roxane Gay, *The New York Times Book Review*

"*Small Great Things* tackles tricky subject matter with grace. . . . [A] gripping read about an issue of urgency" — *The Vancouver Sun*

"A novel that puts its finger on the very pulse of the nation that we live in today . . . A fantastic read from beginning to end, as can always be expected from Picoult, this novel maintains a steady, page-turning pace that makes it hard for readers to put down. It also allows for conversations to be had and for people to sit back and look at their lives, actions (past and present) and wonder how they will move forward. This is a fantastic book not only because it addresses something that happens in America and around the world every day, but it also shows us that change is possible too."

—*San Francisco Book Review*

"Given that Picoult is wrestling with the subject of white privilege, writing Ruth's story in the first person might seem like an exercise of that very prerogative. Can Ruth be the hero of her own story? Or must she be saved by Kennedy? Turns out, this is Picoult's driving concern, too. That *Small Great Things* embraces this question with empathy, hope and humility is no small feat."   —*Newsday*

"The gem of this novel lies in the characterization of Picoult's three narrators: Ruth; Ruth's white public defender, Kennedy McQuarrie, who prefers to keep race out of the courtroom; and Turk Bauer, the baby's father. As the narrators alternate throughout the novel, their perspectives on the case are strikingly distinct."

—*Vox Magazine*

Praise for *Leaving Time*

"This one might actually *be* her best one yet. It's got everything you'd expect from Picoult: the impeccable pacing, the efficient prose, the expertly rendered characters, the brushstrokes of deep emotional brilliance, the carefully presented moral dilemmas. . . . Truly, this is Picoult at the top of her game."

—*The Globe and Mail*

"Jodi Picoult is a powerhouse writer. . . . She tackles important issues . . . from a human perspective. . . . An exploration of love and emotion that won't soon be forgotten."

—*The Vancouver Sun*

"Count on blockbuster novelist Jodi Picoult for two things. First is a smart, accessible yarn with a suspenseful puzzle at its core that will keep readers enthusiastically turning the page. Second is impressive insight into any number of topical issues. . . . Picoult does her homework, and her main themes are thoroughly researched and engrossingly presented. With this new novel, *Leaving Time*, her fans will not be disappointed. . . . Both pierc[es] and uplift[s] the hearts of those willing go along for the ride . . . Picoult's stories reinforce the significance of the bond between mother and child."

—*The Boston Globe*

"Bestselling, reliably entertaining, and thought-provoking, Picoult's newest multifaceted novel is redolent with elephant lore that explores the animals' behavior when faced with death and grief, and combines a poignant tale of human loss with a perplexing crime story that delivers a powerhouse ending."

—*Booklist*

Praise for Jodi Picoult

"Picoult writes with unassuming brilliance."   —Stephen King

"It's hard to exaggerate how well Picoult writes."   —*Financial Times*

"Picoult writes with a fine touch, a sharp eye for detail, and a firm grasp on the delicacy and complexity of human relationships."

—*The Boston Globe*

"Picoult is a master of the craft of storytelling."   —Associated Press

By Jodi Picoult

A Spark of Light

Small Great Things

Leaving Time

The Storyteller

Lone Wolf

Sing You Home

House Rules

Handle with Care

Change of Heart

Nineteen Minutes

The Tenth Circle

Vanishing Acts

My Sister's Keeper

Second Glance

Perfect Match

Salem Falls

Plain Truth

Keeping Faith

The Pact

Mercy

Picture Perfect

Harvesting the Heart

Songs of the Humpback Whale

FOR YOUNG ADULTS

Off the Page

Between the Lines

AND FOR THE STAGE

Over the Moon: An Original Musical for Teens

A Spark of Light

a
spark
of
light

A NOVEL

Jodi
Picoult

VINTAGE CANADA

VINTAGE CANADA EDITION, 2019

Published by Vintage Canada, a division of Penguin Random House Canada
Limited, in 2019. Originally published in hardcover by Random House Canada,
a division of Penguin Random House Canada Limited, Toronto, in 2018, and
simultaneously in the United States by Ballantine Books. Distributed in Canada by
Penguin Random House Canada Limited, Toronto.

Vintage Canada with colophon is a registered trademark.

Scripture quote "The Lord brings death and makes alive" on pg. 164 is from
THE HOLY BIBLE, NEW INTERNATIONAL VERSION®, NIV®
Copyright © 1973, 1978, 1984, 2011 by Biblica, Inc.® Used by permission. All
rights reserved worldwide.

www.penguinrandomhouse.ca

Library and Archives Canada Cataloguing in Publication

Picoult, Jodi, 1966-, author
A spark of light / Jodi Picoult. — Vintage Canada paperback edition.

Originally published: Toronto: Random House Canada, 2018.
ISBN 978-0-345-81342-8 (softcover)

I. Title.
PS3566.I372S68 2019   813'.54   C2018-901805-4

Book design by Susan Turner
Cover design by Laura Klynstra
Author photograph: © Nina Subin

Printed and bound in the United States of America

2 4 6 8 9 7 5 3 1

 Penguin
Random House
VINTAGE CANADA

For Jennifer Hershey and Susan Corcoran

If you're lucky, you wind up with colleagues you love.

If you're luckier, they feel like sisters.

XOX

The question is not whether we will be extremists,
but what kind of extremists we will be. Will we be extremists
for hate or for love?

—Reverend Dr. Martin Luther King, Jr.

Five p.m.

THE CENTER SQUATTED ON THE CORNER OF JUNIPER AND MONTFORT behind a wrought-iron gate, like an old bulldog used to guarding its territory. At one point, there had been many like it in Mississippi—nondescript, unassuming buildings where services were provided and needs were met. Then came the restrictions that were designed to make these places go away: The halls had to be wide enough to accommodate two passing gurneys; any clinic where that wasn't the case had to shut down or spend thousands on reconstruction. The doctors had to have admitting privileges at local hospitals—even though most were from out of state and couldn't secure them—or the clinics where they practiced risked closing, too. One by one the clinics shuttered their windows and boarded up their doors. Now, the Center was a unicorn—a small rectangle of a structure painted a fluorescent, flagrant orange, like a flag to those who had traveled hundreds of miles to find it. It was the color of safety; the color of warning. It said: *I'm here if you need me.* It said, *Do what you want to me; I'm not going.*

The Center had suffered scars from the cuts of politicians and the barbs of protesters. It had licked its wounds and healed. At one point it had been called the Center for Women and Reproductive Health. But there were those who believed if you do not name a thing, it ceases to exist, and so its title was amputated, like a war injury. But still, it survived. First it became the Center for Women. And then, just: the Center.

The label fit. The Center was the calm in the middle of a storm of ideology. It was the sun of a universe of women who had run out of time and had run out of choices, who needed a beacon to look up to.

And like other things that shine so hot, it had a magnetic pull. Those in need found it the lodestone for their navigation. Those who despised it could not look away.

TODAY, WREN MCELROY THOUGHT, WAS not a good day to die. She knew that other fifteen-year-old girls romanticized the idea of dying for love, but Wren had read *Romeo and Juliet* last year in eighth-grade English and didn't see the magic in waking up in a crypt beside your boyfriend, and then plunging his dagger into your own ribs. And *Twilight*—forget it. She had listened to teachers paint the stories of heroes whose tragic deaths somehow enlarged their lives rather than shrinking them. When Wren was six, her grandmother had died in her sleep. Strangers had said over and over that dying in your sleep was a blessing, but as she stared at her nana, waxen white in the open coffin, she didn't understand why it was a gift. What if her grandmother had gone to bed the night before thinking, *In the morning, I'll water that orchid. In the morning, I'll read the rest of that novel. I'll call my son.* So much left unfinished. No, there was just no way dying could be spun into a good thing.

Her grandmother was the only dead person Wren had ever seen, until two hours ago. Now, she could tell you what dying looked like, as opposed to just dead. One minute, Olive had been there, staring so fierce at Wren—as if she could hold on to the world if her eyes stayed open—and then, in a beat, those eyes stopped being windows and became mirrors, and Wren saw only a reflection of her own panic.

She didn't want to look at Olive anymore, but she did. The dead woman was lying down like she was taking a nap, a couch cushion under her head. Olive's shirt was soaked with blood, but had ridden up on the side, revealing her ribs and waist. Her skin was pale on top and then lavender, with a thin line of deep violet where her back met the floor. Wren realized that was because Olive's blood was settling inside, just two hours after she'd passed. For a second, Wren thought she was going to throw up.

She didn't want to die like Olive, either.

Which, given the circumstances, made Wren a horrible person.

The odds were highly unlikely, but if Wren had to choose, she would die in a black hole. It would be instant and it would be epic. Like, literally, you'd be ripped apart at the atomic level. You'd become stardust.

Wren's father had taught her that. He bought her her first telescope, when she was five. He was the reason she'd wanted to be an astronaut when she was little, and an astrophysicist as soon as she learned what one was. He himself had had dreams of commanding a space shuttle that explored every corner of the universe, until he got a girl pregnant. Instead of going to grad school, he had married Wren's mom and become a cop and then a detective and had explored every corner of Jackson, Mississippi, instead. He told Wren that working for NASA was the best thing that never happened to him.

When they were driving back from her grandmother's funeral, it had snowed. Wren—a child who'd never seen weather like that in Mississippi before—had been terrified by the way the world swirled, unmoored. Her father had started talking to her: *Mission Specialist McElroy, activate the thrusters.* When she wouldn't stop crying, he began punching random buttons: the air-conditioning, the four-way flashers, the cruise control. They lit up red and blue like a command center at Mission Control. *Misson Specialist McElroy*, her father said, *prepare for hyperspace*. Then he flicked on his brights, so that the snow became a tunnel of speeding stars, and Wren was so amazed she forgot to be scared.

She wished she could flick a switch now, and travel back in time.

She wished she had told her dad she was coming here.

She wished she had let him talk her out of it.

She wished she hadn't asked her aunt to bring her.

Aunt Bex might even now be lying in a morgue, like Olive, her body becoming a rainbow. And it was all Wren's fault.

You, said the man with a gun, his voice dragging Wren back to the here and now. He had a name, but she didn't want to even think of it. It made him human and he wasn't human; he was a monster. While she'd been lost in thought, he'd come to stand in front of her. Now, he jerked the pistol at her. *Get up.*

The others held their breath with her. They had, in the past few hours, become a single organism. Wren's thoughts moved in and out of the other women's minds. Her fear stank on their skin.

Blood still bloomed from the bandage the man had wrapped around his hand. It was the tiniest of triumphs. It was the reason Wren could stand up, even though her legs were jelly.

She shouldn't have come to the Center.

She should have stayed a little girl.

Because now she might not live to become anything else.

Wren heard the hammer click and closed her eyes. All she could picture was her father's face—the blue-jean eyes, the gentle bend of his smile—as he looked up at the night sky.

WHEN GEORGE GODDARD WAS FIVE years old, his mama tried to set his daddy on fire. His father had been passed out on the couch when his mother poured the lighter fluid over his dirty laundry, lit a match, and dumped the flaming bin on top of him. The big man reared up, screaming, batting at the flames with his ham hands. George's mama stood a distance away with a glass of water. *Mabel*, his daddy screamed. *Mabel!* But his mama calmly drank every last drop, sparing none to extinguish the flames. When George's father ran out of the house to roll in the dirt like a hog, his mama turned to him. *Let that be a lesson to you*, she said.

He had not wanted to grow up like his daddy, but in the way that an apple seed can't help but become an apple tree, he had not become the best of husbands. He knew that now. It was why he had resolved to be the best of fathers. It was why, this morning, he had driven all this way to the Center, the last standing abortion clinic in the state of Mississippi.

What they'd taken away from his daughter she would never get back, whether she realized it now or not. But that didn't mean he couldn't exact a price.

He looked around the waiting room. Three women were huddled on a line of seats, and at their feet was the nurse, who was checking the bandage of the doctor. George scoffed. Doctor, my ass. What he did wasn't healing, not by any stretch of the imagination. He should have killed the guy—*would* have killed the guy—if he hadn't been interrupted when he first arrived and started firing.

He thought about his daughter sitting in one of those chairs. He wondered how she'd gotten here. If she had taken a bus. If a friend had driven her or (he could not even stand to think of it) the boy who'd gotten her in trouble. He imagined himself in an alternate universe, bursting through the door with his gun, seeing her in the chair next to the pamphlets about how to recognize an STD. He would have grabbed her hand and pulled her out of there.

What would she think of him, now that he was a killer?

How could he go back to her?

How could he go back, period?

Eight hours ago this had seemed like a holy crusade—an eye for an eye, a life for a life.

His wound had a heartbeat. George tried to adjust the binding of the gauze around it with his teeth, but it was unraveling. It should have been tied off better, but who here was going to help him?

The last time he had felt like this, like the walls were closing in on him, he had taken his infant daughter—red and screaming with a fever he didn't know she had and wouldn't have known how to treat—and gone looking for help. He had driven until his truck ran out of gas—it was past one A.M., but he started walking—and continued until he found the only building with a light on inside, and an unlocked door. It was flat-roofed and unremarkable—he hadn't known it was a church until he stepped inside and saw the benches and the wooden relief of Jesus on the cross. The lights he had seen outside were candles, flickering on an altar. *Come back*, he had said out loud to his wife, who was probably halfway across the country by now. Maybe he was tired, maybe he was delusional, but he very clearly heard a reply: *I'm already with you.* The voice whispered from the wooden Jesus and at the same time from the darkness all around him.

George's conversion had been that simple, and that enveloping. Somehow, he and his girl had fallen asleep on the carpeted floor. In the morning, Pastor Mike was shaking him awake. The pastor's wife was cooing at his baby. There was a groaning table of food, and a miraculously spare room. Back then, George hadn't been a religious man. It wasn't Jesus that entered his heart that day. It was hope.

Hugh McElroy, the hostage negotiator George had been talking to for hours, said George's daughter would know he had been trying to protect her. He'd promised that if George cooperated, this could still end well, even though George knew that outside this building were men with rifles trained on the door just waiting for him to emerge.

George wanted this to be over. Really, he did. He was exhausted mentally and physically and it was hard to figure out an endgame. He was sick of the crying. He wanted to skip ahead to the part where he was sitting by his daughter again, and she was looking up at him with wonder, the way she used to.

But George also knew Hugh would say anything to get him to surrender to the police. It wasn't even just his job. Hugh McElroy needed him to release the hostages for the same reason that George had taken them in the first place—to save the day.

That's when George figured out what he was going to do. He pulled back the hammer on the gun. "Get up. You," he said, pointing to the girl with the name of a bird, the one who had stabbed him. The one he would use to teach Hugh McElroy a lesson.

HERE WAS THE PRIMARY RULE of hostage negotiation: Don't fuck it up.

When Hugh had first joined the regional team, that's what the instructors said. Don't take a bad situation and make it worse. Don't argue with the hostage taker. Don't tell him, *I get it*, because you probably don't. Communicate in a way that soothes or minimizes the threat; and understand that sometimes the best communication is not speaking at all. Active listening can get you a lot farther than spouting off.

There were different kinds of hostage takers. There were those who were out of their head with drugs, alcohol, grief. There were those on a political mission. There were those who fanned an ember of revenge, until it flared up and burned them alive. Then there were the sociopaths—the ones who had no empathy to appeal to. And yet sometimes they were the easiest to deal with, because they understood the concept of who's in control. If you could make the sociopath believe that you were not going to cede the upper hand, you'd actually gotten somewhere. You could say, *We've been at this for two hours* (or six, or sixteen) *and I get what's on your mind. But it's time to do something new. Because there is a group of men out here who think time's up and want to address this with force.* Sociopaths understood force.

On the other hand, that approach would fail miserably with someone depressed enough to kill himself and take others with him.

The point of establishing a relationship with a hostage taker was to make sure that you were the only source of information, and to give you the time to find out critical information of your own. What kind of hostage taker were you facing? What had precipitated the standoff, the shoot-out, the point of no return? You might start trying to build a relationship with innocuous conversation about sports, weather, TV. You'd gradually find out his likes and dislikes, what mattered to him. Did he love his kids? His wife? His mom? Why?

If you could find the *why*, you could determine what could be done to disarm the situation.

Hugh knew that the best hostage negotiators called the job a ballet, a tightrope walk, a delicate dance.

He also knew that was bullshit.

No one ever interviewed the negotiators whose situations ended in a bloodbath. It was only the ones with successful outcomes who got microphones stuck in their faces, and who felt obligated to describe their work as some kind of mystical art. In reality, it was a crapshoot. Dumb luck.

Hugh McElroy was afraid his luck was about to run out.

He surveyed the scene he had spearheaded for the past few hours. His command center was an event tent the department had used a few weeks ago at a community fair to promote safe child fingerprinting. Beat cops were posted along the building's perimeter like a string of blue beads. The press had been corralled behind a police barricade. (You'd think they'd be smart enough to get further out of the range of a madman with a gun, but no, the lure of ratings was apparently too high.) Littered on the sidewalk like empty threats were placards with giant pictures of babies in utero, or hand-drawn slogans: ADOPTION, NOT ABORTION! ONE HALF OF PATIENTS WHO ENTER AN ABORTION CLINIC DO NOT COME OUT ALIVE!

Ambulances hunkered, manned by EMTs with foil blankets and portable IVs and hydration. The SWAT team was in position waiting for a signal. Their commander, Captain Quandt, had tried to boot Hugh off the case (who could blame him?) and take the shooter by force. But Hugh knew Quandt could do neither of these things in good conscience, not if Hugh was on the verge of getting George Goddard to surrender.

This was exactly what Hugh had been banking on when he broke the second rule of hostage negotiation five hours ago, screaming onto the scene in his unmarked car, barking orders to the two street cops who'd been first responders.

The secondary rule of hostage negotiation was: Don't forget that this is a job.

Hostage negotiation is not a test of your manhood. It is not a chance to be a knight in shining armor, or a way to get your fifteen minutes of fame. It may go your way and it may not, no matter how textbook your responses are. Don't take it personally.

But Hugh had known from the get-go that was never going to be possible, not today, not this time, because this was a different situation altogether. There were God knew how many dead bodies in that clinic, plus five hostages who were still alive. And one of them was his kid.

The SWAT commander was suddenly standing in front of him. "We're going in now," Quandt said. "I'm telling you as a courtesy."

"You're making a mistake," Hugh replied. "I'm telling you as a courtesy."

Quandt turned away and started to speak into the walkie-talkie at his shoulder. "We're a go in five . . . four . . ." Suddenly his voice broke. "Stand down! I repeat—*abort!*"

It was the word that had started this disaster. Hugh's head flew up, and he saw the same thing Quandt had noticed.

The front door of the clinic had suddenly opened, and two women were stepping outside.

WHEN WREN'S MOTHER STILL LIVED with them, she'd had a spider plant that she kept on top of a bookcase in the living room. After she left, neither Wren nor her father ever remembered to water it, but that spider plant seemed to defy death. It began to spill over its container and grow in a strange verdant comb-over toward a window, without playing by the rules of logic or gravity.

Wren felt like that now, swaying on her feet toward the light every time the door opened, drawn to where her father stood in the parking lot outside.

But it wasn't Wren who was walking out of the building. She had no idea what it was that her father had said to George during their last phone conversation, but it had worked. George had pulled back the trigger and told her to move the couch that he had used to buttress the door. Although the hostages couldn't talk freely without George hearing, a current had passed among them. When he instructed Wren to open the lock, she had even begun to think she might get out of here in one piece.

Joy and Janine had left first. Then George told Izzy to push out Dr. Ward in the wheelchair. Wren had thought that she'd be released then, too, but George had grabbed her by her hair and yanked her back. Izzy had turned at the threshold, her face dark, but Wren had given a small shake of her head. This might be Dr. Ward's only chance to get out, and he was hurt. She had to take him. She was a nurse; she knew. "Wren—" Izzy said, but then George slammed the door behind her and drove home the metal bolt. He released Wren long enough to have her shove the couch in front of the doorway again.

Wren felt panic rise in her throat. Maybe this was George's way of getting back at her for what she'd done to him. She was alone in here now, with this animal. Well, not quite—her eyes slid along the floor to Olive's body.

Maybe Aunt Bex was with Olive, wherever you go when you die. Maybe they were both waiting for Wren.

George sank down on the couch in front of the door, burying his face in his hands. He was still holding the gun. It winked at her.

"Are you going to shoot me?" she blurted.

George glanced up as if he was surprised she would even ask that question. She forced herself to meet his gaze. One of his eyes pulled the tiniest bit to the right, not so much that he looked weird, but enough that it was hard to focus on his face. She wondered if he had to consciously pick which view he took in. He rubbed his bandaged hand across his cheek.

When Wren was little, she used to hold her hands to her father's face to feel his stubble. It made a rasping sound. He'd smile, while she played his jaw like an instrument.

"Am I going to shoot you?" George leaned back on the cushions. "That depends."

IT ALL HAPPENED SO FAST. One minute Janine Deguerre was a hostage, and the next she was in a medical tent, being checked over by EMTs. She looked around, trying to find Joy, but the other hostage with whom she had walked outside was nowhere to be seen.

"Ma'am," one of the first responders said, "can you follow the light?"

Janine snapped her attention back to the kid, who in fact probably wasn't much younger than she was—twenty-four. She blinked at him as he waved a little flashlight back and forth in front of her face.

She was shivering. Not because she was cold, but because she was in shock. She'd been pistol-whipped earlier across the temple, and her head was still throbbing. The EMT wrapped a silver metallic blanket around her shoulders, the kind given to marathon runners at the finish. Well, maybe she had run a marathon, metaphorically. Certainly she had crossed a line.

The sun was low, making shadows come to life, so that it was hard to tell what was real and what was a trick of her eyes. Five minutes ago Janine had arguably been in the worst danger of her life, and yet it was here underneath a plastic tent surrounded by police and medical professionals that she felt isolated. The mere act of walking past that threshold had put her back where she had started: on the other side.

She craned her neck, looking for Joy again. Maybe they had taken her to the hospital, like Dr. Ward. Or maybe Joy had said, as soon as Janine was out of earshot: *Get that bitch away from me.*

"I think we should keep you for observation," the paramedic said.

"I'm okay," Janine insisted. "Really. I just want to go home."

He frowned. "Is there someone who can stay with you tonight? Just in case?"

"Yes," she lied.

A cop crouched down beside her. "If you're feeling up to it," he said, "we're going to take you back to the station first. We need a statement."

Janine panicked. Did they know about her? Did she have to tell them? Was it like going to court, and swearing on a Bible? Or could she just be, for a little longer, someone who deserved sympathy?

She nodded and got to her feet. With the policeman's hand gently guiding her, she began to walk out of the tent. She held her metallic blanket around her like an ermine cloak. "Wait," she said. "What about everyone else?"

"We'll be bringing in the others as soon as they're able," he assured her.

"The girl," Janine said. "What about the girl? Did she come out?"

"Don't you worry, ma'am," he said.

A surge of reporters called to her, shouting questions that tangled together. The cop stepped between her and the media, a shield. He led her to a waiting police car. When the door closed, it was suffocatingly hot. She stared out the window as the policeman drove.

They passed a billboard on the way to the station. Janine recognized it because she had helped raise money to erect it. It was a picture of two smiling, gummy-mouthed babies—one Black, one white. DID YOU KNOW, it read, MY HEART BEAT EIGHTEEN DAYS FROM CONCEPTION?

Janine knew a lot of facts like that. She also knew how various religions and cultures looked at personhood. Catholics believed in life at conception. Muslims believed that it took forty-two days after conception for Allah to send an angel to transform sperm and egg into something alive. Thomas Aquinas had said that abortion was homicide after forty days for a male embryo and eighty days for a female one. There were the outliers, too—the ancient Greeks, who said that a fetus had a "vegetable" soul, and the Jews, who said that the soul came at birth. Janine knew how to consciously steer away from those opinions in a discussion.

Still, it didn't really make sense, did it? How could the moment that life began differ so much, depending on the point of view? How could the law in Mississippi say that an embryo was a human being, but the law in Massachusetts disagree? Wasn't the baby the same baby, no matter whether it was conceived on a bed in Jackson, or on a beach in Nantucket?

It made Janine's head hurt. But then, so did everything right now.

SOON IT WOULD BE GETTING dark. Wren sat on the floor cross-legged, keeping an eye on George as he hunched forward on the couch, elbows balanced on his knees, and the gun held loosely in his right hand. She tore open the last packet of Fig Newtons—all that was left of the basket of snacks taken from the recovery room. Her stomach growled.

She used to be afraid of the dark. She'd make her dad come in with his gun in his holster and check out the whole of her bedroom—beneath the bed, under the mattress, on the high shelves above her dresser. Sometimes she woke up crying in the middle of the night, convinced she had seen something fanged and terrible sitting at the foot of her bed, watching her with its yellow eyes.

Now she knew: monsters *were* real.

Wren swallowed. "Your daughter," she asked. "What's her name?"

George glanced up. "Shut your mouth," he said.

The vehemence of his words made her scoot back a few feet, but as she did, her leg brushed something cold and rigid. She knew right away what it was—*who* it was—and swallowed her scream. Wren willed herself to inch forward again, curling her arms around her bent knees. "I bet your daughter wants to see you."

The shooter's profile looked ragged and inhospitable. "You don't know anything."

"I bet she wants to see you," Wren repeated. *I know*, she thought, *because it's all I want.*

SHE LIED.

Janine sat in the police station, across from the detective who was recording her statement, and lied. "What brought you to the Center this morning?" he had asked gently.

"A Pap smear," Janine had said.

The rest that she had told him was true, and sounded like a horror film: the sound of gunfire, the sudden weight of the clinic employee slamming into her and knocking her to the floor. Janine had changed into a clean T-shirt that the paramedics had given her, but she could still feel the woman's hot blood (so much blood) seeping into her dress. Even now, looking down at her hands, she expected to see it.

"Then what happened?"

She found she could not remember in sequence. Instead of linked moments, there were only flashes: her body shaking uncontrollably as she ran; her hands pressed against the bullet wound of an injured woman. The shooter jerking his pistol at Janine, while Izzy stood next to him with a heap of supplies in her arms. The phone ringing, as they all froze like mannequins.

Janine felt like she was watching a movie, one she was obligated to sit through even though she had never wanted to see it.

When she got to the part where the shooter smacked her with the gun, she left out why. A lie of omission, that's what they used to call it when she was a little girl going to confession. It was a sin, too, but of a different degree. Still, sometimes you lied to protect people. Sometimes you lied to protect yourself.

What was one more lie to add to the others?

She was crying as she spoke. She didn't even realize it until the detective leaned forward with a box of tissues.

"Can I ask *you* a question?" she said.

"Of course."

She swallowed. "Do you think that people get what's coming to them?"

The detective looked at her for a long moment. "I don't think anyone deserves a day like today," he said.

Janine nodded. She blew her nose and balled the tissue into her hand.

Suddenly the door opened, and a uniformed officer stuck his head inside. "There's a gentleman out here who says he knows you . . . ?"

Behind him, Janine could see Allen—his florid cheeks and broad belly, the one that made him joke that he knew what it was like to be pregnant. Allen was the leader of the local Right to Life group. "Janine!" he cried, and he pushed past the cop so that he could fold her into his arms. "Sweet Jesus," he sighed. "Honey, we've been praying for you."

She knew they prayed for every woman who walked through the doors of the Center. This, though, was different. Allen would not have been able to make peace with himself if anything had happened to her, because he had been the one to send her inside as a spy.

Maybe God had been listening, because she had been released. But so had Joy, and Izzy, and Dr. Ward. And what about those who didn't make it out alive? What kind of capricious God would roll the dice like that?

"Let me take you home and get you settled," Allen said. And to the detective, "I'm sure Miz Deguerre needs a little rest."

The detective looked directly at Janine, as if to see whether she was okay with Allen calling the shots. And why shouldn't she be? She had done what he wanted from the moment she arrived in town, intent to serve his mission any way she could. And she knew that he meant well. "We're more than happy to give you a ride wherever you need to go," the detective said to her.

He was offering her a choice; and it felt heady and powerful.

"I have to use the restroom," she blurted, another lie.

"Of course." The detective gestured down the hallway. "Left at the end, and then third door on the right."

Janine started walking, still clutching her foil blanket around her shoulders. She just needed space, for a second.

At the end of the hallway was another interrogation room, much like the one she had been in. What had been a mirror on the inside was, from this vantage point, a window. Joy sat at a table with a female detective.

Before she realized what she was doing, Janine was knocking at the window. It must have made a sound, because Joy turned in her direction, even if she couldn't see Janine's face. The interrogation room door swung open, and a moment later a female detective looked at her. "Is there a problem?"

Through the open doorway, she met Joy's gaze.

"We know each other," Janine said.

After a moment, Joy nodded.

"I just wanted to . . . I wanted to see . . ." Janine hesitated. "I thought you might need help."

The detective folded her arms. "We'll make sure she gets whatever she needs."

"I know but—" Janine looked at Joy. "You shouldn't be alone tonight."

She felt Joy's eyes flicker to the bandage at her temple. "Neither should you," Joy said.

* * *

IN THE HOSPITAL, THERE WAS a piece of tape stuck to one of the slats of the air-conditioning vent overhead. It fluttered like a ribbon, like an improbable celebration, as Izzy lay on her back pretending she didn't feel the doctor's hands on her.

"Here we go," the OB murmured. He moved the wand left, and then right, and then pointed to the fuzzy screen, to the edge of the black amoeba of Izzy's uterus, where the white peanut of the fetus curled. "Come on . . . come on . . ." There was something urgent in his voice. Then they both saw it—the flicker of a heartbeat. Something she had seen multiple times in other women's ultrasounds.

She let out a breath she didn't know she'd been holding.

The doctor took measurements and recorded them. He wiped the gel off her belly and pulled the drape down to cover her again. "Miz Walsh," he said, "you are one lucky lady. You're good to go."

Izzy struggled onto her elbows. "Wait . . . so . . . that's it?"

"Obviously, you'll want to make sure that you don't have any cramping or bleeding in the next few days," the doctor added, "but given the strength of that heartbeat, I'd say that little guy—or girl—is planning on sticking around. Definitely takes after its mama."

He said he'd write up some discharge orders and ducked out of the curtain that separated her ER cubicle from the others. Izzy lay back on the gurney and slipped her hands underneath the scratchy blanket. She flattened them on her stomach.

As soon as she had gotten outside the clinic, the EMTs had put her on a stretcher beside Dr. Ward, even as she had tried to tell them she wasn't hurt. He would have none of it. "She's pregnant," he insisted. "She needs medical attention."

"*You* need medical attention," she argued.

"There she goes again," Dr. Ward said to the young paramedic inspecting his tourniquet. "Won't give me a moment's peace." He caught her eye. "For which," he said quietly, "I am supremely grateful."

That was the last she had seen of him. She wondered if he was in surgery; if he would keep the leg. She had a good feeling about it.

Maybe some people simply were destined to survive.

She had grown up with a chronically unemployed father and a mother who struggled to take care of Izzy and her twin brothers, in a house so small that the three kids shared not just a room but a bed. But for a long time, she didn't even know she was poor. Her mother would take them on a spare change hunt. They'd go fishing for dinner. Occasionally they celebrated Colonial Week—when they used candles instead of electric lights.

When Izzy thought about her life, there was such a clear break between then and now. Now, she lived with Parker in a house three times larger than her childhood home. He was, on paper, the prince from the entitled family who'd fallen for a debt-ridden nursing-student Cinderella. They had met when he was in traction with a broken leg. Their first date, he liked to say, had been a sponge bath.

Parker had gone to Yale like his father and grandfather and great-grandfather. He had grown up in Eastover, the snobbiest neighbor-hood in the whole state. He went to private schools and dressed in miniature blazers and ties even as a child. He *summered*. Even his job—a documentary filmmaker—was possible only because of his trust fund.

Izzy still ordered the cheapest thing on a menu if they ate out. Their freezer was packed with food, not because she couldn't afford to go grocery shopping now, but because you never stopped antici-pating another lean time.

They might as well have come from different planets. How on earth were they supposed to raise a child together?

Izzy wondered if now—finally—the fault line of her life would no longer be the first day she earned a paycheck. It would now be today's shooting; she would divide everything into *before* and *after*.

A nurse entered the cubicle. "How are you feeling?"

"I'm good," Izzy said, glad that her shaking hands were still tucked under the blanket.

"I got some information on that patient you asked after . . ."

"Dr. Ward?" Izzy sat up.

"No. The woman. Bex something? She came out of surgery okay," the nurse said. "She's in intensive care."

Izzy felt tears spring to her eyes. *Thank God.* "And what about Dr. Ward?"

The nurse shook her head. "I haven't heard anything yet, but I'll keep an eye out." She looked at Izzy with sympathy. "I guess y'all went through Hell together."

They had. In trying to save Bex's life, Izzy had pushed her finger through the other woman's chest wall; had felt for the pillow of her labored lungs. She had been covered in Dr. Ward's blood.

"The police want to talk to you," the nurse said. "They've been waiting. But if you're not feeling up to it, I'm happy to tell them."

"Can I use the restroom, first?"

"You sure can," the nurse replied. She helped Izzy off the gurney and led her through the curtain to a single-person bathroom. "You need any help?"

Izzy shook her head. She closed the door and locked it, leaned against the wood. The shakes had migrated from her hands to the rest of Izzy's body. Her teeth were chattering now.

Textbook shock.

"Pull yourself together," she commanded, and she ran water in the sink and splashed it on her face. She blotted her skin dry with paper towels, looking at the bathroom mirror, and immediately wished that she hadn't. Her hair had long ago escaped its braid and was a hot red frizz around her face. The scrubs they had given her to replace the bloody ones she had been wearing when she was brought in were too big, and the top was slipping off one shoulder, like a really poor version of a sexy nurse fantasy. Although she had washed off most of the blood that covered her arms and neck, she could see the spots she had missed.

She scrubbed until her skin was raw and then walked back to her little cubicle. Hovering outside the curtain was a police officer. "Miz Walsh? I'm Officer Thibodeau. I was hoping you might be able to just give a short statement?"

She drew back the curtain and sat down on the gurney, her legs dangling. "Where do you want me to start?"

Thibodeau scratched above his ear with his pen. "Well, I guess at the beginning," he said. "You went to the clinic this morning?"

"Yes."

"How long have you worked there?"

Before she could respond, there was a voice demanding to know where Izzy was.

Parker.

Izzy's legs slid off the table and she stepped forward as he pushed past the nurse and the resident who were trying to keep him out of the secure patient area.

"Parker!" she shouted, and his head snapped toward her.

"Izzy, my *God*." He took three giant steps and crushed her into his arms. He held her so tight she almost couldn't breathe. But she only noticed that when she touched him, she finally stopped shaking.

When the paramedics had first brought Izzy in and the intake nurse asked her who they could call as next of kin, Parker's name had slipped out of her mouth. That was telling, wasn't it?

Maybe there was a way to stop worrying about what might drive them apart, and to focus on what bound them together.

"Are you okay?" he asked.

She nodded against him.

"You're not hurt?" Parker pulled away, holding her at arm's length. There were dozens of questions written across his features, and he stared into her eyes as if he were trying to find the answers. Or the truth. Maybe they were even, for once, the same.

This was not how—or where—she had thought her day would end. But somehow, it was exactly where she needed to be. "I'm fine," Izzy said. She took his hand and flattened it against her belly, smiling. "*We're* fine."

Suddenly Izzy's future no longer seemed impossible. It felt like the stamp of a passport when you reached your own country, and realized that the only reason you'd traveled was to remember the feeling of home.

WHEN ONE OF THE JUNIOR detectives brought the word that his older sister Bex was out of surgery, Hugh winged a silent thank-you to a God he had long ago stopped believing in. The part of his brain that had been worrying about her could go back to focusing on Wren, who was still in there with a murderer.

First the two women had been released. Then the nurse and the injured abortion doctor.

Hugh had waited. And waited. And . . . nothing.

He paced the command center from where he had made the call to give the shooter a few more minutes, in the hope he would make good on his promise to release *all* the hostages. The question was, had he made a bad decision? A fatal one, for Wren?

Captain Quandt approached once again, blocking Hugh's path. "Okay, I'm done waiting. He released most of them. Now we're flushing him out."

"You can't do that."

"The hell I can't," Quandt said. "I'm in charge, Lieutenant."

"Only on paper." Hugh stepped closer, inches away from him. "There's still a hostage. Goddard doesn't know you from a hole in the wall. You go in there and we both know how this will end."

What Hugh didn't say was that it might still end that way. What if George had agreed to release the hostages, planning all along to go back on his word? What if he wanted to go out in a blaze of bullets, and take Wren with him? Was this going to be his ultimate fuck-you to Hugh?

Quandt met his gaze. "We both know you're too close to this to be thinking clearly."

Hugh remained immobile, his arms crossed. "That's exactly why I don't want you blasting through that goddamn door."

The commander narrowed his eyes. "I will give him ten more minutes to release your daughter. And then I will do everything in my power to make sure she is safe . . . but we're ending this."

The minute Quandt walked away, Hugh picked up his cellphone and dialed the clinic number, the same one he had been using for hours now to speak to George. It rang and rang and rang. *Pick up*, Hugh thought. He had not heard any gunshots, but that didn't mean Wren was safe.

After eighteen rings, he was about to hang up. Then: "Daddy?" Wren said, and he couldn't help it, his knees just gave out.

"Hey, sweetheart," he said, trying to tamp down the emotion in his voice. He remembered when she was a toddler, and she had fallen. If Hugh looked upset, Wren would burst into tears. If he seemed unfazed, she picked herself up and kept going. "Are you all right?"

"Y-yes."

"Did he hurt you?"

"No." A pause. "Is Aunt Bex—"

"She's going to be fine," Hugh said, although he did not know this for sure. "I want you to know I love you," he added, and he could practically hear the panic rise in his daughter.

"Are you saying that because I'm going to die?"

"Not if I have anything to do with it. Would you ask George," he said, and then he swallowed. "Would you ask him if he'd please speak to me?"

He heard muffled voices, and then George's voice was on the line. "George," Hugh said evenly, "I thought we had a deal."

"We did."

"You told me you'd release the hostages."

"I did," George said.

"Not all of them."

There was a hitch in the conversation. "You didn't specify," George replied.

Hugh curled his body around the phone, like he was whispering to a lover. "You want to tell me what's really going on, George?" A pause. "You can talk to me. You know that."

"It's all a lie."

"What's a lie?"

"Once I let your kid go, what happens to me?"

"We'll talk about that when you come outside. You and me," Hugh said.

"Bullshit. My life's over, either way. Either I go to jail and rot there forever or they shoot me."

"That won't happen," Hugh promised. "I won't *let* it happen." He glanced down at the notes he'd scribbled after his last discussion with George. "Remember? You end this, and you get to do the right thing. Your daughter—hell, the whole world—will be watching, George."

"Sometimes doing the right thing," George said quietly, "means doing something bad."

"It doesn't have to," Hugh said.

"You don't get it." George's voice was tight, distant. "But you will."

That was a threat. That definitely sounded like a threat. Hugh glanced at the SWAT team commander. Quandt was staring at him from the corner of the tent. He lifted his arm, pointed to his watch.

"Let Wren go," Hugh bargained, "and I will make sure you come out of this alive."

"No. They won't shoot me as long as I've got her."

What Hugh needed to do was offer a viable alternative, one that did not involve Wren, but let George still believe he was protected.

Just like that, he knew what to do.

Hugh looked at the captain. There was no way Quandt would go for this. It was too risky. Hugh would lose his job—maybe his life— but his daughter would be safe. There was really no choice.

"George," he suggested, "take me instead."

BEX WAS DEAD. SHE HAD to be dead, because everything was white and there was a bright light, and wasn't that what everyone said to expect?

She turned her head a fraction to the left and saw the IV pole, the saline dripping into her. The light overhead was fluorescent.

A hospital. She was the very opposite of dead.

Her throat tightened as she thought about Wren and about Hugh. Was her niece all right? She imagined Wren, knee bent, drawing on the white lip of her sneaker. She pictured Hugh leaning over her in the ambulance. That was how Bex saw the world, in images. Had she re-created it in her studio, she would call it *Reckoning*. She would highlight the cords of tension in Hugh's neck, the vibration of Wren's moving hand. The background would be the color of a bruise.

Bex had installations with collectors as far away as Chicago and California. Her works were the size of a wall. If you stood at a distance, you might see a feminine hand on a pregnant belly. A baby reaching for a mobile overhead. A woman in the throes of labor. If you stepped closer, you saw that the portrait was made of hundreds of used, multicolored Post-it notes, carefully shellacked into place on a grid.

People talked about the social commentary of Bex's work. Both her subject—parenthood—and her medium—discarded to-do lists and disposable reminders—were fleeting. But her transformation of that heartbeat, that particular second, rendered it timeless.

She had been famous for a brief moment ten years ago when *The New York Times* included her in a piece on up-and-coming artists (for the record, she never up and went anywhere, after that). The reporter had asked: since Bex was single and had no kids, had she picked this subject in order to master in art what was so personally elusive?

But Bex had never needed marriage or children. She had Hugh. She had Wren. True, she believed all artists were restless, but they weren't always running in pursuit of something. Sometimes they were running away from where they had been.

A nurse entered. "Hey there," he said. "How are you feeling?"

She tried to sit up. "I need to go," she said.

"You aren't going anywhere. You're ten minutes out of surgery." He frowned. "Is there someone I can get for you?"

Yes, please, Bex thought. *But they are both currently in the middle of a hostage standoff.*

If only it were that simple to rescue Wren. She couldn't imagine what Hugh was feeling right now, but she had to believe in him. He'd have a plan. Hugh *always* had a plan. He was the one she called when the toilets in her house all stopped working at once, like a cosmic plot. He trapped the skunk that had taken up residence under her ancient Mini Cooper. He ran toward the scream of a burglar alarm, when everyone else was fleeing. There was nothing that rattled him, no challenge too daunting.

She suddenly remembered him, fifteen or sixteen, riveted by a comic book and completely ignoring her. Only when Bex grabbed it from him did he look up. *Damn*, Hugh had said, one syllable with equal parts shock, respect, and sadness. *They killed off Superman.*

What if she lost him? What if she lost them both?

"Can you turn on the television?" she asked.

The nurse pressed a button on a remote control and then settled it underneath Bex's palm. On every local channel there was a live report about the Center. Bex stared at the screen, at the orange Creamsicle stucco of the building, the ribbons of police tape blocking it off.

She couldn't see Hugh.

So she closed her eyes and sketched him in her imagination. He was silhouetted by the sun, and he was larger than life.

Bex could still remember the first time she realized that Hugh was taller than she was. She had been in the kitchen, making dinner, and had dragged a chair toward the cabinet so that she could reach the dried basil on the highest shelf. From behind her, Hugh had just plucked it off its rack.

In that moment, Bex realized everything was different. Hugh had grown up, and somehow she had gone from taking care of him to becoming the one who was being taken care of.

"Well," she had said. "That's handy."

He'd been fourteen. He'd shrugged. "Don't get used to it," Hugh had said. "I won't be here forever."

Bex had watched him jog up the stairs to his room. And then, soon after, she had watched him go to college, fall in love, move into his own home.

No matter how many times you let someone go, it never got any easier.

HUGH HUNG UP THE PHONE. "I'm going in," he announced. "Alone. He wants a hostage? He can have me."

"Absolutely not," Quandt said, turning to a member of his squad. "Jones, get your team to—"

Hugh ignored him and started walking. Quandt grabbed Hugh's arm and spun him around.

"If you storm in there, there *will* be casualties," Hugh said. "I am the only one he trusts. If I can get him to walk out with me, it's a win."

"And if you can't?" the commander argued.

"I won't condone an action that risks my daughter," Hugh snapped. "So where does that leave us?" His fury was a shimmering curtain, but there were glimpses of what he was hiding behind it.

The two men stopped, staring at each other, a standoff. Finally, Hugh glanced away. "Joe," he said, his voice broken. "You got kids?"

The SWAT leader looked down at the ground. "I'm here to do a job, Hugh."

"I know." Hugh shook his head. "And I know I should have walked away as soon as I found out Wren was inside. God knows this is hard enough when you don't have a personal stake. But I *do*. And I can't sit on the sidelines, not if she's in there. If you won't do this for me, will you do it for *her*?"

Quandt took a deep breath. "One condition. I get a couple of snipers into position first," he said.

Hugh held out his hand, and the men shook. "Thank you."

Quandt met his gaze. "Ellie and Kate," he said, just loud enough for Hugh to hear. "Twins."

He turned away, calling over two of his men and pointing to the roof of a building across the street and a spot on top of the clinic. As they strategized, Hugh walked back underneath the tent. He saw the young detective who had brought him news of Bex. "Collins," he called. "Over here."

She hurried to the command tent. "Yes, sir?"

"That patient in the hospital—Bex McElroy, my sister? I need you to give a note to her."

The detective nodded, waiting while Hugh sat down at his make-shift desk. He picked up a pen and ripped a page off his legal pad.

What did you say to the woman who'd basically raised you? The one who had nearly died today only because she had been trying to help his own daughter?

He thought of a dozen things he could tell Bex.

That she was the only one who laughed at his terrible dad jokes, the ones that made Wren cringe. That if he was on death row, his last meal would be her chicken Parmesan. That he could still remember her making shadow puppets on his bedroom wall, trying to bribe him to go to sleep. That, at age eight, he hadn't known what the Savannah College of Art was—or even that she had given up her scholarship to come take care of him when their mother went to dry out—but that he wished he'd said thank you.

But Hugh had never been good at putting his feelings into sentences. It was what had led him to this very point, this very instant.

So he wrote down a single word and passed it to the detective. *Goodbye*.

LOUIE WARD WAS UNCONSCIOUS, AND in the ocean of his memory, he was not a fifty-four-year-old ob-gyn but a young boy growing up beneath a canopy of Spanish moss, trying to catch crawfish before they caught him. He had been raised to love Jesus and women, in precisely that order. In southern Louisiana, he was reared by two ladies—his grandmama and mama—living in a small cottage that was, as his grandmother pointed out, still a palace if the Lord dwelled there among you. He was a practicing Catholic, as was everyone else he knew, the result of a long-dead white landowner who had come from France with a rosary in his pocket and who had baptized all his slaves. Louie had been a sickly child, too skinny and too smart for his own good. He had wheezy lungs that kept him from tagging along with the other kids, who snuck at midnight into nearby houses rumored to be haunted, to see what they might find. Instead he followed his grandmama to Mass every day and he helped Mama with her piecework, using tweezers to pinch tiny links into gold chains that wound up around the necks of rich white women.

Louie had never met his father, and knew better than to ask about him since his grandmama referred to him as the Sinner, but whatever hole his father's absence had left in him was, by age nine, well plastered over.

Louie knew how to open doors for ladies and to say please and thank you and yes, ma'am. He slept on a cot in the kitchen that he made with tight hospital corners, and helped keep the house tidy, because as his grandmama had taught him Jesus was coming at any moment and they'd best all be ready. Mama had spells where she could not muster the courage to get out of bed, and sometimes spent weeks cocooned there, crying. But even when Louie was alone, he was never alone, because all the ladies in the neighborhood held him accountable for his behavior. It was child raising by committee.

Old Miss Essie came and sat on their porch every day. She told Louie about her daddy, a slave who had escaped his plantation by swimming through the bayou, braving the alligators because relinquishing his body to them would at least have been his decision. He had not only survived with all his limbs, he had hidden along the Natchez Trace, moving only by the light of the moon and following the instructions of everyday saints who had helped others get free. Eventually he had reached Indiana, married a woman, and had Miss Essie. She would lean forward, her eyes bright, and hammer home the moral of this story. *Boy*, she told Louie, *don't you let nobody tell you who you can't be.*

Miss Essie knew everything about everybody, so it was no surprise that she could tell tales about Sebby Cherise, the hedge witch rumored to be descended from the voodoo priestess Marie Laveau. What *was* a surprise was that Louie's mama had been the one doing the asking. The bayou could be easily split between those who believed in gris-gris and those who believed in the Lord, and Grandmama had set her family squarely in the latter camp. Louie had no idea what his mama could possibly want from Sebby Cherise.

His mama was the most beautiful woman in the world, with sad eyes you fell into, and a voice that sanded all your rough edges. For the past few months he'd noticed that she hadn't cried, and instead had been rising as if helium were pulsing through her veins. She hummed when she wasn't aware, melodies woven through her braids. Louie rode the outskirts of her good mood.

When Mama knelt beside him and asked if he could keep a

secret, he would have followed her to Hell and back. Which, as it turned out, was not that far from the mark.

That summer was a parched throat, and as Louie and his mama hiked to the witch's home, his clothes became a second skin. Sebby Cherise lived in the bayou, in a hut with a porch that was draped with dried flowers. There were crudely lettered signs that said KEEP OUT.

Sebby Cherise traded in miracles. Jimsonweed, cut with honey and sulfur and crossed by the path of a black cat, could root out cancer. Dixie love perfume could net you the man who slipped into your dreams. Five-finger grass set a ward around your house to keep it safe. Louie wondered if it was one of Sebby's potions or pouches that accounted for his mother's recent good spirits.

He also knew, from his grandmama and the priest, that the deals you made with the devil came back to bite you. But just like his mama seemed willing to overlook that, so was Louie, if it meant she stayed this way.

His mama told him to stay on the porch, so he only had a glimpse of Sebby Cherise, with her long red skirt and the scarf wrapped around her head. She might have been twenty years old, or two hundred. She beckoned Mama inside, and the bangles on her arm sang. Her voice sounded like fingernails on wood.

It didn't take long. Mama came out clutching a small packet on a string. She looped this around her neck and tucked it in under her dress, between her breasts. They went home, and that afternoon, Louie went to Mass with his grandmama and prayed that his mother had gotten whatever she needed, and that Jesus would forgive her for not going to Him instead.

One week later, it was so hot that Grandmama stayed at church between morning and evening Mass. Mama told Louie she was going to take a nap. Near dinnertime, Louie went to wake her up, but she didn't answer at his knock. When he turned the knob he found his mother lying on the floor, a widening triangle of blood pooling between her legs. Her skin felt like marble, the only cool surface in the world.

THE OUTPOURING OF GOODWILL IN the aftermath of Mama's death had given way to the whispers Louie heard when he passed folks in church, or walked down the street holding fast to his grandmother. Something about Mama and Mr. Bouffet, the mayor, who Louie knew only for his marshaling of the Mardi Gras parade with his pretty blond wife and matching blond daughters at his side. And something else about *abortion:* a word he had never heard before.

His grandmama would squeeze his hand to keep him from looking at the people who murmured behind their hands and stared.

She squeezed his hand a lot those days.

She was squeezing now.

Dr. Louie Ward's eyes flew open and he immediately struggled against his surroundings—the soft beep of a heart monitor, the snake of tubing in his IV. He didn't feel pain in his leg, as he expected, but then if he was in a hospital he probably had some kind of nerve blocker. The only thing that hurt like hell was his hand, which was being clutched by a skinny girl with pink hair and a ring of hoops climbing the cartilage of her left ear. "Rachel?" he rasped, and her head flew up.

The administrative assistant at the clinic had pinched features that always reminded Louie of a badger. "I'm sorry, Dr. Ward," she sobbed. "I'm so sorry."

He glanced down at his leg, thinking for one panicked moment that perhaps it had been amputated, and that was the source of Rachel's hysterics—but no, it was there, if swathed in batting like a cloud of cotton candy. Thank *God* for that nurse at the clinic. "Rachel," he said, raising his voice over the sound of her weeping. "Rachel, I already feel like I was run over by a truck. Don't give me a headache, too."

But the girl showed no signs of quieting. He didn't know her very well—he flew to many clinics around the country, and the staff often blurred with each other. He was pretty sure Rachel was a grad student at Jackson State. She worked part-time as what the antis called a "deathscort"—guiding women from the parking lot inside the clinic. She also helped Vonita, the clinic owner, with administrative work. There was so much to do at the Center that they all pitched in, wherever they had to.

"I'm sorry," Rachel repeated, wiping her nose on her sleeve.

Louie was used to crying women. "You got nothing to be sorry about," he said. "Unless your alter ego is a middle-aged white anti with a gun."

"I ran, Dr. Ward." Rachel mustered the courage to glance at him, but her gaze slid away again. "I'm a coward."

He had not even known that she was in the building at the time the shooting began. Of course, she would have been up front, and he was in the rear in a procedure room. And naturally she wanted to believe she would have been a hero, when push came to shove. But you never knew what path you'd take until you got to that crossroads. Hadn't Louie heard this a thousand times before, from patients who had come to the Center, who seemed shell-shocked to find themselves there, as if they'd awakened in someone else's life?

"You're alive to tell the story," he said. "That's what matters." Louie was aware, even as he spoke, of the irony. He turned his own words over in his mind. Coal, with time and heat and pressure, will always become a diamond. But if you were freezing to death, which would you consider the gem?

I DIDN'T CLEAN THE HOUSE, Joy thought, as she unlocked the door of her apartment. Breakfast cereal had dried to a crust in a bowl on the kitchen table; there were empty glasses on the coffee table in front of the television; a bra dangled from the arm of the couch. "The place is a mess," she apologized to Janine.

Then again, Joy had not expected to bring home an anti-abortion activist on the day she went to terminate her own pregnancy.

When the door opened, there was a scatter of mail on the floor. Joy started to bend down gingerly but Janine moved faster. "Let me," she said.

Let me drive you home.

Let me get you settled.

Janine had taken over like a mother hen, which was odd given that they were probably close to the same age. She watched Janine gather the bill and flyers. "Perry," Janine said, and she offered a small smile. "I didn't know your last name."

Joy looked at her. "Same."

"Deguerre," Janine answered. She held out her hand. "Nice to meet you. Officially."

Joy smiled awkwardly, uncomfortable with the forced intimacy. All Joy really wanted to do was strip down, get into her pajamas and fuzzy socks, have a glass of wine, and cry.

Janine set the mail on the kitchen table and turned. "What can I get you? Are you hungry? Thirsty? How about some tea?" She paused. "Do you *have* tea?"

Joy couldn't help it, she laughed. "Yeah. Cabinet over the stove."

While the water boiled, Joy went to the bathroom. She had to change her sanitary napkin, but after a moment of panic realized she didn't have any. She had been told to bring one to the Center since they didn't provide them, and it had been the last in the box. She'd been planning to swing by the drugstore on the way home.

Frustrated, she tore apart the closet, the medicine cabinet, scattering pills and ointments and lotions.

The last thing she pulled out of the recesses of the drawer beneath the sink was a dusty, crusted bottle of calamine lotion. Calamine lotion. For fuck's sake. She had *calamine lotion*, but not a pad?

Joy grabbed the bottle and hurled it at the bathroom mirror, shattering it.

There was a soft knock on the door. Janine stood there, holding her knapsack. She had left it locked in the trunk of her car that morning, so unlike the rest of the possessions of the hostages, it hadn't been part of a crime scene. "I thought you might need this," she said, and she held out a small, square wrapped Kotex pad.

Joy took it, closed the door, and went to the bathroom. She was angry that her savior—again—had been Janine. As she washed her hands, she looked into the fractured mirror. Her freckles stood out in relief from her pale skin; her hair looked like a small animal had taken up residence in it. There was blood on her neck. She rubbed it off with a washcloth. She kept rubbing until she hurt on the outside as much as she did on the inside.

When Joy came out of the bathroom, Janine had picked up the living room so that the newspapers were stacked neatly and the dirty dishes removed to the sink. She told Joy to sit down and carried over two steaming mugs of tea. Each bag was tagged with an inspirational quote. "May this day bring you peace, tranquillity, and harmony," Janine read. She blew on the surface of the tea. "Well. Screw that."

Joy looked at her own tag. "Your choices will change the world." She stared at the words until they swam. She felt a rolling wave of relief.

The room was painfully silent. Janine felt it, too. She reached for the television remote. "What do you think is going on?"

The picture blinked to life on the last channel Joy had been watching, which now showed the exterior of the clinic. It was dark, but police lights were still flashing. A reporter said something about a SWAT team, and there was a grainy photo of a marksman on a distant roof. Joy felt as if she were being suffocated. "Turn it off," she said roughly.

The screen went blank. Janine set the remote down between them. "I just moved here. I don't really know anyone in Mississippi," she suddenly admitted. "Except, you know . . . the people I was with."

"What do we do now?" Joy blurted out.

"What do you mean?"

"Tomorrow. I mean, how do we go back to normal?" Joy shook her head. "*Nothing's* normal."

"I guess we fake it," Janine said. "Till we forget we're faking." She shrugged. "I'll probably just do what I did before. Hold signs. Pray."

Joy's jaw dropped. "You'll keep protesting?"

Janine's glance slid away. "Who knows if the clinic will even open again."

If after all *that*, other women didn't have the opportunity to do what Joy had done, then why had she lived through it at all?

Joy felt a surge of heat. How could Janine not recognize that it was rhetoric spouted by herself and her cronies that led to violence? When they passed judgment on people like Joy, it gave license to others to do it. And this time, the person who had done it had been wielding a gun.

"In spite of what happened today," Joy said, incredulous, "you still think you're right?"

Janine looked her in the eye. "I could ask you the same thing."

Joy stared at this other woman, who believed the polar opposite of what she believed, yet with the same strength of conviction. She wondered if the only way any of us can find what we stand for is by first locating what we stand against.

"Maybe you'd better go," Joy said tightly.

Janine stood up. She looked around, located her knapsack, and headed silently for the door.

Joy closed her eyes and leaned back on the couch. Maybe there just *wasn't* any common ground.

Did all babies deserve to be born?

Did all women deserve to make decisions about their own bodies?

In what Venn diagram did those overlap?

She heard the knob turn, and then Janine's voice. "Well," she said, miffed, as if *she* were the one whose morality had been attacked. "Have a nice life."

Joy wondered how you get someone you think is blind to see what you see.

It certainly can't happen when you're standing on opposite sides of a wall.

"Wait," Joy said. She dug her hand into the pocket of her sweatpants. "Can I show you something?" She didn't wait for Janine to respond. Instead she smoothed out the ultrasound picture on the coffee table. Her fingers touched the white edges.

She heard Janine close the door and walk back toward the couch. Janine looked at the grainy image, bearing witness.

"It's—it was a boy," Joy murmured.

Janine sank down beside her. "I don't know what you want me to say."

Joy knew this wasn't true; that Janine had a dozen responses, all of which were variants of the fact that Joy had made her choice; that she didn't deserve to grieve. She wanted to tell Janine that yes, she had gotten what she wanted, but she also felt the pain of loss, and they were not mutually exclusive.

"Maybe neither of us should say anything," Joy suggested.

Janine covered Joy's hand with her own. She didn't respond.

She didn't have to.

She just had to be here, one woman holding up another.

ALMOST THREE HOURS NORTH OF the hostage standoff, in Oxford, Mississippi, a teenage girl curled on her side in bed at Baptist Memorial Hospital, wondering how she could feel so incredibly alone in a world so crowded with people. Beth rolled over when the door opened—her heart swelling with hope that maybe her father had come back to say that he was sorry, that he forgave her, that she could have a second chance. But it was only her court-appointed lawyer, Mandy DuVille.

Beth glanced at the police guard at the door, and then at Mandy. "Did you find my dad?" she asked.

Mandy shook her head, but that wasn't really an answer. Beth knew (because Mandy had told her) that she couldn't and wouldn't talk to her client while the policeman was present because there was no client-attorney confidentiality. Which was really just as well, because Beth didn't need any more bad news. The charges weren't going to be dropped. The prosecutor wanted to ride Beth's sad little story all the way to Election Day. Beth was only collateral damage.

And what was her crime, exactly? She was a seventeen-year-old girl who didn't want to be a mother, and because of that, she was going to lose what was left of her childhood. She had tried to get a judicial waiver because she knew her father would never sign the consent papers—even though by the time she had the baby, she'd be over eighteen. But her court date had been postponed for two weeks, and by then it would have been too late for her to have an abortion in the state of Mississippi. She'd been forced to take desperate measures.

Maybe if there were fewer laws, Beth thought, she wouldn't have had to break them. Given how hard it was for her to get a legal abortion, why should she be punished for having an illegal one?

Suddenly reality knocked the breath out of her. It felt like the one time her father had taken her to see the ocean on the Georgia coast. Beth had been a kid. She had run toward the waves with her arms wide, only to find herself tumbled head over heels and nearly drowned. Her father had plucked her out of the surf before she could be washed away.

Who was going to rescue her now?

"I'm going to jail," Beth said, her voice small. She was starting to see that nothing she had done, nothing Mandy DuVille could do, was going to untangle her from this mess. It was like when you tried to erase a mistake, and wound up ripping the paper instead. "I'm really going to jail."

Mandy looked at the officer, who had turned around to face them. She raised a finger to her lips, reminding Beth not to speak in front of the cop.

Beth started to cry.

She curled her knees up to her chest, feeling empty inside. She was a husk, a shell, a rind. This was how badly she had fucked up. She had gotten rid of the baby, true, but she had also somehow excised her ability to feel. Maybe taking away the latter was the only way she could have taken away the former. Or maybe this was fate: if the only love you had ever known was conditional, so was the absence of it. She would rot away behind bars, missed by no one. Even if her father came back, it wouldn't be to apologize. It would be to tell Beth how disappointed he was in her.

After a moment, she felt arms folding her close. Mandy was soft and smelled of peaches. Her braids tickled Beth's cheek. *This is what it could have been like*, Beth thought.

After a few minutes, her sobs became hiccups. Beth lay down on the pillow, her fingers still threaded with Mandy's. "You should get some rest," her lawyer said.

Beth wanted to fall asleep. She wanted to pretend that today had not happened. Well, no. She wanted to pretend that today had gone differently. "Can you stay here?" Beth asked. "I don't have—I don't have anyone else."

Mandy met her gaze. "You have me," she said.

As HUGH STARTED WALKING TO the front door of the clinic, he thought of the day that Wren was born. He and Annabelle had been at home watching a Harry Potter marathon when her contractions started. They were getting closer and closer, but Annabelle refused to leave until *The Chamber of Secrets* was over. Her water broke during the credits. Hugh drove like a maniac to the hospital, leaving the car in a loading zone, and got his wife settled on the delivery ward. She was already dilated 9¾ centimeters, which Annabelle saw as a sign.

I'm not naming her Hermione, Hugh had said, after the birth.

I'm not naming her after your mother, Annabelle had countered.

(Even back then, they had fought.)

The nurse, who had been following this conversation, opened a window. *Maybe we all need a little fresh air*, she suggested, just as a bird darted through. It fluttered to the lip of the bassinet where the baby was sleeping. The bird turned its head, fixed a bright eye on her.

Now, that's *a sign*, Hugh said.

Wren was the very best thing that had ever happened to him.

He bought her her first bra. He let her paint his nails. He told her kids were assholes when she wasn't invited to a popular girl's birthday party, and then spitefully gave that girl's mother a ticket the next day for jaywalking.

Every August they hiked to the highest spot in Jackson, waiting to see the Perseids, the meteor shower that made the sky look like it was weeping. They'd pull an all-nighter, talking about everything from which Power Ranger was expendable to how you find the person you want to spend your life with.

Hugh had had trouble with that one. In the first place, his judgment had been off; Annabelle now lived in France with a guy ten years her junior, a master baker who competed in the Bread Olympics, as if that was a *thing*. In the second place, the person he wanted to spend his life with had been placed into his arms by a labor and delivery nurse fifteen years ago.

Now, Hugh glanced over his shoulder. Captain Quandt tilted his head, speaking into a radio. "If you don't get him to meet you partway, my snipers can't get a clean shot," he said to Hugh.

"Not my problem," Hugh replied, moving forward.

"Hugh!"

He stopped.

"You don't have to be a hero," Quandt said quietly.

Hugh met his gaze. "I'm not. I'm a father."

He squared his shoulders and started toward the clinic door. Behind him, the air was stale with heat; the only sound was the buzzing of mosquitoes.

He knocked. A moment passed, and then he could hear furniture scraping the floor.

The door swung open, and there stood Wren. "Daddy," she cried, and she took a step toward him, but was jerked back inside. Hugh reluctantly tore his eyes away from his daughter to look, for the first time, at the man he had been talking to for five hours.

George Goddard was slight, around five-ten. He had a five o'clock shadow and a bandage wrapped around the hand that was holding a gun to Wren's temple. His eyes were so light they appeared transparent. "George," Hugh said evenly, and Goddard nodded.

Hugh was aware of the pulse leaping in his neck. He tried to keep himself calm, to not grab Wren and run, which could be disastrous. "Why don't you step out here, and let her go?"

George shook his head. "Show me your weapon."

Hugh held up his hands. "Don't have one."

The other man laughed. "You think I'm an idiot?"

After a hesitation, Hugh reached down and hiked up his pants leg, revealing the pistol he had strapped there. Keeping his eyes on George the entire time, he tugged the weapon free and held it off to the side.

"Drop it," George ordered.

"Let go of her and I will."

For a beat, nothing happened. June bugs paused midflight, the breeze died, Hugh's heart missed a stitch. Then George shoved Wren forward. Hugh caught her up with his arm, leaving the right outstretched with the weapon dangling. "It's okay," he whispered into his daughter's hair.

She smelled of fear and sweat, the way she had when she was

little and woke up from a nightmare. He drew back, threading the fingers of his free hand with one of hers. On the edge of her palm was a little black star, inked like a tattoo at the juncture of her thumb and pointer. "Wren." Hugh smiled at her, as best he could. "Go on now. Walk to the officers under that tent."

She turned and looked at the command center, then back at him. She realized in that moment that he wasn't coming with her. "Daddy, no."

"Wren. Let me finish this."

She took a breath, and nodded. Very slowly, she started to back away from him, toward the tent. None of the other officers stepped forward to swoop her to safety, as they had the other hostages. This was on Hugh's order. Before, George had been hidden behind the security of his door, but now, he'd feel vulnerable. Seeing an approaching cop might trigger him, make him shoot in self-defense.

When Wren was a few steps away, George spoke. "Put down the gun." He took his own firearm and pointed it at Hugh's chest.

Hugh bent, slowly letting the weapon slip from his fingers. "All right, George," he said. "What do you want to do now? Your call."

He saw the gunman's eyes flicker around the rooftops, and prayed that if the snipers were in position, they were well concealed.

"You told me you'd do anything for your daughter," George said.

Hugh felt his throat tighten. He did not want George talking about Wren. He didn't even want him *thinking* about her. He risked a peripheral glance; she was maybe halfway to the command center.

"You keep saying we're not that different," George continued. "But you don't really believe that."

No matter what Hugh had said to gain George's trust, he was well aware that there was and always would be a seminal difference between them, and it had to do with morality. Hugh would never take a life because of his own beliefs.

He realized with a tiny shock that that exact conviction was what had brought George here today.

"George, this can still end well," Hugh said. "Think of your daughter."

"She'll never look at me the same after this. You don't get it."

"Then make me understand."

He expected George to reach for him, to pull him back into the clinic, where he could barricade the door and use Hugh as a bargaining chip. Or kill him.

"All right," George said.

The twilight was bleeding, it was the seam between day and night. Hugh saw the gun move. He reached for his pistol, sheer habit, and remembered that he was unarmed.

But George's gun was no longer pointed at Hugh. It was aimed at Wren—still twenty feet shy of the tent—a moving target Hugh had arrogantly believed he could keep safe.

WHEN HIS DAUGHTER WAS YOUNGER, George had read to her from the Bible, instead of fairy tales. Some stories, he knew, just don't have happy endings. Better for Lil to understand that love was about sacrifice. That what looked like carnage, from a different angle, might be a crusade.

We are all capable of things we never imagined.

Well, Detective, he thought. *You asked me to make you understand and I did. You and I, we're not that different.*

Not the hero and the villain, not the pro-life activist and the abortion doctor, not the cop and the killer. We are all drowning slowly in the tide of our opinions, oblivious that we are taking on water every time we open our mouths.

He wished he could tell his daughter that he realized this, now.

He pulled the trigger.

Four p.m.

AFTER HOURS OF TALKING WITH THE SHOOTER OVER A SECURE LINE, Hugh had been lulled into complacency. He had mistakenly assumed that it was possible to reason with a madman.

But then there had been another gunshot, and Hugh's only thought was of his daughter.

When Wren was two, he had taken her along when he went down to fix a little dock that sat out behind Bex's property, on the edge of a weed-choked pond. He was hammering treated wood into place while she sat on the grass, playing with a toy her aunt had given her. One minute she had been laughing, chattering to herself, and the next there was a splash.

Hugh hadn't even thought. He jumped off the dock into the water, which was so murky and clogged that he couldn't see a foot in front of him. His eyes burned as he struggled to spot anything that might be Wren. He dove over and over, his hands outstretched and spinning through weeds, until finally he brushed against something solid. He broke through the water with Wren wrapped in one arm, laid her on the dock, fitted his mouth against hers, and breathed for her until she choked up the swamp.

Hugh had screamed at Wren, who'd burst into tears. But his anger was misdirected. He was furious at himself, for being stupid enough to take his eyes off of her.

There had been a gunshot, and Hugh was in that muddy pond again, blindly trying to save his daughter, and it was all his fault.

There had been a gunshot, one that struck his sister hours ago, and he hadn't been there.

There was a gunshot, and what if that meant he was too late, again?

Captain Quandt was immediately at his side. "McElroy," he said. "There's active gunfire. You know the protocol."

The protocol was to engage rather than wait and suffer the loss of more victims. It was also risky as hell. When gunmen felt threatened, they started panicking, firing at random.

Had he been Quandt, he might well have made the same call. But Hugh hadn't yet confessed to Quandt that his own child was inside. That this wasn't random at all.

There had been other hostage situations that had become bloodbaths because the law enforcement agencies were too aggressive. In 2002 Chechen rebels went into a theater, taking hundreds of hostages and even killing two; Russian forces decided to pump an untested gas inside to end the standoff. They killed thirty-nine terrorists but also over a hundred hostages.

What if that happened when Quandt went in?

"It wasn't active gunfire," Hugh said, trying to buy time. "It was a single shot. It's possible that the threat neutralized himself."

"Then there's zero risk," Quandt pointed out. "Let's go." He didn't wait for Hugh to respond, just turned on his heel to organize his team.

There had been several moments in Hugh's experience that changed his life. The day he asked Annabelle out. The night that suicidal kid on the roof turned and gave Hugh his hand. When Wren took her first breath. This would, he knew, be another of those moments: the one that ended his career.

"No," Hugh said, to Quandt's back. "My daughter's one of the hostages."

The SWAT commander turned slowly. "What?"

"I didn't know at first. I found out after I got here," Hugh explained. "But I didn't—I didn't step down. I *couldn't*."

"You're relieved of your position," Quandt said flatly.

"Only my chief can do that," Hugh said. "And I'm in too deep now with the hostage taker to walk away. I'm sorry. I know the rules. I know it's a conflict of interest. But my God, Captain—nobody has greater incentive for this to end well than I do. You understand that, don't you?"

"I understand that when you lied to me, to the chief, to *everyone*— you knew exactly what you were doing."

"No. If I knew what I was doing, she'd be here with me." Hugh cleared his throat and forced himself to look the commander in the eye. "Don't make my daughter pay for my stupidity. Please," he begged. "It's my *kid*."

He was underwater again, and flailing in the weeds. He was drowning.

Quandt stared him down. "Everyone in there," he said, "is somebody's kid."

BEX STARED AT THE FLUORESCENT lights overhead in the hospital's operating room, wondering if she was going to die.

She was worried. Not for herself, but for Wren, for the rest of the people in the clinic. And of course for Hugh, who shouldered this burden. He would blame himself for anything that went wrong today. Some men wear responsibility and some are worn by it; Hugh had always been the former. Even at her father's funeral, when Hugh had been just eight, he insisted on shaking the hand of everyone who came to grieve. He was the last to leave the grave site, walking back to the parking lot with the minister. Bex had settled her sobbing mother in the car and gone back to get Hugh. "I'm the man of the house now," he'd told her, and so she had spent the rest of her life walking behind him, trying to inconspicuously take away some of the load he carried.

It was why she had moved back home, when her mother's grief made her turn to a bottle and neglect Hugh.

It was why she made sure that there was a female presence in Wren's life after Annabelle was gone.

It was why she had brought Wren to the clinic.

The anesthesiologist leaned over her. "You might feel a little burning," he said, "but then you're going to have the best nap of your life."

When Hugh was little, he had never wanted to go to sleep at night. She used to have to create two alternatives that gave him a choice and the sense he was in control: Do you want to walk upstairs to your room, or do you want me to carry you? Do you want to brush your teeth first, or wash your face? Either scenario ended in bedtime. But then he began to get wiser. He would ask her to read three books, and she would counter with one, and he would laugh and tell her he'd been hoping for two all along.

Even at five, he had been a negotiator.

When the anesthesia took effect, Bex was smiling.

JANINE COULD FEEL THE GHOSTS. They were sitting in her lap and in her arms and pulling at the hem of her dress. This building was full of babies without mothers.

She had come to get information. Intelligence. Something that could be revealed online, the way Lila Rose had done, to expose the reality of these murder centers. She was never supposed to get stuck here.

Janine had grown up on the southwest side of Chicago, where you came not from neighborhoods, but from parishes. She was from St. Christina, and she knew from the time she was a young child that a baby was a baby the moment it was conceived. At the very least, it was a human person in progress.

She was not unrealistic. She understood that abstinence wasn't always possible, that birth control sometimes failed, but if a couple decided to engage in an activity that could potentially create a life, they should also be prepared to accept a change in their *own* lives. She knew, of course, that it wasn't just a woman who was responsible for a pregnancy—although it *was* the woman who had to carry the baby for nine months. But nine months was a hiccup in the time line of a woman's life. And it wasn't the child's fault that led to him or her being conceived. So why should he have to pay with his life?

Janine had been told she was anti-woman. That she was ridiculous. That if she didn't want an abortion, she didn't have to have one. But she knew that if a woman killed that same bundle of cells a few months later, there wouldn't even be an argument. She would be vilified and put in jail for life. The only difference was the calendar.

Janine had been twelve when her mother conceived again, an accident, at age forty-three. She remembered how her parents had come home from an appointment with two new bits of knowledge: the baby was a boy, and he had one extra chromosome. The doctor had counseled her mother to terminate the pregnancy, because the baby's life would be full of developmental and health challenges.

She'd been old enough to pick up on her parents' fear. She had googled Down syndrome. Half the kids who were born with Down syndrome also needed heart surgery. They had increased chances of developing leukemia and thyroid problems. By age forty, many had early Alzheimer's. And then there were other complications: ear infections, hearing loss, skin problems, bad vision, seizures, gastro-intestinal disorders.

She believed she knew everything about her baby brother before he arrived. But she didn't know that Ben would have a belly laugh that made her start laughing, too. Or that he would be ticklish on his right foot but not his left. She didn't know that he wouldn't go to sleep unless Janine read him exactly three books. She knew that he would meet milestones later than other kids, that he might need help. But she didn't know how much she would need *him*.

It wasn't all rosy. There were blogs where parents talked about having kids with Up syndrome, and how they'd been given an extra blessing from God in the form of that additional chromosome. That was bullshit. It took Ben three years to be potty trained. He whined when he was tired, like any other little brother. He was bullied in school. One year, Ben had a surgery on Janine's birthday, and her parents completely forgot to give her a cake, a party, a moment of attention.

At college, when she was president of the Students for Life club, she had plenty of conversations about the moral quicksand of abortion, and she used her brother as an example. Ben may not have been the child her parents had expected, but he was the one they got. Having a child is a terrible risk, no matter what. You might have a healthy baby who then gets a heart condition, diabetes, addicted to opioids. You might raise a kid who gets her heart broken, who miscarries her own baby, whose husband dies fighting overseas. If we are meant to only have children who never encounter difficulty in life, then no one should be born.

Had Janine's mother done what the doctor suggested at that prenatal appointment, Ben would never have existed. She wouldn't have seen the triumph on his face when he finally learned how to tie his own shoes, when he brought home his first friend from school. He wouldn't have been there on the day her dog Galahad was hit by a truck, the day everything went wrong, when no one could make her stop crying and Ben just crawled into her arms and hugged her.

Now, Janine glanced at Joy, who was curled sideways in her chair, her face buried in her hands. She wished she had been standing at the fence today when Joy came into the clinic to have her abortion. She might have kept her from making the decision she had.

It was too late for Joy's baby. But that didn't mean it was too late for Joy.

Janine sat up a little straighter. Even Norma McCorvey changed her mind. She had been Jane Roe in *Roe v. Wade*. In the 1970s, when she was twenty-two, she found herself pregnant for the third time. She lived in Texas, where abortion was illegal unless the mother's life was at risk. Her lawsuit went all the way to the Supreme Court, and of course, you know how *that* turned out. She became an abortion advocate, until the nineties, when she did an abrupt one-eighty. From that moment, all the way till she died in 2017, she asked the Supreme Court to overturn their decision on her case.

What led to her change of opinion? She was born again.

Janine smiled to herself.

Born again.

She didn't think it was any coincidence that the term for letting God back into your heart had, at its core, birth.

Izzy sat on the floor beside the body of Olive Lemay. Her hands were still shaking with the effort of trying to resuscitate the woman, but she had known that there wasn't a prayer. The gun had gone off at close range. The bullet had torn through the older woman's heart. Even as Izzy had tried to stanch the flow of blood, she had felt Olive's hand come up to cover hers. She had seen the fear in the woman's eyes.

"That was a very brave thing you did," Izzy whispered fiercely.

Olive shook her head. Her eyes held Izzy's.

Sometimes, being a nurse doesn't matter. Being human does.

So Izzy eased up the pressure on Olive's chest. She grabbed Olive's hand with both of her own and she stared into the woman's eyes, nodding in answer to the question that hadn't been asked.

She had been in this profession long enough to know that people sometimes seemed to need permission before they left this world.

The first death she ever saw was when she had been a nursing student, and had a patient with metastatic breast cancer. The woman was a former beauty queen, now in her fifties. She'd been in the hospital before for palliative care and for rehab after a pathological fracture. But this time, she had come back to die.

One quiet night, after her family left, Izzy had sat down beside the sleeping woman. Her head was bald from the chemo; her face was gaunt, and yet somehow it only served to make her features more arresting. Izzy stared at her, thinking of the woman she must have been, before cancer ate away at her.

Suddenly the woman's eyes blinked open, a lucid and lovely sea green. "You've come to get me, haven't you?" she said, smiling softly.

"Oh no," Izzy replied. "You're not going for any tests tonight."

The woman moved her head imperceptibly. "I'm not talking to you, honey," she said, her gaze fixed somewhere over Izzy's shoulder.

A moment later, the woman died.

Izzy always wondered what she would have seen, had she been brave enough to turn around that night.

She wondered if she would be shot, like Olive.

She wondered how long it would be until an autopsy was done, and someone found out she was pregnant.

She wondered, if her life ended today, whether anyone would be waiting for her on the other side.

*   *   *

IF HE HAD NOT BEEN given detention by the nuns in seventh grade, Louie Ward might never have become an obstetrician. In the school library, he picked up a book that was lying on the table—a biography of the Reverend Dr. Martin Luther King, Jr. Out of sheer boredom Louie started to read. He didn't put the book down until he was finished. Louie was convinced that this man was speaking directly to him.

He began to read everything he could that the reverend had written. *Life's most persistent and urgent question is,* Dr. King had said, *what are you doing for others?* He read those words and thought of his mama, bleeding out on the floor.

Like his mentor, Louie wanted to be a doctor, but a different kind: an ob-gyn, because of his mother. He worked hard enough to get a full scholarship to college, and then another to medical school.

When he was a resident, he came in contact with multiple women who had unplanned, unwanted pregnancies. As a practicing Catholic, he believed life started at conception, so he referred these patients to other doctors, other places. Much later in his career he would learn that although 97 percent of doctors had encountered a patient who wanted to terminate a pregnancy, only 14 percent performed abortions themselves. When the gap was that great, it was not like abortions stopped. They just got done unsafely.

One Sunday, Louie's priest was giving a homily about the parable of the Good Samaritan in the Gospel of Luke. A traveler, beaten and left for dead on the side of the road, was passed by a priest and a Levite—neither of whom stopped. Finally, a Samaritan offered his help, even though historically Samaritans and Jews were enemies.

On the day before Martin Luther King, Jr., was killed, he had talked about that parable. He considered why the priest and the Levite might have walked past the beaten man—maybe they thought he was faking; maybe they were worried for their own safety. But most of all, he mused, the reason they passed was because they were thinking of what would happen to *themselves* if they stopped—not what would happen to that man if they didn't.

Louie knew in that instant, he had to be the Samaritan. So many of the women he met who were seeking abortions were, like him, southerners of color. These were the women who had raised him. These were his neighbors, his friends, his own mother. If he didn't interrupt his own journey to help them with theirs, who would?

It was the one truly miraculous moment of Dr. Louie Ward's life.

At that moment Louie realized why his mama had gone to see Sebby Cherise. It wasn't because she was having the child of a prominent married white man. It was because she had been protecting the child she already had, at the expense of the one she hadn't wanted to conceive. This was a variation on a theme he had heard from patients: *I have a child with a disability; I don't have the time to parent another one. I can barely feed my son; what will I do with a second baby? I already work three jobs and take care of my family—there isn't any more of me to go around.*

So although Louie still went to Mass like clockwork, he also became an abortion provider. He flew several times a month to offer his services at women's clinics. The only person who didn't actually know what he did for a living was his grandmama.

She was in her nineties by the time Louie went back home to confess. He told her about the runner who had worked her whole life to secure a spot on the Olympic team, and then found herself pregnant after a condom broke. He told her about the woman who learned, in an opioid treatment program, that she was twelve weeks along.

He told her about a lady from a small, narrow-minded place who had been so blinded by the sun of a respected married man that she believed he would support her and claim their child as his own, only to learn that wasn't how the world worked. They both knew who Louie was talking about. *Grandmama*, he said. *I think Jesus would understand why I do what I do. I hope you can, too.*

As he expected, his grandmama started to cry. *I lost my baby and my grandbaby*, she said after a long moment. *Maybe now some other woman won't.*

In fact the only objection his grandmama had had to his career was that Louie might be killed by an anti-abortion activist. Louie knew that his name had been published on a website, along with other doctors who performed abortions, with information about where he lived and worked. He had known George Tiller, a doctor who'd been murdered while he was at church. Dr. Tiller had been wearing a protective vest at the time, but the gunman had shot him in the head.

Louie refused to put on a vest. The way he saw it, the minute he did, *they* had won. And yet, every morning he had to run the gauntlet of protesters. He would sit in his car for an extra minute, taking a deep breath, steeling himself for the vitriol and the love bombers—*We're praying for you, Dr. Ward. Have a blessed day!* He would think of George Tiller and David Gunn and John Britton and Barnett Slepian, all killed by activists who were not satisfied to simply stand in a line and hurl insults.

Louie would count to ten, say an Our Father, and then in one smooth movement gather his briefcase and exit the car. He'd hit the power lock while he was walking, face forward, eyes on the ground, refusing to engage.

Mostly.

There was one anti, a middle-aged white man, who repeatedly called out, "Sinful Negro baby killer!" Louie had ignored him, until one day he yelled, "Do I have to call you a *nigger* to get a rise out of you?"

That—well. That stopped Louie dead in his tracks.

"What part of me is most upsetting to you?" Louie asked calmly. "The fact that I am African American? Or the fact that I perform abortions?"

"The abortions," the man said.

"Then what does my race have to do with anything?"

The protester shrugged. "It doesn't. I just threw that in."

Louie almost had to admire the man's scorched-earth tactics.

There was only one reason he got out of his car every damn morning: the women he treated, who had to walk through that same gauntlet. How could he be any less brave than they were?

The antis wanted the women who chose abortions to feel isolated, the only people in the universe who had ever made such a selfish decision. What Louie wanted, for every woman who walked through the doors of the Center, was to make her understand she was not alone, and never would be. The most ardent antis didn't realize how many women they knew who'd had an abortion. Wipe away the stigma and all you were left with was your neighbor, your teacher, your grocery clerk, your landlady.

He imagined what it felt like for them—to have made a decision that came at a colossal emotional and financial cost—and then to have that decision called into question. Not to mention the implication that they were not capable of managing their own healthcare. Where were the protesters at cancer centers, for example, urging chemotherapy patients to steer clear of the risks of toxins? Women were capable of taking aspirin if they had a headache, and the intrinsic risk of aspirin was far greater than that of any of the abortion medications that currently existed. If a woman chose a medication abortion, why did the mifepristone have to be taken in front of a doctor, as if she were an inpatient in a psychiatric ward who couldn't be relied on to swallow a pill?

Louie believed that those white men with their signs and slogans were not really there for the unborn, but there for the women who carried them. They couldn't control women's sexual independence. To them, this was the next best thing.

Louie shifted and cried out as pain stabbed through his leg. The tourniquet had slowed the bleeding, until the shooter had—in a fit of pique—kicked him hard in the spot where the bullet had entered.

It was hell being a physician but being too injured to treat the others who'd been hurt. That had fallen to the other medical professional trapped here—the nurse, Izzy. He hadn't worked with her before, but that wasn't unprecedented. Vonita, the clinic owner, employed a rotating parade of healthcare professionals brave or stupid enough to show up every day in spite of the threats.

Had employed. Past tense.

He closed his eyes, fighting the feelings that rose in him.

Vonita hadn't been the only casualty. Izzy had tried—desperately and fruitlessly—to save the life of Olive, the older woman. This was true collateral damage: clearly a woman in her late sixties wasn't at the clinic to terminate a pregnancy, but she had still been on the receiving end of the shooter's rage. Izzy now drew a cotton drape over the body. At Louie's moan of pain she turned to check the binding around his thigh. "I'm all right," he said, trying to get her to stop fussing, when to his surprise she did. She bolted a few feet to the left and threw up in a trash can.

One of the other women—his last patient, Joy (formerly fifteen weeks along and now, Louie thought with satisfaction, *un-pregnant*)—handed Izzy a tissue from a box on a table in the waiting room. The shooter looked at Izzy in disgust, but didn't speak. He was too busy tending to his own injury. Izzy wiped her mouth and then returned her attention to Louie's thigh. "I'm that bad off, huh?" he said wryly.

She looked up at him, her cheeks flushed. "No, sir. I don't think he caused any major damage when he kicked you. Any *additional* major damage," she amended.

Louie looked down at her hands, pressing gently around the wound. It hurt like hell. "How far along are you?" he asked.

He waited until she looked up at him. "How did you know?"

Louie raised an eyebrow.

"Twelve weeks," Izzy said.

He watched her hand steal to her abdomen, her palm a shield.

"You're gonna get out of here," he promised. "You and your partner are going to have a beautiful bouncing baby."

She smiled, but it didn't reach her eyes.

Louie thought of all the times he'd administered what he called "verbicaine"—just chatting to ease the women who were so tense about what was going to happen. He would ask if a woman made her grits sweet or savory. If she'd listened to Beyoncé's latest album. What sorority she belonged to. He prided himself on being able to get any woman relaxed, while he calmly and professionally performed the procedure. What he heard most often from his patients was "You mean you're already finished?"

But his reassurance had not worked on Izzy.

Izzy didn't believe him when he said she was going to get out of here.

Because, frankly, neither did he.

JOY HAD TOLD ONLY ONE person about her pregnancy—her best friend, a waitress at the Departure Lounge, a martini bar in the Jackson airport. Rosie had been the one who stood beside her in the ladies' room, counting down a timer on her phone, while they watched the little plus sign appear on the stick. "What are you going to do?" Rosie had asked, and Joy hadn't answered.

A week later, she made an appointment at the Center. That same day she told Rosie she had miscarried. The way Joy figured, this was just one minor inaccuracy, a small erroneous footnote. The outcome would be the same.

Even though she knew Rosie would have driven her for her procedure, Joy wanted and needed to do it alone. She had been stupid enough to get herself into this mess; she would be smart enough to get herself out.

The first night that *he* came into the bar, Joy had noticed him right away. He'd been tall, lean, and wearing a suit that fit beautifully; his hair was gray at the temples. Joy had looked at his hands—you could tell a lot about a person from their hands—and his were long-fingered, strong. He looked a little bit like President Obama, if President Obama had been so sad that he sought refuge in the bottom of a bucket of gin martinis.

When Joy came on duty, it was the late shift, and she was the only staff in the lounge—it was cheaper to train the waitresses to mix drinks and lock up for the night than to pay additional employees. She refilled the nuts for a gay couple drinking Negronis and printed out the tab for a woman whose flight was being called. Then she went over to the man, whose eyes were closed. "Can I get you a refill?"

When he glanced up at her, it was like looking into a mirror.

Only someone who has been there—trapped in an invisible prison, desperate to escape—can recognize that expression in another.

When he nodded, Joy brought him another drink. And another. Three more customers came and went, while she kept an eye on the man at the high-top. She knew he wasn't in the mood to talk; she had been a cocktail waitress long enough to read those clues. There were some people who wanted to pour out their troubles as you poured their spirits. There were some who texted furiously on their phones, avoiding eye contact. There were the handsy ones, who grabbed her ass as she walked by and pretended it was an accident. But this man only wanted to lose himself.

When he had been there for three hours she stood beside his table. "I don't mean to bother you," Joy said, "but when's your flight?"

He knocked back his drink past the fence of his teeth. "It landed. Four hours ago."

She wondered if Mississippi was his starting point or his destination. Either way, there was something outside this building that he couldn't face.

When it came time to close up, he paid with cash and gave her a tip equal to the amount of the bill. "Can I get you a cab?" she asked.

"Can't I stay here?"

"Nope." Joy shook her head. "What's your name?"

"Can't tell you," he slurred.

"Why? You in the CIA?"

"No, ma'am," he said. "But this is not appropriate behavior for a representative of the court."

So he was a lawyer, Joy thought. Maybe he had lost a big case, something he'd been working on for months. Maybe his client had perjured herself on the stand. There were a hundred scenarios, and she'd seen them all on *Law & Order*. "Lucky for you, this isn't a courtroom," Joy said. "Although there *is* a bar."

He smiled at that. As she turned away to close out the cash register, he tapped her arm. "Joe," he said after a moment.

She held out her hand. "Joy."

He peered at her with pale blue eyes, so arresting in the face of a Black man, some historical, genealogical evolution that was more likely due to a moment of force than to passion. He wore the scars of his past on his face, Joy realized. Just like she did.

"Y'all don't look very joyous," he remarked.

That's when she made the decision that would change the course of her life. Joy, who never invited anyone to her apartment, decided that this man needed to sleep off his drink, and start over tomorrow. She decided to give him the second chance she never had gotten.

She locked up, and by then, Joe was passed out, his cheek pressed to the polished wood. Rolling her eyes, she found a wheelchair three gates down and half-lifted, half-dragged Joe into it. That was how she got him to her car, too. By the time they collapsed in a tumbled heap onto the couch in her living room, she was sweating and exhausted. Joe started to snore immediately.

When she tried to extricate herself, though, his arms tightened on her. He stroked her hair. He pulled her against him.

Joy did not even know his last name, or what had brought him to

Jackson. But it had been so long since she'd been held, just held. And it had been even longer since she'd felt needed. And so against her better judgment, she'd lain down to sleep with her head on his chest. She made his heartbeat her lullaby.

It was sometime in the dead of night that she woke up to find herself being watched. They were pressed together on the narrow couch and Joe's eyes were soberly focused on hers. "You are a good person," he said after a moment.

He wouldn't say that if he knew how she had grown up, what she had done to survive.

When he kissed her, Joy wanted to believe that her conscience would cause her a moment of hesitation, yet that wasn't true. She was on the Pill for period cramps, but even so, this was a stranger. She should have used a condom. Instead, she grabbed on to his shoulders and made him the center of her storm. And even though it was grief he poured into her, it was better than being empty.

Afterward, they were both wide awake and dead sober. "I shouldn't have—" Joe began, but Joy didn't want to hear it. She couldn't stand being someone's mistake again. She went to the bathroom and splashed cold water on her face. When she came back out, Joe was dressed in his suit. "I called an Uber," he said. "I, uh, got your address off an envelope." He handed her an electric bill that had been on the coffee table with yesterday's mail. He gestured awkwardly toward the bathroom. "Could I . . . ?"

Joy nodded, stepping aside so that he could pass. She told him where he might find aspirin, and he thanked her and closed the door.

Joe returned to the living room. He was tall, she realized, something she had not seen when he was slumped over a table. "I'm not the kind of person who—" she started, but he interrupted.

"I've never done this before."

"Chalk it up to the alcohol," Joy said.

"Temporary insanity."

A car horn honked twice.

"Thank you, Miz Joy," Joe said formally. "For showing me a kindness."

Joy felt like she had shown him her very soul, disfigured as it might be. She looked away as he shrugged into his jacket and presumably out of her life. As she showered that morning, she tried to convince herself that she wasn't the slut her foster mother had always called her; that she was entitled to creature comfort; that they were both consenting adults. She went to her classes, and then to her afternoon job at the college library, and then to her shift at the Departure Lounge, where she found herself looking for Joe although she knew he would not be there.

Until one night he was. That night, he hadn't gotten drunk. He had waited until Joy's shift was over, and accompanied her back to her apartment, where they made love and then shared a pint of ice cream in bed. She learned that Joe was not a lawyer, but a judge. He told her how his favorite moments on the bench were adoptions, when a foster kid got a permanent home. He stroked her hair and said he wished she'd been one of them.

He came back two more times, admitting that he was inventing business in Jackson just to see her again. Joy couldn't remember a time that someone had run toward her, instead of away. She let him quiz her before one of her midterms and cook her a big breakfast before the test.

When you are used to fending for yourself, being taken care of is a drug. Joy became addicted. She texted Joe funny signs she passed on the way to work: the Baptist church with the live Nativity that advertised COME SEE OUR ASSES; the gaily flashing STOP—THREE WAY!; the Taco Bell billboard that said IN QUESO EMERGENCY, PRAY TO CHEESES. Joe wrote her back with daily Darwin Awards, anonymously describing the memorable defendants in his courtroom. When he showed up unexpectedly, she called in sick to work at the library so that she could spend as much time with him as he could spare. He was fifteen years older than she was, and sometimes she wondered if she was compensating for her lack of a father, but then she would realize there was nothing paternal about their relationship. She guardedly began to wonder if this was the moment that her terrible luck turned.

She should have known better.

Biology and evolution and social mores allowed Joe to leave; Joy was the one stuck with the pregnancy. Even though there had been two of them in that bed. Joy realized, in retrospect, she should have expected this. Life had repeatedly served her a big old side dish of miserable anytime she had a taste of anything good.

She had one more year of classes before she graduated with her bachelor's degree—a degree she had fought for by scrimping and saving to pay for her credits. She worked two jobs already in order to make that happen. There was not a world in which she could take care of a baby, too.

That was Joy's reasoning, as she sat in the bathroom at the library and whispered answers to the woman who scheduled her appointment at the Center.

Name. Address. Date of birth. First day of your last menstrual period.

Have you been pregnant before?

Have you had any bleeding or spotting since your last period?

Are you breast-feeding now?

Do you have a history of uterine abnormalities?

Have you ever had asthma? Lung problems? Heart problems? Stroke?

And a dozen more questions, until: Is there anything else we should know about you?

Yes, Joy thought. *I am pathologically unlucky. I'm perfectly healthy, except for this one thing that never should have happened to me.*

The woman explained that because of the state of Mississippi's requirements, an abortion was a two-day procedure. She asked if Joy had health insurance, and when she said no, the woman said Medicaid didn't cover the cost. Joy would have to scrape together $600, if she could get here before she was eleven weeks, six days pregnant. Otherwise, the price jumped to $725 till thirteen weeks, six days. After that, it was $800, till the sixteenth week. After that, the procedure couldn't be done.

Joy was already ten weeks pregnant.

She texted Joe, saying she needed to speak to him, but she didn't want to tell him over text that this had happened. He didn't answer.

She did some math in her head, and scheduled an appointment for a week and a half out. But even after skipping class to double her shifts at the bar and the library, she didn't have enough money by the deadline. So she worked even harder, hoping to schedule an appointment at thirteen weeks. But her carburetor died and she had to pay for it or risk losing both her jobs. Before she knew it she was fourteen and a half weeks pregnant and running out of time. This time she called Joe, instead of texting. When a woman answered, she hung up the phone.

Joy pawned her laptop to get the cash, and rescheduled.

If she'd been richer, she wouldn't have been here today.

She wouldn't have been getting an abortion when a madman stormed the Center and started shooting.

It was just another layer of icing on the shitcake of her life.

This morning, when she had walked past the protesters, one of the women yelled that Joy was selfish. Well, she was. She had worked her ass off to get somewhere after aging out of the foster care program. She had struggled to pay for classes at college. She was determined to not wind up dependent on anyone.

The phone rang. And rang and rang. Joy slanted her gaze to the gunman to see if he would pick it up, but he was struggling—unsuccessfully—to tie a bandage around his bleeding hand.

It's crazy, what puts you on a collision course with someone. You might wind up in an airport, drunk. You might be too poor to pick the appointment date you wanted. You might have the bad fortune to be born to an addict, or to be bounced from foster home to foster home.

What had brought this shooter here today with his gun? Joy had heard bits of conversation when he was on the phone with the police outside. He wanted revenge because his own daughter had come here for an abortion. Apparently she hadn't told him what she was going to do.

Joy hadn't told Joe, either, but then, he hadn't returned her messages.

"What the fuck is your problem?" George asked, looming over her.

Startled, Joy pressed herself back against the chair. After what they had done to him—after what she had seen him do to Olive—she was terrified. She felt sweat trickle down her back. She had not felt this way—paralyzed—since she was eight. Back then the villain hadn't had a gun, just fists. But he had still towered over her; he'd still had all the power.

Joy wondered, again, about George's daughter.

She wondered why the girl had wanted an abortion.

She wondered if the girl was watching the news, if she felt responsible.

She wondered what it felt like to have an act of violence committed because someone loved you too much, instead of too little.

When she was small, Wren had believed her father knew everything. And she had asked him thousands of questions: *Are there more leaves in the world, or blades of grass?*

Why can't we breathe underwater?

If your eyes are blue, do you see everything in blue?

How do you know you're real and not someone else's dream?

How do you get wax in your ears?

Where does the water go when you let the bathtub drain?

Why don't cows talk?

Once she had asked, *Are you going to die?*

Hopefully not for a long time, he had answered.

Am I going to die?

Not if I can help it.

There were so many things she had not asked her father, that now she wished she had. *What is it like to see someone die in front of your eyes?*

What do you do when you realize you can't save them?

Wren lifted her gaze to the man she had stabbed in the hand, the one who had tried to shoot her. The one who had shot her aunt. The one who had killed Olive.

He was wrapping gauze around his bleeding palm, and doing a really shitty job of it. When the gun had gone off, at first Wren couldn't hear anything, and she thought for a second she had actually been shot and this was what death was. But the silence had been her eardrums shutting down, and the blood all over her had come from Olive. By the time Wren *could* hear again, the room bleating in fits and starts, she didn't want to.

The tattered name ripped from Olive's lips, for anyone who would be a messenger.

Janine keening.

Dr. Ward moaning in a yellow haze of pain as Izzy checked his tourniquet.

And a tiny, high whistle that it took Wren a while to figure out was coming from the center of her own body, the sound of fear vibrating through the tuning fork of her skeleton.

She stole a glance at the shooter. He clumsily tied off the bandage, using his teeth.

Just watch. Wren would be the girl who had come to a women's health clinic to get birth control, but still managed to die a virgin.

Suddenly the man lunged forward. Izzy shifted slightly, as if she were willing to throw herself between Wren and the shooter, but Wren would be damned if she let that happen again. She twisted at the last minute so that when he grabbed her forearm and jerked her upright, Izzy couldn't get in the way.

A small cry escaped Wren's clenched teeth, and she hated herself for showing any weakness. She forced herself to look him in the eye even though her knees were knocking together.

Bring it, you motherfucker, she thought.

"Let's go, girl," he said.

She could smell the cellar of his breath.

Where was he taking her? *Where was he taking her?*

He glanced at the others. "Do not move. If *any* of you move, I'll make sure you never move again." As if for punctuation, he glanced down at Olive's body.

"Let go of me," Wren yelled, actively fighting. She tried to pull out of his grasp, but he was too strong. "Let *go of me!*" she shrieked, and she lifted her foot to kick him, but he twisted her around roughly, his arm pressing against her windpipe.

"Do not," he said, "tempt me."

He increased his pressure on her throat until she saw stars.

Stars.

And then it all started to go black.

Suddenly he let her go. Wren fell to her hands and knees, sucking in air. She hated that she was at this man's feet, like a dog he could kick to the curb. "My dad is never gonna let you out of here alive," she gasped.

"Well, too bad your dad isn't with us."

"Oh yeah?" Wren said. "Who do you think that is on the phone?"

For just a moment, everything stopped, like it does at the apex of the roller coaster when you are caught between heaven and earth.

But then, you plummet down.

The shooter smiled. A terrible, reptile smile. Wren realized she did not have the upper hand after all.

"Well," the shooter said. "It's my lucky day."

HUGH LET THE PHONE RING five more times and then slammed it down. He was electric with frustration. The hostages had not come out. George was not answering. Hugh's decision an hour ago to cut the Wi-Fi and block all phone signals except the landline had cost him the ability to text Wren to see if she was all right—or if she had been the one who was shot.

It seemed like yesterday that he had driven Wren to kindergarten in his truck. As they turned in to the half-moon driveway of the school, he would tell her to put on her jet pack, and Wren would wriggle into her oversize knapsack. He'd slow to a stop. *Launching Wren*, he would announce, and she would leap out of the car, as if she were setting foot on a new and unexplored planet.

After Annabelle had left them, for several months Wren had asked when she was coming home. *She's not*, Hugh had told her. *It's just you and me now.*

Then one night, Hugh had gotten called to a domestic that was spiraling out of control. Bex had come to stay with Wren, who was inconsolable. When he got home at 3:30 A.M., his daughter was still awake and sobbing: *I thought you were gone.*

Hugh had pulled her into his arms. *I will never leave you*, he promised. *Never.*

Who would have guessed it might be the other way around?

He felt a shadow fall over him, and looked up to see the SWAT team commander standing shoulder to shoulder with the chief of police. "You should have told me about your daughter," Chief Monroe said.

Hugh nodded. "Yes, sir."

"You know I can't keep you in charge, son."

Hugh felt heat spread beneath his collar and he rubbed his hand on the back of his neck. His cellphone—the one he had been using to communicate with George Goddard—started to buzz on the card table he was using as a desk. He glanced at the incoming number. "It's him."

Quandt looked at the chief and then cursed underneath his breath. Chief Monroe picked up the phone and handed it to Hugh.

In 2006, in the state of Mississippi, sixteen-year-old Rennie Gibbs was charged with "depraved heart" murder when she delivered a stillborn at thirty-six weeks. Although the umbilical cord had been wrapped around the baby's neck, the prosecutor claimed the stillbirth was caused by Gibbs's cocaine use, due to trace elements of illegal drugs in the baby's bloodstream.

The prosecutor was Willie Cork, the same showboat who had been in Beth's hospital room, charging her with murder.

Beth glanced up from the article she was reading over her public defender's shoulder. "Is it true?" she asked. "The prosecutor did this before to someone else?"

"Don't read this," Mandy said, closing her laptop.

"Why not?"

"Because looking up prior cases when you're in legal trouble is like going to WebMD when you have a cold. You'll wind up convinced it's cancer." She sighed. "Willie has major aspirations for the next election. He wants to paint himself as someone who's tough on crime—even for the pre-born."

Beth swallowed. "Did she go to jail? Rennie Gibbs, I mean?"

"No. She was indicted by a grand jury, but the evidence was questionable. In 2014 the case was dismissed."

"That means mine could be, too, right?"

Mandy looked at her. "That means Willie Cork needs a win."

Beth was scared and overwhelmed. She had a hundred questions, and the answer to all of them was probably something she didn't want to hear. She felt tears climb the ladder of her throat, and she turned on her side, closing her eyes, hoping that Mandy wouldn't notice.

She may have fallen asleep. When she heard Willie Cork's voice, she thought at first she was having a nightmare. "What the hell are you doing out here?" he said, and Beth peeked from beneath her lashes to see that the door was open, and he was chewing out the cop who Mandy had convinced to stand outside, so that they could have privacy. "You left them in there *alone?* Get out. I'm having you reassigned," the prosecutor swore, "and I'm waiting until your replacement gets here."

She heard his voice in a one-sided phone conversation with, she guessed, someone at the police station. Mandy got up and stood in the open doorway, waiting for him to hang up. Was it weird that her public defender had sat there the whole time Beth was asleep? Had it been to avoid leaving Beth alone in a room with some male cop she didn't know?

"What are you doing here?" Mandy hissed at Willie Cork.

"I could ask you the same, since I'm guessing that cop didn't wander outside by himself." He crossed past Beth's bed and picked up a silver pen that was sitting on top of the radiator, something she hadn't noticed. "To answer your question, I left this behind by accident." He turned it over in his hand. "Montblanc. My daddy gave it to me when I graduated from law school."

Mandy rolled her eyes. "Keep your voice down. She's sleeping. And you left it behind by *accident?* Come on. You planted that so you could come back and interrogate my client without her lawyer present."

"Now, now, Mandy. You're soundin' like a conspiracy theorist."

"Says the slick son-of-a-bitch who plans to climb to the district attorney's office by trampling on a frightened, innocent girl."

If Beth had had any thoughts of revealing she wasn't sleeping, they vanished. She concentrated on making her breathing even, on not rattling the handcuff against the bed rail.

"Dismiss the charges," Mandy said quietly. "I'm doing you a favor, Willie. Don't ruin a girl's life because you want to get ahead in yours. You're only going to wind up embarrassed, like you did before."

Rennie Gibbs, Beth thought.

"You're trying to elevate the status of a fetus to personhood," Mandy continued, "and we don't have that law in Mississippi."

"Yet," the prosecutor answered.

Beth had been too nervous to really look at him during the arraignment, but now she did, peeking through the seams of her lids. Willie Cork wasn't much older than her public defender, but he already had threads of silver at the temples of his black hair. He probably dyed them that way, just to look the part.

"Mississippi has a long history of violence against people who've been silenced," he said.

Mandy laughed. "Willie, surely even *you* aren't dumb enough to try to play the race card on a Black woman."

"Unborn children are already part of the fabric of legal documents. Why, my granddaddy made sure I had a trust before I was even a glimmer in my daddy's eye."

"You know there's a world of difference between the legal rights of an unborn child and the constitutional rights of a living human being," Mandy whispered, heatedly. "The Constitution may protect liberty and privacy interests, but the Supreme Court has determined that those protections don't take effect until birth, *and* that prior to birth, a fetus is not a person. States may give a fetus legal rights, but that doesn't make it a person."

Beth's head was spinning. These were a lot of words, and most of them she didn't really understand. What she didn't get was why, if this was all about a fetus, *she* was the one who was handcuffed. She stifled the hysterical laugh bubbling: after all she had gone through to not be responsible for a baby, it turned out she still *was*.

"I'm merely elaborating on a time-honored legal tradition of allowing those who don't have a voice to have one in court. You see it every day, when a guardian ad litem is appointed to speak for children, or people with disabilities. We have laws to protect the vulnerable in this country who can't protect themselves. Like, for example, your client's baby."

"My client's *fetus*," Mandy clarified, "which relied on its host to survive."

"And if that host does something to cause harm, there should be consequences. If she had been attacked by someone when she was pregnant and lost the baby, wouldn't you want her attacker pursued? You know if that was the case, you'd be fighting as hard as I am for justice. We're not going to exclude the perpetrator just because her womb happens to house the child."

"What about the mother's rights?" asked Mandy.

"Can't have it both ways, darlin'," Willie Cork said. "You don't get to call her a mother if you aren't willing to call what's inside her a baby."

They were not even whispering anymore, and both lawyers had their backs turned toward Beth. It was as if they had forgotten she was the root of this argument.

It wouldn't have been the first time.

The reason she was here, now, was that everyone else seemed to have the right to make decisions about her—except Beth herself. She was so damn tired of being a bystander in her own life.

"You don't have a case," Mandy challenged.

"Don't I, though?" The prosecutor slipped his phone from his pocket, punched the screen a couple of times, and started to read aloud. "Mississippi code annotated 97-3-19: *The killing of a human being without the authority of law by any means or in any manner shall be murder in the following cases: Subsection A—when done with deliberate design to effect the death of the person killed . . . or Subsection D—when done with deliberate design to effect the death of an unborn child.* And of course, there's precedent."

"That's bullshit."

"Purvi Patel," Willie Cork began. "2016. She took the same pills your client did to terminate her pregnancy, at twenty-four weeks. Got them from a Hong Kong online pharmacy. When the baby died after birth, she was charged with a Class A felony. She was convicted and sentenced to twenty years for feticide and child neglect."

"The evidence wasn't clear in the Patel case that the baby was born alive," Mandy argued. "And the conviction was overturned."

"Bei Bei Shuai drank rat poison to commit suicide when she was thirty-three weeks pregnant. Her baby died, but she didn't, and she was charged with murder and attempted feticide and sentenced to thirty years," the prosecutor replied.

"And the charges against her were dropped after she pleaded guilty to a lesser charge and spent a year in custody." Mandy folded her arms. "Every case you've cited has been thrown out or dismissed."

"Regina McKnight," the prosecutor said. "Successfully prosecuted in South Carolina for homicide following a stillbirth caused by prenatal ingestion of crack cocaine. She got a twelve-year sentence."

"Are you kidding? McKnight wasn't even *trying* to have an abortion," Mandy argued.

"You're not making your point here, darlin'. You're making *mine*. If those women were charged with murder and intent wasn't even involved, imagine how easy it's gonna be to lock up your girl."

The door swung open, and a new cop entered. "You will not leave this room," Willie Cork ordered. "Not even if the building is on fire around you. And *you*," he said to Mandy, "well, good luck, Counselor."

Mandy faced him. "As long as *Roe v. Wade* stands, my client had every right to terminate her pregnancy."

"Yes," the prosecutor agreed. "But in Mississippi, she didn't have the right to do it by herself. That, my dear, is murder."

Murder. Beth flinched, and her handcuff scraped the rail. Both attorneys whirled around at the same moment, realizing she was awake.

"I—I'm sorry," Beth stammered.

"Little late for that, isn't it?" Willie Cork said, and he sailed out the door.

GEORGE GODDARD'S VOICE CRACKLED THROUGH Hugh's phone. "I believe," he said, "that I have something of yours."

He knows, Hugh thought. He knows about Wren.

Hugh shivered, even though it had to be ninety degrees outside. He flicked his eyes over the small group huddled around his command center and nodded. Quandt slipped on a pair of headphones to listen in. "George," Hugh said evenly, not taking the bait. "I heard a shot. What happened? Are you hurt?"

Remind the hostage taker you're on his side.

"Those bitches tried to shoot me."

Hugh glanced at the SWAT commander. "So you weren't the one who fired the gun?"

"I had to. They stabbed me."

Hugh closed his eyes. "Do you need medical help?" he asked, although he really didn't give a fuck if George bled to death.

"I'll live."

Quandt raised one brow.

"What about . . . everyone else? Did someone get hurt?"

"The old lady," George said.

"Does she need medical attention?"

There was a flicker of silence. "Not anymore," George said.

Hugh thought about Bex, about all that blood. "Anyone else, George?"

"I didn't shoot your daughter, if that's what you're asking," George said. "Now I know why you didn't send in the SWAT team."

"No!" Hugh said quickly. "Look. I didn't know she was in there when you and I started talking."

Find a bridge between you.

"She never even told me she was *going* to the clinic," Hugh added. "You know what that's like."

Hugh held his breath. He hated talking this way about Wren. No, he hadn't known she was going to the clinic. Yes, he hated himself for the fact that she had asked Bex to take her, and not him. But he didn't blame Wren for not feeling comfortable. He blamed his own parenting, for not making it clear that no question, no request, *nothing* was off-limits.

How many parents had he sat with in their own living rooms, while the medical examiner's team removed the body of their teenage child behind them, raw with the marks of a noose or the cuts of a razor? *I didn't know*, they would say, dazed. *She never told me.*

Hugh never said it out loud, but sometimes thought: *Well, did you* ask?

And he had. He would poke his head into Wren's room and say, *Anyone picking on you at school? Anything you want to talk about?*

She would look up from her homework. *You mean other than the pipe bomb I'm building in my closet?* Then she would grin. *No suicidal thoughts, Dad. All clear.*

But there were a hundred mines a teenager could step on daily. One of them had slipped through his defense.

Suddenly everything in Hugh went still. Yes, George had a vital piece of information now—that one of his hostages was related to the negotiator. He thought it gave him an advantage. But what if Hugh could use the *knowledge* of that information to tip the scales in his own favor?

"Listen," Hugh said. "Both our kids snuck around behind our backs. You couldn't stop your daughter, George. But you were able to stop mine. You saved her from making a terrible mistake."

It was not true. Wren had not gone to the Center to get an abortion. Hugh knew this. But George didn't.

"You know why I want this to be over, George?" Hugh said.

"You're worried about your kid."

"Yeah. But I also want to meet my grandchild, one day. Because of you, that's possible."

Silence.

"It'd be like getting a second chance. I'm a single parent, George. Just like you. I may not always have been the best father, but I tried to be. You know?"

There was a huff of response on the other end of the telephone line, which Hugh took as assent.

"But I'm also worried about what she thinks of me. I want her to be proud. I want her to think I did everything I possibly could for her."

"We can't both be the hero."

"Hero is just a label," Hugh said. "But honor—that's a legacy. You have a chance, George. A chance to redeem yourself. To do what's right."

He was taking a risk, raising the specter of integrity to a man who had only hours ago gone off the deep end due to a question about his reputation. But then it stood to reason that a person whose dignity had been questioned might crave respect. So much so that he would be willing to surrender in order to get it.

"It's not honorable to quit," George said, but Hugh could hear it—the weakening of bonds between the syllables of his conviction. The *what if*.

"Depends on the circumstances. Sometimes you have to make a choice that isn't what you *want* to do, but what you *have* to do. That's honor."

"You're the guy in the white hat," George scoffed. "You've probably never even run a red light. Everyone looks up to you."

Hugh met Captain Quandt's gaze. "Not everyone."

"You got no idea what you might do when you feel trapped."

George was retreating into his own defensive armor, making excuses for his behavior and using it to sever the connection that Hugh had built with him. He could continue down this rabbit hole, and take all the hostages with him—it would be fast, and it would be bloody, and it would be over.

Or.

Hugh could say something, *do* something, that would make George realize he was not stuck. That there was a way out.

He stared at Quandt, silently begging the man for a grace period. But the SWAT commander took off his headphones and turned to rally his team.

"You told me you started this for your daughter," he said to George. "Now end it for her."

Three p.m.

HUGH STARED AT THE WINDOWS OF THE CLINIC, MIRRORED LIKE aviator sunglasses. He assumed they were a later addition, when the protesters grew in number. This gave the women inside a sense that once they crossed the threshold, their business was their business alone. Those windows were meant to protect, but today they were obstacles. No one knew what was happening inside those walls.

He glanced at the phone in his hand, the line dead. One minute he'd been talking with George, seemingly making progress, and the next, he had been disconnected. He dialed again, and again, but there was no answer. His heart was racing, and not just because he'd lost contact with the hostage taker. The last sound he'd heard before George hung up on him was Wren's voice.

Which meant— Oh fuck, he didn't even want to go there.

He opened to the text thread he'd had with his daughter. *Wren*, he typed. *?*

R U OK

He held his breath, and the three telltale dots appeared.

She was responding.

She was all right.

He sank into the folding chair someone had brought him a couple of hours ago, holding the phone between his hands and willing the response to come faster.

"Hugh?"

At the sound of Chief Monroe's voice, he slipped his phone beneath a stack of papers. He could not let on that Wren was inside. That he *knew* Wren was inside. The minute he did, his neutrality was compromised. "Yeah, Chief?"

He looked up to see a guy in camo approaching. "This is Joe Quandt," the chief said. "He's the SWAT commander. Joe, this is Detective Lieutenant Hugh McElroy."

Hugh recognized Quandt; they'd worked together before.

Quandt held out his hand. "Sorry for the delay," he said.

It was not unusual for a countywide SWAT team to take a bit of time to congregate. The individuals constituting it came from all over the state and after receiving the call of a crisis in progress, had to converge upon it. Hugh had had three hours on his own to manage the situation, but now that Captain Quandt had arrived, there would be a struggle to see who would actually be in charge.

Hugh immediately began to give a rundown of the past three hours. If he acted like he was in charge, maybe it would remain that way.

"Have you got aerial photos?" Quandt asked, and Hugh nodded. It was one of the first things he'd asked for, so that when the SWAT team needed to get snipers into position, they'd know where to place them. He shuffled through the materials on his command desk, surreptitiously glancing at his phone as he did so. Those dots were still there, but no message yet.

• • •

• • •

"I've already instructed my team to take the perimeter," Quandt said. Hugh knew this was a relief to the chief, who didn't have the manpower to block the clinic entrances, restrict the media, and re-route traffic. "We'll be ready to go in in about fifteen minutes."

SWAT teams existed to back up the negotiator, but they also itched to do what they were trained for—end the showdown by force. Negotiators wanted to do what they were trained to do—negotiate.

"I don't think that's wise. He's got the hostages in the front wait-ing room," Hugh said, "and he can see you coming through the mir-rored glass, but you can't see in."

"We could pump tear gas in . . ."

"There are injured people in there," Hugh said, his voice even. *And my kid.*

The chief turned to Hugh. "So what's *your* plan?"

"Give Goddard a little more time," Hugh said. *Let me figure out what's happening inside first. Let me hear from Wren.*

Quandt shook his head. "It's my understanding that there were shots fired . . ."

"But not in the last three hours," Hugh pointed out. "I've been able to keep him calm." He looked at Quandt. "If you go in, can you guarantee that you won't lose a hostage?"

The SWAT team commander's jaw tightened. "Of course not," he said.

Both men turned to Chief Monroe. "Hugh will continue to run with it for now," the chief replied.

Chief Monroe put his hand on Hugh's shoulder, turning him away from the SWAT commander. He spoke in a firm, quiet voice. "You *do* know what you're doing, don't you?"

"Yes, sir," Hugh said, as if hostage negotiation was a set of rules you could follow, rather than a game where the players made up the rules as they went. "I have to get back to . . . I need to . . ."

He moved to his makeshift desk again and grabbed his phone.

There was no message, and the dots were gone, too.

He texted again: *WREN?*

* * *

WHEN THE SHOOTER HAD YANKED open the door to her hiding place, Wren thought her heart was going to burst. She barely managed to hide her phone in her sock before he grabbed her wrist and pulled so hard that she cried out. She managed to claw his face and drew blood, a triumph about which she was supremely happy. He dragged her into the waiting room in the front of the clinic, the one with the windows where you could see out but people on the street couldn't see in. She landed sprawled on her belly in front of a handful of people.

There was a woman in sweats, who had freckles all over her face that stood out because she was so pale right now. There was another girl—maybe in her twenties?—with a giant bruise on her forehead. The redheaded lady in scrubs who had opened the closet door earlier and pretended not to see her. The only male hostage rested his head in her lap and was breathing heavily. His own scrubs had been ripped off at the thigh, and below a belt of fabric and tape, his leg was bloodied.

Her aunt Bex was nowhere.

Wren felt tears spring to her eyes. Was she dead? Had someone dragged her body into another room?

When she was little, and her aunt Bex used to watch her after school while her dad was at work, they did everything Wren wasn't supposed to do. They ate dessert, and skipped dinner. They watched R-rated movies. Her aunt had promised that not only would she take Wren to get a tattoo when she was eighteen, she would design it for her.

What if neither of them survived that long?

"Tie her hands," the shooter yelled. "Now! *You!*" He jerked the gun at the redhead in scrubs.

She took a roll of surgical tape and wrapped it around Wren's wrists. She was trying to do it loosely, but it was tape, and there was no way Wren was getting free anytime soon. "Are you hurt?" she whispered. "I'm a nurse."

"I'm okay," Wren managed. "My aunt . . ."

"The woman with you in the closet?"

Wren shook her head. "No. The lady who was shot. Out here."

"Bex," the nurse murmured. "She got out."

Wren collapsed with relief on an empty couch. Aunt Bex was alive. Or at least she had been.

She hoped that the next time she saw Bex, her aunt reamed her for putting her in this situation. She hoped that Bex yelled so loud Wren was brought to tears. She wouldn't mind if Bex refused to forgive her for the rest of her life. Just so long as she *had* a rest of her life.

Wren had begged Aunt Bex to bring her here. If she had talked to her dad, maybe they could have made an appointment with a gynecologist. Maybe she would be snagging a lollipop from a basket on her way out. (Did gynecologists even have those? Or were they just for pediatricians' offices?)

Then again, she never could have asked her father. He didn't even let her wear spaghetti straps to school. All he knew about Ryan was that they were working together on a chemistry project.

Which was kind of true.

But what was combustible was the two of them. Wren thought about the kisses that made her lips feel like they'd been blistered; about how his hand snaked under her shirt and ignited her skin. She thought of the giddy rush of adrenaline that flooded her when they scrambled apart a breath before Ryan's mother opened the door, her arms full of groceries.

Had she told her father about Ryan, he would have been waiting on the hairpin turn near the high school to give Ryan a ticket for driving too fast or too slow or too erratically. He would have done a background check. He would have convinced himself that this boy did not deserve Wren.

There was nothing her father wouldn't do for her. But there were also things her father *couldn't* do for her. When she had gotten her period two years ago, the cramps had been so bad she'd told her dad she was sick and couldn't go to school. He held his hand to her forehead, dubious, because she didn't have a fever. "I have cramps," she told him flatly, and he went bright red and stumbled out of her room. He returned an hour later with two bags from CVS—Gatorade, Advil, a Matchbox car, a Rubik's Cube, a pack of Bazooka gum, a little puzzle with a picture of a kitten. He set them on the foot of her bed, as if he couldn't bring himself to get too close to her. "For your . . . um . . . *lady-stomach*," he murmured.

Seriously, how could she ask a man who couldn't even say the word *cramps* to bring her somewhere to get birth control?

She had turned to her aunt for help, and it had almost cost Bex her life. It *still* might.

In her sneaker, her cellphone vibrated. She crossed her ankles, wondering if anyone else had heard the buzz, knowing it was probably her dad.

He would not let anything bad happen to her. Even if she could not reach her phone and tell him she was all right.

Sometimes when her father came home from work and was particularly quiet, Wren knew that he'd had a really shitty day. He once told her that being a detective meant you had to peel back the pretty of a town, and see its festering wounds: who was an addict, who was beating his wife, who was drowning in debt, who was suicidal. But he never told her details. She had accused him once of treating her like a baby. *It's not that I want to hide anything from you*, he'd told her. *It's that if I tell you, you'll never look at people the same way.*

Wren turned back to the nurse, and then to each of the other women. "I'm Wren," she whispered.

"Izzy," said the nurse softly. "And this is Dr. Ward."

The man lifted a hand, but that was all he could manage.

The woman with a bruise on her forehead met her gaze. "Janine," she mouthed.

"Joy," whispered the woman in sweats.

"What's he gonna—"

"Ssh," Izzy hushed, as the shooter returned, dragging Olive from the closet and unceremoniously shoving her into the space beside Wren.

"Sorry, ma'am," he said to Olive.

And then he pointed the gun at Wren's face.

IT WAS THE SECOND TIME Olive had come out of the closet, and it was equally traumatic. Now, she glanced around the room. Wren was shaking like a leaf, her wrists bound. There were red marks on her skin where the gunman had yanked her out of their hiding spot. It was a wonder he hadn't dislocated the girl's arm.

Seeing his roughness, Olive had been the most docile, subservient hostage imaginable as he hauled her out of the utility closet, too. She pleaded with him—what could a sixty-eight-year-old woman do to him, after all? And it had worked. Like most men, he saw only her petite frame, and not the strength of her mind. He pushed her into a couch, next to Wren, but he said, *Sorry, ma'am*. And he didn't restrain her as he had Wren. Now her brain—her celebrated retired-professor brain—was working in triple time to find a way out of this situation.

He started waving the gun at Olive and Wren. It bounced between them with each syllable, like the little ball on the screen at a sing-along. "Did you think you could hide from me? Did you?"

Olive was trying to be strong, really she was. Peg, her wife, was always the first to tell her she often worried herself into a panic about things that didn't come to pass. Like, for example, a mark on her shoulder that she was certain was a tick bite heralding the onset of

Lyme disease. (It wasn't.) A news report about another missile fired off by North Korea, which Olive thought would start World War III. (It hadn't.) "Eeyore," Peg would call her, and in this moment of all moments, the thought made Olive smile.

Well, Peg, I'm in a room with a crazy guy waving a gun and five other hostages. Is it all right to panic now?

"You lied to me!" He turned, the force of his anger bending over the woman who was wearing scrubs. A nurse? "You told me that closet was empty!"

The woman cowered, her arms shielding her face. "I didn't—"

"Shut up! Shut your goddamn mouth!" he yelled.

In addition to Olive and Wren, there were three other women. There was a young woman in sweatpants, and another one with a big bruise on her temple. There was the nurse, whose name must have been Izzy, because the man she was tending to kept calling her that. The doctor, maybe? He was in scrubs, like her. He was big enough to take down the gunman, if not for the fact that his leg looked like hamburger below the thigh, and he was in obvious pain.

Wren's aunt was nowhere to be seen.

And then there was the gunman. He was middle-aged—maybe forty, maybe forty-five. He was wiry, but strong. Strong enough to haul a fighting teenager out of hiding. A silver stubble of beard rubbed along the coastline of his jaw. There was nothing about him that would have made Olive look twice at him on the street, unless their eyes had met. Then, she might have just stopped and stared. His eyes were almost colorless. His gaze felt like a sucking wound.

"I'm sorry," Olive said, in her thickest Elderly Southern Lady accent. "I don't think we've been introduced. I'm Miz Olive."

"I don't care who you are," he said.

One of the other women caught her eye and glanced at the television overhead, where the news was streaming in a weird metaphysical mirror, a reporter with this very clinic over his shoulder. GUNMAN IDENTIFIED AS GEORGE GODDARD, a caption below read.

"Well, George," she said evenly, as if they were sitting down to lemonade. "Lovely to make your acquaintance."

He may have been unhinged, but he was from the South, where even the unhinged had mothers and grandmothers who drilled decades of manners into them. Olive did not believe in using her age except for discount prices on movie tickets and to get 10 percent off at Kroger the second Tuesday of the month. And now, apparently, in a hostage situation.

George Goddard was sweating profusely, running his free hand over his brow and wiping it on his pants leg. Olive had a neuroscience background, but she could do armchair diagnosis with the best of them. Grandiose claims about the self. A sense of entitlement. Lack of empathy. A tendency to lash out when they feel like they're not being respected.

Narcissistic personality disorder.

Or homegrown terrorist, Olive thought. Either would fit.

If you could see me, Peg, she thought. Olive was the one who peeked from between her fingers during scary movies, who still sometimes had to check the closet before going to bed to make sure there was nothing lurking inside (and goodness, after this episode, she would be doing that *all the time*). But here she was calmly playing the old lady for all it was worth, the only postmenopausal one in the bunch.

Surely he knew she hadn't come here to get an abortion.

Did it even matter?

The girl beside her burst into tears. Olive wrapped her arms around Wren, trying to will her strength.

The man knelt down, his eyes clouding for a second. "Don't cry," he said to Wren, his voice catching. "Please don't cry . . ." He reached out to her with his free hand.

There was something in the way he was looking at Wren, but wasn't *seeing* her, thought Olive. In his mind's eye, this was someone else, maybe someone about her age, who had come to this clinic against his wishes. After all, what else would have set him off?

If Olive was right, and she usually was, what had happened to that other girl?

She and Peg used to sit at the airport, waiting for their flight, and eavesdrop on conversations between men and women, mothers and children, colleagues. They would take turns making up backstories for them. *He grew up in a cult and hasn't learned how to bond with some-one in a healthy way. She's adopted that five-year-old, who has oppositional defiant disorder. That guy's a sex addict, cheating with his boss's wife.*

"Don't touch me," Wren shrieked, as the man reached out to her. She kicked reflexively, connecting with his knee, and he winced and backed away. "Goddammit," he growled, and he started toward her, but Wren let out a piercing scream. George covered his ears with his hands, his eyes screwed shut.

Wren let a loud wail loose again. And another. Maybe she had figured out that her aunt was dead, and she was inconsolable. Olive squeezed her arm. Clearly every time Wren opened her mouth, it set the gunman on edge. She had to see that, even if she was young. Didn't she?

Her weeping was almost rhythmic.

And . . . was Wren's foot buzzing?

Wren turned to Olive, and Olive realized that in spite of her cries, not a single tear streaked down her cheeks. Her chin nodded imperceptibly to her sock, where a phone screen glowed beneath and vibrated with a text. She was covering up the sounds with her sobs.

Olive waited until George paced past them, and then she covered Wren's ankle with her palm. She slipped her fingers beneath the elastic and felt around for the power button, turning it off.

Wren sagged with relief, resting her head against Olive's shoulder. The movement made George spin around, the gun trained on her.

Peg, I didn't even jump, she would say, when this was all over.

Olive pasted a wide smile on her face. "George," she said, "I remember some Goddards from Biloxi. They were in the brick busi-

ness, family-run. You wouldn't be related, now, would you? I do believe they moved to Birmingham. Or was it Mobile?"

"Shut *up*," he growled. "I should have left you in the goddamn
closet. I can't think when you're yapping."

Olive quieted dutifully, and then she winked at Wren. Because as
George was busy silencing her, he had tucked the gun back into the
waistband of his jeans.

IN THE AMBULANCE, BEX TRIED to speak. "My . . . niece . . ." she
rasped, clawing at the shirt of the EMT.

"Don't try to talk," the young man said. He had soft eyes and
softer hands, and his teeth were a beacon against his dark skin.
"We're gonna take care of you now. We're almost at the hospital."

"Wren . . ."

"When?" he said, mishearing her. "Soon. Real soon." He smiled
down at her. "You got the devil's own luck."

What Bex knew was that this was not luck, but karma. If Wren
did not get out of that clinic, Bex would never forgive herself. She
should have known better than to go behind Hugh's back to the
clinic. But Wren had come to her last week after school, riding her
bike to Bex's studio; she had been finishing a new commission—a
mural going into a skyscraper lobby in Orlando, to commemorate
the Pulse shooting. It was a fourteen-by-fourteen-foot profile of two
men kissing. The pixels were made not of Post-its, as usual, but of
photos of people who had died during the AIDS crisis.

"Cool," Wren had said. "What's it going to be?"

Bex had explained it. "Want to help?"

She gave Wren hundreds of tiny squares of tinted celluloid.
Showing her how to affix them to each photo with glue, Bex instructed her to start at the bottom and screen the last ten rows of
photographs in shades of violet celluloid. The next ten rows above
them would be blue, then green, then yellow, and so on. Standing far

enough away, you would see the kiss, but you would also see a rainbow. Standing close, you'd see all the individual shoulders those two men had to stand on in order to embrace each other openly.

"This isn't even a thing for kids your age, is it?" Bex mused as they worked beside each other.

"What thing?"

"Being gay."

"Well, yeah. It still is, I think, if you're the one who happens to *be* that way. People assume you're cis and straight, so if you're not, you're different. But who says there's only one way to be normal?"

Bex stopped working, her hands stilling over the lips of one of the models. "When did you get to be so smart?"

Wren grinned. "What took you so long to notice?" They worked in silence for a while, and then Wren asked, "Does this piece have a name yet?"

"I was thinking maybe *Love*."

"That's perfect," Wren said. "But not just the word. The whole sentence. Exactly the way you said it." She brushed a line of glue around a violet celluloid. "Aunt Bex? Can I ask you something? Do you believe that you can fall in love when you're fifteen?"

Bex's hands stilled. She lifted the magnifying glasses she wore when she worked so that she could look Wren in the eye. "You bet I do," she said firmly. "Is there something you want to tell me?"

And oh, it had been delicious—the way Wren's cheeks had gone pink when she held his name in her mouth; how she talked about him as if there had never been another boy on earth. What love looked like was this: fledgling and unsteady, fierce and soft-shelled at the same time.

Wren didn't have a mother around to talk to her frankly about sex. Hugh would have probably rather carved out his liver with a teaspoon than have that conversation with his daughter. So Bex asked her niece the questions no one else would: *Have you kissed him? Have you done more than that? Have you talked about protection?*

No judgment, no finger wagging. Just pragmatism. Once the rocket had left the launchpad, you couldn't bring it back.

Wren was fifteen; she was writing his name on the leg of her jeans; she was stealing his sweatshirts so that she could sleep in the ghost of his scent. But she'd also been thinking of birth control. "Aunt Bex," Wren had asked shyly, "will you help me?"

And so it was with the best of intentions that—once again—Bex had done something inexcusable.

She heard a machine somewhere behind her start to beep. The EMT leaned closer. He smelled like wintergreen. "Ma'am," he said, "try to relax."

Bex closed her eyes again, thinking of the bullet that had exploded through her, and the pierce of the scalpel that had maybe saved her life.

This is what it means to be human, Bex thought. *We are all just canvases for our scars.*

WHEN HUGH'S PHONE FINALLY DINGED, he lunged for it. But the text wasn't from Wren—it was from a guy named Dick, a state trooper who had been in his hostage negotiation training sessions. Two hours ago, when George Goddard's license plate was run, Hugh had reached out to Dick, who got a search warrant from a local judge and let himself into the empty house in Denmark, Mississippi. Now Hugh had the results of Dick's search: a blurry photo of a handout about medication abortions that had the name and logo of the Women's Center on it. It was enough for Hugh to connect the dots from George to this clinic.

Where's the daughter? Hugh texted.

There was a beat. And then: *M.I.A.*

Hugh raked his hair, frustrated by the fact that the only person he didn't want to talk to—his sister—refused to leave the site; and that the people he *did* want to talk to were not communicating:

Wren, George Goddard, his missing daughter. Who the hell could negotiate when no one was listening?

What was he missing now? What could he use that he hadn't used before?

Hugh picked up the phone and texted Wren again. He dialed the number of the clinic, his secure line. One ring. Two.

Three rings. Four.

There was a click of connection, and then George's voice. "I'm busy," he said.

Muscle memory took over. "I won't take up too much of your time, George," Hugh replied. "We were talking about your daughter, when we got cut off."

When you hung up on me.

"What about her?"

Hugh closed his eyes and made a leap into the unknown. "She wants to talk to you."

LOUIE WARD KNEW EXACTLY THE moment that something in the shooter had changed. Even though he could only hear half the conversation, he could see that the man grew very still. Hope could do that to a person, Louie knew. Paralyze you inside and out.

"What about her?" the shooter said.

When he—George, his name was George, according to the television still playing in the waiting room—said that, Louie realized two very important things:

1. This was personal, for him. Someone—a wife, a daughter, a sister—had had an abortion.
2. He wanted that someone's approval for today's actions.

Izzy leaned down on the pretense of tightening his tourniquet. *"Her,"* she murmured.

"Mmm," Louie said. "So I heard."

In the handful of times that the phone had rung over the past couple of hours, the people huddled in the waiting room had been able to take a collective breath. George didn't turn his back when he was on the phone—he wasn't that stupid—but he also didn't silence them if they whispered to each other.

"You think it was his wife?" Izzy whispered.

"Daughter." Louie grunted as he shifted and a streak of pain shot up his leg.

"You have either of those?"

Louie shook his head. "I never wanted to make anyone else a target," he admitted. "And eligible ladies don't often celebrate the fact that I spent the day looking into other women's vaginas."

Behind him, Janine shifted. "You don't have to have a personal stake to know that it's wrong to kill an innocent baby."

Eighty-eight percent of abortions happened in the first twelve weeks of pregnancy, Louie knew, but the antis acted like those fetuses were already eight pounds and holding their own bottles.

Joy's eyes widened. "You are *not* defending him," she said to Janine. "After he knocked you out?"

"I'm just saying—if it wasn't wrong, then there wouldn't be psychos like him."

Izzy stared at her. "That's the most ass-backward logic I've ever heard."

"Is it? You want to protect children with laws that punish rapists and molesters and murderers. Why is this any different?"

"Because they're not children yet," Izzy said. "They're embryos."

"They may not be born but they're still human."

"Oh my God," Joy said. "Shut her up before I do it myself."

Janine folded her arms. "I'm sorry. I know that he's insane, but you can't tell me there is ever a valid reason to destroy a child."

Louie looked at her. "She's right," he murmured, and the others all stared at him. "There is never a valid reason to destroy a child."

He thought of what he had seen over the years: The Syrian teen who needed to terminate after being raped as an act of war, but who couldn't get consent from her parents, who had been killed in the same war. The sixteen-year-old who had wanted to have an abortion at eight weeks, whose parents stood in her way with their religion, and so her abortion was delayed for six weeks while she figured out how to get a judicial bypass and to raise the money to terminate. The fourteen-year-old who wanted to keep her baby, but was being pushed by her mother to have the abortion.

A few years back, a twelve-year-old girl came in who was sixteen weeks pregnant. Her hysterical mother and stoic father were with her. She was quiet to the point of disengagement, clutching a tattered stuffed rabbit. She had said that a neighborhood boy got her pregnant, but during the intake process when she was alone with the counselor, she slipped up on her lie and revealed that the baby was her father's. The man was taken off by the police in handcuffs, but that girl, she still needed an abortion.

While Louie performed the procedure he talked to her. He told her, *This is not normal, what happened to you. This is not something you've done.* She didn't respond. She didn't act like a twelve-year-old. She never had been allowed to *be* a twelve-year-old. But he hoped that one day, when she was twice this age, she would remember the kindness of a man who *hadn't* hurt her.

Now, Louie turned to Janine. "What we do here," he said, "what *I* do. Sometimes it lets children be children."

Janine opened her mouth as if to argue the point, but then snapped it shut.

Izzy tried to turn the conversation back to a safer spot. "Well, whoever she is—wife or daughter—maybe she can convince him to let us go."

From the couch further away came the voice of the girl, Wren, who could not have been much older than the child Louie had been remembering. Had she come here to get an abortion? Would they, in other circumstances, have met on the exam table?

"If he was my father," she muttered, "I sure as hell wouldn't talk to him."

FOR A MOMENT, THE ONLY sound in the hospital room was the intravenous pump. Beth lay on her side, her face turned away from her public defender. "I wrapped it up," Beth whispered. "I put it in the garbage. I didn't know what else to do."

She had bought misoprostol and mifepristone, the pills used in a medication abortion, off the Internet. That was illegal in the United States, which Beth hadn't known at the time. Abortion clinics offered medication abortions to women who were up to ten weeks pregnant, but they had to be administered in the clinic. Beth had been sixteen weeks along, and had taken the pills at home. The medication had done its job, but it had also caused enough hemorrhaging to land her in the ER.

Tears slipped down the bridge of Beth's nose. For the first time since she had started talking, she looked at Mandy. "Miz DuVille? It wasn't a baby yet . . . was it?"

Mandy's mouth tightened.

"When I went to the clinic," Beth said, "there was a woman outside who said my baby could feel pain."

The lawyer actually recoiled, and that only made Beth feel even worse. Mandy was an attorney, not a shrink. For all Beth knew, Mandy was against abortion, and was only here to do her job. Didn't lawyers have to defend horrible people—murderers, rapists—all the time, no matter what they felt about them personally?

"I'm sorry," Beth whispered. "I just . . . I haven't had anyone to talk to."

"It's not true," Mandy said flatly. "The pain thing."

Beth came up on an elbow. "How do you know?"

"Science doesn't support it. I've done the research."

Beth frowned, confused. "But you said you didn't even know anything about me before the arraignment."

"I did the research," the lawyer repeated, "for me." She leaned forward, her head bent, propped against the heels of her hands. "I was thirteen weeks pregnant. Just at the point where you can tell people you're having a baby, without tempting fate. My husband and I were at the ultrasound," she said. "I wanted to name her Millicent, if she was a girl. Steve said no little Black girl is named Millicent. He wanted a boy named Obediah."

"Obediah?" Beth repeated.

"Knock, knock," Mandy said.

"Who's there?"

"Obediah."

"Obediah who?" Beth played along.

"Obediah-dore you." Mandy closed her eyes. "Steve told me that joke, and then after that, everything went to hell. The technician came in and turned on the machine and started the ultrasound and just went white as a sheet." She shook her head. "The doctor who came in wasn't my usual doctor. I remember exactly what he said. *This fetus has a genetic abnormality inconsistent with life.*"

Beth sucked in her breath.

"It was called holoprosencephaly. It happens when two sperm fertilize one egg at the exact same moment. There was a heartbeat and a brain stem, but the forebrain had never developed. If it survived birth, it would die within a year." Mandy looked up. "I didn't want to terminate. I was raised Catholic."

"What did you do?" Beth asked.

"I went online and looked up pictures of the babies who had it. It was . . . it was horrible." She looked up at Beth. "I know there are mothers who have kids with profound disabilities, and who see that as a blessing. It was kind of a wake-up call to admit to myself I wasn't one of them."

"What about your husband?"

Mandy looked up. "He said it was a no-brainer."

A laugh burst out of Beth; she clapped her hand over her mouth. "No he didn't."

"He did." Mandy nodded, smiling faintly. "He did and we laughed. We laughed, and we laughed, until we cried."

"Did you . . . do you have children now?"

Mandy met her gaze. "I stopped trying after the third miscarriage."

Silence fell between them. Beth spun through another scenario, one in which she had been brave enough to tell her father she was pregnant, one in which she had carried the baby to term, and given it to someone like Mandy. "You must hate me," Beth whispered.

For a long moment Mandy didn't speak. Then she lifted her chin. "I don't hate you," she said carefully. "If you and I both told people our stories, even the most pro-life advocates would see mine as a tragedy. Yours is a crime." She thought for a moment. "It's funny. The logic goes that as a minor, you can't exercise free will to consent, because you don't have the mental capacity to do so. But in your case, the fetus is getting the protection you're not, as if its rights are worth more than your own."

Beth stared at her. "So what happens now?"

"You're going to get discharged from the hospital, in a day or so. And then you'll stay in custody until the trial."

Beth's heart monitor began to spike. "No," she said. "I can't go to jail."

"You don't have a choice."

I never did, Beth thought.

*   *   *

"YOU'RE LYING," GEORGE SAID. "My daughter isn't here."

Fuck that cop. He might be fishing for information, but that didn't mean George planned to give it to him. Yet now that Hugh McElroy had brought up his daughter, he couldn't stop thinking about her.

Was Lil all right?

Was she looking for him?

"Because she doesn't know what you're doing," Hugh said. "Am I right?"

Lil knew that he loved her. He loved her so much that he had come here to make things right, even though it seemed impossible. George would never meet his grandchild. He just hoped this had not cost him Lil, too.

"How would she feel about you being here, George?"

He had not been thinking about that, clearly, when he came. He was just an avenging angel for her suffering. And he had been thinking of God's word. An eye for an eye.

A life for a life.

"What's her name, George?"

"Lil," he said, the syllable falling from his lips.

"That's pretty," Hugh said. "Old school."

George hated that he'd left her after they argued. He knew she'd be well taken care of in his absence, but he also knew he had fucked up. He'd just never been good with speeches. He didn't know how to say what he was feeling. Pastor Mike used to call him a man of few words, but reminded him that deeds spoke a thousand times more loudly.

That's why he was here, wasn't it?

The drive here had been long, and his thoughts had provided the soundtrack for the journey. He had imagined Lil in all the incarnations of her life—the time she was a baby with croup and he sat up with her all night in a steamy bathroom, the shower blasting hot water; the Father's Day when she tried to make him pancakes for breakfast and set a dish towel on fire; the sound of her voice harmonizing with his when they sang at church. Then he'd pictured himself like an avenger, swollen to comic-book-hero proportions, bursting through the doors of the clinic and leaving destruction in his wake.

He had imagined screams and falling plaster and a haze of dust. But somehow although he could see himself when he started shooting, everything afterward was fuzzy. Revenge, in theory, throbbed with adrenaline and was clean with conviction. In reality, it was rushing into a house on fire, and forgetting to map out your exit.

Behind him, George heard a ripple of conversation. He turned around, the phone still clutched to his ear. "Quiet," he ordered.

"What's going on in there?" Hugh asked.

George ignored him, trying to focus on the scene in front of him. The women were whispering, and the baby killer he'd shot was still lying on the floor, a bandage twisted around his thigh. "Joy needs to use the bathroom," said the kid.

The one who'd scratched him.

He glanced at her hands, making sure they were still tied.

"Well, hold it in," he muttered.

The nurse who was kneeling on the floor looked up. "It's not that," she said. "She needs to check her pad. She just had a—"

"I know what she had," George snapped, interrupting.

"Is everything okay?" asked the cop. There was a strange note in his voice, a vibration.

"I have to go."

"Wait!" Hugh said. "George, I wasn't lying before. I didn't say your daughter was here. I said she wants to talk to you. She's listening to the news, George. And they don't get things right. They're not going to give your side of the story to her. Only you can do that." Hugh paused. "I can make that happen for you. I can get her on the phone."

"Wait," he muttered, distracted.

"What's wrong, George?" the cop asked. "Talk to me."

He was staring at the television that had been on the entire time. When he first got here, there was some daytime food show on. But now, there was a breaking news banner and a picture of a reporter with the clinic behind her. Her lips were moving, but the volume had been lowered; George couldn't tell what was being said.

What if Hugh was right? What if Lil was listening?

"Where's the remote?" he asked. When the women stared at him like he was crazy—was he? Or was he thinking clearly for the first time in hours?—he barked at them again. "The *remote!*"

The old lady pointed to a shelf near the television.

"Get it," he commanded. He was still holding the phone, but he had tuned out the cop's insistent voice.

The old lady was fumbling with the control. She dropped it, picked it up, and pointed it at the television. "I think this is the right button," she said, but nothing happened.

"Faster!" George yelled, and he jerked the gun at her.

The woman screamed and dropped the controller again.

"Leave her alone!" the kid cried.

"George?" Hugh's voice blistered against his ear. "George, who was that yelling?"

"Give her the damn thing," he ordered, pointing to the teenager. "Kids always know how to work stuff like this."

"What kid?" Hugh said.

George let the phone fall in his hand, holding it against his thigh, as the girl managed to increase the volume even with her wrists bound.

". . . given that Goddard *was* in fact dishonorably discharged for killing civilians during his service in Bosnia."

The screen cut to a studio anchor. "So we can say that there's a historical pattern of violence . . ."

"Turn it off," George breathed.

He couldn't even see the screen. His vision was blurred, and all he could imagine was Lil listening to this utter bullshit. "That isn't what happened," he muttered.

He could feel the phone vibrating against his thigh, emitting sounds.

Suddenly it was 2001 and he was in Bosnia and he was doing his job and everyone was out to get him.

He thought of Lil, hearing that bullshit. He thought of how, when she was little, she would always play the princess and he had to be the prince who saved her from the ogre or the quicksand or the evil queen. She had never seen him as anything but a hero. And now?

He reached for the nearest piece of furniture—a lamp—and hurled it against the wall.

The women screamed.

He could hear the cop yelling, trying to get his attention.

He hung up the phone.

Well, fuck. They had his attention now.

HUGH HELD THE PHONE IN his hand, the line dead. He had heard two critical things in the background during this last phone conversation: Wren's voice, and the television report on George's military service.

He sank onto a chair and speared his hands through his hair, making it stand on end. When he was young, Bex was forever smoothing down his cowlicks. That's what it really came down to, wasn't it? Looking presentable to the world, no matter who you were when the cameras weren't rolling and the door was closed.

When push came to shove, was he a hostage negotiator, or a father?

When the two came into conflict, which triumphed?

He looked up, beckoning over a SWAT team member. "Where's Quandt?" he asked.

"I can get him for you, Lieutenant." The man hurried off and Hugh stared down at his makeshift desk, weighing his options.

George Goddard was losing control.

Hugh had heard Wren's voice.

She was still alive.

And this might be his only chance to keep her that way.

A shadow fell over him, and Hugh glanced up to see Quandt standing with his arms crossed. "I can only assume that the reason you want to see me is because you've come to your senses and you're ready for my men to move in," he said.

"No," Hugh replied. "I want you to cut communications."

"What? *Why?*"

"I don't want any comms in that building that don't come directly from us. I want the phone lines cut, except for the hard line to the clinic that connects to me. No TV signal, no Wi-Fi, nothing. I can't risk him seeing anything else on TV that will send him over the edge."

"What if a hostage tries to communicate with us? Say one of them tries to use her cell—"

"I know what I'm doing," Hugh said firmly.

He recognized the risks. But he also realized this decision would isolate George, so that the only information the shooter got was directly from Hugh himself.

Quandt looked at him for a long moment, and then nodded. He walked off, shouting orders to his men, who would reach out to the cellular companies and cable company and effectively make the clinic an island.

Hugh picked up his phone and texted Wren one more time, just in case she saw it.

Trust me, he typed.

OLIVE HAD BEEN A PROFESSOR for thirty-five years before she retired. Her course was on the workings of the brain, and it always had a waiting list. She started each semester by showing a random student a photo of himself or herself at an event or in a certain geographical place. After a few questions, the student was able to remember that moment, and to fill in details. The catch? The student had been Photoshopped into the picture, and had never actually been there.

Olive would explain to her students that the brain is constantly telling us lies. It simply can't record every detail that our eyes see, so instead, the occipital lobe adds what it assumes is there. The brain isn't a video recording—it's more like a photo album, and in between those pictures it fills in the blanks. The result is that false memories can be created more easily than any of us want to believe. There will be incidents you swear on your mother's grave happened a certain way . . . but *didn't*.

She wondered what she would remember of this incident. She hoped very little. With any luck she would be granted a wondrous and selective amnesia. She hoped the same for all the others who were huddled in the waiting room, watching George fight with his own demons.

And what of George, the shooter? What had his brain pieced together inaccurately, she wondered, to bring him here today?

She raised her hand to her brow, surprised to see it come away bloody. When George had thrown the lamp against the wall, it had shattered, and ceramic and glass shards had gone everywhere. Including, apparently, her temple.

"Let me," the nurse said—Izzy, that was her name. She pressed a piece of gauze against Olive's forehead, though they both knew it was nothing more than a scratch. "We have to get out of here," Izzy murmured. "He's losing it."

Olive nodded. "Oh, George," she said, pasting a wide, dizzy smile on her face. "I hate to be a bother . . . but . . . George?" She waited until he looked up. "I'm afraid that my age is getting the best of me. Some parts don't work as well as they used to."

He blinked at her, confused.

"I have to pee, dear," she stated.

At that Izzy turned. "If Olive is going to the restroom, then Joy has to go, too. It's for medical reasons."

"I have an idea," Olive said. "Why don't we all go now? If we get it out of the way, then we won't be any more trouble."

At that, George snorted.

A Hobson's choice, that was what she had to offer George—a choice that wasn't really a choice at all—like the executioner asking if you'd prefer to have your head severed from your body, or your body from your head. Olive smiled at George. "Would you like me to go first, or Miss Joy?"

George took a step forward. "You think I'm an idiot?" he said. "I'm not letting you go into the bathroom by yourself."

"Well, I hardly think you'd care to *watch*," she replied. She got to her feet. "I don't really think I can wait much longer for you to decide, dear. The muscles in the urinary tract just aren't what they used to be—"

"For God's sake," George cut her off. He stepped forward, grabbing her arm. "Come on."

There was a small single-person restroom off the waiting room where they were all sitting. George dragged her toward it and turned on the light, then gave her a rough pat down. "Go," he said, but when Olive tried to close the door, he pushed it back open. "If you don't want to do it this way, you don't get to do it at all."

Olive considered arguing with him, but in the end she just nudged the door closed a bit. It remained open for all intents and purposes, but she was mostly shielded from the view of everyone.

Think, Olive. Think. She did not have a lot of time. She couldn't stand on the toilet and try to send a signal through the small window. George would hear her scrambling, and could poke his head in at any time. She pulled up her skirt, wriggled her underpants down, and sat on the toilet seat.

Beside it was a small cart with specimen bottles and labels and a Sharpie, so that you could write your name on the plastic.

Olive grabbed the pen and unspooled the toilet paper.

There are six of us and one of him, she wrote across three of the squares. *We need a plan. Thoughts?*

She knew that whatever the others plotted, she would be at a disadvantage. But she also knew to look for a signal. And to act.

Olive pulled up her panties and flushed the toilet. She rolled the paper back up, with the writing carefully tucked in a way that it couldn't be seen until it was unspooled. She washed her hands and opened the door and smiled at George. "There," she said. "That wasn't so bad, was it?"

WHEN OLIVE CAME OUT OF the bathroom, Joy stood up, letting herself be manhandled by that crazy asshole before she stepped inside. While she peed, she looked at the pad in her underpants, which was soaked but not soaked through, and this was a good thing since she didn't have a replacement. Then she pulled the roll of toilet paper to ball it up in her hand.

Except, she didn't.

She read.

Then she took the Sharpie, and began to write.

JANINE HAD HOPED THAT THE shooter would cut her a little slack. Forgo the pat down, or let her close the door. After all, they both believed in the same sanctity of life—even if he had a pretty bad track record with that at present. Instead, he treated her just like one of the other women.

Janine unraveled the toilet paper roll. She looked at the notes in different handwriting. Olive's first statement, and then Joy: *What if we jump him?*

She could do one of two things right now. She could take all the toilet tissue and flush it, sabotaging the work of the other women.

Or she could admit that through a strange twist of fate, her goals had aligned with theirs.

Right now, Janine was not holding a sign with a picture of an unborn child on it. She was not praying for the mothers who were walking past her. She was the person being prayed for. On any given day, she could have told you that, inside this clinic, lives were at risk. Today, the life was hers.

She reached for the Sharpie. *Trip him*, she wrote. *And go for the gun.*

WHEN WREN WAS GROWING UP, she thought there was nothing worse than having a mother who had actually *chosen* a life that did not include her. Her mom still hit the high-water marks—birthday, Christmas—with a card and a present, usually something from Paris that was so not Wren's style, she buried it in the back of her closet, not having the heart to throw it away. Her mom had hinted that, now that Wren was older, maybe she wanted to come spend summers in France. Wren would have rather vacationed on the front lines of a war zone. She may have owed her mother for the nine months she carried her in her womb, but that was it.

On the other hand, if there was some divine power, He or She had made up for the loss of her mother by giving her a father who was there for her 200 percent. Unlike her friends, who were always complaining that their parents didn't *get* them, Wren actually liked being in her dad's company. He was the first person she texted when she got an A on a test she had been sure she failed. He told her, honestly, if a pair of jeans made her hips look wide. He taught her about the night sky.

Her dad was also the person you wanted next to you in an emergency. When she went to Lola Harding's birthday party and a few idiots were getting drunk and a kid accidentally sliced his hand open cutting limes and everyone was freaking out, Wren had called her father, who called 911 and came over and took control and didn't go ballistic and call everyone's parents, but somehow managed to put the fear of God into the guy who'd brought the Jägermeister. When Wren was ten and had, on a dare, tried to climb a rose trellis and wound up in the hospital with a broken leg, her father had sat beside her trying to comfort her when the painkillers didn't. *Pant sweat*, he had said, and she'd been distracted enough to stop crying and obsessing over the fact that she could see her bone through the break in her skin. Her dad had tugged at the leg of her sweatpants. *There are just some compound words that you should never reverse.*

Finger chicken, she had said.

Litter kitty.

Pot coffee.

All things considered, she wished he was here. She had liked being able to text him—it was the next best thing. But since she and Olive had been dragged from their hiding place, that wasn't a possibility.

Except now. The second it was her turn to go to the bathroom, she was going to fire up her phone again and tell her dad everything that was going on.

From where she was sitting on the couch, Wren narrowed her eyes and stared at George. He had been on the phone with her dad, but now the phone was on the receptionist's counter. He held the gun in his right hand. He was sweating.

He had ghost eyes, so light, with the pupils just pinpricks. Almost like you could see right through him.

And if the doctor and Izzy were right, he had a daughter. That may even have been the reason he'd come here. Wren knew better than anyone that you couldn't choose your parents, but she wondered what it would be like if she had grown up with this man, instead of her father.

She wondered what his daughter was thinking right now.

Suddenly he was waving the gun in her face. "What are you waiting for?" he said. "Get moving."

She stood and held up her bound hands. "I can't . . . *you know* . . . like this."

For an awful second she thought he was going to tell her to deal with it. Then he scrabbled at her wrists, feeling for the edge of the tape, and unraveled her. Wren felt blood flood to her hands; she shook them at her sides. "Do not," he said, "do anything stupid."

Wren nodded, but she had a feeling that what she thought was stupid and what he thought was stupid were two very different things.

The door was left open. She sat down on the toilet lid and fished in her sock for her phone. Olive had managed to turn it off, so that it wouldn't keep buzzing. When she powered it up again, though, it would make a noise. Wren reached toward the sink and began to run the water to mask it.

She held her breath, muffling the phone against her shirt. She waited for a signal, so that she could text her father.

No service.

That made no sense; she'd had a full signal when she was in the closet. And her phone had buzzed when she was taken into the waiting room, before Olive had turned it off for her. Wren fiddled with the cellular settings. She tried to find a Wi-Fi network.

Nothing.

When her aunt had been shot, Wren had turned into a statue. She hadn't been able to move. She probably would have stood there, just waiting to be killed, if Olive hadn't dragged her into the closet. Her heart had been pounding so hard she thought it would break the cage of her ribs. She had never been so scared in her life, and every time she closed her eyes, she saw that bright banner of blood unfurl on Aunt Bex's chest. But being able to text her father—knowing her father was right on the other side of that brick wall—well, it had tethered Wren to sanity.

Now that was gone.

What if she never got out of this clinic? She was fifteen years old.

She hadn't had sex. She hadn't gone to prom. She hadn't smoked a joint or pulled an all-nighter.

Her dad was always telling her to be careful—that he saw far too many mangled car wrecks or drunk drivers who were teens who thought they were invincible. Maybe it sounded ridiculous, given the fact that she had been jerked out of the closet and had a gun pointed at her face, but for the first time Wren now really understood she could die.

A fresh wave of terror settled over her, and she started to shake.

She grabbed one hand with the other. She closed her eyes tight, and tried to imagine every detail of her father's face.

If her dad were here, he'd tell her to take a deep breath. He'd say, *Make sure you're safe. Make sure everyone else is, too.*

He'd say . . .

He'd say . . .

Bed water, she thought.

She let a tiny smile slip out from inside that knot of fear.

Way high.

Paper toilet.

For the first time since she had been in the bathroom, she looked at the toilet paper roll. She saw the message thread, and began to read.

"What the hell is taking you so long?" George said, and he yanked open the door. Wren did the first thing she could think of. She dropped her phone in the toilet, along with the paper in her fist. "I'm al-almost done," she stammered.

His face receded and Wren doubled over. She stood up and fished for her phone in the bowl, but it was ruined. Then again, it hadn't been working anyway and it was better to have it hidden than on her—she knew from watching the others that they had received pat downs from George when they left the bathroom, too. Holding the device by a dripping corner, she lifted the toilet tank cover and hid the phone inside.

She looked down at the soggy mess of toilet paper in the bowl. Wren took the marker on the side table and wrote on the roll, succinctly, what Izzy would need to know. She and the doctor were the only ones who hadn't gone to the bathroom yet, and the doctor probably couldn't even get to his feet. *We can take him down. Trip him. Go for the gun. Everyone's in.*

She rolled the words back up, flushed the toilet, rinsed her hands, and stepped outside.

George was waiting, tapping the gun against his thigh. She felt lost without her phone. *Untethered.*

She could remember asking her dad once what happened during a spacewalk if an astronaut became untethered from the spacecraft. He explained that they wore backpacks they could fire up, with jets to propel them back to the vehicle. They were called Simplifed Aid for EVA Rescue. SAFER.

She took a step toward the couch, feeling the shooter's eyes on her.

"Did you forget something?" he said.

Wren drew in her breath and shook her head. Had he seen her holding the phone?

George grabbed her by the wrist and pulled her toward the others. "Tape her up," he ordered Izzy.

"I'm sorry," Izzy said. The tape roll went around twice, three times. Then Izzy tried to tear it. When that didn't work, she leaned forward, her hair falling over her face and Wren's wrists as she bit the edge of the tape with her teeth.

Izzy looked up, catching Wren's eye for a moment. Then she turned to George. "I believe it's my turn?"

Wren stumbled back to the couch, gingerly sitting down beside Olive again. She gently settled her bound hands in her lap and looked down at them. Clasped between her palms was a scalpel Izzy had managed to pass to her, with a tiny, lethal blade.

* * *

DISHONORABLY DISCHARGED. THE WORDS CHASED themselves around George's mind. What if Lil had heard that? She knew that he had been in the army—and she also knew that he didn't like to talk about his time there. But shit, neither did anyone who had seen combat.

He had been in Bosnia, stationed in a hellhole where he was supposed to be keeping the peace but even he knew, early days as it was, that there was no way they could win this one. It had been the end of a long day at the end of a long week and he was drinking at a bar. He'd gone outside to take a piss and had heard a woman's scream.

He should have ignored it. But he thought about his wife, back home, and instead rounded the corner to find two men holding down a Muslim woman. No, make that a girl, a Muslim girl. She couldn't have been more than twelve. He assumed, given the ethnic conflict, that the men were Serbs, but they all looked alike. One held his hand over her mouth and pinned her shoulders, the other was vigorously pumping between her thighs.

George pulled him off, sending him sprawling into the dust. His friend came after George, who landed a solid punch. The man staggered and fell, his head smacking against the curb. George was dimly aware that the girl had scrambled off. The rapist got to his feet and came toward George, who leveled his weapon. By then, the commotion had drawn a crowd. What they saw was an American soldier holding a Croatian civilian at gunpoint, while a second civilian bled to death at his feet.

He was court-martialed. He explained that he had interrupted a rape, but the girl's family insisted that she had not been sexually assaulted. And why would they admit she had, since it would make her forever unmarriageable in their culture? Instead, there was testimony from the bystanders who had seen George pointing a gun wildly at a man who had fallen to the ground with his hands up.

George was convicted of manslaughter, and dishonorably discharged, goddammit, for doing the right thing.

When he came home he had a wife who didn't understand his anger and a baby who screamed all the time, and he couldn't get any sleep. He got fired from his job and maybe drank more than he should. One night, when he fell asleep on the couch, Greta had leaned over him to wake him up but he had been dreaming and saw instead that girl, the Muslim girl, and he grabbed her by the throat with all his frustration. *Why didn't you tell them the truth? I* saved *you. Why didn't you save me?*

It wasn't until Greta started to go slack beneath him that he realized where he was, who he was. When he let go of his wife, she ran to the bedroom and locked the door. He begged for forgiveness. He promised he'd go to counseling. She didn't answer, just stayed away from him, wearing a necklace of bruises. When he called her name the next day, she jumped in fear. She did everything she could to avoid him. George took to sleeping in the baby's room, because he knew Greta wouldn't leave without Lil.

Until one night she did.

He glanced up at the television screen. It was dark now, turned off at his command—but he could still hear the words of the reporter ringing in his head. *Dishonorable discharge is reserved for the military's most reprehensible conduct*, the man had said. *Desertion, sexual assault, murder . . . egregious violence.*

Egregious violence.

George felt sweat trickle down his back. He pulled at his collar. Egregious fucking violence. There was nothing egregious about it. They didn't know what went down in Bosnia. They didn't realize it hadn't been Greta's face he saw that night, when he tried to strangle her. They didn't understand what had happened to Lil that had led him here.

He could not hear anything except that reporter's voice, ringing in his ears. "Egregious violence," George muttered. "*This* is egregious violence," he said, and he slammed his boot into the injured leg of the doctor.

When George's hearing returned, it was with the man's scream.

THE GUNMAN WAS OUT OF control. He was muttering to himself; he had stomped on Dr. Ward's leg. Izzy bent down over the poor man, soothing, trying to do something—anything—to stave off the pain. Dr. Ward was shivering, sweating, in shock. The false comfort of the status quo had been shredded, and what would happen next was anyone's guess.

She glanced over at Wren. The girl had her eyes screwed shut as if she was trying to will this into a nightmare, instead of reality. She must still be holding the scalpel. Izzy had known she had to get rid of it as soon as she saw the shooter doing full body checks before and after each woman went to the bathroom.

She blotted Dr. Ward's forehead with a strip of gauze. On the pretense of ministering to him, she said loudly, "Ssh, it's all right. It will help if you focus on something else right now . . ." Izzy looked up, as the other women turned at the sound of her voice. She made eye contact with each of them in turn. "Think of a nice beach maybe. Down on the Gulf Coast. I don't get down there very much myself, but my boyfriend and I, we keep talking about taking a *trip*."

If the shooter noticed that she stressed that last word, he didn't show it.

There was a charged moment of silence. They had all read the missive in the bathroom, but there hadn't been an explicit plan of action.

Suddenly Joy grabbed her belly and jackknifed forward. "Ow," she moaned. "It hurts. It hurts like *crazy*." She began rocking back and forth.

"Shut her up," the shooter commanded. He turned to Izzy. "Do something."

Izzy moved toward Joy. "Do you still feel the pain?"

"Yes," Joy said, squeezing Izzy's hand three times. A sign. "Right *now*." She screamed.

"Shut her up," George said. "Shut her up or I'll . . ."

He stepped forward, either to threaten or to coldcock her, but as he did Janine stretched out a foot.

Just like that, George Goddard went sprawling.

Now NOW NOW NOW NOW.

Wren watched him trip, and when he did, he dropped the gun.

When she was very little, she used to imagine what it would feel like to fly. On windy days she would unzip her raincoat and spread her arms and leap into the air and know, just *know*, that she was airborne for an extra heartbeat.

Now, she flew.

She leaped off of the couch and dove for the gun at the same time George did. Her hands were still tied so she went down like a stone and wriggled on her elbows. It was a tenth of a second and, at the same time, an eternity. She felt her fingertips graze the barrel of the gun and he knocked it away from her.

Wren raised her bound hands and slammed them down as hard as she could into his outstretched palm.

He howled, and the scalpel stuck deep in his flesh, sliding from between Wren's palms.

"You *bitch*," he cried. He yanked the blade from his hand and then grabbed the gun.

Wren couldn't get up. Her hands were still tied—the angle of the scalpel, when she had held it, had made it impossible to cut the tape, although she had tried like hell. She scooted backward on the carpet, slipping in the fresh blood from Dr. Ward's injury. In that moment all she could see was the shooter's red, red eyes and the twist of his face and his thumb pulling back the trigger. She wondered if it would hurt, when she returned to stardust.

WHAT WE KNOW, OLIVE COULD tell you, is not what we think we know.

One year, she had run a psychological study in which she told her collegiate subjects that scientists had discovered a chemical that had antiaging benefits. When told that the scientists didn't really know how that worked yet, the students reported not understanding how the antiaging effects occurred. But when told that scientists had figured out the methodology, the students reported an understanding of the process—even without being given the details.

It was almost as if knowledge was contagious. People constantly claimed to "know" something when they didn't have the facts and tools to uphold their claims.

Maybe for this reason, she'd thought that at this moment she would be reliving the high-water marks of her life, the memories of love and joy and justice. She thought she would see her first kiss with a girl made of moonlight in a lake at summer camp; or her last kiss with Peg, when each put a bookmark in her reading material and curled toward the other like parentheses before they turned out the light.

Olive thought, and therein lay the mistake.

When it came down to it, at the end, you did not think. You felt.

What did she feel?

That you will never cease to underestimate yourself.

That love is fleeting.

That life is a miracle.

That the reason she had come to this clinic, on this day, at this hour, was *this*.

Acting purely on instinct, Olive Lemay threw herself in front of the bullet.

Two p.m.

THE SUNLIGHT WAS OVERWHELMING.

Izzy watched it glint off the silver bars of the wheelchair. She was temporarily blinded and then forced herself to put one foot in front of the other, to push the wheels over the threshold of the clinic door.

It wasn't just the sunlight, though—it was cameras and shouted questions as someone emerged from the belly of the beast. Izzy froze, unsure of where to go and what to do.

She was supposed to wheel Bex outside, and then walk back through those doors. But it would be so easy to save herself.

She could lean forward, low and dynamic, and run. She could bring Bex to the ambulance and leap inside, and really, what could the shooter do?

Her vision cleared as a man stepped forward. In silhouette he was tall and broad-shouldered, and for just a moment she thought: *Parker*. But Izzy was not the one being rescued now, and anyway, in her fairy tale, she was still afraid that any moment the prince might realize she was just a poor villager, posing as a princess.

The hostage negotiator held out a hand and beckoned her forward.

She felt like she was suspended between what could be, and what was. Just like always.

It was that way for all people who grew up poor, she imagined. Izzy had vivid memories of her birthday being celebrated two weeks after the fact, because that's when they could afford a box of cake mix. Of always adding water to the milk to stretch it. Of being giddy when the food stamps came in and you could go to the grocery store; and being ashamed when you had to actually use them to pay.

When Izzy was in first grade, her family couldn't afford school supplies, so she pretended that she had forgotten them at home. Then one day, when she opened her little flip-top desk, there was a brand-new box of Crayola crayons. They were still pointy at the top and smelled like wax and had a *sharpener* on the back. Izzy had no idea if it was her teacher who'd given them to her, and she never found out. But she did realize, then, that her family was different from other families. Most kids didn't go to Sam's Club for lunch when you weren't even a member, because you could make the rounds for free samples. Ketchup sandwiches, with packets stolen from McDonald's, weren't normal. Her mother rummaged through her brothers' backpacks and threw out the flyers for the Scholastic Book Club, for field trips, for dances, for anything that was an additional expense. When they ate dinner, Izzy would pretend to be full because she knew her mother wouldn't have any food if she didn't leave some behind on her plate.

As she worked through high school, she was determined to have a different life. She couldn't afford an SAT prep course, so she asked another student for the syllabus, and then got books through interlibrary loans and taught herself. She applied for more than a hundred scholarships that she found online using the library's public Internet. She didn't get them all. But she got enough for a free education.

She went to nursing school on student loans and she scrimped and saved.

And then she met Parker—who had taken her on her first vacation.

Who couldn't believe that she'd never gone to a doctor growing up—only the school nurse, who didn't require insurance.

Who had found her adding water to the shampoo so it lasted longer.

Who had proposed, in spite of all this.

If she had told Parker about the pregnancy, he would have been thrilled. He would have used it as leverage, to make her say *yes*, instead of *I need more time*.

But then she would never stand on her own two feet financially. Or pay off her own nursing school loans. Or buy a house, just because she had the credit to do it. And she could not get him to understand why that was so important.

The man who was beckoning to her was waving his arms, trying to get her to start moving again. If she ran, now, she could save herself.

Izzy felt Bex reach for her hand. She could imagine the effort and pain that cost the woman, and she gently laced her fingers with Bex's and squeezed. She leaned down. "You're going to be fine," she said. She drew a deep breath, and took another long step forward.

Once, when her brothers had been fighting over who got more spaghetti for dinner, her mother had said, *You don't look at another person's plate to see if they have more than you. You look to see if they have enough*.

Izzy thought of Dr. Ward, bleeding on the floor, still inside. She let go of the handles of the wheelchair, turned, and ran back to the gaping mouth of the clinic door.

BEX COULD TELL THE MOMENT Hugh realized that she was the woman in the wheelchair. He took a step forward, and as if that had triggered it, Izzy turned and ran.

Bex couldn't speak. Her eyes filled with tears as Hugh started to run toward her, but before he could reach her side, the paramedics were there, hoisting Bex out of the wheelchair and onto a gurney and loading her into an ambulance. She twisted, trying to see Hugh, trying to reach her hand toward him. But she was surrounded by people who were prodding and poking and shouting at each other.

What if she got taken off to the hospital before she could talk to Hugh?

"What's your name, ma'am?" an EMT asked.

"Bex."

"Bex, we're going to take care of you."

She grabbed at his arm. "Need to . . . tell . . ."

"We'll contact your family as soon as we get you settled at the hospital—"

Bex shook her head. The double doors started to close, and then suddenly she heard Hugh's voice. "I have to speak to her," he said.

"And I have to get her to an OR."

She, who knew his face better than perhaps anyone, saw the struggle etched in his features—the desire to connect with her warring with the determination to get her treated.

"Hugh," she managed. "Need . . ."

He turned, sending her a warning in his gaze. "You need to tell me something, ma'am?" Hugh glanced at the EMT. "I'll need a moment of privacy," he said, dismissing the paramedic, and then they were alone.

She swallowed, emotion damming all the words she had thought she might never get a chance to say to Hugh. "Bex," he moaned, leaning closer, trying to figure out how to embrace her and settling for folding his hands around her own. "Are you all right?"

"Been . . . better," she said. "Wren . . ."

"Is in there," Hugh finished. "I know. Is she . . ."

"Alive. Hiding."

A small sob escaped, and his head bent until his hair brushed her cheek. Bex looked at him and saw the shadow of Hugh as a boy: jack-knifed with grief when his dog died, frustrated by a calculus problem set, furious when he didn't make the varsity football team. She wanted to reach out and pull him into her arms like she used to; to tell him that tomorrow would be easier, but she couldn't. This time, she was the cause of his pain.

"Nobody knows," he said, his voice a whisper. "Nobody *can* know. Do you understand that? If it gets out that my daughter is inside, I'm off the case. I have no control over the outcome here. Period." He stared down at her, his eyes dark with pain. "Why, Bex? Why did you bring her here?"

She thought of Wren—the way she smiled and raised her right eyebrow, like she had a secret; how she painted her nails in different colors because she could never pick just one; the time she reprogrammed all the SiriusXM radio channels in Bex's car after decreeing that her aunt needed to move past the eighties. "She asked."

Hugh's hands bit into her skin. She knew he was fighting to maintain control. "Wren needed . . . she had to have . . ." He couldn't force the words from his throat.

"No!" Bex said. "Birth control. She . . . didn't want you . . . to know."

He closed his eyes.

Were some betrayals kinder than others? Bex searched his face, waiting for a shimmer of forgiveness.

Before she could find it, however, the EMT had reappeared. "Lieutenant?" he said. "Are you finished?"

Were they?

Bex willed him to speak. To absolve her of blame.

Instead, he let go of her hands, jumped out of the ambulance, and shut the doors.

* * *

IT FELT LIKE IT TOOK a hundred years for Izzy to run the last five steps back to the clinic door. She forced herself to stare at the black seam that separated freedom from captivity, until a hand reached out and grabbed her by her braid, yanking her inside again.

George let go of her long enough to close and lock the door, pile the furniture back against it. "Smart gal," George said. "If you hadn't come back here, well, who knows how angry I might have got."

Izzy's head swam. She could still smell the pavement, baking in the afternoon heat. She could see the necks of all the cameras trained on her as she walked away from the clinic door. She could hear Bex's shallow breathing as they went over each crack in the sidewalk.

What kind of idiot tastes freedom and spits it out?

She heard a groan behind her and turned to find Dr. Ward's wound trickling blood. Izzy met George's gaze. "Can I . . . ?"

He nodded, and she got to her knees beside Dr. Ward, unwrapping the soaked tourniquet to replace it with a fresh one. As soon as the pressure was relaxed, blood poured from the wound. Izzy wondered how long she had before she needed to beg the shooter to let Dr. Ward get real medical attention. She had a feeling it was different from Bex; that George would see the doctor's death not as regrettable collateral damage, but as revenge.

With quick efficiency she began to tighten the makeshift bandage again by using the Sharpie as a winding key. She secured it into place with tape. Dr. Ward groaned when she moved his limb, and she tried to distract him with banter. "You know, when I was a kid and my brother broke his arm, I just splinted it and told him to use the other one."

"Where I grew up we were so poor we didn't even have wood to *make* a splint," Dr. Ward said.

Izzy smiled a little. "Pretty sure I had the flu for a whole year, because we couldn't afford a trip to the pediatrician."

"We only went to the dentist if a cavity was so bad it made you throw up."

"And braces," Izzy said. "They might as well have been tooth jewelry."

Dr. Ward offered a wobbly smile. "Girl, I know what you're doing and you can't use my own medicine on me."

"I have no idea what you're talking about."

"You're trying to distract me from what's really happening down there with my leg."

"You know what's happening down there," Izzy said.

"Yeah," he sighed. "If it's much longer, I could lose it."

Izzy tried not to think about that. More important, she had to make Dr. Ward not think about that. "You talk like you're my only patient." She jerked her chin toward Janine, still unconscious from the blow George had given her with the butt of the gun. "Any change?"

"No," Dr. Ward said, sobering. "I've been watching."

Izzy made a small noise in the back of her throat. "Well," she said, "I wouldn't mind if she stays unconscious."

Dr. Ward frowned. "Do you know I only once refused to perform an abortion?"

"Was it for a pro-life protester?" Izzy asked.

He hesitated, then shook his head. "It was a racist. A woman came in and saw me and said she preferred a white doctor. Problem was, I was the only person doing procedures that day, and she couldn't wait any longer to have it done."

Izzy sat back on her heels. "What happened?"

"I have no idea. Even after she decided my skin color mattered less than her getting that abortion, I said no. I was self-aware enough to know that I had to treat myself like an impaired physician. I was intoxicated with anger, the same way I would have been if I had swigged a fifth of gin. I couldn't touch her any more than I would have touched a patient if I were drunk. What if she was uncomfortable during the procedure? She might think I was intentionally trying to cause her pain because of what she'd said. And what if there was a complication, and it reinforced her beliefs that I was less than qualified because of my skin color?" He shook his head. "Like Dr. King said: *It may be true that the law cannot make a man love me, but it can keep him from lynching me, and I think that's pretty important.*"

"I would think that when it comes to abortion, race is the last thing on anyone's mind."

Dr. Ward glanced up, surprised. "Why, Miss Izzy. When it comes to abortion, race is first and foremost in everyone's minds." He nodded toward Janine. "She's the anomaly, you know. The average anti-choice protester is"—he lowered his voice—"a middle-aged Caucasian male."

Izzy looked at George Goddard. He was polishing the shaft of his gun with the hem of his shirt. They'd heard him talk about his daughter; they knew he had some personal connection to this clinic. But surely that wasn't true of every protester who fit that profile. "Why?"

"Because they're trying to make America white again."

"But more women of color have abortions than white women—"

"Doesn't matter. They don't care about the fertility of Black women. They're using them, the way Black women have been used for centuries, to further a white agenda. You've seen those Black genocide billboards?"

Izzy had. They sprouted on the highways in the Deep South. They showed a picture of a beautiful little Black baby and a slogan: THE MOST DANGEROUS PLACE FOR AN AFRICAN AMERICAN IS IN THE WOMB. A picture of President Obama and the words EVERY 21 MINUTES OUR NEXT POTENTIAL LEADER IS ABORTED.

"White people are the ones who put those up. Race isn't exactly a walk in the park in this country," Dr. Ward said. "If the antis frame their opposition to choice as antiracism, it looks like they're trying to help Black women. But a law that keeps Black women from having abortions also keeps white women from having them. The only person who can give birth to a white baby is a white woman. Those same white women are working outside the home and bucking tra-ditional family values, and by 2050 whites will be in the minority. When you look at it like that, it's a little clearer who those billboards are really benefiting." He looked at Izzy's expression and smiled a little. "You think I've lost too much blood."

"No. No. I just never thought of that before."

Dr. Ward leaned back against the frame of the couch. "It's *all* I think about." He glanced at her tourniquet. "You are one damn fine nurse."

"Stop flirting now."

"You're a little skinny and pale for my tastes," he joked.

"Well, too bad. You're a unicorn—a smart guy who isn't threat-ened by women. I think you might be the biggest feminist I've ever met."

"You bet I am. I love women. All women."

Izzy cut a glance toward Janine, still passed out on the floor. "All women?"

"All women," Dr. Ward repeated. "And you should, too." He turned to Izzy. "Like it or not, you're in this fight together."

WREN HADN'T COME HERE FOR an abortion. The numbing relief Hugh felt knowing that was eclipsed by the truth that she was still being held hostage, because she wanted to get birth control.

But she hadn't wanted him to know.

Hugh would have taken her, if she had just asked.

Why hadn't she asked? Why had she gone to Bex? Why hadn't his sister confided in him?

He knew Bex had been looking for mercy, for Hugh to say, *This wasn't your fault.* But he hadn't been able to do it. Because if it wasn't Bex's fault that Wren was in there, then Hugh had to admit that it might be his own.

He wouldn't have flown off the handle if Wren had come to

him. It wasn't in his DNA. In fact he was so good at plastering his emotions with a thick layer of calm that it took someone who had known him all his life to know there were cracks beneath the surface. When Annabelle left Hugh, she had slapped him to see if she could get a rise out of him. Hugh had told Bex, afterward. *She said no one could blame her for leaving me for someone with human emotions.* He had rested his elbows on his knees and buried the heels of his hands in his eyes. *The thing is, if you saw the stuff I do every day on the job, you'd do anything to not feel.*

Bex. How the hell could Bex have brought his daughter here?

He knew the answer to that. What his sister had envisioned was a free clinic, a half-hour appointment, and a prescription for the Pill. The only person who would get hurt in this scenario was Hugh, for not being in the know. Bex hadn't thought about protesters or gunmen. She wouldn't have, swimming in the back of her consciousness, statistics of violence at other women's health clinics. Only someone who had been doing what Hugh had been doing for years would assume the worst could happen.

The thing was, the worst hadn't happened . . . yet. Bex was safe, now. And Wren *would* be, no matter what it cost him.

Beyond the command tent, the reporters had formed a line, each faced by a cameraman, like they were arranged for some courtly dance. Hugh heard the closest reporter spout absolute and total bullshit to fill up time on a live feed. "The question, of course," the reporter said, "is where did the gun come from? Who sold him the gun? It's worth remembering that a dishonorable discharge may be a military court ruling, but it's still a felony, and for Goddard to have a gun would be illegal—"

Hugh closed his eyes. He pushed away the voices of the reporters and thoughts of Bex and Wren hiding from a lunatic with a gun. *No distractions,* he told himself. *No distractions.*

He dialed his phone, and George picked up on the third ring. "That was great," Hugh said. "You released someone who really needed help. I knew you and I could work together." Hugh wiped his forehead. It was hotter than Hell.

"I'm not working with you," George said. "You're a fucking cop."

Hugh closed his eyes. It was going to be considerably worse when the SWAT team arrived, which could be any minute now. Which meant he had limited time to woo his hostage taker.

"I'm a negotiator," Hugh corrected. "You're the only reason I'm here."

He forced himself to block out the people around him—emergency personnel and media. If he was going to do his job, he had to create a space that was just him, George, and no one else. It was a seduction, and Hugh would say anything he had to in order to reach the endgame.

"Look," Hugh said, "a lot of these guys out here, they make assumptions. Not me. I know you're smart. The fact that you let that woman get medical attention proves it."

That woman.

As if Bex hadn't basically raised him after his father died and his mother started drinking.

He hesitated, waiting to see if George would take the bait. "Are there others inside who need help?"

"I'm not letting anyone else go."

"This could be a win-win, George. If there are more people in there with you who are hurt, and you send them outside, then you don't have to worry about them . . . and it makes you look compassionate to everyone out here."

A young detective tapped Hugh on the shoulder. She held up a cellphone. "His pastor," the detective whispered.

Hugh nodded and held up a finger for her to wait a moment. "George, is anyone else in there hurt?"

"Why should I tell you?"

"Because you opened the door, and I kept my promise. I waited. I didn't rush the clinic and storm in. You can trust me."

"To do what? Screw me over in the end?"

The detective scribbled on a piece of paper and waved it beneath Hugh's nose. *BORN AGAIN.*

"No. To do unto others as you would have them do unto you," Hugh said.

"You a Christian?"

"Yes," Hugh said, although he wasn't a religious man at all. "Are you?"

He could hear George's breathing. "Not anymore."

Hugh looked down at the piece of paper that the detective had handed him. "God will forgive you for what you've done, George."

"What makes you think I'll forgive *Him*?" George said, and the line went dead.

Hugh grabbed the cellphone from the detective. "Hugh McElroy," he said. "Who am I speaking to?"

"Pastor Mike Kearns," a man replied. "I lead the Eternal Life Church up in Denmark."

"Thanks for calling, Pastor. I understand you know George Goddard?"

"George used to be our church handyman. Landscaping, carpentry, you name it. I don't think there's anything he can't fix."

"When did he stop working for you?"

"Six months ago, give or take?" Shame crept into the pastor's voice. "We had some storm damage and the budget got tight. Now, we have volunteers doing what George used to do."

"Have you been watching the news today, Pastor?"

"No, I've been officiating at a funeral—"

"George Goddard shot up the Center in Jackson—the abortion clinic—and is currently holding several hostages."

"What? No. No, that isn't the man I know."

Hugh didn't have time for this man's existential crisis. "Did he exhibit any violent tendencies when you employed him?"

"George? Never."

"Was he pro-life?"

"Well," the pastor said, "our congregation believes in protecting the rights of the unborn—"

"Enough to kill people to get your message heard?"

The pastor drew in his breath. "I don't appreciate being tried for my faith, Officer—"

"Lieutenant. Lieutenant McElroy. And I don't appreciate people who waltz into a clinic and start killing innocent bystanders."

"*Killing?* My God."

"You can have Him," Hugh said under his breath. "Listen, Pastor, I don't mean to attack you. But there are people in that clinic who might die. Anything you can tell me about George Goddard that could help me understand him and his motivations would be greatly appreciated."

"I met him a little over fifteen years ago," Pastor Mike said. "He showed up one night in the church, carrying his baby. She was sick, feverish. His wife was gone."

"Dead?"

"No. She left him, but he never would say why."

Hugh's mind began to turn, mixing possibilities. Had she run because her husband was violent? Had he stolen the baby and left her? Was she still alive somewhere?

"Do you know her name?" Hugh said, pulling the cap of a pen off with his teeth.

"No," the pastor said. "He wouldn't even speak of her. It was always just George and Lil."

"Lil?"

"His daughter. Good girl. Used to sing in the church choir."

All Hugh had known about George's daughter was that she had come here for an abortion. But now, he also knew her name. Hugh held his hand over the speaker of the phone. "Lil Goddard," he barked at the young detective. "Find her."

* * *

HUGH KNEW ALL THE WAYS to find someone who didn't want to be found. You looked at bank records and credit card receipts and phone records. You followed aliases and money trails. The primary advantage a detective had was that he was pursuing a truth, while the person hiding was living a lie. Truth tends to gleam, like the glint of a penny. Lies, on the other hand, are a series of loops—eventually they will trip you up.

It had been the car radio that tipped him off. He had taken Annabelle's minivan to get the registration renewed and on the way punched at the five preprogrammed radio buttons to find NPR. There was an oldies station, an acoustic station that always made him feel like he'd nod off at the wheel, a classical music channel, and one that played nonstop Disney tunes for Wren. The NPR station, however, had been reprogrammed to a country station.

Hugh had punched through the buttons again. True, he was rarely in this car, but Annabelle hated country music.

He could still remember her lying with her head in his lap when they were dating, telling him that what she hated most about the Deep South was the constant barrage of songs about men with trucks, men with cheating wives, men with cheating wives in trucks.

Hugh had reset the radio channel to NPR, got his wife's car registration, had the oil changed, and even went through the car wash. He didn't think about it again for a week, until he came home early from work. He knew Wren would still be at school, and when he heard the shower running, he grinned and stripped off his clothes, planning to join Annabelle. It wasn't until he reached the bedroom that he heard her belting out "Before He Cheats."

He was still standing at the threshold of the bathroom when the water turned off and Annabelle opened the door, wearing a towel. "Hugh!" she shrieked. "You scared me to death! What are you doing here?"

"Playing hooky," he said.

Annabelle laughed. "Naked?"

"That was a happy accident," he replied.

He put his arms around her and started to kiss her. He tried not to wonder about her sudden interest in country music or whether it was his imagination that she had stiffened at his touch.

When Annabelle left to pick up Wren at school, Hugh pulled on a pair of shorts and sat down at the computer. He logged in to their AT&T account, the family plan that included his phone and Annabelle's. Her call history was password-protected, but he knew her password—Pepper, her childhood dog's name. As the list of numbers scrolled onto the screen, he looked past her mother's number and his work number and others he recognized. His eyes rested on the repeat calls to Brookhaven, Mississippi. The calls were lengthy—an hour at times. There were texts to that number, too.

Hugh wrote it down, put on a T-shirt and sneakers, and jogged five miles back to the police station. His secretary, Paula, glanced at him as he walked into his office, streaming with sweat. "Didn't you just sneak out of here?"

"Can't stay away from you," he joked.

In criminal cases, Hugh could subpoena the phone company to release the name of a cellphone subscriber. He wrestled with the morality of using his power to check up on his wife, and lost. A day later he had a name: Cliff Wargeddon. He ran a DMV check and got the license plate number of a white Ford pickup truck and an address.

He arrived at nine P.M. The house was a small ranch on a cul-de-sac, with carefully tended gardens and little gnome statues and colorful pinwheels catching the wind. The white pickup was in the driveway. There was a doormat that said, THE PEOPLE INSIDE THIS HOME ARE BLESSED. On the stoop, two potted plants dripped with begonias.

When a woman in her seventies opened the front door and came out with a small dog on a leash, Hugh began to wonder if he'd made a mistake. She walked the dog around the block and then went back inside. Hugh was about to abandon his post when the door opened again and a young man walked out, shouting something into the house before he walked to the white pickup truck and got inside.

He was younger than Hugh. Maybe by ten years. Hell, he still lived with his mother. Hugh followed him to a bakery in Jackson. The man went through an employee entrance in the back. He didn't emerge for another six hours, just as dawn was breaking, his arms and pants dusty with flour.

It took two more days of trailing him before Wargeddon parked his white pickup truck down the street from Hugh's house, in the middle of the day, when Wren was at school and Hugh was at work.

It took him a while to work up the courage to follow Wargeddon inside.

The first thing he noticed was that Wargeddon had a tattoo on his right shoulder blade, a scorpion. The second thing he noticed was the music playing softly from the clock radio beside the bed. He looked at Annabelle. "Since when," he said, "do you like Carrie Underwood?"

There had been times since Annabelle left that he wondered what would have happened if he hadn't tracked down proof of her infidelity. Would he ever have known? Would she have tired of Cliff, instead of moving with the boy-man to Paris, where he studied the art of baguettes and she took up smoking and worked on a novel he never even knew she had wanted to write? Would Wren have been better having a flawed mother, rather than no mother at all?

Sometimes, in the broken breath of night, Hugh wondered if it was better to leave some things hidden.

He wondered if George Goddard had gone after his runaway wife.

He wondered if, against all odds, he had yet another thing in common with that man after all.

* * *

JANINE'S HEAD WAS THROBBING. SHE tried to sit up, but winced when she felt the sharp stab of pain in her jaw and temple. "Shh," she heard, a whisper like cotton batting. "Let me help you."

She felt an arm slide beneath her shoulders to elevate her to a sitting position. Slowly, she cracked open one eye, then the other.

She was still in Hell.

The shooter was pacing, muttering to himself. The nurse was re-dressing the bandage on the doctor's thigh. She peeled back the soaked gauze from the wound, and Janine turned away so she wouldn't have to see any more.

Her cheek fell into a cupped hand. Janine found herself staring at Joy.

Suddenly it all came flooding back—what she had said, what had happened. She looked at her wig, lying like roadkill a few feet away. She felt her face flame with embarrassment. "Why would you take care of me?"

"Why wouldn't I?" Joy replied.

They both knew the answer to that.

Janine scrutinized Joy. "You must hate me," she murmured. "All of you. Oh my God."

Joy gingerly touched a spot on Janine's cheekbone. "You're gonna have a hell of a bruise," she said. She hesitated, and then looked Janine in the eye. "So you didn't just say that stuff to get out of here? You're really anti-choice?"

"Pro-life," Janine automatically corrected. In this war, labels meant everything. She had heard so many on the other side take umbrage when they were called pro-abortion. *It's pro-choice*, they always said, as if there was something wrong with being pro-abortion. And wasn't that exactly the point?

Joy stared at her. "So . . . you didn't even *have* to be here."

Janine met her gaze. "Neither did you."

Joy didn't move away from her, but Janine could feel the line between them solidify. "I came to get . . . evidence," she explained. "Audio. Proof of people being forced into . . . you know."

"I wasn't forced," Joy said. "It was necessary."

"That's not how your baby felt."

"My baby felt nothing. It wasn't even a baby."

Janine knew that there wasn't a moral difference between the embryo you used to be and the person you were today. So the unborn were smaller than toddlers—did that mean adults deserved more human rights than children? That men were due more privileges than women?

So the unborn weren't fully mentally aware—did that preclude people with Alzheimer's or cognitive deficits, or those in comas, or those sleeping, from having rights?

So the unborn were hosted in the bodies of their mothers. But who you are is not determined by where you are. You are no less human if you cross state lines or move from your living room to your bathroom. Why would a trip from womb to delivery room—a voyage of less than a foot—change your status from nonhuman to human?

The answer was because the unborn *were* human. And Janine, for the life of her, could not understand how people like Joy—like all the others in this clinic—couldn't see what was so clear.

But somehow, it didn't seem like the time or place to have this fight. Especially with someone who was resting your aching head in her lap, and gently stroking your hair.

Unbidden, the thought came into Janine's mind: *Joy would probably have been a good mother.*

"Would you have tried to stop me?" Joy asked. "If you had been outside?"

"Yes."

"How?"

Again, all the arguments against abortion in which Janine had been tutored floated to the tip of her tongue, but instead, she looked at Joy and spoke from the heart. "You might not have given birth to the next Einstein or Picasso or Gandhi," she said. "But I bet whoever he was, he would have been amazing."

Tears welled in Joy's eyes. "Don't you think I know that?"

"Then . . . there must have been another way. There's always another way."

Joy shook her head. "Do you think I *wanted* this? Do you think anyone wakes up and says, *I think I'll go get an abortion this morning*? This is the last stop. This is the place you go when you run through all the scenarios and you realize that the only people who say there's another way are the ones who aren't standing there with a positive pregnancy test in their hand. I did it. I don't regret it. But that doesn't mean I won't think about it every day of my life."

Janine struggled to sit up, her head pounding. "Doesn't that sort of prove, on some level, that it's questionable?"

"It's completely legal."

"So was slavery," Janine replied. "Just because it's legal doesn't mean it's right."

Their whispers were getting louder. Janine worried that they'd attract the shooter's attention. She wondered if she would die here, today, a martyr for her cause.

"All that legal protection you want for the unborn," Joy said. "Great. Give it to them. But only if you can find a way to not take it away from me."

It made Janine think of King Solomon, suggesting that a baby be split down the middle. Obviously that wasn't a solution. "If you carried the baby to term, yes, maybe you'd have some problems to solve, but it wouldn't threaten your existence. There are plenty of women who can't have children, who would do anything to adopt."

"Really?" Joy said. "Then where the fuck were they when *I* was in foster care?"

* * *

When Joy was eight years old, her prized possession had been a Walkman cassette player she had bought at a church yard sale for two dollars, with a cassette still inside: Steely Dan's *Can't Buy a Thrill*. Joy didn't particularly like Steely Dan, but beggars could not be choosers. Every night she fell asleep to "Reelin' in the Years," because it blocked out the other sounds in her house.

There had been crying. Shouting. Joy would turn up the volume of her Walkman and pretend she was somewhere else. Then, in the morning, her mother would wake her up, sporting a bracelet of bruises on her arm, blisters on her palm. *I'm so clumsy*, she would say. *Fell right off the step stool. Put my hand down on the stove when it was still hot.*

Joy had never known her daddy, but there had been a parade of men in the apartment since she was small. Some stayed for a week, some for years. Some were better than others. Rowan had brought her coloring books and stickers. Leon had a dog, an old coonhound named Foxy, that she used to feed scraps to underneath the table. But Ed had liked to watch Joy when she slept, and more than once she woke in the night to find him sitting on her bed, stroking her hair. And Graves, the man who was with her mama now, was mean as a trapped cat.

One night Joy heard the voices escalating and turned up her Walkman volume only to have it garble and fade and then quit entirely. She opened the little battery pack and saw one of the two double As frothing at the tip. Setting aside the cassette player, she realized the house had gone silent, which was somehow even worse.

Joy slipped out of bed. She crept into the kitchen.

The reason her mama wasn't screaming was that Graves had his hands wrapped around her throat. Her face was flushed, her eyes rolled back in her head.

Joy grabbed a knife out of the kitchen drawer and plunged it into his back.

With a cry Graves whirled around, grabbing for the hilt of the blade, reaching for Joy. She danced away from him, backing out of the kitchen even as her mama collapsed.

Later, Joy would not remember running out of her apartment and banging on the other doors in the hallway. She did not recall Miz Darla opening the door wearing her head scarf and housecoat; how she washed Joy's hands and face with lukewarm water. When the police came to take her away, Joy noticed the small bloody handprints marking every door on the fourth floor.

She was taken to a foster home, a couple called the Grays, who looked like they sounded: thin and bled colorless by the four kids they housed. Her mother was allowed to visit her once a week. She showed up only once, and Joy begged to be taken back. Her mother said this wasn't such a good time, and that's how Joy realized that Graves was still living in their apartment.

Her mother never returned.

Joy went to three other foster homes just that first year. The Grays' biological daughter bullied her, and when she finally decked the girl, she was placed somewhere else. She loved her second home, but the couple moved out of state because of the father's job. At the third home, one of the other foster kids—a thirteen-year-old named Devon—made her touch him places she didn't want to, and threatened to say she was stealing from the foster family if she didn't.

By age ten, Joy was a husk of the girl she had been. When she cut her wrists at age eleven, it wasn't because she wanted to kill herself. It was because she wanted to feel *something*, even if that was only pain.

Staring at Janine all these years later, Joy sure as hell *felt*. She felt volcanic anger—for having been born to a parent who couldn't or wouldn't take care of her. For being judged by a stranger who acted holier than thou. How dare she think Joy was selfish, when in fact, she was being selfless—knowing she didn't have the resources to raise a child, giving up the one person who might love her unconditionally?

"I was in foster care for ten years," Joy said. "Trust me. There are not people lining up to adopt the children other parents don't want."

"If you didn't want to get pregnant, then why did you . . ." Janine's voice trailed off.

"Have sex?" Joy filled in.

Because I was lonely.

Because I wanted to.

Because I wanted fifteen minutes where I was the center of someone's world.

But Joe, bless his heart, had neglected to mention that he was already married.

The fourth week he came through Jackson, Joe told her that he and his wife had been having problems for a while, and that she had finally accused him of having an affair. For one beautiful, breathless moment Joy had imagined the rest of her life—one in which Joe admitted that he was in love with Joy, chose to be with her, lived happily ever after. But he had come to say goodbye.

It was good, Joe said. *To get everything out in the open.*

He had looked at her with his beautiful eyes, which no longer reminded Joy of seas she might travel, but of pale glaciers, an ocean of ice.

I should have told you. I would have if . . . His voice trailed off.

If what? Joy thought. What condition had to exist for her to be loved?

We're going to Belize. Some place Mariah found that's off the grid, so that we have nothing to do but talk. I'm taking a two-week leave of absence from the bench.

Mariah, Joy thought. That's her name.

She thanked God for her prescription for Ortho-Novum.

A few weeks later she discovered she was one of the 9 percent of women who still got pregnant while using the Pill.

She had not let herself think about Joe. Telling him about the pregnancy might have been morally right, but to what end? He had made it clear that it was over.

But now, she gave herself a hiccup of space to imagine where he was at this moment, and what he was doing. She wondered if he had heard the news about a shooter at an abortion clinic. She wondered if she would be a casualty, if when the victims' names were read by a reporter, he would grieve.

"You want to know why I had sex?" Joy repeated. "Because I made a mistake."

"Babies are born flawless. They deserve the world." To Joy's surprise, Janine started to cry. She reached for Joy's hands. "Babies are born flawless," she repeated, "and they deserve the world. I'm not talking about . . . what you did today. I'm talking about *you*. I'm sorry that you got stuck in foster care. I'm sorry you didn't feel safe. Just because you didn't get that protection doesn't mean you were born any less than perfect."

Joy had not cried the night she stabbed a man.

She had not cried when she was taken away to a foster home.

She had not cried when she was told her mother had died of a broken neck after an "accidental" fall.

She had not cried when she was sexually abused or when she woke up in the pediatric psych ward, her wrists wrapped with bandages.

She had not cried when she found out she was pregnant.

She had not cried during this morning's procedure. Or afterward.

But now, Joy sobbed.

OLIVE'S EYES WERE TIGHTLY SHUT, even though the closet was dark. She was trying to block out the heated conversation on the other side of the door by picturing Peg, the shape of her face, the smell of her hair when she just came out of the shower, the sound of her name in Peg's mouth, blurred by her southern accent: *Olive. Olive. I love.*

"Are you afraid of dying?" Wren whispered, pulling Olive out of her reverie.

"Isn't everyone?"

"I don't know. I never thought about it until now."

This girl was so young; younger, even, than Olive's students. They had been wedged together on the floor of the utility closet for three hours now.

"I think what I'm afraid of," Olive said, "is leaving everyone else behind."

"Do you have a husband? Kids?"

Olive shook her head, unsure what to say. There were still places in Mississippi where she introduced Peg as her roommate. And she would never have walked down the street in broad daylight holding Peg's hand.

"Not in the cards for me," she murmured.

"Same for my aunt," Wren said. "I never asked her if she was lonely."

"You'll be able to, when you get out of here."

"*If* I get out of here," Wren whispered. "My dad used to actually tell me to make sure I was wearing clean underwear. I mean, what a cliché, right?" She hesitated. "I'm wearing Friday."

"Beg pardon?"

"It's Tuesday. And my day-of-the-week underwear says Friday."

Olive smiled in the dark. "Your secret is safe with me."

"What if I get shot? I mean, it's clean, but it's the wrong day." Wren laughed, a little unhinged. "What if I'm bleeding all over and the paramedics notice that—"

"You won't get shot."

In the dark, Olive could see the fierce shine of the girl's eyes. "You don't know that."

She didn't. *To live* was always a conditional verb.

There was a flurry of footsteps outside the closet door, and the phone rang. Both Olive and Wren held their breath. Olive grabbed Wren's hand.

"I don't wanna talk to you." It was the shooter's voice. It got fainter as he moved away again.

Olive squeezed Wren's fingers. "Peg," she breathed. "That's the name of the woman I love."

"The . . . oh, okay," Wren replied. "That's cool."

Olive smiled to herself. Yes, Peg was cool. Cooler than she was, anyway. She made fun of Olive for not wearing white after Labor Day and for waiting a half hour after eating before she swam. *Live a little*, Peg would say to her, laughing.

Right now that was all Olive wanted to do.

"I just wanted to say her name out loud," Olive added softly.

"At least you got to fall in love," Wren whispered.

"Isn't that why you're here?"

Wren ducked her head. "I don't know. If I do survive, after this, I may *never* have sex."

Olive grinned. "If I survive," she replied, "it's *all* I'm going to do."

GEORGE ANSWERED THE PHONE ON the second ring. "You know," Hugh began, as if George had not hung up on him before, "I used to go to church with my kid. Not every week—I wasn't as good a Christian as I could have been. But always Easter services and Christmas Eve."

George snorted. "That's like putting gravy on Skittles and saying you made Thanksgiving dinner."

"Yeah, I know. It was my fault. I have a hard time sitting still. And I couldn't handle the holier-than-thous. You know, the guys who sit right up front in the pews and act like they've got some special VIP pass to God?"

"It don't work that way," George said.

"Hell, no," Hugh said. "Anyway, it must drive you crazy when you see people acting like that, too. People taking liberties that belong to a greater power."

"I don't follow."

Hugh looked down at the slip of paper one of the detectives had given him. "The Lord brings death and makes alive."

"Samuel 2:6," George said.

"Is that why you came here today? Because you felt people in this clinic didn't have the right to end a life?"

There was silence on the line.

"Vengeance is mine, saith the Lord," Hugh said softly. "Not yours. The Lord's."

"That's not why I came," George said. "It's why *you* came."

"I came to talk to you—"

"You came," George interrupted, "to decide who lives today, and who dies. So, tell me . . . which one of us is playing God?"

GEORGE WAS SIX YEARS OLD when he learned how fine the line was between life and death. It had been one of those beautiful fall days in Mississippi. The colors had peaked, and the trees were a jeweled necklace wrapped around the lake. He was walking through the woods, liking the crunch of the red maple and hickory and bur oak leaves under his sneakers. He was kicking an acorn when he found the bird.

It was not a baby, but some kind of sparrow that had broken its wing. It hopped in small circles on the ground.

He picked it up as if it were made of glass and carried it all the way back to his home. There, he found a cigar box and lined it with Kleenex. For three days, he hid the little bird under his bed, trying to give it water, and bringing it leaves and grubs and anything else he thought might be appetizing.

The bird did not improve. It barely moved. He could hardly see the rise and fall of its breast.

He needed help, so he went to his father.

What he hadn't known, at the time, was that his daddy was in one of his moods, sleeping off last night's excesses.

It's not getting any better, he explained. *Can you fix it?*

You bet. His father lifted the bird with the gentlest of touches. One long finger stroked from the crown of the bird's head to its crooked tail. And then he snapped its neck.

You killed it! George cried.

His father pushed the limp creature back and corrected him. *I put it out of its misery.*

George couldn't stop sobbing; he hadn't stopped, not when he buried the cigar box in his mother's melon patch; not when she made him catfish for dinner; not when he lay down in his pajamas after saying his prayers for the departed soul of the bird. He could hear his parents arguing in the hall.

What kind of father does *that?*

Back then he had wondered if his father truly thought he was doing the right thing by ending the bird's suffering.

Now, George looked around the clinic waiting room at the motley collection of people whose fate he held in his hand.

Violence, from one angle, looked like mercy from another.

TEN YEARS EARLIER, HUGH HAD been one of a dozen cops on the ground twenty-two stories below the Regions Plaza. He squinted up at the roof, where a slight guy in a windbreaker wavered. The chief was talking into a bullhorn. "Step away from the edge," he said. "Don't jump."

It seemed to Hugh that the last thing you wanted to say to someone in this situation was *Don't jump.* It was like you were planting the seed more firmly in his head, when what you really needed to do was distract him.

"Chief," he said, "I've got an idea."

Within minutes, Hugh had climbed a set of stairs from the twenty-second floor to the roof of the building and crept to the edge where the man sat. Except he wasn't a man. He was a boy, really. Eighteen, if that.

Hugh sat down beside the kid, facing the opposite direction, away from the edge. He turned on the digital recorder in his pocket. "Hey," Hugh said.

"They sent you?"

"*They* didn't do anything. I came up here because I wanted to."

The boy glanced at him. "And you just happen to be wearing a cop uniform."

"My name is Hugh. How about you?"

"Alex."

"Is it okay if I call you that?"

The boy shrugged. The wind ruffled his fine hair.

"You okay?"

"Do I *look* okay?"

Hugh thought back to when he was a teenager, and such a smart-ass that once, Bex had made dinner and set an extra plate at the table. *That's for your attitude*, she had said, *and feel free to leave it behind when you're done eating.*

Hugh noticed the familiar colors of an Ole Miss T-shirt peeking from behind the boy's half-zipped windbreaker. "Ole Miss, huh?"

"Yeah. Why?"

"Because if you were a fan of Mississippi State, I might have had to push you off."

A laugh burst out of the kid's throat, surprising him. "If I was a fan of Mississippi State I would have jumped."

Hugh leaned back a little, like he had all the time in the world, and started talking about who was going to replace the quarterback after he graduated. It went on from there, like they were just two guys shooting the breeze.

After a couple of hours had passed, Alex said, "You ever wonder why they call them stories? The floors of a building?"

"No."

"I mean, then why isn't a building called a book?"

Hugh laughed. "You're pretty smart," he said.

"If I had a dime for every time I heard that," Alex said, "I'd have a dime."

"I find that hard to believe. Come on. You're funny, and intelligent, and you clearly root for the right football team. There's got to be someone out there who's worried about you."

"Nope," Alex said, his voice catching. "Not a single one."

"Wrong. There's me."

"You don't know me at all."

"I know I was off the clock an hour ago," Hugh said.

"So go."

"I'd rather stay here. Because your life, it's important," Hugh said. "I can't pretend that I know what's going on with you, Alex. And I won't disrespect you by claiming I do. But I do know that my own shittiest days were usually followed by better ones."

"Well, tomorrow, I'm not gonna be any less gay. It took me fifteen years to figure it out and another two to get the nerve to tell my parents." Alex picked at a thread on his jeans. "They threw me out of the house."

"If you need a place to stay, I can help you figure that out. If you need someone to talk to, we'll get you someone to talk to."

Alex looked into his lap. "I wish my dad was like you," he said softly.

"That's nice of you to say," Hugh replied. "Especially since my dad was the biggest asshole on this planet."

The kid's head snapped up. "What did he do to you?"

"I'm not real comfortable talking about it . . . but I think you'd get it. I'll just say that no kid deserves to be hit all the time. And no parent should be drunk all the time."

"How did you . . . do you still talk to him?"

"Nope," Hugh said. "Once I told people what was going on, they were willing to help me. I took their good advice, and their support." He looked at Alex. "The world turned out to be a whole lot bigger than my dad."

For the first time in over two hours, Hugh reached out his hand. Alex looked down at it, and then grabbed on. Hugh pulled the kid away from the edge, and into his embrace.

It wasn't until a week later that Chief Monroe called Hugh into his office and said he was recommending him as a candidate for hostage negotiation school. "You're a natural," he said. "What you did on the roof with that kid . . ." He gestured at the transcript from Hugh's digital recorder, the conversation between him and Alex. As Hugh started to leave, the chief's voice called him back. "I didn't know about your dad. I'm sorry."

Hugh paused in the doorway. "My dad was the greatest guy. He never touched a drop of alcohol in his life, Chief." He inclined his head. "I was just selling hope."

BETH WATCHED THE STRANGER WHO was supposedly going to be able to keep her out of jail. And based on what had just happened in front of the judge, it didn't look promising.

The woman was short, maybe five-three, African American. She had her hair in dozens of braids that were clipped back from her face. She was wearing a navy suit that didn't flatter her curves. And she was still about five feet away from the bed. Beth didn't know if this was supposed to be for the lawyer's safety, or her own.

The stenographer packed up her machine and left with the security guards. The male lawyer—the one who wasn't on her side—sauntered up to Beth's public defender. "Always a pleasure, Mandy."

"For you, maybe."

He laughed. "See you in court."

The door hadn't closed behind him before Miz DuVille turned to the cop who was stationed in her room, like some kind of creepy-ass stalker. He didn't even leave when the nurses came in to check her *down there*. "Nathan," her lawyer said, "I must talk to my client."

"Nope."

"It'll take two minutes, tops."

"What word didn't you understand?"

"You can stay here. I'll whisper into her ear so you can't hear me."

"N," the cop spelled out, "O."

She took a step closer, refusing to give an inch. "If you do not allow me a private conversation with my client, I will tell everyone at the station that you shit your pants during your fitness test run because you had bad Chinese for lunch."

"You would not—"

She folded her arms.

He frowned. "If you tell anyone that I'm stepping outside to let you do this, you will never get the cooperation of a single person in my department."

"Cross my heart," the lawyer said, and with a swear, the policeman left them alone.

"Nathan's my cousin," the public defender explained, and she grinned.

"Miz DuVille—"

"Mandy." She walked to the side of the bed. "I'm going to need you to tell me everything that led up to this point. But first, you must have some questions."

Some questions? She had dozens. Why were they treating her like a criminal? Was she really going to have to go to prison? What would her dad say, when he found out?

How long did she have to stay in the hospital? What would happen if she tried to leave? Where would she even go?

Instead, she looked at Mandy and said, "Is God going to have mercy on me?"

The lawyer blinked. "I beg your pardon?"

"What the judge said. Do you think God will have mercy on me?"

"I'd be more worried about whether Judge Pinot will," Mandy said. "We call him the Pinot-lizer, because he has a fondness for maximum sentences. He's not exactly a great justice to draw. You're a minor, but you can be tried as an adult." She sighed. "Look, I'm not going to lie. The odds are not in your favor. You ordered pills illegally on the Internet, and medical termination of pregnancy is something that can be done only with a doctor's supervision. But that's just the tip of the iceberg. We live in a state that considers an embryo a person, for purposes of a homicide statute. That means if you intentionally cause the death of a fetus growing inside you, you could be prosecuted in Mississippi for murder."

Beth shrank back against the pillows. She closed her eyes, seeing the white tile of the bathroom floor and the blood smeared across it.

"You may not have known you were doing something wrong, but that's not how the law sees it."

"I don't get it," Beth murmured. "I thought abortion was legal."

The lawyer took out a pad and pen. "Why don't we start at the very beginning?"

Beth nodded, and suddenly she was back at Runyon's, the market where she worked as a checkout girl. It was a tiny grocery, not a chain, the kind that sold slices of homemade pie right at the register. It was an ordinary shift, meaning that the patrons were old white ladies with hairnets on and their young Black companions pushed the cart. *Tessie, how much are those green beans?* Beth would hear, and then, *Well, Miss Ann, I think they are on sale.* The bagger at her station was a Black man named Rule, and when Mr. Runyon came around and pinched Beth on her ass Rule would duck his head so he didn't see. You didn't have to go any further than the market to realize that America had not changed much in hundreds of years.

Every day at Runyon's was the same, which was why, when the stranger entered, it felt like a lightning bolt. He was at least six feet tall, wearing a blazer—even in the infernal heat—with his button-down oxford shirt. He walked right up to her counter, holding a six-pack of beer. "Well, hello," he said, looking at her name tag. "*Beth*."

His accent rose and fell like birds with their wings clipped. "I'm going to need to see your ID," she said.

"I'm flattered. But I could also just tell you my name, if you want to know."

He had a smile that was a torch. "I'm guessing you're not from around here," Beth said.

"U of Wisconsin. We're here for a track meet." He smiled. "You go to the college?"

Beth was seventeen. She wasn't at Ole Miss. She didn't even know if she'd go to college. But she nodded.

"Then maybe you'll come cheer me on." He picked up a wedge of pie wrapped in plastic and frowned. "Buttermilk pie? That sounds terrible."

"Actually, it's sweet."

"Not as sweet as you."

Beth rolled her eyes. "Does that line actually work in Wisconsin?" she said. "I'm still going to need your ID."

He fished in his pocket for his wallet and pulled out a license. Beth scanned the birth date and then the name. "John Smith," she said dryly.

"Blame my parents." He winked at her, took his beer and his pie, and then turned back just before he walked out of the market. "You should come to the meet."

And then he was gone, and with him, all the air in the market.

She knew better. She had been counseled her whole life about how when the devil came to you, he would come in a form you couldn't resist—like a Yankee boy who seemed to glow like a Roman candle when he grinned. The way Beth *knew* it was the devil was that he made her lie to her father, saying she had a double shift, when instead she went to the university and sat in the bleachers and watched him in the 4 x 100 relay. Every time he rounded the corner, it seemed he was running straight to her.

What Beth didn't know—in spite of all the hours she had gone over it in her mind since then—was how, in the moment, it felt like a door had opened on a whole new world—yet, afterward, she was nothing but a cliché. He had spread his fancy blazer on the ground beneath the bleachers like a picnic blanket, he had given her her first beer, and when her head was full of stars, he had laid her down and kissed her. When he peeled off her blouse and touched her, she transformed into someone else—a girl who was beautiful, a girl who wanted more. When he pushed inside her, burning, and then suddenly he stopped, Beth panicked. She had not told him he was her first, but it wasn't the only lie between them. *I'm sorry*, she told him, and he kissed her forehead. *I'm not*, he said.

He promised that he would come visit her and that this wasn't a onetime deal. He put his phone number and his name into her contacts. She floated home, wondering if everyone in Mississippi could see how different she was now, as if being loved left a patina on your skin.

Two days later he had still not texted, so she gathered up all her courage and made the first move. One second later her phone buzzed with the news that the text was undeliverable. She dialed the number, only to have an elderly lady pick up and tell her that there was no one there by that name.

There were too many John Smiths on Facebook to count. There was a John Smith at the University of Wisconsin, but an Internet search revealed him to be a professor of comparative literature in his mid-seventies.

"That rat bastard," Miz DuVille said, shaking Beth out of her reverie.

"Yeah, that was only the start," Beth replied. "I missed my period."

"No condom?"

"No, but Susannah at church—who volunteered with me for the little kid Sunday School—told me you can't get pregnant the first time."

"That's not—" The lawyer shook her head. "Never mind. Go on."

"I figured I was all right. But I missed another period, so I took a pregnancy test." She looked up, sheepish. "Actually, three."

"Then what?"

Beth shifted. "I kept putting it off. I thought, *Something will happen. It'll go away.*" Her eyes filled with tears. "I prayed. I prayed for a miscarriage."

"Is that what happened?"

Beth shook her head. "I called the clinic and made an appointment."

"Didn't they ask your age?"

"Yeah. I said I was twenty-five. I was afraid they'd tell me they couldn't help me." Beth shrugged. "They asked when my last period was, and they told me I was fourteen weeks and they did procedures up to sixteen weeks. They said it would be eight hundred dollars for the procedure."

"But the Center is—"

"Two and a half hours away. I took a bus, and all the savings I had from my job—a whopping two hundred and fifty dollars. I didn't tell anyone. I *couldn't*." Beth took a deep breath.

"How were you going to raise the rest of the money?"

Beth shook her head. "I don't know. I figured I'd steal, if I had to. From my dad. Or the cash register at work."

"I'm confused. If you went to the Center—"

"They asked for picture ID, which would have given away that I was a minor. I started to cry. The lady at the front desk said if I couldn't tell my parents, I could get a judicial waiver, and then come back. She gave me a form to fill out."

Mandy DuVille frowned. "But you didn't. And that's why you wound up here."

"I *tried*," Beth said. "But the day before, someone from the judge's office called and told me my hearing was canceled. They said the judge was having a personal emergency and going to Belize with his wife."

"That doesn't make sense," the lawyer said. "There's always a judge on call, for restraining orders for domestic violence cases or anything else life-threatening—"

"I guess my life wasn't being threatened," Beth said. "Not the way they thought, anyhow. The lady who called me from the judge's office said the quickest she could get me in was in two weeks. But I couldn't wait that long."

"Because the Center only does abortions up to sixteen weeks of pregnancy," the lawyer said.

Beth nodded. "I had to do something. I read online about a girl who said she got ulcer pills from her bodega that could cause a miscarriage. I didn't have a bodega anywhere near me, though. So I posted on a message board online."

She remembered what she had typed: *How do I get rid of a pregnancy without my parents finding out?*

The responses had been horrible:

Throw yourself down the stairs.

Broomstick.

Good old-fashioned hanger.

You sick bitch, kill urself not ur baby.

But buried somewhere in the responses saying she was a sinner who should have kept her legs together was a girl who told her she could purchase abortion pills online.

"They came from China with instructions," Beth said. "It only took five days to come in the mail."

She'd thought it would be easy. Like taking Imodium when you had the runs, and then they magically were gone. She did everything the way she was supposed to, tucking the pills high into her cheeks like a chipmunk, and she sat down on the toilet and waited. She threw the packaging into the trash. When the cramps started, she was so happy, she burst into tears. But soon they were so strong she had to run the water in the sink to drown out her moans. She staggered off the toilet and sank into a squat to try to make the pain go away and that's when it happened.

"I wrapped it up," Beth sobbed, "and I put it in the garbage. I didn't know what else to do."

She needed someone to tell her that she wasn't a terrible person; that she hadn't done the unthinkable. She wiped her eyes on the blanket and looked at her lawyer for the absolution she feared she would never have.

"Miz DuVille," she whispered. "It wasn't a baby yet, was it?"

LIL GODDARD HAD EITHER VANISHED off the face of the earth or had never existed. In spite of the pastor's description of her, and George's own comments about his daughter, no one had been able to turn up any information about the girl.

Hugh was multitasking—still trying to win George's trust on the phone while scanning the notes and the reports that were being fed to him by detectives. Lil Goddard wasn't at her home. She had never gotten a traffic ticket and didn't have a vehicle registered to her name. The only hit a Google search retrieved was from ten years ago, when she played an angel in a Christmas pageant at her church and had a captioned photo in the local paper. It wasn't uncommon for minors to leave very faint trails, but Lil had also never been enrolled in any public school in the state of Mississippi. Then again, many kids of evangelicals were home-schooled. And all Hugh really knew about Lil was that she had, at some point, had an abortion at this clinic—but the records were not accessible online, so it could have been yesterday or a month ago.

Hell, for all Hugh knew, George Goddard had killed Lil in a fit of rage and buried her in the backyard.

But if they could find her, maybe she could convince George to end this.

"I could get a message to your daughter." Hugh hesitated. "I could be an intermediary. I'm sure you want to explain to her what's happening."

"I can't," George said, his voice cracking.

Because she wouldn't listen? Hugh thought. *Because she's dead?*

"Man, I hear you. Seems like me and my daughter can't even agree that the sky is blue sometimes."

Hugh had a sudden vision of him lying on his back on a field, with Wren's nine-year-old head pillowed on his belly, as she pointed at the clouds in the sky. *That one looks like a condom,* she'd said. He had barely controlled himself from bolting upright. *How do you know what a condom is?* Wren had rolled her eyes. *Dad. I'm not a baby.*

"I could help you," Hugh suggested. "Maybe I could even get her to come here and talk in person . . . if you were willing to give me something in return."

"Like what?"

"I want all the hostages safe, George. But this isn't about me. It's about you. And your daughter. She's the reason you came here today. Clearly, she's pretty special to you."

"You ever wish you could turn back the clock?" George said softly. "It's like yesterday she was begging me to braid her hair. And now . . . now . . ."

"Now what?"

"She's all grown up," George whispered.

Hugh closed his eyes. Sometimes when he walked past Wren's room and heard her FaceTiming with a friend and laughing, her voice sounded like Annabelle's, like a woman instead of a girl. "Yeah," Hugh said. "I know."

WREN COULD HEAR HER FATHER. For whatever reason, the shooter had turned on the speakerphone.

Seems like me and my daughter can't even agree that the sky is blue sometimes.

Did he really think that? Or was this part of the role he played as a negotiator? Wren used to tell him that he was basically just a really poorly paid actor, making up whatever he thought the person he was talking to wanted to hear. *Yeah*, her father said. *But the best acting comes from some grain of truth.*

Did her dad think they fought a lot?

There had been a point when her father had been the center of her universe, and she had followed him around like a shadow, helping him fix the dryer or mow the lawn, but mostly just getting in his way. He never told her to get out of his hair, though. Instead, he showed her how to check the dryer vent for lint and how to change the spark plugs on the mower. Then she went to school, and began to hang out at friends' houses, and learned that there was a whole slice of life she had been missing—like messing around in your mother's makeup drawer and trying on her heels and pretending to be a grand duchess; or watching soap operas instead of police procedurals. It was her friend Mina's mother who bought her her first box of tampons, and stood outside the bathroom door coaching her on how to use them. Wren knew her father could and would do anything for her, but there were just some things that were not in his wheelhouse, and so Wren had found them elsewhere.

Now he thought they didn't get along?

She tried to remember the last time they'd spent a good amount of time doing nothing but be together. It was a month and a half ago, mid-August. They had a standing date for the Perseid meteor shower; every year they would hike to the highest point in the Jackson area—her dad carrying the telescope and Wren lugging the tent. They'd pull an all-nighter, watching the show that the sky put on for them, and then have pancakes at a diner at sunrise, and sleep the rest of the day away. But this year Wren had been invited to the movies with Mina and they'd heard that Ryan was going to be there with a group of guys from school. She and Mina had made an elaborate plan about how to best get Wren to sit beside Ryan in the theater, and to share a bucket of popcorn. Maybe their hands would brush. Maybe he would put his arm around her.

Wren almost backed out of the meteor overnight. She in fact had gone to break the news to her dad when she found him in the basement, wrestling with an inflatable sleeping pad. "I figure after all these years we deserve some creature comfort," he said. "No more stones underneath our sleeping bags." He looked up at her. "What's up?"

She didn't have the heart to cancel. So she called Mina and told her she had to do something with her dad. And it all worked out, because Ryan asked her to go to the movies alone a week later, and he didn't just put his arm around her—he kissed her, during the credits, and Wren had felt the way she imagined a star did when it exploded.

On the night of the Perseid meteor shower, Wren and her father had hiked to their usual spot and pitched the tent and spread the bedrolls and arranged the sleeping bags. Her dad cooked hot dogs on sticks over a campfire, and they roasted marshmallows. They set up the telescope, and Wren scanned the night sky.

"Do you remember when I showed you Betelgeuse," her father said, "and you asked which came first, the star or the movie?"

"I was, like, seven," Wren protested.

He laughed.

She stepped away from the scope and stretched out beside him. "It's dying, isn't it?"

"Betelgeuse? Yeah. It's a red giant. So it's cooling."

"That's kind of sad."

Her father grinned. "You won't be around to see it die, if that makes you feel any better."

"I guess if you have to go, a supernova's a flashy way to do it." One day Betelgeuse would explode in a tremendous spark of light, leaving behind a planetary nebula. And as all that dust and gas cleared, all that would remain of it would be a tiny white dwarf star. A core, without fire.

"Nothing lasts forever," her father said.

She and her father had seen plenty of white stars through the telescope. She wondered which ones from her childhood were gone now, and whether they were actually dead, or if they were just too faint to emit light. Did you have to be missed to exist?

When the first streak of light had grazed the sky, she'd sat up, breathless. What followed was a visual symphony, strafing the dark, as if someone had shaken the constellations like dice and rolled them across the night. "Sometimes I forget how beautiful it is," she whispered.

"Me, too," her father said, his voice tight. When she turned he wasn't looking at the meteors. He was looking at her.

If she died, she would be missed.

Wren felt her eyes well up. What had she been doing this morning that was so important that she hadn't spent an extra five minutes at the table with her father, telling him she loved him? Or, for that matter, about Ryan? Or that lately she woke up with the blankets tangled around her feet and her heart racing because she was afraid of not finding her tribe in high school and that she'd bomb her PSATs and never go to college and suddenly everything was happening too fast.

Last year for her birthday, her father had gotten her tickets to a Neil deGrasse Tyson lecture. They had traveled to Atlanta to hear him speak. The astrophysicist had talked about dark energy. It was a real, measurable pressure in the universe that scientists didn't truly understand yet, which was forcing the universe to expand beyond our horizon. One day, he said, astronomers would only be able to track the stars of the Milky Way, and not other galaxies—they would have moved out of sight, like the last chapter of a book that had been torn away. Maybe we were already only seeing part of the story, already missing chapters.

You don't know what you don't know, Neil deGrasse Tyson had said, a year ago.

But now, for the first time, Wren really understood.

It had been Pastor Mike's wife, Earlene, who first mentioned the problem to George: Lil's hair. It was unmanageable.

He, too, had noticed that her baby-fine curls had somehow become matted in places. He had tried to brush it, but the bristles caught on the snarls and Lil would start to cry. Then Earlene stopped him when he was cleaning out the gutters of the church on a summer day that was easily a hundred degrees. She stood below the ladder with a glass of lemonade for him. He thanked her, and as he drank, she looked off in the distance to where Lil and some of the other kids from the church were playing on a swing set. "You know, one of mine had hair like that. Just as uncontrollable as she was." Earlene laughed. "I used to wash her hair in the tub at night with shampoo and conditioner and braid it wet, so it couldn't get tangled while she slept." She took the empty glass from him and smiled. "Don't you go getting sunstroke on me, hear?"

Earlene had the sweetest way about her, finding ways to make suggestions without being critical. George had never met a woman like that. Certainly his mama wasn't that way, and if his wife had been more like Earlene, maybe he wouldn't have gotten so angry all the time.

That night when he gave Lil her bath, he told her she was going to Daddy's Hair Salon. He tugged a comb through her damp hair, working conditioner into the places where the tangles were tough, and razoring away one spot that had turned into the beginning of a dreadlock. Then he divided her hair into three sections, clumsily crossing his fists over each other to make a lopsided braid. He secured it with a rubber band, and tucked her in.

The next morning when he unwound the braid, Lil's hair spilled over her shoulders like a shining waterfall.

"Daddy," she said that night, "braid it again."

George bought hair ribbons at the drugstore, and elastics that didn't catch on Lil's fine hair. It became a twice-daily ritual: He would sit her on a kitchen stool and stand behind her, brushing her hair rhythmically, and braiding it for bed. In the morning, he'd comb through the waves. As he got braver, he made a part, and fashioned pigtails. He learned how to pull her hair back into a barrette. He went to the library and watched videos on the Internet about how to do a French braid, a bun, a fishtail.

There was no question that he took pride on Sundays, when at church mothers came up to him and complimented him on Lil. Or when people were surprised to find out that she was being raised by a single father. He was a man who'd been told he'd done wrong all his life, and this was balm on a wound. But what George loved the most was the magic that happened between him and Lil when it was just the two of them, running the brush through her curls. George knew he was a quiet man, not given to, well, chitchat. But when he was standing behind his daughter, with his hands in her hair, she talked to him. And he started to talk back.

They talked about silly things: whether they'd rather have a fire pole in the house to get from upstairs to downstairs, or a swimming pool full of Jell-O; what they'd buy if they won the Powerball, if

Batman would kick Wonder Woman's butt, or vice versa. There was something about standing behind Lil and not making eye contact that made talking easier for them both, even when the conversation turned tougher—standing up to the girls at church who bullied her for wearing the same dress every Sunday; understanding that a boy who stuffed a frog down her shirt might have actually been trying to get her to notice him; talk of her mama.

George lived for those moments, twice a day, when he did his daughter's hair.

Then one night, when Lil was fourteen, she didn't come into the kitchen after her shower. George found her in her room, her elbows twisted behind her head, weaving her hair into a braid. "It seems silly for you to do it," she said, "when I can do it myself."

George didn't know how to say it wasn't about that, but about the moments he spent with her. He didn't know how to explain that each sweep of a brush could jog something in a teenager that she didn't even know she was holding inside. He didn't know how to say that seeing her fix her own hair filled him with a terrible heaviness, as if this was the beginning of the end.

So he said nothing at all.

If Lil had still let him braid her hair, would he be here now? Or would she have realized that there was nothing she could do or say that would make her seem less perfect to him? Would she have known that whatever knot she had gotten into, they would untangle together?

He had put down the telephone receiver because it hurt his ear. It was on speakerphone now, and he was pacing in front of the desk where you signed in. But Hugh McElroy had stopped talking, and so had George, both lost in their thoughts.

"You still there?" George asked.

"Of course," Hugh replied.

And then, from somewhere behind the desk, he heard a sneeze.

* * *

IMMEDIATELY, IZZY SNEEZED, TOO. SHE faked a series of sneezes, an allergic jag that should have won her an Oscar. If she could convince the shooter that it had been her, instead of the two people hiding in the supply closet behind the desk, then maybe they would stay safe.

If the shooter found them, he'd also realize that Izzy had lied to his face when she told him it was empty.

He spun around, stalked to the closet, and yanked open the door.

"GEORGE?" HUGH SAID. HE COULD hear commotion and shouting and something clattering. "George, talk to me." His heart began to pound. *What the fuck is going on?*

Hugh heard a grunt. A scuffle. "Get up. Get *up!*" George yelled.

"George, what's going on?" Hugh tried again. He swallowed his worst suspicions. "Are you all right? Did something happen?"

There was a crash and a cry and then Wren's voice: *No, no, no . . . don't!*

All of the air left Hugh's lungs. He was paralyzed, terrified for her. His only hope lay in calming George down before he did the unthinkable.

"George," he urged, "I can help. I can—"

"Shut up," George said, and there was a clatter, and then the line went dead.

One p.m.

THE SHOOTER HAD HUNG UP, BUT HUGH WAS STILL TRIUMPHANT. HE had the first puzzle piece he needed for this negotiation. George Goddard had revealed—maybe intentionally and maybe not—what had brought him to the Center today. The greatest weapon a negotiator had was information; knowledge was power.

Wasn't that what he always told Wren?

When Wren was in middle school, and he still packed her lunches, he used to include a sandwich, a bottle of water, an apple, and a nugget of knowledge. On a piece of paper, he'd write a fact: *There's a planet where it rains glass. If you cry in space, the tears stick to your face. There's a tiny aluminum sculpture on the moon. Your body is made out of bits of stars that exploded. Atoms are mostly extra space, and if you squeezed all that space out of the atoms that make up humans, the rest of the mass could fit in less than one square inch. The Milky Way has four arms, not two.*

None of these facts had included how to hide in a hostage situation. How to protect yourself if someone comes at you with a gun and you're unarmed. Hugh could have easily filled her head with *that* wisdom because it was the bulk of his career knowledge. But for reasons he could not fathom right now, he had instead fed her information that would make her the hit of a cocktail party.

Knowledge was power, and he had left his daughter without a weapon. Which meant this was up to him to fix.

"You," he called to a young detective. "Find out what George Goddard does for a living. If he's married. How long he's lived in Mississippi. If there's a bar he hangs out at. Where he bought his gun. If he has any priors." The woman blinked at him. *"Now!"*

She scurried off, and Hugh sank down on the folding chair behind him. He buried his face in his hands. He might already be too late to help his sister. He could not afford to make a mistake. It wasn't just his professional reputation on the line, this time.

The Milky Way has four arms, not two.

It wasn't that the silhouette of the galaxy had changed. It was that often you couldn't see the shape of something when you were stuck inside it. You couldn't be objective if you were too close.

It was why doctors did not operate on relatives and judges recused themselves from matters that involved them and hostage negotiators stepped back from situations where they had a vested, personal interest.

Well, Hugh thought. *Fuck that.*

BEX LAY ON HER BACK, feeling the soup of her breathing, drowning even on dry land. Everything hurt: inhaling, exhaling, blinking. She was dizzy and faint and felt as if a pike had been driven through her chest.

At least Wren was safe, still. If Bex had to die to keep it that way, she would do it.

She should have told Hugh. She could have told him what Wren had asked her to do, and made him swear not to tell Wren that she had said anything. Then he would have known they were going to the clinic, at least.

He would know she was in there.

But Bex knew from personal experience that the minute a father realized his baby girl wasn't a baby anymore, something infinitesimal changed in the relationship. Even if it seemed outwardly solid and unaltered, you could still sense it, like the broken bone that never properly healed, or the hairline crack in the vase to which your eye was unerringly drawn. And so she had kept Wren's secret.

She was good at that.

She felt herself starting to shiver. Did that mean she was in shock? That she had lost too much blood?

Everyone in this room, she realized, had a story that ended within these walls. If today hadn't happened, many of those stories would have gone untold. There were a hundred different paths that led to the corner of Juniper and Montfort—from pregnancies that were unwanted to those that were cherished, but impossible to carry through; from young girls who were trying to do the right thing to the relatives who lied for them. Here was the one thing all these women had in common: they hadn't asked for this moment in their lives.

It was getting harder to breathe. Bex tried to turn her head toward the closet, just in case Wren could miraculously see her through the slats. It hurt so much that the edges of her vision went a hot, searing white.

Bex made a promise to herself: if she got out of here—if she survived—she would tell Hugh the truth.

All of it.

GEORGE STARED DOWN AT THE gun in his hand. Now what?

He had imagined his vengeance as if it were a movie he had seen long ago, where someone wronged took justice into his own hands. He saw himself bursting through the front door of the Center with his gun raised like Stallone or Willis; he saw a doctor cowering under the heel of his boot; he saw an apocalyptic landscape of destruction left in his wake as he emerged, the vanquisher.

Here is what had not been part of his vision: the ringing in his ears when the gun fired, the spray of people's blood, the way they begged for mercy.

George glanced at the group of people huddled in the waiting room. The doctor, injured. The nurse who was hovering near him. The blond girl who kept tugging at her hair. The one who had just killed her baby. The lady who was struggling to breathe. He had done that to her. It made George feel sick, watching her suffer. In the abstract, eliminating everyone who was tied to the Center had seemed masterful, necessary. In truth, it was messy.

These people were puppets and their strings were made of terror. Their whispers died the minute he looked at them. *I'm not who you think I am,* George wanted to say, but that was no longer true. He was exactly who these people thought he was.

His frustration and fury had been a live grenade, dropped into his hands. What was he supposed to do with it? Let it tear him to pieces? Instead, he had run. Far and fast, behind enemy lines. And then he had thrown it right back at them.

They huddled together in the waiting room, leaving as large a gap between themselves and George as they could. They seemed to be waiting for something from him—a demand, a tantrum, an explanation.

They had all heard him talking to the cop. They knew there was someone out there who wanted to rescue them. Hope was a pretty damn good weapon.

On the other hand, George had this pistol. When he waved it they jumped, they cried, they shivered. They listened to him.

He just had no idea what to say.

He started to pace. He had come here with intention, but not with a plan. Somehow he hadn't imagined that there would be people left when he finished teaching his lesson of retribution. He knew how these things ended. In a standoff, with him and a bunch of cops in flak jackets.

But then, he had more leverage than just the gun.

He had hostages.

WREN HUGGED HER KNEES TO her chest in the closet and cursed herself for being conscientious. Who knew that trying to be responsible was deadly?

She could have been like most teenagers on the planet and just waited until things got so intense between her and Ryan that it was too late to plan ahead. She could have brought a pack of condoms to the register at the Rite Aid, or she could have told Ryan that it was his problem. But there had been a girl in her homeroom last year who'd gotten pregnant and had stayed in school until her water broke during gym class. Wren had sat on the bleachers with her till the ambulance arrived, holding her hand while the girl's fingernails squeezed little half-moons of pain into her skin. *Is there anything I can do?* Wren had asked, and the girl had turned to her, panting, and said, *Yeah. Use anything but Trojans.*

So instead, she and Ryan had talked about It. When to do It. Where to do It. Since Ryan was the one who was working out those logistics, Wren volunteered to be the one in charge of birth control. Which, as it turned out, was easier said than done when you were a minor and trying to keep your private business private.

So much for not being a risk taker. You could take all the precautions in the world, and bad things still happened.

That made her think of her aunt.

When Wren's dad went to hostage negotiator training for a few days, and Bex babysat, she'd let Wren skip school. She called it a mental health day. They would lie wedged together in her hammock in the backyard, like peas in a pod, and play a game of choice: *Would you rather grow a tail, or grow a horn?*

Would you rather always be too hot, or always be too cold?

Would you rather stay overnight in a haunted mental hospital or have to ride a broken roller coaster?

Would you rather eat nothing but stuffing, or drink only gravy?

Would you rather know the day you're going to die, or know how you're going to die?

For Wren, the answers were obvious. A tail, because you could hide it in clothing. Be too cold, because you could add layers to get warm. Stay at the mental hospital, because being terrified beats getting killed. Stuffing, because it was *stuffing*. And knowing the method of your death would be better, she had been sure, than counting down how much time you had left.

Wren was currently rethinking that last answer.

Now, Wren thought of another one: *Would you die if it meant someone else could live?*

Was that what her aunt had done for her?

Wren shivered in the closet beside Olive, who smelled like lemons and was being really nice, but all things considered, the odds that they could avoid getting caught hiding were pretty slim.

At least Olive was old. That sounded terrible, Wren knew, but it was true. Olive had lived her life, or most of it anyway. There were hundreds of things Wren hadn't done. Sex, for one, but that was a given. She'd never broken her curfew. She'd never gotten trashed. She'd never gotten a hundred percent on a math test or climbed up the water tower at Jackson State.

She hadn't gotten her license, either. She had a learner's permit— she'd applied for it the day she turned fifteen. Her father knew she had been waiting for this moment, and when she bounced into the kitchen on the morning of her birthday, he was already wide awake, as if he'd been waiting for her. He intentionally took his sweet time eating breakfast and finishing his cup of coffee while Wren squirmed, desperate to be taken to the DMV. "Give me a lesson," she begged, as they walked out of the building with that sacred piece of paper.

"Now, why didn't I think of that?" he said, grinning, and he drove her to the police station parking lot, way out back, where they had summer Friday barbecues. He had set up an obstacle course of orange cones. He showed her how to adjust her mirrors and check her blind spots, and for ten minutes alone they practiced shifting the car from park into drive with her foot firmly on the brake.

Eventually he let her inch between the orange cones, moving five miles per hour. "You want to stay toward the middle around the corners," he told her. "You never know who's on the other side."

"Got it."

"But seriously, Wren. There could be a biker."

"Okay."

"And maybe there's not a bike lane, so you turn the corner, and you clip him and he goes flying off his bike and smacks his head on the pavement and then you get out and call 911 and follow him to the hospital and you find out that he's dead and you have to tell his family you're the reason why."

She glanced at him. "Dad."

"Eyes on the road!"

"This isn't even a road!"

He put up his hands in surrender. "Sorry. Turn left."

She put on her blinker and rotated the steering wheel.

"You know that you don't have the right of way."

"There aren't any other cars."

"But if you jump out in front of someone who's going straight, and they T-bone you, it will probably take the Jaws of Life to get you out of the wreckage. And by then, your ribs could be broken and penetrating your heart and you could slowly bleed to death—"

"*Dad.*"

"Sorry. It's just that there are a million drivers I don't know and don't trust . . . and there's only one *you.*"

Wren put the car into park. "I'm not going to die in a car wreck," she vowed.

Her father looked out the window, eyes straight ahead. Then he smiled, the same kind of half smile she had seen on his face when she told him that she could read to herself at night now; the same kind of smile he'd had when she crossed the auditorium in fifth grade to get a silly graduation certificate; the same kind of smile as when she came downstairs for the first time wearing mascara and lip gloss. "I'm gonna hold you to that," he said softly.

THE SHOOTER HAD HERDED THE five of them into the waiting room. The front desk was littered with glass. There were pamphlets scattered all over the place and smears of blood on the carpet. Furniture had been piled against the front door as a barricade—a coffee table, a file cabinet, a couch. The television overhead was playing *The Chew*.

Joy had left her purse and her phone in the recovery room when she ran away from the shooter. His name was George. She had heard him say it, on the telephone. He looked like any of the male protesters who had been standing outside yelling at her as she ran into the clinic. She didn't listen to a single word they said. But she remembered a man holding a baby doll upside down by the foot, with a knife sticking out of its belly.

To be here today, she had switched shifts at the bar and said she was going to Arkansas to visit her family. If anyone else were going to be a casualty of a pro-life shooter, he'd pick the woman who'd just had an abortion. Was this the karmic price she had to pay? A life for a life?

Would anyone even notice she was gone?

"Hey." Dr. Ward's voice floated toward her. "You all right?"

She nodded. "Are *you*?"

"I'll live. Maybe." He grinned faintly at his own joke. "It's Joy, right? It's gonna be okay."

She didn't know how he could say that with such authority, but she appreciated it, the same way she'd appreciated his kindness during the procedure.

If she died today, she'd be a footnote in a newspaper.

She wouldn't finish her associate's degree.

She wouldn't know what it was like to fall in love.

She wouldn't have a chance to be the kind of parent she never had.

A hysterical laugh bubbled in her throat. She was a hostage, at the mercy of a lunatic with a gun. The soles of her feet were literally soaked with the blood of others. She had stepped over a dead woman to get where she was sitting, and she might very well watch more people die before her eyes. She might even be one of them.

But at least she wasn't pregnant.

To say this wasn't good was an understatement.

Izzy knelt down in front of Bex. She had managed to get the woman out of her blouse and could see the exit wound of the bullet. It had gone through the right breast and out just above her right shoulder blade. But even with Janine pressing gauze onto the wound, Bex's bleeding hadn't slowed.

"We're going to take good care of you, Miz Bex," Izzy said, smiling down at her.

The woman's breathing was labored. "I'm . . . I . . ."

"Don't try to talk," Dr. Ward said. "We'll patch you up like new. I can't risk sullying my reputation as a physician."

That, at least, brought a smile to the woman's face. Izzy squeezed her hand.

"Can I . . . ?" Janine looked up at her. The girl's hands were covered with Bex's blood, and quivering with the effort she was making to stanch the flow.

"No," Izzy said tightly. "You can't."

The phone rang again, and they all turned to stare at it. Last time, Izzy had been the one who answered it. The shooter had directed her to do it by jerking the gun in her face.

"Don't touch it," he barked now.

The phone rang twelve more times; Izzy counted.

Bex's breathing was tighter, soupy. "Hard," she said. "To . . . catch . . . my . . ."

Izzy reached for Bex's wrist, counting heartbeats for her pulse, and doing the math: 240 beats per minute; Bex was tachycardic.

"She probably has a tension pneumothorax," Dr. Ward said. "We have to get the air out of her chest cavity so she can breathe freely." He twisted, trying to haul himself upright on his good foot, but he lost his balance and crashed onto his bad leg.

Izzy took the bulk of his weight. "The last thing we need right now is for you to play hero."

"What we need is a trauma doctor," he said, meeting her gaze. "And it looks like that's going to be you."

Izzy shook her head. "I'm not a doctor."

"That's just a bunch of letters after your name. You know what you're doing, I bet."

Izzy had seen needle decompressions done before in a hospital setting, when they had sterile conditions and all the proper equipment. She also knew that Bex was not long for this world without some kind of immediate medical intervention. As air entered her pleural space from the wound, the pressure would increase and collapse the lung, which in turn would compress the heart and shift the mediastinum. That meant her heart wouldn't pump effectively and the vena cava—the big vessel that returned all the blood to the heart—wouldn't do its job.

Bex started wheezing, fighting for air. Her body shook with the effort. Izzy grabbed Janine's hand and pressed it down harder on the gunshot wound. Then she stood, summoning all her courage. "This woman needs medical attention," she told the shooter.

He stared at her.

"Do you want her to die?"

What a stupid question. Of course he did. He wanted them all to die. It was why he'd come in with a gun.

"I can treat her. But I need to get instruments in the procedure room."

"You think I'm an idiot? I'm not going to let you go off by yourself."

"Then come with me," Izzy said, desperate.

"And leave them alone?" He gestured around the waiting room. "I don't think so. Sit back down."

"No," Izzy said flatly.

He raised his eyebrows. "What did you say?"

"No." She began to walk toward the shooter. The gun was pointed at her belly, and her legs were like noodles, but she managed to take one step and then another until the barrel of the pistol was six inches away from her. "I will not sit down. Not until you let me get supplies so I can save that woman's life."

He stared at her for a moment that lasted days. Then he suddenly grabbed Joy and kissed the pistol to her head. "I'm counting to ten. If you do anything stupid, or if you don't come back, this woman dies."

A small, wounded whimper escaped Joy. Behind her, Bex was outright gasping for air. "One," the shooter said.

Two. Three.

Izzy spun on her heel and raced down the hall to the procedure room. *Four.* She scrambled through drawers, flinging open cabinets, blindly grabbing whatever she could lay hands on as if this were a macabre supermarket sweep. *Five.* She lifted the hem of her scrubs top and dragged her booty off the counter and into the makeshift basket. *Six. Seven.*

She scrambled back to the waiting room, dumping her treasures all over the floor.

The shooter let go of Joy, who fell, trembling, onto the couch and drew her knees up to her chest.

"Pick those supplies up," Izzy said to Janine. She pulled off the johnny she had draped over Bex. The woman's eyes were wide and terrified; they fixed on Izzy as if she were the only mooring in a storm. "Bex," she said firmly. "I know you can't breathe. I'm going to fix that. I just need you to try to stay calm."

Janine settled an armful of items beside Izzy: gauze and tubing and a number 15 stab blade, a Kelly clamp and a tenaculum, a curette.

Izzy was a pro at fixing problems. When the stove broke, you made a campfire and boiled eggs by holding them up to the steam coming out of a kettle. When there was no milk for cereal, water worked. When you wore through the bottom of your shoe, you made an insole out of cardboard. If growing up poor teaches you anything, it's ingenuity.

She picked up a 22-gauge needle. She had seen needle decompressions done before, but with bigger needles. This one was delicate, meant to inject lidocaine. It wasn't long enough or stiff enough to provide a release for the air building up inside Bex's chest cavity.

"Not gonna work," Dr. Ward corroborated. "You're going to have to put in a chest tube."

She met his gaze over Bex's body and nodded.

Izzy pulled the tubing from its sterile plastic packet. She reached for a Kelly clamp, and then picked up the stab blade. She wished she'd had the foresight to grab Betadine or an alcohol wipe, but this would have to do. Lifting Bex's right arm, Izzy trailed her fingers to a spot between the fourth and fifth ribs and paused.

Just because she had seen this done didn't mean she was qualified to do it herself.

"Go on now," Dr. Ward urged. "Make the cut."

She drew in her breath and pressed the scalpel deeply into Bex's skin. A thin line of blood rose. Izzy stuck her left index finger into the incision and felt for the chest wall, blocking out Bex's scream. She lifted the Kelly clamp with her other hand and slipped it through the incision.

"You're going to have to push hard," Dr. Ward said.

Izzy nodded and maneuvered the nose of the clamp above the rib, then punched through the chest wall with a pop. Immediately there was a whoosh of air, and blood spattered into her lap. Bex gasped, finally able to breathe.

It had been not just a pneumothorax but a hemothorax. Blood, not air, had filled her pleural cavity.

Izzy opened the clamp and twisted it back and forth to make a bigger opening in the chest wall. With her index finger, she felt the balloon of Bex's lung as it rose and deflated. She pulled out the clamp, keeping its nose open so that she didn't accidentally snag the lung. Keeping her finger still inside the chest cavity, she inched the suction tubing into the incision until it reached the tip. Only then did she slide her finger out.

Izzy didn't have anything to hold the tube in place, or any way to suture it in. So she grabbed the plastic package that the tubing had come in and pressed it up against Bex's side to make an occlusive seal. Dr. Ward reached for the tape that she'd used to secure his tourniquet and ripped off two pieces for her to secure the plastic.

"Miss Izzy," he said, impressed, "if I didn't know better, I'd think you were born to the ER."

The tube had done its job: blood was running from the tube and dripping on the floor. Izzy wrapped a towel around the end of it, wishing for a container. With a container she could monitor how much blood Bex had lost. Eventually, if Bex didn't get a transfusion, she would die.

Izzy felt a hand grab her shoulder. She turned to find the shooter holding a wastebasket. "Put it all in here," he said, jerking his head toward the discarded instruments on the floor.

She gathered the needle, the tenaculum, the bloody Kelly clamp, and the items she hadn't used, and threw them inside.

"Is that it?" he demanded.

Izzy nodded.

He waved the gun, gesturing that he wanted her to step back so that he could see for himself. Satisfied that nothing had been left behind, he backed away and set the wastebasket beneath the receptionist's desk.

Bex grabbed her hand. She already looked more alert, and definitely more comfortable. "Thank . . . you," she murmured. She tugged until Izzy leaned down.

Her voice was a prayer. *Save my niece.*

Izzy drew back, looking at her face. She nodded.

Izzy fussed with the edges of the tape where it met Bex's skin. With her free hand, she reached beneath Bex's hip and retrieved the scalpel she had hidden there after making the incision. She leaned closer, her hands folded between her and Bex, so that only the two of them could see Izzy retract the blade and slip it through the neck of her scrubs, tucking it into her bra.

ALTHOUGH HUGH HAD ORDERED THE police to clear the area, there were still stragglers. The media, who were too stupid or ambitious to leave. Gawkers, with their cellphones out, recording footage to post on social media. There were still a few of the protesters, too, although they'd moved a safer distance away to hold a prayer circle. Littered on the ground they'd ceded were the hallmarks of their beliefs: a sign that proclaimed ABORTION IS HOMICIDE; dolls painted with fake blood and abandoned in haste, limbs twisted on the concrete in their own miniature crime scene.

Hugh couldn't remember the last time the cops had been called to an altercation here at the Center. For years the employees had coexisted with the protesters the way that oil and water settled in a jar: in the same space, but separate. Each side had an odd, grudging respect for the fact that in spite of the obstacles, they both showed up every day to do the work they believed needed to be done. The protest had mostly been nonviolent and civil.

Except, Hugh noticed, right now.

A ripple of surprise ran through the protesters, triggering some innate reflex he had for impending trouble. He turned around in time to see a young woman with pink hair break through their little sanctimonious tangle. It was the girl he had interviewed an hour ago, the employee who had called 911 after running out of the Center when shooting began. Rachel. She stood toe-to-toe with one of the protesters, a tall, round man with a shock of white hair.

"Please," the man said. "Come pray."

Hugh watched her poke the man in the chest. "Allen, you do *not* get to act like this wasn't all your fault."

He was mildly surprised to realize she knew him by name.

"He's not one of us," Allen replied.

"How can you even stand here and say that?" she cried. "If people like you didn't spout the bullshit you do, people like *him* wouldn't exist."

Hugh took a step forward. "This is an active hostage situation," he said. "You all need to go home."

"I can't," Rachel sobbed. "Not until I know everyone in there is safe."

"That's why we're praying. There's someone pro-life inside," said Allen.

Hugh ran a hand through his hair. "Clearly."

The protester shook his head. "Someone *else*," he clarified. "She's a hostage."

IN TENTH-GRADE DEBATE CLASS, JANINE had to debate *Roe v. Wade*. She argued to overturn it, her knees trembling as she pressed them together, and said that abortion was ending a life. She had lost the debate, according to her teacher, who was pro-choice. But afterward a girl named Holly came up to her and asked if she was busy Saturday morning. Which was how Janine wound up with her arms linked to those of two strangers who were part of Holly's church, forming a human "life chain" that stretched for a mile.

Over the years, Janine had not wavered in her belief that life starts at conception. And yet, it was something she usually kept secret, because when you admitted you were pro-life people started looking at you like you were not so smart, or like you were part of a religious cult. Or they said they were personally opposed to abortion, but believed in a woman's right to choose. That was like insisting, *I'd never abuse my kid, but I'm not going to tell my neighbor he can't beat his son.*

Janine had kept coming back to this truth like a lodestone. It was what brought her to Mississippi to work with Allen. They were so close—only one clinic away from ridding the state of abortion facilities.

She liked the other protesters. In addition to Allen, there was Margaret, who had CP, and who said the rosary as patients passed. There was the professor, who taught at the university. Ethel and Wanda handed out blessing bags as the women walked into the clinic.

It had been Allen's idea that as their youngest member, Janine should start a vlog in which she explained, from a millennial point of view, why abortion was murder. Her first installment was going to be called "Inside the Abortion Factory."

She had wanted to get up close and personal. But she had never anticipated *this.*

Janine had nearly thrown up when the nurse, Izzy, cut into Bex's flesh. Without anesthesia. With Bex wide awake. The skin beneath the scalpel had divided to become a howling mouth, red and angry.

Janine looked down at her own arms, covered to the elbows in blood, and suddenly it all hit her. She had had her hands in another woman's chest. She was trapped with a gunman who didn't realize that one of his hostages was just as disgusted by abortion as he was. She started to weave on her feet.

Izzy looked up as Janine grabbed on to the wall for support. "Are you going to faint?" she asked.

Her own voice was distant and buzzy, like that of the conductor on a train you could never really hear. *I have to get out of here.* Izzy put a reassuring arm around Janine's shoulders. "I have to get out of here," Janine said more firmly.

"Let's take some deep breaths," Izzy said, with a note of warning in her voice. She flicked her eyes toward the gunman, who had turned around to stare at them.

"No." Janine wrenched away. She walked toward the shooter, who held the gun at waist level, pointed at her. "Sir, excuse me, but I don't belong here," she said, smiling at him.

"Sit the hell down," he growled.

"I'm like *you*, not them. I'm not a patient. I was here because . . . Well, it's a long story." She reached up and took off her blond wig, revealing a pixie cut of dark hair. "I think abortion is a sin. They kill babies here, and they deserve . . . they deserve . . ." She glanced around to find everyone in the waiting room staring at her in shock. "Please let me go," she begged.

"Be quiet," the shooter demanded.

"I promise I won't—"

"Stop *talking*—"

"I'll tell them you're a reasonable man. A *good* man. With a good heart, trying to give a voice to the unborn." She took a step forward, emboldened. "You and I, we're on the same side—"

Janine saw the shooter lift his weapon. And then everything went black.

NOBODY MADE A MOVE TO help the girl who'd been coldcocked. Had he not been immobilized with a tourniquet, Louie couldn't even say for sure that *he'd* have done it, the Hippocratic oath be damned.

She must have come here to try to trap them. For years now,

the antis had infiltrated clinics, trying to find proof of the mythology that fetal parts were being sold and that employees were forcing women to terminate late-term pregnancies. The result? People believed them . . . so much so that it inspired violence. In Colorado, a man shot up a Planned Parenthood because he was certain they were selling baby organs and tissue.

Who knew what lies had driven the shooter here, today?

Louie knew all the protesters; it was really a matter of self-preservation. There were too many dark roads in Mississippi, too many places for his car to be driven off into a culvert, like they used to do to civil rights activists. So Allen had complimented him on his haircut recently. Wanda offered donuts to the staff every Monday. Raynaud, who wore the sandwich board with photos of body parts, didn't make eye contact with anyone. Mark only came on Tuesdays and sat on his walker, his oxygen tank in tow for his emphysema. Ethel, who knit the booties and caps that went into the blessing bags, had once given Louie a pair of mittens at Christmas.

There were those who were more disruptive: protesters who took photos of the license plates of cars parked in the lot and published them on websites so that they could be harassed; protesters who had created a geo-fencing mechanism so that as you came within a couple hundred feet of the clinic, your phone's browser would be filled with anti-abortion advertising. (When Louie checked Facebook at work, a pop-up reminded him that he could keep his baby.) Davis, a young minister, blocked incoming cars with his body and screamed at the patients, telling them they were going to Hell. Reverend Rusty, from Operation Save America, drove down from Wichita every couple of months in an old VW bus with a group of followers he could excite into a frenzy with his horsewhip voice and rattlesnake eyes.

Every now and then there was someone new. Last March, a Christian college had a spring break trip to Mississippi, and a busload of fresh-faced college students picketed for a full week. There was a man who showed up for a few days with a snarling pit bull, but he disappeared as quickly as he'd come. There was the time, about a year ago, when a crazy protester barreled into the clinic and chained himself to an ultrasound machine—not realizing that they were portable and could be wheeled out, which was exactly how the police transported him from the building to arrest him. And, apparently, there was Janine.

With that wig off her head, he recognized her as an anti. He couldn't believe that they had been under the same roof and he *hadn't* recognized her, until that moment. It made him feel foolish. Violated.

When Louie was a boy, Miss Essie would come visit and sit on their porch and complain about the head of the ladies' auxiliary at church, yet every Sunday she'd be cozying to the woman as if they shared a twin bed. *Better the devil you know than the devil you don't*, she would say, when his grandmama called her on her hypocrisy.

Then find yourself more suitable company, his grandmama used to argue.

Louie imagined that this young lady had been trying to save her own skin. Clearly, it had backfired. When she regained consciousness, would she apologize to the women who'd come to this Center because they had reached the end of their ropes? Or to Izzy and himself, who fought society and politics and, yes, violence, to give those women a last chance?

She could apologize a thousand times to Vonita, the clinic owner, but it wouldn't bring her back to life.

This woman lying feet away from him would probably be surprised to know that she was not the first pro-lifer to walk into the Center. He had personally performed abortions on at least a dozen.

Louie did not know a single colleague who hadn't done the same. These women claimed to be pro-life and insisted the fetus was sacred, until it happened to be inside them and didn't square with their life expectations. They would come into the procedure room and say that it was different, for them. Or they would bring their daughters and say that obviously this was an exception. Louie wanted to point out that everyone who walked through the Center's door was someone's daughter. But he didn't.

If these women burst into tears on Louie's table because they never imagined themselves there, he did not call them hypocrites. Any of us can rationalize the things we do. But he hoped empathy would spread, an invasive weed of compassion.

A day or two later, after he performed their abortions, these same women would call him a killer again as he walked from his car into his place of work. He did not consider them frauds. He understood why they felt they had to go back to being who everyone else in their social circles believed them to be.

Indeed, when pro-lifers came to him to terminate a pregnancy and told him that they did not believe in abortion, Louie Ward said only one thing:

Scoot down.

PROBLEM SOLVED, JOY THOUGHT BITTERLY. Want to clear up a divisive issue? Throw all the parties into the crucible of a hostage situation, and let them simmer.

She looked down at the unconscious body of the woman who had been suffering beside her. Never in a hundred years would it have occurred to her that she was an undercover anti-choice protester. If she *had* known, would Joy have even given her the time of day?

This was karma, in its purest form. It wasn't as if Janine had just wandered into the wrong place, like Joy had.

Yesterday, she had gone to the wrong clinic. Like the Center, it was painted orange. It was literally around the corner from the Center. The sign even said THE WOMEN'S CENTER, as if they were deliberately trying to confuse patients.

The waiting room was filled with posters of fetuses in different stages: I AM SIX WEEKS AND I HAVE FINGERNAILS! I AM TEN WEEKS AND I

CAN TURN MY HEAD AND FROWN! I AM SEVENTEEN WEEKS—I JUST HAD A DREAM! It had seemed patently cruel to her, to have these posters on the walls, but maybe they were meant to weed out the women who were still unsure of their decision. Joy closed her eyes, so that she wouldn't have to look at them.

She heard her name called, and a smiling woman with a dark cap of hair led her back to a cubicle. The woman wore a lab coat and had the name Maria embroidered over her heart in loopy script. "How about we start with an ultrasound!" Maria said, and Joy realized she was one of those women who spoke only in sentences with exclamation points. "To see how far along your baby is!"

On the examination table, Joy watched Maria squirt gel onto her belly and then rub the ultrasound wand around. "Look at your little miracle!" Maria said, turning the screen toward her. On the screen was a fully formed, chubby black-and-white baby.

Joy had looked on the Internet; she knew her fifteen-week fetus was about the size of an apple, maybe four inches long. But this thing on the screen, it was sucking its thumb. It had hair and eyebrows and fingernails. It looked like it could crawl already. As she stared at the ultrasound screen, she noticed that the movements and twitches of the fetus were repetitive. It was playing on a loop.

Joy cleared her throat. "I think maybe there's been a misunder-standing," she said. "I'm here for an abortion."

"You know if you get an abortion, you probably won't be able to have children . . . ever! And that's if you survive in the first place," Maria said.

She went on: "Do you go to church? Does your boyfriend?" Even these questions sounded enthusiastic. "If you've let Jesus into your heart," Maria said, "He doesn't want you to kill your baby!"

By now Joy was utterly confused. "I think I've made a mistake."

Maria grasped her arm. "I am so glad to hear you say that. We can help you, Joy. We can help you and your child. We have lots of resources on adoption!"

A suspicion crept into Joy's head. "I . . . need to think about it," she said, pulling down her shirt and sitting up.

Maria brightened. "There's no rush!"

Even that was a lie. Joy knew she had exactly four days before she could no longer legally have an abortion in the state of Mississippi.

It wasn't until she was out on the street, breathing hard, that she looked up and saw the actual Center across the street. She ran past the protesters who shouted at her and repeatedly pressed the intercom button. The electronic door lock buzzed, and Joy hurried inside.

"Is this the Center?" she asked the woman at the reception desk, who nodded. "You're sure?"

"I better be, since I own the place. Do you have an appointment?"

She had a name tag—VONITA. When Joy apologized for being late, Vonita knew exactly what had happened. "Goddamn pregnancy crisis center," Vonita said, "pardon my French. They're like weeds—sprouting up next to every abortion clinic, to purposely confuse patients."

"I'm pretty sure they're a bunch of quacks."

"I *know* they are," Vonita said. "The state's got us jumping through a hundred legal hoops just to keep our license, and they're completely unvetted. They tell you we don't have real doctors here? And that you'll probably bleed to death?" She shook her head. "You're more likely to be hit by a bus crossing the street to get here than you are to die from complications from an abortion."

You're more likely to die from sneaking into an abortion clinic to make some kind of moral point.

With a sinking feeling, Joy realized that Janine had gotten what she wanted. It may not have been the way she intended, but in all likelihood this clinic was now going to close—if not permanently, then temporarily. Vonita, the owner, was dead. And who would be willing to come here after this? What would happen to women like

Joy, who were fifteen weeks pregnant and scheduled for an abortion tomorrow or the day after?

Joy glanced down at Janine's sprawled body again. It just went to show you: there was no right way to do the wrong thing.

Except to not do it at all.

She could feel the prickle of everyone else's eyes on her as she slowly knelt on the carpet in front of Janine.

Go figure. When you cradled a liar's head in your lap, it felt just like anyone else's.

In a way, Olive thought, being in the dark was even harder than being out there with the others. She could hear conversations, stomping, crashes. She knew when the shooter was angry and she knew when someone was in pain. But because she couldn't actually see with her own eyes, she began to paint pictures in her mind of what was happening. And what she could dream with a fertile imagination had to be much worse than the reality.

Right?

Beside her, Wren shuddered. "Do you think he killed her?"

There was no need to ask who. The woman who had been babbling about how they kill babies here had fallen silent after a heavy thud.

"He didn't shoot her," Olive whispered.

"That doesn't mean she's alive."

"The brain can do a lot of things," Olive said, "but it can't distinguish between what's really happening, and what you're imagining. That's why scary movies scare you and why you cry at Nicholas Sparks books."

"Who?"

"Never mind."

"You talk like a teacher," Wren said.

"Guilty as charged," Olive said. "I used to teach at the college."

She considered the woman who'd insisted she did not belong here. Olive could have said the same. The Center was all about reproductive choices, and she didn't have any of those left. But she would never have jeopardized Wren's life by throwing open the closet door to save her own skin.

"If I die," Wren murmured, "they'll make a shrine at school."

Olive turned at the sound of her voice.

"They'll put flowers underneath my locker. And posters saying REST IN PEACE, and photos of me doing stupid things, like with my face painted for Spirit Day or dressed like Supergirl for Halloween. It happened last year, with a girl who died of leukemia," Wren said softly. "All these people pretending they miss me, when they never even knew me."

Olive reached for her hand and squeezed it. "You're not going to die," she said.

As if to punctuate her promise, Wren's phone buzzed.

R U STILL SAFE? HUGH texted.

Those three dots appeared, scrolling, and he let out the breath he was holding.

There was someone yelling & then a thud & now it's quiet.

He wondered how many women were in there, other than his daughter and his sister.

He knew his responsibility was to every hostage inside the Center, but the truth was, he was thinking only of Bex and Wren.

Aunt Bex? he typed.

??? don't know.

When he was a kid, and he'd gone somewhere after school, Bex used to insist that he call her when he arrived. He hated it—it made him feel like he was the biggest loser. It wasn't until he had Wren, and worried about her every minute she wasn't with him, that he understood why his sister had been so vigilant. The reason you hold on to someone too tightly isn't always to protect them—sometimes it's to protect yourself.

Hugh stared down at his phone, as if he could will Wren courage, strength, hope. *Stay calm*, he texted.

• • •

• • •

Daddy, Wren wrote, *I'm scared.*

She had not called him Daddy for a long time.

When Wren was little, Hugh had come upstairs to find her scrubbing her face with lemons, trying to get rid of her freckles. *I have spots*, she had said. *I'm ugly.*

You're beautiful, he'd told her, *and those are constellations.*

The truth was, she was his universe.

Parenthood was like awakening to find a soap bubble in the cup of your palm, and being told you had to carry it while you parachuted from a dizzying height, climbed a mountain range, battled on the front lines. All you wanted to do was tuck it away, safe from natural disasters and violence and prejudice and sarcasm, but that was not an option. You lived in daily fear of watching it burst, of breaking it yourself. Somehow you knew that if it disappeared, you would, too.

He wondered if the women who'd come to the Center thought differently.

Then, reconsidering, he imagined it was *exactly* what they thought.

I'm here, he texted Wren, and he hoped that would be enough.

BETH STARED AT THE STRANGE man in her room. A cop. Not outside the door, but inside it, and watching her. It was creepy as fuck. As if it weren't bad enough that she was handcuffed to the bed rail.

She wanted her father. She wished she could text him, apologize, cry, beg, but her phone had been taken away by the police. Was he in the hospital cafeteria, or taking a walk, or just sitting in his car and replaying the horrible things they had said to each other? Beth knew that if she could see his face, talk to him directly, she could make him see that nothing had changed; that she still needed him as much as, if not more than, before. She would spend a month in church with him, if he wanted, atoning for her sins. She would do anything to go back to the way it had been.

When the door opened, she turned, hope swelling. But she hadn't conjured her father at all. It was a strange man in a suit, with a shock of dark hair. He was followed by a stenographer, who set up a machine in the corner near the radiator.

"Hello, Beth," he said. "I'm Assistant District Attorney Willie Cork. How are you doing?"

She looked from this man to the cop, and then her eyes settled on the stenographer, a woman. When she was little and had to go pee, her father used to ask a woman to take her into the ladies' room. He used to say if she ever felt like she needed help, she should find someone who looked like a good mother.

Which, she realized with a shock, disqualified Beth herself.

Maybe he was her lawyer. She had asked for one. She wasn't quite sure how that worked. "Hello," Beth said softly, and at that moment, the door flew open again and a small tornado cycled in. She was tiny and Black and the air crackled around her.

"Your pasty manhood might get you a pass in just about everything in this country, Willie, but even you know better than *this*. You don't get to talk to my client without representation present."

"Such a warm welcome, Counselor," the ADA drawled. "Guess you've missed me."

"Willie, when it comes to you, a tiny bit goes a long way. Like arsenic. Or nuclear fallout." She glanced down at the hospital bed. "My name is Mandy DuVille, I'm your public defender. You're Beth, yes?"

Beth nodded.

"Okay, Beth. Do not talk to anyone unless I'm present, understand?" She faced the prosecutor. "Why are you even here? Don't you have bigger things to do? Like passing a bogus voter ID law or gerrymandering the districts before your next election . . ."

"Officer Raymond here called me down to the scene, and rightly so," Willie Cork said. "I have never seen anything so disturbing in all my years serving Lady Justice. We had an arrest warrant within the hour."

Mandy slid a glance toward the cop at the door. "Nathan," she greeted.

"Cuz," he said.

The prosecutor handed Mandy a file. "Knock yourself out," he said, and Beth's lawyer opened the folder and began to read, her eyes flying back and forth.

"Self-abortion," Mandy read. "Pills?" Her lawyer snapped the folder shut and focused her gaze on Beth's handcuffed wrist, awkwardly balanced on the rail. "She's a child. Maybe a hundred pounds soaking wet. Is that really necessary?" she asked Willie.

"This woman is a murderer," the prosecutor said.

"*Alleged* murderer."

Beth's eyes darted from person to person. It was like they were playing tennis, and she was the ball being volleyed back and forth. She shifted, jingling the chain on her wrist. "I didn't—"

"Stop talking," Mandy interrupted loudly, holding up her palm. "Nathan," she asked, "can I please lean over and whisper to my client for a moment of confidentiality?"

"That's Officer Raymond to you," Nathan said, "and no. You'll stay two feet away from the defendant at all times."

The public defender rolled her eyes. "Beth, I need you to tell me if you understand what the state is saying you did. Not whether or not you actually did it."

Beth blinked at Mandy, utterly confused.

"Okay. I'm going to enter a not guilty plea on your behalf, and waive the bail argument until you're released from here and transported to the prison."

Beth's jaw dropped. *"Prison?"*

Just then, the door to the room opened and a hospital security guard crammed himself inside, followed by a bailiff who was easily seventy and another man who changed the entire tone in the room. Immediately, both lawyers stood a little straighter. The cop put his hand on his weapon and wedged himself between Beth and the judge; the other security guard pushed Mandy further away from Beth to clear a path. "She's not Charlie Manson," Mandy murmured.

"All rise," the bailiff announced, and Beth looked down at her legs in the hospital bed. "The Honorable Judge Pinot of the Third Circuit Judicial District Court."

The prosecutor offered Pinot an oily smile. "Your Honor," he said. "Did I hear that you shot under eighty last week at the country club?"

"None of your damn business, Cork," the judge muttered. "I hate hospital arraignments." He stared down at the only chair in the room, which was occupied by the stenographer. "Is there not another seat?"

"There isn't much room in here," the bailiff said.

"Maybe we make some by getting rid of what's extraneous. Starting with you."

"But, Your Honor," the bailiff insisted, "I'm here to protect you."

Beth wondered what they thought she was going to be able to do, chained to the hospital bed. The hospital security guard got a swivel chair from somewhere and crammed it into the room, which pushed Mandy even *further* away from Beth.

"For the love of all that's holy," Judge Pinot said, "are we *ready*?"

Beth wondered if anyone would be brave enough to point out that he was the cause of the delay. But no.

"Yes, we're ready, Your Honor," Mandy said.

"Indeed," the prosecutor said.

The judge slipped on a pair of reading glasses and read the complaint out loud. Beth's name wasn't part of it, just her initials.

"Do you understand what's going on here today?" the judge asked.

Beth shook her head.

"This proceeding is being recorded, ma'am," the judge prompted. "You need to answer the question audibly."

"Not really," she murmured.

"Well, pursuant to Mississippi Code section 97-3-37, section 1, and Mississippi Code section 97-3-19, section D, you're being charged with homicide for intentionally causing the death of a child in utero. Under our state law, murder is defined as the killing of a human being without the authority of law when done with deliberate design to effect the death of the person killed. Also under our state law, the term *human being* includes an unborn child in every stage of gestation, from conception to live birth. The charge is punishable by imprisonment for not more than twenty years or a fine of not more than seventy-five hundred dollars or both, because your conduct resulted in the miscarriage of that child."

Twenty years? thought Beth. *Seventy-five hundred dollars?* Both numbers were incomprehensible.

"The only miscarriage here, Your Honor, is a miscarriage of justice," Mandy interrupted.

He leveled a glance at her. "I do suggest you watch yourself, Miz DuVille." To Beth he added, "How do you plead?"

"I can explain—"

"No," Mandy instructed. "Beth, I know you have things to say, but don't tell them to anyone but me. I can keep what you tell me private. They can't. All you have to do now is say guilty or not guilty."

"Not guilty," she whispered.

"Where are the parents? Who brought her here?" the judge asked.

Beth waited for someone to ask her; they were acting like she wasn't even there. "Damned if I know," Willie Cork said.

"Your bail recommendation, Counselor?"

"Given the serious nature of this violent crime against a voiceless, unborn child, and given the grave indifference that the perpetrator seems to show, I would request that she be held without bail pending trial."

"You bastard," Mandy muttered.

"I beg your pardon, Miz DuVille?" The judge raised a brow.

"I said he must be plastered. To think that." She waved an arm in Beth's general direction. "I'd respectfully request to waive a bail argument until my client is transported to jail. This isn't grave indifference, Your Honor. This is shock. This defendant is a child, Your Honor. A seventeen-year-old *child*, who had an abortion in the confines of her own home."

"My God, you yourself were once in the same position as that poor defenseless baby," Willie argued. "The difference is that *you* were given a chance to exist."

"Your Honor, if it please the court, may I say something?"

Judge Pinot settled more heavily on his swivel chair. "Something tells me you're gonna whether I say yes or not."

Mandy faced the prosecutor. "Willie, you can stand on top of Mount Everest and shout that life begins at conception all you want, but if this hospital was burning down and you had to decide between saving a fertilized egg in the IVF lab or a baby in the maternity ward, which would you choose?"

"That's a false equivalence—"

"Which would you choose?" Mandy repeated.

"Nobody is trying to say it's all right to kill a child in place of an embryo. This is about allowing the embryo to be born and—"

"Exactly. Thank you for proving my point. No one *truly* believes that an embryo is equivalent to a child. Not biologically. Not ethically. Not morally."

For a moment, the room was still. Then Willie said, "Unfortunately for you, the state of Mississippi *does* believe they're equivalent." He flicked his eyes toward Beth. "There is no distinction in the law between whether she killed a grown adult or a fetus—"

"Allegedly killed," Mandy murmured by rote.

"—except that had she murdered an adult, he could have cried for help."

The judge cleared his throat. "Miz DuVille, we are a court of law, and in this state all that need concern us is that the child that was in the defendant's body is now dead, and she was the proximate cause. For this reason I am setting bail at five hundred thousand dollars. The defendant will have twenty-four-hour surveillance while she is in the hospital, and upon discharge, she will be released to the county jail. Court is adjourned." He hefted himself out of the chair and pushed past everyone else with the bailiff close on his heels. At the door, he turned to Beth. "And you, young lady—may God have mercy on you."

Beth was a devout Christian. She had worshipped Jesus, she had prayed to Him, she had trusted Him.

She believed in God.

She had her doubts, though, about whether God believed in her.

IT HAD BEEN NEARLY AN hour since Izzy put the chest tube into Bex, and she was running out of time. So much blood had drained out that it had soaked through two towels.

"Favor," Bex said.

Izzy leaned down. "Anything."

"You tell my niece . . ." she wheezed. "That this isn't her fault."

"You're going to tell her yourself, Bex."

A smile played over her lips, a shadow behind her pain. "I think we both know that isn't so," she said. She closed her eyes, and a tear slid down her cheek. "It's not the goodbye that hurts the most. It's the hole you're left with."

Izzy stared at her. She knew what it felt like to go without; it had been the guiding premise of her childhood. But she had never been what was missing. Once she told Parker it was over, she would be, though. Breaking someone's heart, it seemed, caused equal damage to your own.

She didn't know anything about Bex, except for the fact that she was an artist, and that she had a niece who was somehow still miraculously hidden. Bex's life was a thread in someone else's tapestry, and that was really all that mattered.

Izzy stood up and approached the shooter. "This woman is going to die without medical help," she said.

"Then fix her."

"I've done what I can, but I'm not a surgeon."

She looked around the waiting room. It had gotten painfully silent since he had smacked Janine across the brow and knocked her out. Joy was sitting with her. Janine had stirred a few times, so Izzy knew she wasn't dead. "I heard you on the phone," Izzy blurted out.

"What?"

"You know what it's like to lose someone you love." She stared into his empty eyes. "All of us, we have families, too. Please. We have to get her to a hospital."

Before she could wonder if he would listen or shoot her, the phone rang.

The first time George realized he was a superhero, Lil was only six months old. They had both gotten sick with the flu, and exhausted, George let her sleep next to him. But her fever had broken sometime before his, and she woke up and started to roll off the edge of the mattress. Even though he would have sworn he had still been asleep, George's hand snapped out and grabbed the baby by her foot before she could fall.

He supposed that all fathers were like that. There was the time she was a toddler and got her foot stuck in the narrow slats of a fence in the pastor's backyard. Earlene had been babysitting while George had gone to get some fertilizer for the church gardens, and when he came back for Lil, he'd heard her hysterical cries. George was out of the car before he'd even finished slamming it into park. Earlene had tried everything and was in tears herself. "I've called 911," she told him, trying to soothe the baby.

"Fuck 911," George said, and he smashed through the slats with his fist, grabbing Lil and cradling her against him even as his bleeding hand stained her dress.

Some of the hurts in the world weren't even physical. When Lil was eight, some little shit of a boy in Sunday School told her she couldn't play pirates with them because she was a girl. He had done for Lil what Pastor Mike did for him when he thought he was worth nothing.

He began by pretending he had forgotten how to turn on the stove to boil the water for the spaghetti. "Dad," she said, rolling her eyes. "You just turn the knob!"

"Can you show me?"

And she did.

Then he pretended that he couldn't remember how to use a hammer correctly. She curled her hand around his and patiently explained how to hit the nail, just a few taps at first, so that you didn't hurt yourself.

He pretended that he didn't know how to replace a lightbulb, how to clean the fishbowl, how to mix plaster, how to fly a kite. A few months later, they went to a church fair. "I don't think I remember the way back to the cotton candy," he told Lil. He held out his hand, but this time, she shook her head.

"Daddy," she said, "you have to try. I won't always be here."

Her words had struck him so hard that he couldn't move, and panicked as she walked off and was swallowed up by the crowd. But she made her way to the cotton candy, just like he knew she would.

It was one of the few times since he had come to the Eternal Life Church that he truly doubted the existence of God. What twisted deity would grant you the superpower of fatherhood to protect someone who, one day, would not need you?

ON THE TWELFTH RING, GEORGE picked up the phone again. "Hello," Hugh said calmly. "Everything okay in there?"

"Don't act like you're on my team."

"I am, though," Hugh replied. "I'm gonna make sure everyone listens to what you have to say, so that this ends well for all of us."

"Oh, I know how this ends," George said. "You call in your SWAT team and wipe me out like a mosquito."

"There's no SWAT team here," Hugh said, which was actually true. They were still assembling; they had only been called forty-five minutes ago.

"You think I believe that you're the only cop out there?"

"There are other police officers here. They're concerned, but no one here is going to hurt you."

"I bet you have a sniper trained on the door right now."

"Nope."

"Prove it," George said.

A shiver went down Hugh's spine. Finally. A bargaining chip. "I can prove it to you, George, and give you peace of mind. But I think you should have to give me something, too."

"I'm not coming out."

"I was thinking of one of the people inside." *I was thinking of my daughter. My sister.* "It's true they are pressuring me, George, to have a SWAT team assembled. But I said that you and I are having a rational conversation, and that we should wait. If you send out a hostage, that's going to go a long way to convincing my chief that I'm right."

"You first."

"Do I have your word?" Hugh asked.

There was a long pause. "Yes."

Proof there's no sniper. Now that he'd promised it, how did he execute that?

Hugh scrambled out of his command tent, still holding his phone. He ran down the sidewalk away from the clinic, blindly grabbing the first cameraman he could. "Dude," the guy said, backing up. "Hands off."

"Who do you broadcast for?"

"WAPT."

"Film me," Hugh demanded. "*Now*." He lifted the phone to his ear again. "George? You still there?"

"Yeah . . ."

"Is there a TV?" *Please, God, let there be a television.* "Turn on channel sixteen."

He heard a scuffle, and a yell, and the voice of a woman. "George?" he asked. "What's going on?"

But he could hear his own voice coming from the TV inside the Center now. The cameraman had the black eye of the camera trained on Hugh's face. "George, it's me. You can see what's going on behind me, right?" To the cameraman, he said, "Film that way. Pan around me."

Hugh kept narrating. "It's like I promised, George. No snipers. No SWAT team. Just some cops who are controlling the scene." The camera swung back to focus on his face. "So. We have a deal, right? Who are you going to send out?"

GEORGE FOUND HIMSELF TRANSFIXED BY the face on the television screen. Hugh McElroy was one of those men who looked tall, even if you couldn't see his whole frame. He had black hair that was military short, and eyes that looked like the blue heart of a flame. He was staring into the camera as if he could see right into George's mind.

If he could, he would know what George was thinking. All those years with Lil that he'd believed himself to be her champion? He wasn't a hero.

Hugh started speaking as if he could indeed read George's thoughts. "Whatever you did, George, and why ever you did it— doesn't matter. That's over and done with. What matters is what you do now."

George had given his word. He didn't believe that it meant anything to Hugh, really. But the fact that he'd asked for it had made George feel . . . well . . . respected.

For once.

George stalked toward the nurse, the bitch who kept reminding him that there were people bleeding all over the floor as if he couldn't see it himself, and hauled her upright by her arm. "Pick one," he said.

IZZY LOOKED AT LOUIE WITH her heart in her eyes. He nodded. Even if it felt like a Sophie's choice, Bex was the hostage who should be released. The rest of them stuck in this room might die. But Bex, if she stayed, *would* die. "You've got to get her out," Louie said.

"Bex," Izzy chose.

The shooter started dragging the couch and chairs and tables away from the front door where he'd stacked them like a barricade.

Louie watched him, his eyes narrowed. He looked like any of a hundred white male antis Louie had seen outside clinics. The vast majority of protesters were men, and it made perfect sense to Louie—the male of the species felt threatened by the biology of women. Even in the Bible, normal female biological functions were made pathological: You were unclean when you had your menses. Childbirth had to occur in pain. And there was the questionable nature of those who bled regularly—but did not die.

There was, of course, the history, too. Women had been property. Their chastity had always belonged to a man, until abortion and contraception put control of women's sexuality in the women's hands. If women could have sex without the fear of unwanted pregnancy, then suddenly the man's role had shrunk to a level somewhere between unnecessary and vestigial. So instead, men vilified women who had abortions. They created the stigma: good women want to be mothers, bad women don't.

Vonita, God rest her soul, used to say that if men were the ones to get pregnant, abortion would probably be a sacrament. The Super Bowl halftime show would celebrate it. Men who had terminated pregnancies would be asked to stand and be applauded at church for the courage to make that decision. Viagra would be sold with a coupon for three free abortions.

God. Louie missed Vonita already.

Forty years ago, Vonita had had an abortion. It wasn't legal then, but everyone knew there was a woman in Silver Grove who worked out of her garage. When the woman died in the 1980s and her property got sold and the new people tried to put in a garden, they dug up hundreds of tiny bones, the size of a bird's.

Vonita told Louie that she herself dreamed of the baby she didn't have. She dreamed so vividly of arguing with her lost daughter that she woke up with her throat raw; once, she had dreamed of her daughter braiding her hair and woke up with it in neat cornrows.

She was well aware that although abortion had been legalized, the stigma still existed, even though one in four women would have one. Vonita thought it was her personal calling to create a place where a woman could safely get an abortion if she needed one, a place where a woman could be supported and not judged.

She had opened the clinic and when she couldn't find a local abortion doctor, she'd tracked Louie down and asked him to fly in to provide services. He had never considered saying no.

"I can't carry her," Izzy said, interrupting his thoughts.

"There's a wheelchair." Louie pointed to a spot where one was crammed beside a file cabinet, beyond Vonita's body.

The shooter jerked his gun at Izzy, indicating she could get it. She ran behind the reception desk, past Vonita. She dragged the chair to where Bex lay, straddled the woman, and slipped her arms under Bex's armpits to lift her. With a struggle that Louie watched, helplessly, she managed to get the woman into the wheelchair and retaped the plastic seal over the chest tube.

Bex coughed and then fought for breath, adjusting to her new position.

"You walk her out," the shooter said, "and then you come right back. Or I start shooting." He grabbed the doorknob from the inside and swung it toward him, so that he was hidden behind the slab of wood. Sunlight fell into the room, silhouetting Izzy and Bex.

That slice of light inched close to Louie as the door opened. He leaned a little to the left, wincing, until he could cup the ray in his palm. Suddenly he was seven years old again, sitting on the porch while his grandmama snapped beans. The air was sticky and the wood under his thighs was hot enough to sear the backs of his legs. He stretched out his small hand, trying to catch the sun that spilled through the leaves of the cypress trees. He wondered if it had come to dance for him alone, or if it would put on its show even after he was gone.

Noon

Hugh had been the third police officer to arrive. His unmarked car screamed to a stop behind a cruiser. He was immediately approached by two wide-eyed beat cops, who'd been the first to reach the Center after Dispatch's all-hands-on-deck call reporting an active shooting. "Lieutenant," one of the cops said. "What do you want us to do?"

"What do we know so far?"

"Nothing," said the second officer. "We got here ten seconds before you did."

"Have you heard any gunfire?"

"No."

Hugh nodded. "Until more backup arrives, position yourselves at the northwest and southeast corners of the building in case the shooter tries to leave the building."

The cops hurried away. Hugh started running a checklist in his mind. He would need the street cordoned off. He would need a command center. If the shooter wasn't coming out, he would need a direct line inside to speak to him. He would need to get rid of the people lining the street who thought this was entertainment.

His personal cellphone was buzzing frantically in his pocket, but he ignored it as he reached into his car and called Dispatch. "I'm on-site," he told Helen. "I'm securing the scene. Shooter's still inside, presumably with hostages. Has anyone gotten hold of the chief?"

"Working on it."

"Call the regional SWAT team and get them here," Hugh said. "And get me aerial photos of the Center."

As he hung up the radio, three more squad cars arrived. He reached into his breast pocket, pushing the button on the side of his phone to dismiss whoever wouldn't leave him the fuck alone while he tried to keep a nightmare from becoming even more disastrous.

When others were paralyzed by panic or overwhelmed by adrenaline, Hugh kept calm, steady, clearheaded. He didn't yet know if there were survivors inside the building, nor did he know what had happened that brought this gunman into a collision path with him today. But he would find out fast, and he would move heaven and earth to get the guy to put down his weapon before there was any more damage.

Even as he instructed additional beat cops on how to secure the perimeter and what materials he needed to do his job, Hugh was praying. Well, maybe not praying, but pleading to the universe. Praying was for people who hadn't seen what Hugh had in his line of work. Praying was for people who still believed in God. He was fervently hoping that this asshole with a gun was one who could be easily defused. And that the shots he'd fired might have struck plaster or glass, and not people.

Within minutes, Hugh was managing thirty-odd police officers. He tapped impatiently on his thigh. He needed to have the area secure before he initiated contact with the shooter. This was his least favorite part of the process: waiting to begin the work.

His phone began to buzz again.

Hugh drew it out of his pocket. There were twenty-five messages from his daughter.

There is a moment when you realize that no matter how well you plan, how carefully you organize, you are at the mercy of chaos. It's the way time slows the moment before the drunk driver crosses the median line and plows into your vehicle. It's the seconds that tick by between when the doctor invites you to take a seat, and when she gives you bad news. It's the stutter of your pulse when you see another man's car in the driveway of your house in the middle of the day. Hugh looked down at the home screen of his phone and felt the electric shiver of intuition: he knew. He just *knew*.

He clicked on Wren's messages.

Help

There's someone shooting.

I'm here with Aunt Bex.

She's hurt. I don't know where she is.

Dad? Are you there?

DAD THIS IS AN EMERGENCY

I DON'T KNOW WHAT TO DO

DAD

He stopped reading. His hands felt like lead and all his blood was pooling in his gut. Why was Wren in there? Why was *Bex* in there? He managed to type out a response:

Where are you?

The longest moment in Hugh's life was the breath he held until he saw those three little dots that meant she was typing.

Hiding, she wrote.

Stay there, Hugh typed. *I'm coming.*

He should recuse himself. The whole point of hostage negotiation was to be clearheaded, and he couldn't be objective if his own daughter was a hostage. Staying in charge here would be against the rules.

He also knew he didn't care. There was no way he was going to trust Wren's life to someone else.

He started to run toward the clinic.

To BEX, AIR HAD BECOME fire, and every breath was charring her raw. Some tiny cell of self-preservation warned her to crawl somewhere, anywhere, that she could hide. But when she tried to roll to her side the agony that stabbed through her made it impossible; the world went white at the edges.

She stared overhead, her brain making patterns of the fluorescent lights and the tiles of the dropped ceiling. That was what artists did, they arranged the unarrangeable into something that made sense.

When she created her canvases, with their giant pixels, she was filtering impressionism through technology. The key to her technique was that the human eye—the human *brain*—did not have to see individual parts to imagine the whole. It was called Gestalt theory. Similarity, continuation, closure—these were some of the principles that the mind craved. It would complete lines that weren't fully drawn; it would fill in boxes that were empty. The eye was pulled to what was missing, but more important, the eye finished it.

Maybe Hugh would be able to do that, too, if she were gone. Finish her work.

And yet she also knew that there was another tenet of art: the observer could easily miss what wasn't obvious. An optical illusion worked because the brain focused on the positive space of a chalice, and not the negative silhouettes of the two profiles that formed it. But just because the viewer saw a goblet didn't mean the artist, while creating the piece, hadn't been wholly focused on those faces.

Maybe one day Hugh and Wren would hold a gallery retrospective of her work. Maybe she would achieve fame by dying relatively young. And only then, maybe, would they realize they were the subjects of every one of her pieces.

This was the worst pain she had ever felt.

She opened her mouth to say their names, but found her throat was filled with the words of Leonardo da Vinci: *While I thought that I was learning how to live, I have been learning how to die.*

HUGH WAS HALFWAY TO THE front door of the clinic when he crashed into a cop. "Lieutenant?" the officer said. "This is Rachel Greenbaum. She's the one who called in the shooting."

He blinked. He had to shake his head a few times to clear it, to let go of Wren's name, which was caught like a bit between his teeth.

What had he been thinking? Well, obviously, he *hadn't* been. Charging inside was a mistake. He couldn't help Wren if he got himself shot.

"Ms. Greenbaum," he said, taking a breath. "Why don't you come with me?"

Slowly, he loosened his death grip on his phone and slipped it into his pocket. He led her in the other direction (away from the clinic; away from Wren and Bex, goddammit) to a spot where two officers were hastily erecting a Tyvek canopy over a card table and a couple of folding chairs. There was also a laptop.

He sat down and offered her a chair as well. The girl—he put her in her twenties, maybe—had cotton-candy pink hair and a hoop in her nose. Her mascara had run, giving her raccoon circles under her eyes. She was wearing a pinny with buttons on it: THINK OUTSIDE MY BOX. MAY THE FETUS YOU SAVE TURN OUT TO BE A GAY ABORTION PROVIDER!

"You work at the Center?" he asked, reaching for a pad and a pen.

She nodded. "I'm a jack-of-all-trades. I do everything from escorting people in from the parking lot to admin to holding the hands of patients during procedures."

"You were there when the shooter came in?"

Rachel nodded and started to cry.

Hugh leaned forward. "I know how hard this must be for you. But anything you can tell me is going to make the odds much greater that we can help your friends inside."

She wiped her eyes with her wrist. "I came in late this morning because my car broke down. I had just arrived."

"Can you describe in detail what you saw?"

"The waiting room was pretty empty," Rachel said. "That meant the group info session was finished."

"Group info?"

"We have to do one every day for the next day's procedures. It's the law," she explained. "There were only a couple of patients left, I think."

Was one a young girl? Hugh thought desperately. *Or a woman with eyes the same color as mine?* But the cop who had brought Rachel Greenbaum over was an arm's length away. He could not risk him overhearing.

"Vonita was at the front desk." Rachel looked up. "Vonita's the owner of the clinic," she said, and then she started to cry again. "She . . . she's dead."

"I'm so sorry," Hugh said evenly, but his heart tripped. Wren had said that Bex had been shot. Was she dead, too?

"She was drinking a diet shake. She hates—*hated*—diet shakes. We were joking around and then the buzzer rang, and it was *him*." Rachel glanced at Hugh. "We're not like Planned Parenthood, with security guards and metal detectors. I guess we operate on hopes of southern gentility. We have protesters, but they keep to their side of the fence, and the Center door is always locked and there's an intercom. If you don't come in with a known escort, all you have to say is that you're there for an appointment, or that you're with someone who's there for an appointment, and then whoever is at the desk will push a button and let you in."

"Was it unusual to have a man show up?"

She shook her head. "We get boyfriends and husbands coming to pick up patients all the time."

"Did he say he was there to pick up a patient?"

"No," Rachel said quietly.

"What did he look like?"

"I don't know. Ordinary. Shorter than you. Brown hair. Plaid shirt. A jacket." She could have been describing half the citizens of Mississippi.

"What kind of gun was he carrying?"

"I-I didn't see one."

"Handgun, then," Hugh said. "Not a rifle."

Rachel wiped her eyes as another police officer approached. "Lieutenant? Dispatch came back with the plate registrations."

His first order had been to run the plates of every car in the parking lot. There were only a dozen. Now Hugh shuffled through the driver's license photos, subtracting out the women. "Any of these ring a bell?"

Rachel hesitated at the first one. "This is Dr. Ward," she said. "He works for us." Then she turned the page. "That's him."

"George Goddard," Hugh read. "Excuse me a minute." He picked up his phone and pushed a few buttons. "Dick? Yeah, I know. Listen, I have an active situation I'm working and the hostage taker's got a car registered in Denmark. Can you do a drive-by?" He glanced down at the screen after he hung up. Wren had not texted again.

"Did he say anything?" Hugh asked.

"I was going to lock up my backpack in Vonita's office," Rachel said. "I heard him come in, and come up to the desk, and Vonita asked if she could help him. I expected him to say he was looking for his wife, or picking up his girlfriend or something. But he said, 'What did you do to my baby?' and he started shooting."

" 'What did you do to my baby?' " Hugh repeated. "You're sure?"

"Yes."

"Did he say anything else? Did he mention anyone by name?"

"I don't know."

"Did it seem as if he'd been to the Center before?"

"I-I'm not sure."

"Did he seem like a local? Have an accent?"

She looked up at him. "Do any of us, here in Mississippi?"

"Then what happened?"

Rachel buried her face in her hands. "He shot Vonita. I ducked under her desk. I heard more shots. I don't know how many."

"Did you see anyone else injured?" *Did you see my sister?*

"No. I tried to take care of Vonita, but she didn't . . . she wasn't . . . ." Rachel swallowed hard. "So I ran." She started sobbing.

"Rachel, listen," Hugh said. "You got us onto the scene fast. And thanks to you, now I know that the shooter isn't in there because he's on a philosophical crusade. This is personal, which will help me connect with him." He leaned forward, his elbows on his knees. "You're lucky you got out."

The tears started falling harder. "I'm not lucky." She sucked in the truth like she was breathing through a straw. "I saw him, through the one-way glass. And he was wearing a coat. I noticed it, because who wears a coat when it's eighty-five degrees? But I didn't stop to think about it. I just buzzed him in." She folded into herself, an origami of grief. "What if I was the one who could have stopped it from happening?"

"This is not your fault," Hugh said, but it wasn't just Rachel he was trying to convince.

THEY HAD SHOWN JOY INTO a recovery room after her abortion, where she had changed back into her sweatpants and baggy T-shirt, and sat down to rest. As she reclined in a leather chair, she dozed, dreaming of when she used to babysit for a toddler named Samara, who lived next door to her foster family. Samara had the roundest cheeks and tiny Bantu knots and little white raptor teeth. She would do the hand motions to "Itsy Bitsy Spider" if you sang it to her, and she didn't like crusts on her sandwiches. Her mama went out twice a week to night school, which was when Joy would come over, feed Samara dinner, and put her to bed.

Samara's mama, Glorietta, took a half hour to say goodbye to her daughter. She would smother her face with kisses and act like she was going to be gone for a year, not three hours. When she got home, she would go check on Samara and inevitably wake her up with her touches and hugs, even when Joy had worked hard to get her to go down. Sometimes, Glorietta would come home in the middle of her class, saying she missed her baby too much and needed to be with her. She always paid Joy for the full amount of babysitting time, so it was a win-win, but Joy thought it was kind of strange all the same.

One night Joy came home from practice to find six police cars on her street, and an ambulance pulled up in front of Glorietta's house. Samara was dead. Glorietta had smothered her in her sleep. She told the police it was so that her daughter would stay an angel forever.

You never knew what went on behind closed doors, as any foster kid could tell you. Joy hadn't thought about Samara in years. But now she wondered: If a child died, in the afterlife, did they keep growing up? Would Samara be there with Joy's child now? Would she babysit him?

A scream woke Joy up. The sad woman was gone from the waiting room and the playlist had ended. Just then, she heard a crash, the sound of glass shattering. "Hello?" she called, but there was no answer.

She slowly inched to her feet. She felt the pad in her underwear shift as she stood, and the hot rush of blood that came with being upright.

Then came gunshots.

She couldn't move fast enough. Her limbs weren't working properly; it was as if she were swimming underwater.

She struggled down the hallway with jerky, furtive movements. Her pulse was so loud, like a timpani keeping count, as she tried to remember the way out of the clinic, but the sound of footsteps approaching had her grabbing for the nearest doorknob and ducking into a room. She closed the door and locked it and rested her forehead against the cool metal.

Please, she prayed. *Please let me live*.

GEORGE GLANCED DOWN AT THE redheaded nurse, who flinched.

He would have killed her. He could have killed her, to get to the doctor. Except, if he killed her, he would also be killing her baby.

Which would make him no better than the asshole bleeding out on the floor.

Frustrated, he looked away and took note for the first time of his surroundings. The procedure room. Had this been where Lil was? Had she been scared? Crying?

Had it hurt?

He had only met one woman who had ever gotten an abortion. Alice belonged to their church and she and her husband had just found out that they were going to have a baby when she learned she had lymphoma. The congregation had prayed hard, but that hadn't stopped the advanced cancer diagnosis and the medical necessity to have surgery and start chemo. Pastor Mike had told her that God would understand if she terminated the pregnancy, and it was proven true a year later when she was cancer free and pregnant again.

George remembered how once, he had come into the church early one morning during the week to find Alice, now healthy and eight months pregnant, sitting in a pew and sobbing her heart out. He had never been one for crying women, so he passed her his handkerchief and shifted uncomfortably. "Can I get the pastor for you?" he'd asked.

She'd shaken her head. "Maybe just sit with me?"

It was the last thing George wanted to do, but he lowered himself into the pew. He glanced at her belly. "Guess it won't be long now."

Alice started to cry, and he fell all over himself to apologize. "I know it's a blessing," she sobbed, "but it's not a replacement."

Two, George realized now.

He knew *two* women who had had abortions.

Izzy cowered as the gunman turned to her, abruptly, and dragged her to her feet. A bolt of pain shot through her arm. "Who else is here?" he demanded, his breath hot on her face. "How many people?"

"I-I don't know," Izzy stammered.

He gave her a hard shake. "Think, dammit!"

"I don't know!" She felt like she was made of sawdust.

"Answer me!" he ordered, waving his gun in her face.

He wrenched her arm again, and tears came to her eyes. "This is everyone!" she burst out.

Just like that, he let go of her. She stumbled, managing at the last moment to not fall on top of the doctor's wounded leg. She lay on her side, her eyes shut tight, waiting to wake up from this nightmare. Any minute now, she would. Parker would be shaking her shoulder, telling her she'd been making sounds in her sleep, and she would sit up and say, *I had the most horrible dream.*

The shooter sank to his knees. He rubbed the barrel of his gun against his temple as if he had an itch, and this was an extension of his finger. Then he lowered the pistol and stared at it as if he was wondering how the hell it got into his hands.

Could she rush him, right now? Could she grab the gun, and hold it against him?

As if he could hear her thoughts, he leveled the gun at her again. "How can you be pregnant and work here every day and be okay with what happens?"

"Please, you don't understand—"

"Shut up. Just shut up. I can't think." He got up and started to move in a small circle, muttering to himself.

Izzy inched toward the doctor. She could tell from the trickle of blood at his leg that he needed a better tourniquet. She felt his neck for a pulse.

"What are you doing?"

"My job," Izzy said.

"No."

She looked up at him. "I'll do whatever you want. But let me help these people before it's too late."

The shooter glanced down at her. "First, you round up everyone else, and get them all into one place. The front area. With the couch."

The waiting room. Izzy winced as the shooter dragged her down the hall. They stopped in front of a bathroom. "Open it," he demanded, and when Izzy hesitated his fingers bit deeper into her flesh. "Open it!"

Please be empty, she thought.

With a shaking hand, she pushed open the door, and revealed a squat toilet, a pristine sink. No one.

"Come on," the shooter said. He pulled her from the bathroom to the changing room—empty, the recovery room—empty, and the consultation room, where the sonograms were done. There, another woman was sprawled on the floor—the social worker at the Center. Izzy didn't have to get any closer to know she was dead.

Fighting the urge to throw up, she let herself be pulled down the hall. The shooter paused at the one door they hadn't opened yet. Izzy turned the knob, but it was locked. She looked at him, and he cocked the hammer and shot the doorknob clean off the door. Even with her hands belatedly covering them, Izzy felt her ears ringing. When she stepped inside, she saw a pale woman cowering in the corner of the lab, her mouth rounded in a scream.

Sound came back in fits and starts. She could hear herself trying to calm the woman down. "I'm Izzy," she said.

"Joy." Her gaze darted to the shooter.

Izzy tried to redirect the woman's attention. "Are you hurt?"

"I just had . . . I had . . ." She swallowed. "I was in the recovery room."

"He wants us to go to the waiting room, but I need help carrying the doctor, who's been wounded. You feel strong enough to help me, Joy?"

Joy nodded, and they backtracked. Izzy was well aware of the gun pointed at her. "Make it fast," the shooter said.

In the procedure room Joy froze, staring at the dead nurse. Dammit. Izzy had forgotten to warn her.

"Oh my God. *Oh my God oh my God oh my*—" She turned away from the body and gasped. "Dr. Ward?"

He was conscious now, but clearly in pain. "Miz Joy," he managed.

"This is not a goddamn ice cream social," the shooter yelled. His anger lit a fuse in Izzy. She scrambled around the room, opening drawers and grabbing as much gauze and tape as she could and shoving it into her scrubs top, which ballooned out with the items where it was tucked into the waistband of her pants.

She got to her knees and looped the doctor's arm around her neck, then caught Joy's eye to get her assistance. Joy looped the doctor's other arm around her neck. Together they got him upright and began to drag him down the hall, his leg leaving a trail of blood.

As they approached the waiting room, Dr. Ward looked past the reception desk and saw the body of the clinic owner. "Vonita," he moaned, just as the shooter grabbed Izzy by her braid. Tears sprang to her eyes and she lost her grip on Dr. Ward, so that Joy had to bear the bulk of his weight. They tumbled to the floor, the doctor landing on his bad leg. His makeshift tourniquet popped free of its knot, and blood began to run freely.

Izzy immediately knelt to fix the tourniquet, but the shooter wouldn't let her. "You're not finished," he said. "I want *all* of them where I can see them."

"Joy," Izzy cried out, "tie that tubing!" As she spoke, she crawled to Bex, the lady who'd been shot near the reception desk. Janine, the young woman she had ordered to apply pressure to the wound, was still there, pressing down on the injury to slow the flow of blood.

Izzy looked up at the gunman. "I can't move her."

"I'm not the one who cares if she dies."

Gritting her teeth, Izzy dragged Bex, apologizing for causing her pain. Janine watched her struggle for a moment. When Izzy stared at her in disbelief, she scrambled to help.

They positioned Bex beside the doctor on the waiting room floor. "Okay, start again with the pressure," Izzy told Janine. She was young, but it was clear that she was wearing a blond wig, and not a particularly good one. *Chemo?* Izzy wondered, and on the heels of that came a wash of empathy.

She immediately turned her attention to the doctor again. Joy had wrapped the tubing around his leg and was holding it in place with her hand. Izzy ripped off the bloody pants leg of his scrubs and began to twist it into a rope.

"You're. Not. Finished," the shooter growled. "Check the rest of the rooms!"

Izzy's hands stilled as the pistol nudged her between the shoulder blades.

Lifting her palms in surrender, she sent a silent plea to Joy to keep her vigil over the doctor and got to her feet again. With sharp, angry strides she walked to the bathroom that she had gone into earlier to be sick. She flung the door wide. "Empty," she announced.

The shooter didn't come to verify her claim. He couldn't, without turning his back on his hostages. Instead he stood at a distance with the gun, bouncing his aim between Izzy and the others.

She yanked open a supply closet, the only other door in the waiting room. On one side was a pile of boxes, and a stack of cleaning supplies. On the other side hung three long white lab coats and a barricade made of a vacuum, a mop, and a bucket. From where she was standing, Izzy could also see two faces, pinched and pale, blinking up at her. One, an older woman, held a finger to her lips.

Izzy turned, blocking that side of the closet with her own body. "Empty. Happy now?" she said, and she slammed the doors shut. She folded her arms, mustering courage she didn't feel. "*Now* can I go back to doing my job?"

FOR A MINUTE WREN WAS sure she was a goner. When that closet door opened, she had turned to stone. She stared up at the woman, who clearly noticed them, but didn't give away their hiding place. She stayed utterly frozen until they were plunged into darkness again, and then felt Olive's fingers gripping hers, papery and powdery, the way old ladies' hands always were. Wren's phone vibrated and she lifted it in the darkness.

Still safe?

Yes, she texted back to her father.

Where r u?

In a closet

Alone?

No, she wrote. *With Olive.* She didn't explain who Olive was. It was enough that her father realized she wasn't sitting here alone and terrified.

Can you see Bex?

No.

Don't move, her father wrote. *Don't speak. Listen and tell me what u hear.*

Wren tried, but with the closet doors closed, it was all muffled. *There were shots*, she wrote after a moment. *Aunt Bex fell down. I think it went into her chest.*

Which side?

Wren blinked. She tried to think; where had the red spread? She moved her hand over her own chest, mapping the memory. *Right.*

She realized, as she typed it, that her father was feeding her hope. The right side of your chest didn't hold your heart. There was a chance that her aunt was still fighting.

People were crying, Wren typed. *A lady wearing scrubs opened the closet door and she saw us but she made sure he didn't.*

A warning popped up on her screen. *You only have 10% battery left. Would you like to go into Save mode?*

Yes, Wren thought. *Yes, I very much would.*

Dad, she typed, *I'm sorry.*

It had been her decision to get birth control. Her decision to keep that little tidbit of information from her father. Her decision to ask her aunt to bring her here secretly. She waited for her father to absolve her, to say that it was all right, that it wasn't her fault.

Tell me what else is happening, he wrote.

Wren felt something sink inside her. What if she got out of here, and things were never the same between the two of them? What if she had broken everything with one mistake?

She was going to live, she decided, if only to prove to her father that she could grow up *and* still be his little girl.

Wren started typing. *The woman who saw us had blood all over her clothes.*

Was she hurt?

I don't think so, Wren wrote. *But other people are.*

Did you hear the shooter say anything? Did he mention any names? When was the last time you heard the gun go off? How many injured did you see before you went into hiding?

Her father's questions rolled in like thunderclouds, fast and thick. Wren closed her eyes and pressed the power button to darken the screen and save some of the limited juice she had left. She thought, instead, of all the questions he wasn't asking her.

Why are you in a women's health center in the middle of the school day?

Why is your aunt with you?

Why didn't you tell me?

Her earliest memory was when she was four years old, when she still had a mother and a normal nuclear family. She was at nursery school, and a boy on the playground kissed her smack on the lips underneath the jungle gym that looked like a pirate ship and announced that he wanted to make babies with her. Wren had drawn back her fist and punched him right in the mouth.

Her parents were called to school. Her mother was mortified and kept saying that Wren didn't have a violent bone in her body, which made her wonder if other people had violent bones, and if they were tucked in among the ribs or pressed down under the foot when you stamped it. "Wren," her mother said, "what did you *do*?"

"I did what Daddy told me to," she answered. Her father laughed so hard he couldn't stop, and her mother told him to go stand outside, like he was the one in trouble.

Her mother wanted to punish her. Her father took her out for the biggest ice cream sundae, instead.

Dad, she texted, *are you still there?*

• • •

• • •

• • •

Always, he wrote, and she exhaled.

THE SHOOTER HAD TAKEN EVERYONE'S cellphones and thrown them into the trash. He barricaded the front door with the couch and seats and coffee tables. Breathing hard, he turned around, leveling the gun at the others. "Do what I say," he muttered, "and no one will get hurt."

"No one *else*," Izzy corrected under her breath.

She knew that he was watching her; his eyes felt like lasers. But Izzy didn't care. She had kept up her end of the bargain, and there were people here who were hurt. She'd be damned if she sat back and let them suffer.

Janine still had her hands pressed on Bex's chest. Izzy bent down, trying to see how much the wound was still bleeding. The woman's whisper fell into her ear. "My niece. Closet."

Izzy thought of the two faces, pinched and terrified, that had been staring up at her when she opened those doors at the gunman's directive. She leaned over farther on the pretense of listening to Bex's labored breath. "She's okay," Izzy murmured.

Bex's eyes fluttered closed. "Need to tell Hugh."

"Tell me what?"

Bex coughed, and then cried out from the pain that must have shot through her lungs and ribs. Izzy tried to distract her, because there was damn little else she could do but keep the woman comfortable. "What do you do, Bex?"

"Artist," the woman whimpered. "Hurts."

"I know," Izzy soothed. "The less you can move, the better." She glanced at Janine, and silently directed her to maintain her position. "I'm going to tend to someone else," Izzy said, "but I promise I'll be back."

She inched across the carpet to Dr. Ward. The tourniquet that Joy had tied needed to be tighter and more durable.

"Vonita," he said softly. "She's gone?"

Izzy nodded. "I'm sorry."

"So am I," he murmured. "So am I." He looked over his shoulder, as if he could see past the barrier of the front desk, where the body lay. "These women, they were all the daughters Vonita never had.

Drove her husband crazy, how hard she worked at this place. He used to say they'd carry her out of here in a coffin." His voice broke on the last word. "She would hate knowing that he turned out to be right."

Izzy rolled the fabric from Dr. Ward's pants leg around his thigh and tied it just above the wound. "Hold still, Doctor," she said.

He raised a brow. "You just ripped my scrubs off. I think you can call me Louie, don't you?"

Izzy placed a Sharpie she'd found under the couch at the center of the knot, then tied the fabric again. She began to twist the Sharpie, which wound the cotton around, tightening the new tourniquet. The blood flow trickled, stopped. "There," she said. "That's more like it." She grabbed a roll of tape, awkwardly tugging it with her teeth so that she could secure the tourniquet in place. Then she looked at her wrist. It was just after twelve-thirty. Now, the countdown began: she had stopped Dr. Ward from bleeding out, but without arterial flow, there would eventually be ischemic damage to the tissue. If that binding stayed in place longer than two hours, there could be muscle or nerve injury. Six hours, and he would have to have his leg amputated.

Maybe by then they'd be rescued.

Dr. Ward patted her hand as she finished taping the tourniquet. "We make a good team," he said. "Thank you." He lifted his leg onto a chair so that it would be elevated above his heart.

She looked at Bex, still lying on the floor, deathly pale but stable.

Now that Izzy didn't have a medical emergency to occupy her hands, they started shaking. She grabbed her right with her left.

"I haven't seen you here before, have I?" Dr. Ward murmured.

Izzy shook her head. She started to answer, but then hesitated as the shooter passed by, talking to himself under his breath.

When he was on the other side of the room, the doctor spoke again. "You got a husband out there worrying about you?"

He was speaking quietly, creating a bubble of conversation just big enough for the two of them. "No," she said. "Just a boyfriend."

"Just a boyfriend?" he teased.

"Maybe a fiancé . . ."

"Maybe like you can't remember?" Dr. Ward chuckled. "Or maybe like you haven't decided yet?"

"It's complicated."

"Girl, I got nothing but time." Dr. Ward grinned.

"It's not that easy. We come from really different places," Izzy explained.

"Palestine and Israel?"

"What? No . . ."

"Mars and Venus?" Dr. Ward asked. "Union and Confederacy?"

"Parker grew up eating caviar. I grew up eating when we had enough money for food." Immediately, Izzy flushed beet red. She didn't talk about her upbringing. She tried, on a daily basis, to forget it.

She and Parker had been together for three years. They hardly ever fought, and when they did, it always came down to the difference in their backgrounds.

There was the time they had only been dating a few weeks when she had come across him scrolling through social media on his phone. He'd murmured, *Valencia looks nice.*

Let me guess. She's someone you went to school with. Jealousy had bristled through Izzy. Women with names like that had trust funds and ski instructors.

Parker had held out his phone to show her that it was the name of the new Instagram filter.

Someone's jealous, he had teased.

I told you I'm not perfect.

Nope, Parker had said. *But you're perfect for me.*

Another time, they had just moved in together and he'd put his glass on the coffee table they had just bought at a yard sale. *How could you not use a coaster?* she'd snapped.

It's a twenty-dollar table, he had said, incredulous.

Izzy could not imagine spending that much on an item and not treating it like it was precious. *Exactly*, she'd said.

All the fight had gone out of him.

I'm an asshole, he had told her, and she never caught him without a coaster again.

She knew damn well why she had fallen for Parker. She just couldn't, for the life of her, understand why he had fallen for her. One day, Parker would be embarrassed by her in the company of his friends, when she did something that revealed her upbringing. Or he would leave her and she'd be broken. Better to be the one to do the breaking.

Dr. Ward reached for her steady hand. "Well, look at that," he said. "Someone's forgotten to be scared."

During this whispered conversation, which they might have been having anywhere and anytime, rather than in the middle of a hostage crisis, Izzy had stopped shaking. "What do you think he's going to do to us?" she whispered.

"I don't know," the doctor replied. "But I do know you're going to survive it." He winked at her. "You can't leave that poor boy of yours hanging."

You don't know the half of it, Izzy thought.

TRUTH BE TOLD, JANINE HAD been waiting for this day. She knew God would punish her; she just hadn't thought it would be with quite this much irony.

She kept her hands pressed to the chest of the woman who had been shot. If she pushed hard enough, there wasn't any blood. If she pushed hard enough, maybe she could shove back the secret that had been buried so far it felt like a false memory.

Janine had not had many friends. Having a brother with Down syndrome was time-consuming. It meant she had to be home after school when her parents were working, to be a babysitter. It meant explaining to everyone why Ben had to tag along, and sometimes she just didn't have the energy or inclination. And it also meant defending him against stupid comments people made—calling him the *R* word, or saying *But he* looks *pretty normal*, or asking why her mother hadn't had prenatal testing. It was easier to just not have anyone over to the house, to remain a loner in school.

Which was why, when she was sixteen and somehow got paired in biology with the queen bee of the sophomore class, she expected the worst. Instead, Monica took her under her wing, as if she were a clueless little sister, dragging her into the girls' room to teach her how to do a cat's eye with liquid liner; sharing YouTube videos that were supposed to make her laugh. It was the first time she was in on the joke instead of the butt of it, which was why when Monica invited her out on a Friday night, she went. She told her mother that she was studying for her bio midterm with her lab partner, which was only partly a lie. She met Monica, who gave her a fake ID to use that had belonged to her cousin, who looked like Janine with longer hair if you squinted hard. They were going to sneak into a frat party at the college.

Janine had only drunk wine at communion, and that night's fare was grain alcohol punch. It tasted like Kool-Aid and there was always a boy pressing another drink into her hand. The night became a collage of images and moments: a red Solo cup, a heartbeat made of music, boys who danced so close that the hair on the back of her neck stood up the way it did before a thunderstorm. Their hands on her shoulders, a massage. Teeth scraping her neck. The realization that most people, including Monica, had gone home. The green nap of a pool table on her bare thighs. Someone holding her down while another moved between her legs, splitting her in two. *Don't tell me you don't want this*, he said, and while she was trying to figure out whether the answer that would get him off her was a yes or a no, a dick was shoved into her mouth.

When she awakened, alone, bruised and oozing, she pulled down her dress. Her underwear was gone. The sun stabbed at the horizon as she let herself out of the frat house. The lawn was littered with beer cans, and one of the bros was passed out on the porch. She wondered if he had been on her, in her. At that thought she leaned over and threw up violently, until she believed there was nothing left inside.

She was wrong about that.

She found out she was pregnant the usual way—a skipped period, tender breasts, exhaustion. But beyond all that, she just knew. She could feel them, still inside her, dirty. Taking root.

No one knew. Monica had only said, *Well, when I left you were surrounded by guys. You sure looked like you were having fun.* Her parents still thought she had been studying. Janine was determined to keep it that way.

Where they lived, it was easy. She still had the fake ID. She used it to make the appointment at a clinic in a part of Chicago she had never been to before. She scheduled it during the afternoon, when she was supposed to be home watching Ben. *I have to run an errand,* she told him, *and if you don't tell Mom, I'll let you watch TV the whole time.*

She stole money from the jar in the kitchen cabinet that her parents used for emergencies. She took a cab there. They asked at the front desk if there was a father, and Janine did a double take, thinking they meant her dad. Then she realized—the father of the baby. But it wasn't a baby to her. It wasn't a human being. It was a wound that had to be closed.

The doctor was an Indian woman with perfume that smelled like a garden. There was a pinch, and then pressure, and she panicked and kicked her foot out of the stirrup. After that, a nurse came in to help hold her down, and that only made her think about Them and she fought harder. Finally the doctor sat back and looked at her. *Do you want this,* she asked dispassionately, *or don't you?*

Don't tell me you don't want this.

She held it together during the procedure, and in recovery, and afterward, when she took another cab home. But when she saw Ben on the porch with their next-door neighbor, she panicked.

The neighbor picked up a blanket-wrapped bundle on the ground. "Galahad was run over," he said. "I'm really sorry."

Their terrier was supposed to stay in the house unless he was on a leash. "You were taking a long time and I went to see if you were back and he ran outside before I could stop him," Ben said. "He won't wake up."

She wrapped her arms around him. "It's not your fault."

Janine took the bundle from her neighbor. It was the first time she had ever held anything dead. Galahad's weight felt slight, as if he were evaporating. That morning she had yelled at him because he was chewing on her sock. She had so many orphaned socks because of that dog, she had taken to wearing them in mismatched pairs. Even now, she had on a blue spotted one and a red one with tiny penguins on it. Janine was sick thinking about it, dizzy, the way you felt when you perched at the edge of a cliff. That's all that stood between death and life, a single misstep.

She carried the dog to the backyard and, using one of her mother's gardening spades, dug a hole. Ben watched. He asked why she was putting Galahad's face into the dirt.

She didn't know how to explain life and death to her brother. She didn't know how to keep from thinking that this was her punishment, for what she had done. Had the baby inside her been like this, alive one moment, dead the next? It was the first time—the only time—she had thought of it as a person and not a problem.

When Janine was finished, her hands black with dirt, she sat down in the backyard and sobbed. That was how her mother found her when she got home from work. She was inconsolable, and everyone in her family thought they knew why.

It turned out that if you surgically removed a memory, you might stop feeling for the edges of its scar. You might even come to believe that you had never been raped, had never been pregnant, had never gotten an abortion. The more distance that grew between that day and Janine's future, the more she believed that she was different from other women who had found themselves with an unwanted pregnancy. She had been the victim. She had whitewashed the stain with years of pro-life activism. She didn't think of herself as a hypocrite. That thing inside her had not been a baby. It was something they'd left behind.

Janine had pretended that if she never told a soul where she had been that afternoon, it would be like it hadn't happened. But of course God knew. And that was why this shooting was her fault.

Coming here undercover had been a bad idea. It was as if the Center were Pandora's box. She'd opened the door, and had released all the evil into the world.

Ninety-nine percent of Hugh's job as a hostage negotiator involved being a good listener, but this hadn't always been a skill he possessed. When he and Annabelle broke up, she had accused him of constantly interrupting her and not taking her feelings into account. "That's ridiculous," he had blustered, cutting her off midsentence. Annabelle had held up her hands, as if to say, *I told you so*. The space between them had filled with shock, with Hugh's bitter realization that she was right. "Maybe if you'd let me finish a thought," Anna said into the silence, "I wouldn't have had to find someone else who did."

Hugh had not become a negotiator until after Annabelle left him. But he was bound and determined not to make the same mistake in his professional life that he had in his private one. He had been trained to stay calm, even when his adrenaline was pumping. He knew to keep his voice even, to stay engaged with what a person was saying, attuned to every detail.

He knew, too, to acknowledge when someone else spoke. To accept. To say, *All right, yes, okay.* But he did not say *I understand*, because he understood nothing, particularly what brought any particular person to any particular cliff.

It had always been easier for Hugh to be measured and dispassionate during a hostage standoff than he had been with Annabelle. He supposed it was because at work, he had nothing personal at stake.

Until now.

"McElroy." He turned at the sound of the chief's voice. "What the holy fuck is going on?"

Chief Monroe was still dressed in his coat and tie from his luncheon. "Hostage situation," Hugh said. "I already called in the SWAT team, and we have a name and address. George Goddard."

"Any priors?"

"No. It seems to be a personal grudge, based on information from an eyewitness."

He did not say the words that were on the tip of his tongue: *The two people I love most in the world are in there. I don't trust anyone but me to get them out.* The minute he admitted that, he would be booted off this case. But luckily, part of Hugh's training was knowing how to lie convincingly.

The chief looked from the cordoned-off clinic to the line of police officers securing the perimeter. "You tell me what you need," he said, ceding authority to Hugh.

"I'm good, for now," Hugh said, and he lifted a megaphone that had come from one of the cruisers.

He was not a fan of throw phones—heavy Gator cases that were typically delivered to the front door via an armored vehicle. The cops would retreat while the gunman took in the box and lifted the receiver. Instead, he just needed the shooter to know that he was going to be the one calling him.

"Hello," he boomed. "This is Detective Lieutenant Hugh McElroy of the Jackson Police. I'm going to call the landline in there in one minute." He held up his cellphone, in case anyone was watching through the mirrored windows.

In the silence that followed his words, Hugh could hear the symphony of June bugs and the throaty contralto of cars on the highway in the distance. He imagined Wren, hidden in a closet, straining to hear his voice. He was addressing the shooter, but in his heart, he was speaking directly to his daughter.

"I just want to talk," Hugh said, and then he put down the megaphone, and dialed.

GEORGE HAD ALWAYS BELIEVED HIMSELF to be an honorable man—a good Christian, a good father. But what about when being good got you nowhere? When you were still lied to, shit on, when nobody listened to you?

They'd listen now.

As if he'd willed it, a tinny, amplified voice seeped through the walls of the clinic. *This is Detective Lieutenant Hugh McElroy of the Jackson Police.*

He felt it: the electrified optimism that sizzled through the group. Help had arrived. They were not alone.

George had known, on some subconscious level, that it would come to this: Someone would come to save these people. It was up to him to save himself.

Once, as a kid, George had found a bloody trail in the woods and traced it to an illegal trap, where a coyote had chewed its own leg off to escape. For months after that he had woken up sweating in the middle of the night, haunted by that severed paw. He'd wondered if the coyote had lived. If it was worth making a sacrifice that great for a fresh start.

He didn't blame Lil. She was a child, for God's sake. She didn't know what she was doing. He could easily lay fault at the feet of the people in this clinic who had *done* it to her.

The pistol felt like an extension of his arm, like his own limb. He couldn't chew it off and hope to survive. This was a trap of his own making.

On the reception desk, beneath the glitter of shattered glass, the phone began to ring.

IT WAS THE MODERN-DAY EQUIVALENT of the trolley problem, that old ethics conundrum. There's a trolley whose brakes have failed barreling down a track. Ahead are five people who are unable to move, and the trolley is going to hit them. You have the ability to pull a lever and swing the trolley to an alternate track. However, on that track is a single person who is similarly unable to move. Do you let the trolley stay on course and kill five people? Or do you pull the lever and kill one person who would otherwise have been safe?

Until today, Hugh would have said that the lesser of two evils would be the loss of a single life, rather than five lives. But things changed when you had your hand on that lever and the doomed person on the alternate track was someone you loved.

It was as if Bex was on one track and Wren on another. What if trying to engage the shooter via negotiation took so much time that Bex, injured, didn't survive? What if he attempted to get Bex help quickly, disarming the situation via force, and wound up putting Wren in the line of fire?

Hugh dialed the number of the Center and listened to it ring, and ring, and ring. He knew, thanks to Wren, that the lack of response was not because everyone inside had been killed, including the gunman. So he hung up, and waited a moment before dialing again.

When Wren was born, Hugh had been sure there was something

wrong with him. He just couldn't get excited about a drooling, pooping bundle of flesh. Even when people came over to exclaim at her big blue eyes or her thick head of hair, he smiled and nodded and secretly thought she looked like a tiny alien. Of course he adored her. He would have laid down his life for her. He understood the duty that came with being a parent, but not the visceral pull he'd heard others describe.

Just you wait, Bex had told him, and like always, she was right.

That miracle had happened when Wren was three and her nursery school teacher casually mentioned how cute it was that she and a little boy named Saheed played house together. *Who's Saheed?* he had asked that day, driving her home. *Oh*, Wren had said. *My boyfriend.*

The first time he had seen Wren on the playground, holding hands with Saheed, Hugh had very clearly felt the world shift. That was the moment he realized that Wren did not belong to him. In fact, Hugh belonged to *her*.

One day, she would not need him to help her decide if she should wear leggings with candy corn on them, or foxes. One day, she would remember all the words to "Bohemian Rhapsody" without him filling in the gaps as they sang along in the car. One day she wouldn't ask him to get the Goldfish crackers from a shelf she could not reach. One day she would not need him anymore.

Sometimes you can't tell how consuming love is until you can see its absence. Sometimes you can't recognize love because it's changed you, like a chimera, so slowly that you didn't witness the transformation.

As Hugh watched Saheed following Wren like a loyal subject, he thought of all the crap he had pulled when he was trying to get a girl's attention, and he vowed never to let any guy treat her the way he had treated girls in high school. But he also knew that he couldn't protect her. That she would be heartbroken one day, and he would have to see her cry.

That was fatherhood. Fatherhood was wanting to put his daugh-

ter in a bubble where she could never be hurt, while knowing that
he had hurt someone else's daughter, once. Fatherhood was plot-
ting the future murder of a sweet kid named Saheed because he had
the wisdom to see that nobody else in the world was as awesome as
Wren.

Now, Hugh scrolled through forgotten conversations in his
mind. In any of them, had Wren mentioned a boy?

Wren had said she was here with Bex. But this was an abortion clinic. Bex was too old to need one. Maybe his sister had come
here for another reason, but why would she have taken Wren out of
school to accompany her?

Unless . . .

He couldn't even finish that sentence in his mind.

He decided that after he saved Wren's life, he would find out
who the boy was. And then maybe kill him.

Hugh dialed the phone number of the Center again. This time,
on the third ring, a woman answered. Not Wren.

But he had made first contact. *Now*, he thought. *Go.*

"This is Lieutenant McElroy with the Jackson Police. Am I on
speakerphone?"

"No."

"Who am I speaking with?"

"Um, my name is Izzy . . ."

"Izzy," Hugh said, "I'm here to help you. Can I talk to the person
who might be able to resolve this situation?"

He heard her say to someone: "It's the police and they want you."

And then: "Yeah?"

The voice of the shooter rumbled like a stick drawn across fence
posts. Just that one syllable opened a cave Hugh could peer into.
The word was deep, boiling, wary. But it was also one word, rather
than a barrage of them. Which meant he was listening.

"This is Detective Hugh McElroy of the Jackson Police Department. I'm with the hostage negotiation unit. I'm here to talk to you and ensure the safety of you and everyone else in the building."

"I have nothing to talk about," the shooter said. "These people are murderers."

"Okay," Hugh replied, no judgment. An acknowledgment. "What's your name, sir?" he asked, although he already knew. "What would you like to be called?"

"George."

In the background, Hugh could hear an agonized cry. *Please let it not be Bex*, he thought. "Are you hurt, George?"

"I'm fine."

"Is anyone else hurt? Does someone need a doctor? It sounds like there might be some people in pain."

"They don't deserve help."

Hugh felt the eyes of Chief Monroe and at least a dozen other officers on him. He turned his back. The relationship he needed to build with George Goddard was between the two of them, and no one else. "Whatever happened in there, George, you're not to blame. I know that there are other people at fault here. Whatever happened, happened. That's over and done. But you and I can work together, now, to make sure no one else gets hurt. We can resolve this . . . and help you . . . at the same time."

Hugh waited for a response, but there wasn't one. Well. It beat *Fuck you*. As long as George was still on the line, he had a chance.

"Here's my phone number, in case we get disconnected," Hugh said. He rattled off the digits. "I'm the one in charge out here."

"Why should I trust you?" George asked.

"Well," Hugh said, having known this question would come, "we haven't stormed the building, have we? My gun is still in my holster, George. I want to work with you. I want us to both get what we want."

"You can't give me what I want," George answered.

"Try me."

"Really."

Hugh could hear the sarcasm in George's voice. "Really," he confirmed.

"Bring my grandchild back to life," George said, and he hung up the phone.

Eleven a.m.

IT WASN'T AS IF THE WAITING ROOM OF THE CENTER SCREAMED, *We do abortions here*. It reminded Wren a little of her dentist's office: bad art on the walls, magazines from the Stone Age, a television playing some dumb talk show. There was a couch and a smattering of chairs, none of which matched. The coffee table had deep grooves in it, as if it had come from a previous, careless home.

Then again, not everyone was here to have an abortion. *She* wasn't. Her aunt wasn't. The other woman in the waiting room clearly wasn't either: an older woman with sleek silver hair and red-rimmed eyes.

Wren wondered if that woman was making the assumption that she was pregnant, that she had gotten herself "in trouble." She was here for the exact opposite reason.

Could people tell that she was a virgin? Did hooking up with a guy change you, somehow, from the inside out? Would she come downstairs the morning after *It* happened and would her father instantly know by looking at her?

The thought embarrassed her. What if her dad could tell, and he asked her about it? *Could you pass me the salt, and who the hell did you sleep with?*

It wasn't really that she was afraid he'd kill Ryan. (He might *want* to, but he was an officer of the law, through and through.) It was that for so long it had just been the two of them. Even though she didn't think things would change—and didn't want things to change—it felt like there would always be someone else between them now.

The lady at the front desk who had checked her in was chatting with a pink-haired girl who had just come into the Center. "Sorry I'm late, Vonita," the girl said.

"Thank the Lord you're here. I don't have a single escort out there."

"What happened to Sister Donna?"

"She didn't show," Vonita said. "Maybe the Vatican finally got her to quit."

Aunt Bex nudged Wren with her shoulder and raised her eyebrows. Wren smirked, an entire conversation without words. It had always been like that between them. "A *nun*?" Bex whispered.

"And you thought *you* were the least likely person to be here," Wren replied. "How much school do you think I'm going to miss? Another whole period?"

"Aren't you here to keep that very thing from happening?" Bex smiled. "I don't know what you're complaining about. Personally, I am riveted by the reading material."

On the coffee table beside them was a stack of pamphlets: "The Gynecological Visit and Exam—What to Expect."

"For Parents and Male Partners and Friends: After Her Abortion."

"What Is HPV?"

There was also a Sharpie marker. Wren hiked her knee up and, with the marker, began to draw stars on the sole of her Converse sneaker. One star, two. A constellation—Virgo. Just for the sheer sarcasm.

She knew that her aunt wasn't as calm as she was making herself out to be. Aunt Bex had told Wren repeatedly that she didn't feel comfortable coming inside, and would drop her off and wait in the parking lot. Until they'd gotten here, that is, and had seen the row of protesters. Then Aunt Bex had decided there was no way she was sending her girl in solo.

Last week in Aunt Bex's studio she had heard something awesome on NPR: for the first time ever scientists had watched two neutron stars collide over a hundred million light-years away. It was called a kilonova, and it was such an enormous crash that gravitational waves were created, and light was released. The dude being interviewed said that it took a collision of forces that giant to create the particles that made up gold and platinum. Wren thought that was something her dad would love: to know that the most precious materials came from the clashes of titans.

She had to remember to tell him that. So she inked a tiny star on the crescent of skin between her thumb and index finger. At dinner, he'd see it and say, *You're probably going to die of ink poisoning, you know,* which would remind Wren to tell him about the kilonova. She'd conveniently omit the part about where she was when she'd drawn it on herself.

That's what you did for people you loved, right? You protected them from what they didn't want to know.

AFTER OLIVE'S APPOINTMENT, SHE HAD walked into the waiting room. Staggered, really. She didn't know how she had gotten from the examination room to here. One minute she had been sitting with Harriet, the nurse practitioner she'd been seeing for years for her checkups, and trying to absorb what she had been told. Then just like that, her brain had hit its overload capacity. Somehow she had said goodbye, stood up, walked down the hall, and stood in front of the reception desk, her features blank.

Vonita, the lovely woman who ran the Center, had come from her desk and wrapped her massive arms tight around Olive. "Miss Olive," she said. "How you holding up?"

How could she answer that?

Vonita steered her toward a seat in the waiting room, near a young girl who was tapping her foot anxiously. "You don't have to leave yet," Vonita said. "You just sit here, get your bearings."

Olive nodded. It wasn't her bearings that needed readjusting. Her brain, about which she knew more than the vast majority of people on this planet, was just fine. It was the rest of her body that felt foreign to her.

She had been betrayed by it before, but in a much different way. It had been ten years ago, when she was still living with a woman who, like a tide, was wearing her away at the edges. She pretended she was happy, but what she really meant was that she was settled. That this was easier than wondering, again, if there would ever be anyone for her.

Then she had gone to a faculty mixer at the university to celebrate the start of the new year. Her partner didn't come—she hated these things, where no one seemed to ask the right questions about her and her career designing, as she called them, workable kitchens (but weren't they all?). So Olive had attended alone, planning to stay just long enough to be seen by the head of the department, and then go home and indulge in a glass of wine or maybe a bottle. But then she noticed a woman at the bar with long hair, so long that it was unfashionable, like a seventies flashback. Like Lady Godiva, Olive thought, as she watched the woman throw back three shots of bourbon and ask the bartender for a fourth.

You okay? Olive asked her.

Yes. On the other hand, Peg replied, *the dean of the engineering school is a misogynistic dick.*

Olive didn't answer. She, who had never cheated and had never wanted to, was watching Peg's lips form the words, mesmerized.

Oh fuck, Peg said. *You're his wife, aren't you?*

Um, nope. Not even close. She moved closer and rested her elbow on the bar. *Did you know that drinking doesn't actually make you forget anything? When you're blackout drunk, the brain just temporarily loses its ability to make memories.*

Does that line ever work? Peg asked.

Don't know. I'm road testing it.

Peg laughed. *So. If I keep up this pace, I might not remember meeting you?*

That's about right.

She pushed away that last shot glass, and held out her hand to introduce herself.

Now, Olive buried her face in her hands. Oh, Jesus. Peg. How would she tell her?

The thought chased itself around and around in her mind, like a squirrel in the eaves. Olive could feel panic closing in on her. She took a deep breath and closed her eyes and tried to remind herself that what she was feeling was perfectly normal. The brain could only hold so much; it took roughly ninety minutes to clear its proverbial cache.

On the heels of that came another tidbit of knowledge, one she had often quoted when she handed back the first multiple-choice exam to groans of disappointment. Studies have shown that when presented with a list, the default of the brain is to pick whatever is first.

The same holds true for voting, and ballots.

But sometimes there *are* no choices, Olive realized.

What does the brain do when you've run out of options?

IT WASN'T EASY TO VOMIT quietly, but the bathroom that Izzy had ducked into was located right off the waiting room. When she finished, she wiped her face with toilet paper and rinsed her mouth out. Then she stood there, taking a moment.

The bathroom was decorated like the rest of the building—as if the art had been picked up from garage sales or worse, from the Free boxes of items that didn't sell. On the wall was a photograph of what looked like the French Riviera, a technically weak oil painting of a sad clown, and a detailed, biologically correct pen-and-ink illustration of a shrimp.

All three of them made her think of Parker.

Last weekend, his parents had come to visit and had taken them out to a meal that cost half of what she made in a week. It was one of those steak and seafood houses where the food was airlifted in from the North Sea or a ranch in New Zealand, where you could keep a private wine cellar with your own special vintage. Parker's father had ordered a seafood tower for the table that looked like a wedding cake: tiers of oysters and mussels, ribbons of smoked mackerel and bluefish dip, buttons of sweet baby scallops, crowned by a whole lobster. It was dazzling, excessive, and completely out of Izzy's purview.

Parker's mother talked about the work she did with the hospital auxiliary, and Parker's father asked Izzy all sorts of questions, like whether she always wanted to be a nurse and where she went to school. They talked about their recent trip to Paris and asked Izzy if she had ever been there, and when Izzy said no, they said they hoped she and Parker could come along next time. Clearly Parker had told them that she was important to him.

She watched Parker dribble down oysters and use a fish knife and never have to stress about which plate was for the bread and which drinking glass belonged to him, when Izzy still had to stick her hands under the table and form a lowercase *b* and *d* with her left and right hands to remind herself. The things that were instinctual to him were foreign to her, and vice versa. She doubted that Parker had ever had to gauge if moldy bread could still be consumed without making him sick. She was certain he had never fished a half-finished sandwich from the trash to eat, or gone into the laundromat to feel in the machines for quarters others left behind.

She could tell he sensed her unease, because every now and then he would reach for her hand and squeeze it underneath the tablecloth. He put a small collection of seafood on her plate, so she wouldn't have to worry about whether it was completely gauche to pick up a mussel shell with her fingers.

There was no denying that he calmed her. When his thumb rubbed over her knuckles, absentmindedly, she could breathe more easily. She let him coax her into the conversation as if it were a frigid pool.

She got so comfortable that for a moment, she forgot who she had been. Parker's father told a stupid dad joke, just like the ones her own father used to tell: *What do you call it when you feed dynamite to a steer? Abominable. Get it? Say it slowly* . . . Parker's mother slapped him lightly on the shoulder and rolled her eyes. *For God's sake, Tom, you'll scare her off.* It felt so normal, so similar to her own parents' behavior, that she made the mistake of thinking she and Parker actually did have common ground.

Laughing, she lifted a shrimp from her plate and took a bite.

It crunched, which was weird, but then lots of food rich people liked was weird: caviar, pâté, raw beef. It wasn't until she noticed Parker's parents staring at her that she realized her mistake. She'd never had a shrimp in her life—how was she supposed to know to peel the shell?

"Excuse me," she muttered, and she fled to the ladies' room.

She hid there, thinking about telling Parker about the pregnancy test she had taken. If he knew she was pregnant, he would never let her go. She was doing what was best for him. Even if he thought Izzy was what he wanted right now, it was only a matter of time before he decided he'd rather be with someone from the same background as him. Someone who'd eaten shrimp before, for God's sake.

"Iz?" It was Parker's voice.

"You're in the ladies' room," she said.

"Am I? Damn." He paused. "You gonna come out?"

"No."

"Ever?"

"No."

A woman walked into the bathroom and squeaked. "Sorry, can you give us a minute?" Parker asked. Izzy heard the door open, the buzz of the restaurant before it got quiet again. "You know what? I fucking hate shrimp. It's like eating something prehistoric," he said. "The point is, I don't care."

"I do." That was it, in a nutshell. "Parker, go back to your parents. There's nothing you can say that's going to make this any better."

"Nothing?" Parker replied.

She heard shuffling and shifting, and then Parker's hand slipped under the stall door, his fist opening like a blossom to reveal a diamond ring. "Izzy," he said, "will you marry me?"

ONLY ONE OTHER WOMAN HAD been in the recovery room when Joy was brought in. She wore an Ole Miss sweatshirt and pool shoes, and she was crying. "You have a seat in that chair, honey," the nurse said, flicking a glance at her other patient. Harriet handed Joy a juice box and a packet of Fig Newtons. "You got your azithromycin?" Joy nodded. "Good. You take that as directed. You can also take Motrin or Advil in two hours, but no aspirin, okay? It thins the blood. And here's a prescription for Sprintec, that's the birth control you picked, right?"

Joy nodded absently. She couldn't stop staring at the other woman, who was sobbing so hard that Joy felt rude for intruding on someone's visible grief. What did it say about Joy, who *wasn't* crying? Was this the proof that she had been looking for, that she would have been a lousy mother?

"Will you excuse me a second?" Harriet said, and she went over to the woman's chair and put a hand on her shoulder. "Are you all right? Are you in pain?"

The woman shook her head, past speech.

"Are you sad that you had to make this decision?"

Who wasn't? Joy thought. What hellish tributary of evolution had made reproduction—and all the shit that came with it—the woman's job? She thought about all the women who had sat in the very chair she was in, and the stories that had brought them here, and how, for one brief chapter, they all intersected. A sisterhood of desperation.

The woman took a Kleenex from a box that Harriet offered her. "Sometimes we have to make choices when we don't like any of the options," the nurse said. She drew the woman into an embrace. "You've been here long enough. I can get your driver if you're ready to go."

A few minutes later the woman was signed out. A boy (he really was no more than that) stood awkwardly beside her as she got up and started to walk down the hall. He put his hand on her shoulder, but she shrugged it off, and Joy watched them until she couldn't see them anymore, moving in tandem with six fixed inches of distance between them.

Joy put in her earbuds and filled her head with music. Had anyone asked, she would have said she was listening to Beyoncé or Lana Del Rey, but the truth was she was listening to music from *The Little Mermaid*. At one of her foster homes, she had been given that CD as a birthday gift and had memorized every last word of it. When things got really bad, she used to put the pillow over her head and whisper the lyrics.

Wouldn't you think I'm a girl, a girl who has everything?

"Miz Joy?" the nurse said. "Let's get some vitals." She came and stood beside Joy's oversize armchair in the recovery room.

Joy let Harriet stick the thermometer into her mouth and Velcro the cuff around her arm. She watched the red numbers blink on the machine, proof that her body, battered as it was, was still functional. "One-ten over seventy-five, and ninety-eight point six," the nurse said. "Normal."

Normal.

Nothing was normal.

The whole world had changed.

She had had two hearts, and now she did not.

She had been a mother, and now she was not.

GEORGE SAT IN HIS TRUCK, his hands fisted on the steering wheel, going nowhere. The ignition was off, and he had two choices. He could start the engine again and drive back home and pretend he'd never come. Or he could finish what he'd started.

He was breathing heavily, like he'd run here, instead of driving hundreds of miles to distance himself from a truth he couldn't absorb.

He thought about how he and Lil had once been part of a Thirty Days for Life vigil with the church: where the congregation took shifts round the clock, huddled in a prayer circle in front of the state capitol. They had brought blankets and lawn chairs and thermoses of hot chocolate and had held hands and asked Jesus to help lawmakers see the right path. Lil had been a child—maybe eight or nine— and she and some other kids in the congregation had run around while the adults prayed. He could remember watching them spell out their names with sparklers in the dark, and thinking this was what the movement for life was all about.

How could Lil have gotten an abortion?

She had to have been pressured. Someone here must have told her this was the right thing, the only thing, to do. She couldn't have possibly believed that he wouldn't have helped her, raised the child, done anything she wanted.

In the back of his mind was a thought like a worm in the core of an apple: *what if this* was *what she wanted?*

George didn't believe it; he couldn't. She was a good girl, because he had been a good father.

If the first half of that statement wasn't true, didn't it negate the second half?

Lil had accepted Jesus Christ as her Lord and Savior. She knew that life began at conception. She could probably rattle off five Bible verses proving it. She was kind, generous, beautiful, smart, and everyone fell in love with her when they met her. Lil was, quite simply, the one instance of perfection in George's life.

He realized, of course, that everyone was a sinner. But if there was any splinter of evil in his daughter, he knew where it had come from.

Him.

George, who had spent nearly two decades trying to scrub clean the stains from his soul by giving himself to the church. George, who had been told forgiveness was divine; that God loved him no matter what. What if all that had been a lie?

George shook his head clear. It was this simple: something terrible had happened; someone was to blame for it. This was a test from God. Like the one Job faced. And Abraham. He was being asked to prove his devotion to his faith, and to his daughter, and he knew exactly what was expected of him.

He slipped on his coat and zipped it up halfway. Then he took the pistol out of the glove compartment and tucked it into his waistband, concealing it beneath the fleece. His pockets were already full of ammunition.

He started sweating almost immediately, but then again, it was easily eighty degrees outside. He began moving toward the hazard-orange building. It was garish, a scar on the cityscape. George ducked his head, pulled his collar up.

There was a fence around the Center, and on that perimeter was a cluster of protesters. They held up signs. There was a woman sitting in a folding chair, knitting; and a big man holding a sandwich in one hand and a baby doll in another. George thought about Lil. He wondered if he was walking the same path she had.

A Black woman was leaving the clinic. Her husband or boyfriend had his arm around her. As they passed the protesters, he folded her more protectively into the shell of his body. He crossed paths with the couple, and kept walking. The big man eating the sandwich called out to him. "Brother," he said, "save your baby!"

George continued to the front door of the Center, thinking, *I will.*

OUT OF SHEER BOREDOM, WREN was eavesdropping.

"Dr. Ward's been at it since nine-thirty," Vonita was saying. "We had a fifteen-week come in for Cytotec this morning and she's in the back now."

"All that while I was sitting home eating bonbons?" The girl with pink hair laughed.

"Bonbons," Vonita sighed. "I wish." She took a sip from her tumbler.

"What's in there?"

"I hope it's the ground-up bones of supermodels," Vonita said sourly. "This crap is the work of the devil."

"Why do you even drink that garbage?"

Vonita gestured to her generous curves. "Because of my torrid love affair with food."

Aunt Bex stood up. "I think I'm growing roots," she said, starting to walk in small circles. "How long can it take to give someone a prescription?" Wren watched her lift her arms over her head, bend at the waist, and do it over again.

Oh my God. Her aunt was doing old-person yoga in *public.*

A buzzer hummed on the reception desk, and Vonita glanced up over her reading glasses. "Now, who does this one belong to?" she mused.

Wren craned her neck. The glass window in the door of the Center was specially made, so that they could see out but whoever was on the outside could not see in. She glimpsed a middle-aged man squinting into the mirrored surface.

She heard a click, the buzz of a lock being released, like Wren had seen in movies about New York apartments. "Can I help you?" Vonita said.

About a year ago, Wren and her father had been driving a deserted road near Chunky, Mississippi, when suddenly all the hair stood up on the back of her neck. The next minute, a doe had bolted from the woods and slammed into the car. They had been hit hard enough for the airbags to deploy and for the windshield to shatter. It was the one truly prescient moment of her life.

Until now.

Wren felt a shiver of electricity, the brush of an invisible icy finger. "What did you do to my baby?" the man said, and then the air around her cracked into pieces.

She fell to the floor, covering her ears. It was as if her body had reacted on instinct, while her brain was still struggling to catch up. She couldn't see Vonita anymore, but there was a pool of blood spreading where the reception desk met the floor.

Wren tried to will herself to move, but she was frozen in ice, she was trapped in tar.

"Wren," Aunt Bex cried, reaching out her hand.

To pull her up? To drag her out the door? To embrace her?

Wren didn't know. Because then her aunt's eyes went wide, and she was struck with a bullet. She tumbled to the floor as Wren scrambled closer, screaming, her hands shaking as they hovered over the bright blood on her aunt's blouse.

Aunt Bex's eyes were wide. Her mouth was open, but Wren couldn't hear any sound coming out.

She read her aunt's lips. *Wren. Wren. Wren.*

Then she realized what her aunt was actually saying.

Run.

THE OTHER CLINIC HAD BEEN nothing like this one, Janine thought. It had been in a different state, in a different life, in a part of town full of drunks and Vietnam vets fighting PTSD. There had been someone smoking a bowl in the alley next to the building, and the lobby had smelled like Chinese food. But none of the differences could make Janine shake the fact that she had willingly—once again—entered an abortion factory.

Janine sat on the ultrasound table, her phone tucked in a pocket of her dress, where it was taping the entire conversation between her and the social worker.

Her name was Graciela, and she had the most beautiful black hair Janine had ever seen. It reached her waist. By contrast, the cheap wig that Allen had given her for camouflage was itchy and brassy. Janine scratched her temple. "Still . . . you think I should get an abortion, right?"

The social worker smiled a little. "I can't answer that for you. You'll know in your gut what to do."

"But I don't."

"Well," Graciela suggested, "you're early, right? Only seven weeks? Take a walk. Go outside. Clear your mind. Sleep on it. Sleep on it again if you have to. Write down what you're feeling to sort through your emotions. Scream into your pillow. Cry. Let it out. Talk to friends or family. Ultimately, the decision is all yours, Fiona."

Fiona? Janine frowned, and then remembered that was the name on the fake ID she had used at the reception desk.

Graciela reached for her hand and squeezed. She was being so kind that it made Janine feel sick inside. Why wasn't she saying something incriminating?

Why hadn't there been someone like Graciela when she had . . .

"It's not about making the right choice," Graciela said. "It's about making the right choice for *you*."

"But I'm really scared," Janine said. She needed evidence. She needed to collect proof that they coerced people into killing babies.

"Every woman who's ever been in your shoes has been scared," Graciela assured her. "You're not alone."

"My family would be so disappointed in me." Janine felt tears burn in her eyes. Not because she was such a stellar actress, though. Because it was the truth.

"It's going to be okay," Graciela promised. "I know it doesn't feel that way right now, but I promise you—no matter what your decision is, it's going to be the right one." She drew back, holding Janine at arm's length, and gestured in the direction of the ultrasound machine. "We don't have to do this today."

Janine paused, trying to figure out what to do next. She couldn't have the ultrasound without revealing that she wasn't pregnant. But she didn't want to go back to Allen empty-handed.

In the silence there was a sound, like books dropping. Then a shriek and a crash. Graciela frowned. "Will you excuse me?" She opened the door to the consultation room as Janine reached into her pocket to check the recording. Suddenly, Janine was knocked flat on her back. Dropping the phone, she struggled upright, pinned by the social worker, tangled in her river of hair. She finally freed herself as Graciela fell to the floor, landing on her belly. "Graciela?" Janine said, crouching down. She reached for the woman's shoulder and shook, and when Graciela didn't respond, she turned her over.

Graciela had been shot in the face.

Janine screamed, noticing for the first time the blood on her hands and her clothing. She couldn't breathe. She couldn't think. With a whimper, Janine scrambled to her feet, stepped over the body, and ran.

* * *

WHEN SHE WAS DRIVING WITH Wren once, Bex had slammed on the brakes and instinctively had thrown out her right arm to protect the precious cargo in the passenger seat. The Mom Arm, Wren had called it. Even if her actual mom had not been especially devoted.

Today, as soon as the man came in, Bex's body moved of its own accord. Something was not right, she had seen it in his body language, sweat beaded on his forehead and matting down his hair. She had *known* on some visceral, cellular level; and just as when her car spun on the ice, without any conscious thought, Bex had reached toward her niece.

She saw the blink of the silver pistol as he drew it from the folds of his coat. She even saw the burst of lightning from the barrel of the gun, which ripped a hole in the fabric of the room, and sucked all the sound out of it. She was aware that she was watching a pantomime, that her eardrums were full of pressure and a pulsing silence, but somehow she was an actor in this show and she had a line. Bex felt the scream stream from her throat, and even though she couldn't hear it, the man must have. He pivoted, and Bex felt herself shoved backward before she even realized that the bullet had struck.

Don't shoot don't shoot don't shoot, she said over and over, even though he already had. But Bex really meant, *Don't shoot Wren.*

Then Wren was leaning down over her. "Aunt B-bex, get up . . ." Her eyes were like Hugh's.

Her hair, though, that came from her mother. It brushed Bex's cheek, like a fall of silk, a curtain that closed them off from the world.

Last year Bex had opened an art installation in the center of Smith Park. From the limb of a tree she hung a tiny striped circus tent, just big enough for one. If you slipped inside, you saw an easel with a white canvas, and a scatter of colored Sharpies. BEFORE I DIE, Bex had painted across the top, I WANT TO . . .

Over the course of two weeks, people who came to the park to eat lunch or skateboard or read a book had wandered inside out of curiosity, and had contributed their own answers.

. . . swim in all five oceans.

. . . run a marathon.

. . . fall in love.

. . . learn Mandarin.

When Bex took down the installation she had, at the very bottom of the canvas, finished her own open sentence, painting the word

Live.

She stared up at Wren and imagined a parallel universe where she could still breathe, where she could still move. Where she put her palm against the cheek of her beautiful girl. Where she got to turn back the clock, and do it over.

BEFORE OLIVE HAD RETIRED FROM the university, the dean had handed down a protocol for a school shooting. Mississippi allowed concealed carry of weapons, and even if you weren't supposed to bring one onto a college campus, that didn't mean it wouldn't happen. However, as she had told Peg that night, she didn't want to have to go to work every day wondering if today would be the one she had to Run-Hide-Fight. It was the first time she had ever felt weary of her work, and it was the first seed planted in her mind that perhaps it was time to stop teaching, and to take up gardening or bread making. The world was changing; maybe she should step aside for someone else, who could not only talk about neural plasticity, but do so while escaping a maniac with a semiautomatic rifle.

It hadn't sounded like a shot. That was all Olive could think as she swam up from the gauzy tunnel of her thoughts. It was like popcorn in a microwave. It wasn't until she heard a scream that she even looked up and saw a pink-haired girl race past her and out the front door.

Then she looked down to find a woman bleeding on the carpet with a teenager huddled over her.

There was a crash in the back of the clinic.

The teenager turned, her eyes enormous. "Help."

Run.

Olive stood and glanced around wildly. She could see an arm flung bonelessly past the base of the reception desk, a dark arm with a festival of gold bangle bracelets, swimming in a pool of blood. Sweet Jesus; that was Vonita.

Olive grabbed the girl's wrist, pulling her toward the front door, but the girl was steadfastly clinging to the woman who'd been shot. "We have to get out of here," Olive said to her.

"Not without my aunt."

Olive grimaced and tried to pull the other woman up, but even with Wren's help, they couldn't move her more than a few inches. The cry that tore from the woman's throat was a red flag that would draw the shooter again. "If we leave, we can get her an ambulance."

That convinced the girl. She scrambled to her feet as Olive pulled on the door handle, but it was locked. You had to be buzzed into the clinic, was it possible you had to be buzzed out? She threw all her slight weight into the mechanism, even pounding on the door, but it didn't give.

"We're stuck here?" the girl asked, her voice shimmying up a scale of panic.

Hide.

Olive didn't answer. She opened the first door she could find. It was a supply closet, filled with boxes on one side and cleaning supplies on the other. Olive crouched down, pulling the girl in with her, and shut the door.

This was where her knowledge of the shooting protocol got fuzzy. She had left her purse in the waiting room, and with it her phone. She couldn't call 911. Should she try to barricade the door? If so, with what?

She couldn't help but note that had she not been sitting in a waiting room contemplating mortality, her life would not be in danger right now.

Beside her, the girl's teeth were chattering. "I'm Olive," she whispered. "What's your name?"

"Wr-Wren."

"Wren, I want you to listen to me. We can't make a sound, understand?"

The girl nodded.

"That's your aunt out there?"

She jerked her head. "Is she . . . is she going to die?"

Olive didn't know how to answer that. She patted the girl's hand. "I'm sure the police are already on their way."

In truth, she was not sure about this at all. If she had thought that the gunshots sounded like bubble wrap being stomped on, why would anyone outside the clinic even assume anything was wrong? *Fight*, she thought, the last step of the protocol. *When your life is in imminent danger and you cannot run away or hide, take action.*

The directive seemed particularly relevant today.

Suddenly in the dark there was a small rectangle of light.

"You have a phone," Olive whispered with wonder. "You have a *phone*! Call 911."

In the reflection of the screen, Wren's face was set, determined. Olive watched her thumbs fly. "I can do better than that," she said.

IZZY HEARD WHAT SOUNDED LIKE balloons bursting, and then a cry for help. She opened the bathroom door and saw a woman bleeding on the floor of the waiting room.

She was conscious, and clearly in pain. "What happened?"

"Shot," the woman ground out.

Izzy pressed down on her chest. "What's your name, ma'am? I'm Izzy." The bullet had gone in the right side, which was good, because it most likely meant her heart was not affected.

"Bex," the woman gasped. "Need to get . . . Wren . . ."

"Let's take care of you first." Izzy reached onto a side table, scrabbling by feel for a box of tissues, and wadded them up to press into the wound.

Within seconds, they were soaked through. "I'll be right back," she said, and she stood up. From this angle she could see a second victim—Vonita, the clinic owner. Izzy started toward her and then saw the open, vacant eyes, the blood pooled beneath her head. There was nothing she could do.

Izzy ran into the bathroom and pulled the little decorative shelf from the wall. She smashed it into the paper towel holder so that it cracked open, and the wad of towels fell like an accordion around her feet. Gathering them, she rushed back to Bex, using these to soak up the blood.

With every subsequent gunshot she heard, Izzy's limbs became more liquid. It was only by doing something rote—taking care of a patient—that Izzy was able to keep herself from falling apart. She needed to get out of here, and it needed to be now. But Bex was a large woman, and Izzy couldn't lift her alone. She could save herself, but that would mean leaving Bex behind.

Or she could help Bex—stabilize her wound with bandages. But if she went to get those, she was risking her own life *and* Bex's, because someone had to stay and apply pressure to the wound.

What she needed, really, was someone to help.

JUST AS JANINE TURNED THE corner and saw the mecca of the Center's front door, she saw a dead woman. The clinic owner. She gasped, scrambling away from the body, and when another hand gripped her she screamed like a banshee. She opened her eyes and saw a woman with a frizzy red braid and blood streaking her scrubs. "Listen to me," she said. "I'm a nurse and I need your help. This woman needs your help." She nodded toward another lady lying with a pool of blood staining the floor beneath her right shoulder.

Janine could barely force out the words. "B-but . . . there's a sh-shooter . . ."

"I know. I also know that she could bleed out. I need to get supplies to help her. Please, just press down where my hand is. I promise it will only take a minute, and then you can go."

Janine looked at the door; the nurse followed her gaze.

"You could save your own life," the nurse said, "or you could save hers, too."

If the only lives Janine cared about were those of the unborn, that would make her a hypocrite. She got to her knees beside the nurse, who positioned her hands against the wound.

"I'm Izzy. What's your name?"

"Janine."

"This is Bex," she said. "Press hard." Just like that, she was gone, leaving Janine with her hands pushing hard on the chest of a stranger.

Bex was staring up at her. "Am I hurting you?" Janine asked.

The woman shook her head. "You . . . should go." She jerked her chin up toward the door.

Janine realized that this woman was giving her a literal out, a way to rescue herself. If she left now, she'd survive. She just might not be able to live with herself.

She settled more firmly, covering one of her hands with the other, the way Izzy had shown her. Blood welled between her fingers. "Bex?" Janine asked, smiling as if she weren't terrified. "Do you pray?"

GEORGE WAS GASPING FOR AIR, as if he'd run a four-minute mile. He leaned against the wall, hands shaking. This had to be done, and he knew God would forgive him. It was right there in Isaiah 43:25: *I,*

*even I, am he who blots out your transgressions, for my own sake, and re-
members your sins no more.*

But there was a difference between the righteous anger that had
accompanied him on his long drive and the actual feeling of the pistol recoiling in his hand when he shot. And even though he knew it
was ridiculous, the recoil seemed harder when his bullet struck flesh
versus when it only struck plaster.

When he looked down, his jeans were spattered with blood.

Well, he wasn't the one who'd spilled it first.

There was no way anyone could claim that he didn't have a moral
high ground. He couldn't undo what had been done to Lil. But he
could have retribution. He could teach them the lesson he had not
been able to teach her: life is something only God should give and
take.

George looked down again at the pistol in his hand.

He had forgotten what it was like to watch someone die. In
Bosnia, that man who struck his head on the curb had grabbed at
George's arm and stared into his eyes as if there were a cord stretched
between them, and as long as he didn't blink, he would be able to
stay in this world.

It had been the same when he opened fire at the clinic and struck
the receptionist—he had seen her eyes the moment they went dark,
like a candle at the end of its wick. The second woman he shot, well,
that was an accident. He hadn't even noticed her when he walked
inside. He had only looked at the front desk and what was beyond it.
But when she started yelling, he had to shut her up. He had to. His
body had just taken over.

George told himself this was no different from being a soldier. In
war, killing wasn't murder, it was a mission. Today he fought for the
army of God. Angels weren't always messengers. They could destroy
a city with a twitch of the hand. Sometimes violence was necessary
to remind the fallen of God's power. If people didn't lose His grace

every now and then, they wouldn't realize how lucky they were when they had it.

Still, George wondered if the angels who had flattened Sodom and Gomorrah, or the one who had killed Sennacherib's army, had trouble sleeping at night. He wondered if they saw the faces of the dead everywhere.

When he'd shot the woman in the waiting room, she had stepped forward like a sacrifice.

I am doing this for you, he thought, catching his daughter's name between his teeth as he wrenched himself forward.

I am doing this for you.

WHEN BETH WAS LITTLE, SHE would throw couch pillows on the floor and pretend the world was lava, and she had to jump from island to island. Now that she was older, the world was still a boiling soup of injustice, and Beth was just trying to get through it as best she could.

She had never felt so alone in her life, but that was her own fault.

She thought about how, when she wrapped it in the towel, it had a soft, slight weight. It was the first time she had ever thought of it as something real, instead of abstract.

When Beth closed her eyes she could still see the blue translucence of its skin. The road map of circulation. The shadows of its organs. Her pulse began to race, and a moment later Jayla, the nurse, came into the room. She pushed a button on a monitor.

"Is my father back?" Beth asked.

Jayla shook her head. When Beth had first come in, Jayla had held her hand, stroked her brow. There seemed to be a barrier between them now, and Beth bit her lower lip. Even when she wasn't trying, she seemed to screw things up.

Just then two policemen filled the doorframe.

"Nathan?" Jayla swayed toward one of the cops, a question caught in that one word.

He shook his head the tiniest bit, and then turned. "You're Beth?"

She drew her knees to her chest, afraid to look at him.

"You're being charged with homicide, for the killing of an unborn child."

Beth had already felt the bottom drop out of her world. It was a shock to realize that had been a false landing, that she had further to fall. She tried to put together the pieces, but they didn't fit. She was in a hospital. She had lost so much blood. She had almost died. The only people who even knew she had been pregnant were medical personnel.

She turned to Jayla, shocked. "You called the police," she said.

"What was I supposed to do?" she exploded. "You claimed you weren't pregnant, but you had so much hCG in your blood that couldn't be true unless you'd just delivered . . . so there was a chance a newborn was out there somewhere."

"What about patient confidentiality?" Beth said.

"HIPAA doesn't matter if a life is in danger," Jayla answered. Her eyes suddenly swam with tears.

"You have the right to remain silent," Nathan said. "Anything you say can and will be used against you in a court of law. You have the right to an attorney. If you cannot afford an attorney, one will be provided for you."

The second policeman stepped forward and handcuffed Beth's right arm to the rail of the hospital bed.

Help.

Daddy, help.

Wren must have written fifty times to her father, but he wasn't answering.

She knew he would save her. He always did. There was the

birthday party at the bowling alley when her hand was about to be crushed between two balls, and he pretty much leaped over a table, a metal divider, and a bachelorette party to stick his own hand in the gap. There was the month she was certain there was an alien living in her bedroom closet, when he diligently slept on the floor beside her bed. There was the banana bike race she had competed in at age eight, when her brakes failed and she was careening down a hill into a street with traffic. Somehow her father had caught up and plucked her off the seat with one arm a hot second before it became a pretzel.

Dad reflexes, he called it.

She just thought it was love.

Help, Wren wrote again.

ABOUT TWENTY MINUTES AFTER HIS impromptu birthday party, Hugh was called to Chief Monroe's office for actual business. He leaned back, already knowing where this conversation was going. "I've got to leave for lunch in fifteen minutes," the chief said. "With Harry Van Geld."

Hugh raised his brows, playing dumb. "The selectman?"

"Yeah. I understand his kid was picked up last night? What can you tell me?"

"Well," Hugh said. "He's an asshole, for one."

"That's not going to help me explain to his father why he was written up."

"DUI," Hugh said. "But he refused to blow."

"How come he was stopped?"

"He took the corner too fast and hit the curb. It was two A.M. Kept saying his dad was going to have my job. I didn't even know who the hell he was, at first, until I put two and two together."

The chief steepled his hands on the desk. "So we could amend the charge to reckless operation, if we don't have enough for a DUI?"

Hugh grimaced. "If you want to go that route."

"What's that supposed to mean?"

"He was drunk, Chief." Hugh shrugged. "He reeked of alcohol. And he's got a reputation."

He felt his phone buzz in his pocket, and silenced it with the push of a button.

"What about video?"

Hugh shook his head. "It's been down in the cruiser for a week. Still trying to get it fixed."

"So no breath test, no video, and we know that Van Geld is a dickhead who's going to be pissed if we charge his kid with a DUI." He frowned at Hugh. "What."

"*What* what?"

"What's the look for? You're acting like I just said I'm going to drown your puppy. If the kid had blown a 3.0, that would be one thing. But he didn't, and you don't have a BAC. He *might* have been drunk. He *definitely* was reckless. Consider it erring on the side of caution. We don't need heat from the selectboard. It's not worth it. Do me a solid here, Hugh. Amend it before the arraignment."

"Because he didn't kill anyone last night?" Hugh asked. "How about tomorrow?"

His phone vibrated again.

Chief Monroe stood up and grabbed his sports jacket. "Consider yourself lucky that you don't have to have lunch with his father."

"Guess that's why you make the big bucks." Hugh leaned back in his chair.

"Keep the town running smoothly for me, will you?" the chief said. He had a habit of taking his lunches with the radio chatter turned low, trusting the daily run of the station to Hugh when necessary.

Hugh shook his head. "The guys are going to feel like you sold them out," he said as the chief walked through the door.

"Not if you explain it to them," Monroe called back over his shoulder.

Hugh shook his head. "Definitely above my pay grade," he muttered. He stood up and reached in his pocket for his phone.

Stand by for a Code Red message . . .

The voice of the dispatcher piped through the intercoms of the
building. Hugh let his phone drop back into his pocket. From the
window of the chief's office, he saw Monroe's car pull out of the lot.

*Be advised, we have an active shooter incident taking place at the
corner of Juniper and Montfort. All sworn members are to report to the
Command Post at 320 Juniper, the Pizza Heaven parking lot, and await
further instructions. All responding members are to ensure they have their
body armor. This is an active shooter situation. I repeat, all sworn members
are to report—*

Hugh didn't hear the rest of the announcement. He was already
running out the door.

LOUIE WAS WRITING DOWN NOTES in Joy Perry's file when Harriet
came back into the procedure room. She had settled the patient in
recovery and had moved the products of conception to the lab room,
where she would do a second review. Now she started stripping the
paper from the examination table, getting it ready for the next patient. You could never say that their nurses didn't work their asses
off, that's for sure. "You got any Halloween candy?"

Harriet laughed. "If you keep taking my stash, there won't be
any by the time it's Hallo—"

Whatever she said faded away as a rain of bullets exploded outside the procedure room.

Louie grabbed Harriet and pulled her down to the floor behind
the examination table. He put his finger to his lips, for silence. He
should have closed the door. Why hadn't he closed the door?

He knew, right away, what was happening. This was the nightmare that he couldn't remember when he woke up in a cold sweat;
this was the bogeyman, all grown up; this was the other shoe drop-

ping. It was not that he had obsessed about violence as an abortion provider, but he had been aware of the possibility. He had had colleagues who were hurt. Louie couldn't let himself worry over what might happen to him if he was going to keep doing his job. He knew abortion doctors who wore masks to work to conceal their identities; he had never wanted to be one of those people. What he did was honorable and just. What he did was human. He wasn't going to hide.

It was not that he had naïvely believed this day might not come. In 1993, an arsonist had burned down the Center, and Vonita had had to rebuild. In 1998, after the abortion clinic in Birmingham was bombed by Eric Rudolph, Louie had gone to offer his support. He remembered the ATF mapping out the trajectory of the bomb, which had been full of nails: pink string, pulled tight from where the bomb had been placed to every chair in the waiting room and the receptionist's desk, a spider's web of intended damage. And yet he had listened to the phone ring as new appointments were made and had watched women march right past news trucks to have their abortions. After that, Vonita had contemplated putting bulletproof glass around the reception desk, like her husband had told her to do, but if the patients were strong enough to push past the protesters who told them they were going to Hell, shouldn't the staff be brave enough to meet them face-to-face?

Now, Louie was shaking, hard. He tried to hear where the shots were being fired—if they were getting closer—but there was a strange distortion in the sound. It wasn't, he thought, like the movies made it out to be. On the heels of that: this was a fact he wished he had never had to learn.

On his first day at the Center, Louie had arrived early. He walked across the parking lot, where he ran into a little old lady carrying a chair. *May I?* he asked, taking it from her. She thanked him, and a few hundred feet later said that this was her spot. Louie unfolded the chair and realized he was smack in the center of a group of protesters.

He walked away and ducked into Lenny's Sub Shop across the street, where he ordered a chicken salad sandwich and a Diet Coke and sat at the counter. A few minutes later he realized that someone was standing at the window taking his picture—the old lady he'd helped. *Do you know her?* the waitress asked, and Louie said no, he had never been in Mississippi before today, but that he worked across the street at the Center. The waitress rapped on the window. *If you ain't buying anything, stop loitering*, she said. She turned to Louie. *Those people need to mind their own business*, she said.

When Louie finished his sandwich, the old lady was waiting for him. She followed him across the street, shouting the whole time. *You should be ashamed of yourself. You're not a real doctor. You're a butcher.*

Louie realized two things that day: that the waitress might not be an abortion doctor or even go to a pro-choice rally, but she was an activist all the same. And that you could not underestimate an anti. Had that sweet old grandma wanted to, she had been close enough to shank him.

When he had gotten inside the Center that day, he had broken out in a sweat. For the past ten years, he had been careful. He didn't leave the building until the end of the day. He ordered food in. As long as he stayed in the Center, it was a safe space.

Until now.

Harriet was crying. Her hand shook as she reached for her phone and typed out a text. To her husband, maybe? Her kids? Did she *have* kids? Why didn't Louie know that?

Louie's phone was locked up in Vonita's office, along with his wallet. Who would he contact, anyway? He had no family left, no significant other—for this very reason. Because it was enough that he put himself on the front lines every day, doing the work he did. It wasn't fair for someone else to suffer by sheer proximity. Dr. King's words floated into his mind: *If a man has not discovered something that he will die for, he isn't fit to live.* Would he die, today, for his principles? Or had he already died years ago, by pledging himself to his work and cutting himself off from others who might get close to him? If his heart stopped beating today, would it just be a belated announcement of a death that had already happened?

Sometimes, at bars or conferences or weddings, he met women who were impressed by his bravado. They asked if he was worried about violence at clinics, and he shrugged it off. He'd say, *Life is fatal; none of us are getting out of here breathing*.

It was easy to make that joke, in response to a hypothetical question. But now?

He did not want to die, but if he did, he hoped it would be swift and not lingering.

He did not want to die, but if he did, he believed he'd been as good a man as he could have been.

He did not want to die, but if he did, he would have gotten more time than Malcolm or Martin had.

And yet. Goddammit. He wasn't finished yet.

A high-pitched whine wheezed out of Harriet; Louie was sure she didn't even know she was making the sound. He grabbed her hands and forced her to meet his gaze. "Harriet, you all right?" She shook her head, tears running. "Harriet, look at me."

Louie could see over her shoulder into the hallway. He flicked his glance away from the nurse, scanning for movement, for shadows. Five minutes passed. Or fifteen. He couldn't tell.

"Dr. Ward," Harriet whispered, "I don't want to die."

He squeezed her hands. "Harriet. You just keep your eyes right on me, you hear?"

She nodded, swallowed. Her eyes fixed on his, wide and brown, trusting. He held her faith tight, even as he saw through his peripheral vision the silhouette that rose behind her in the doorway; the twist of the pistol; the grim slash of a mouth as the man's features came into focus.

Louie's leg exploded in pain. The world narrowed to the throb of his thigh and the fire licking through the muscle. Then Harriet fell on top of him. He sucked in the smell of gardenia on her skin, tasted the copper of blood.

Footsteps. Closer.

Louie pretended to be dead. Or maybe he wished it to be true.

He held his breath, waiting to die. He counted to three hundred. And then he cracked open one eye. The shooter was gone.

He found himself looking at Harriet. There was a bullet hole, neat as a thumbtack, in the center of her forehead. A feathered fan of blood sprayed the wall behind her.

Louie turned his head and vomited.

He pushed himself up on his forearms, intent on hiding, grunting at the pain that tore through his leg. Dr. King's words beat in his head: *If you can't fly, run. If you can't run, walk. If you can't walk, crawl. But by all means, keep moving.* Based on the radiating center of the pain and the rhythmic pulse of the bleeding, Louie would guess that he'd been shot in the superficial branch of the femoral artery, that his femur had been shattered. He might be able to crawl somewhere and conceal himself, but he'd bleed out unless he could fix this first. He gritted his teeth and inched forward on his elbows, until he could grab the handle of a cabinet.

Inside was the sterile tubing used to connect the cannula to the suction machine. He tore the packet with his teeth and tried to tie the clear rubber around his thigh. It was like trying to make a Christmas gift bow alone, though—no matter how hard he worked at it, he couldn't knot it tight enough. And the pain, it was like no pain he'd ever felt.

The edges of his vision began to go dark, like the borders at the end of one of those old-time silent movies, just before they shrank into a pinpoint of darkness. Louie's final thought before he passed out was that this was indeed some crazy world, where the waiting period to get an abortion was longer than the waiting period to get a gun.

* * *

IZZY CREPT DOWN THE HALLWAY, certain that she had fallen into a mirror universe of chaos and discord and gore. The shooter had left macabre breadcrumbs—shattered windows, smears of blood, empty shells. Every instinct told her to turn around and run in the other direction, but she couldn't. It wasn't heroism that drove her toward the supply closet but the fear of learning that she was not the woman she had always believed herself to be.

The procedure room door was ajar and she could see the rows of glass cabinets filled with gauze and tape. She could also see two bodies.

She fell to her knees, rolling the nurse over, feeling for a pulse and finding none. She did the same with the doctor, who moaned, unconscious. He had been shot in the leg and someone had tied plastic tubing around his thigh, a makeshift tourniquet. It had probably saved his life. "Can you hear me?" she asked, as she tried to tighten the tubing.

She was attempting to gauge whether she could drag him to safety when she heard the click of the hammer.

The shooter stood behind her, in the doorway. Izzy froze.

He was older than she was—maybe in his forties. He had brown hair with a neat part. He was wearing a buffalo plaid fleece jacket, even in this infernal heat. He looked . . . ordinary. The kind of man you let cut in the supermarket line because he only had a few items. The kind of man who sat next to you on the bus, said hello, and then left you alone for the rest of the trip. The kind of man you didn't really notice.

Until he stormed into a clinic holding a gun.

There had been several times in the past when Izzy believed she might die. When there wasn't food for a whole week. When the heat was cut off and the temperature dipped into the teens. Yet she had known, as a kid, that there was always something you could do: eat from the neighbor's trash; sleep in layers of clothes, nested between your siblings. As a nurse, she had cheated death on behalf of her patients, reminding a stopped heart of how to beat or breathing for someone with her own lungs. Nothing had prepared her, however, for a situation like this.

Izzy wanted to beg for her life, but she couldn't; she was trembling so hard that her mouth wouldn't form words. She wondered if the girl and the woman in the waiting room would survive; if they would tell the press how brave Izzy was, running toward the sound of the gunfire just so that she could help others. She wondered how long it would take before Parker heard. She wondered if the people who would have come to their wedding would come to her funeral, instead.

"Get away so I can finish him," the shooter said, and she realized that his weapon was pointed not at her, but at the doctor.

There are moments in your life that change you. Like when Izzy stole a hot dog from a gas station, because she hadn't eaten in four days. When she opened a savings account. When, three years ago, she walked into Parker's cubicle in a hospital.

She wasn't going to die without putting up a damn good fight.

Izzy threw herself square in front of the doctor's body, spreading her arms as if she could create a shield.

The shooter laughed. "I have enough bullets for you both," he said.

I can't stop a bullet, Izzy thought. *But I can stop him from firing one.*

Izzy forced herself to look him in the eye. He was a basilisk; she could be turned to stone. But he was also a gunman in an abortion clinic; presumably he was pro-life. She gathered all the threads of courage she could find, and drew them together into a fierce knot. "You can't shoot me," she said. "I'm pregnant."

Ten a.m.

As BEX PULLED INTO THE PARKING LOT OF THE CENTER, A PROTESTER jumped out in front of her car. Bex slammed on the brakes. He shouted, waving his hands over the hood. In the passenger seat, Wren watched, wide-eyed. "I thought you said they had people to help you get inside," Bex said to her niece. "I don't see anyone in a pink pinny."

"Maybe it's too early," Wren said. As Bex moved at a snail's pace into the lot, Wren craned her neck. In the rearview mirror Bex watched the man go back to the others on the far side of the fence. An elderly lady poured him a cup of coffee from a thermos.

Bex pulled into a parking spot and flexed her hand on the steering wheel. "You could walk me in," Wren suggested, her voice small.

Bex looked at her, tortured. She'd do anything for Wren. "Honey, I . . ."

"Forget it. You can wait in the car. It shouldn't take very long."

Bex drew in her breath. "I believe a woman should do whatever she wants with her own body, I do. But I can't say I'd personally make that choice."

"You do remember I'm not here to get an abortion?" Wren said.

"Well, of course. But . . ."

She couldn't say what she was thinking. That even if Wren was headed inside for a completely benign reason, there were still other women in there, maybe women who hadn't had aunts to bring them here, who had run out of options. Women who were creating secrets they would hide from others. It made her sick to her stomach.

Wren set her unfinished chocolate crème donut on the console between them. "Don't get any ideas," she warned.

Bex watched her walk toward the Center. But then a truck crossed her field of vision. It stopped dead in front of her Mini, blocking her view.

Bex honked her horn and gestured: *What the hell?* The man in the truck glanced at her dismissively. She wondered if he was lost. He was alone in the cab; there was no woman with him who might have an appointment.

She saw Wren approach the chain-link fence and the line of pro-lifers. One woman leaned over, reaching for her.

Oh, hell no.

Bex was out of the car and huffing toward the Center faster than green grass through a goose. She caught up with Wren and looped her arm around her niece, anchoring her tight to her side.

Wren turned, surprised. "But—"

"No buts," Bex said firmly. "You're not going in there alone."

"You're late," said Helen, the dispatcher, as Hugh walked into the police department.

Hugh checked his watch. "I'm ten minutes early," he said.

"Not for the staff meeting."

"*What* staff meeting?"

"The one that's going on in the staff room," Helen replied.

"Shit." Hugh waited for Helen to buzz him in, and then took

the stairs two at a time to the basement, where the staff room was. The last time he'd missed a staff meeting, the chief had gone off on him for not taking his position seriously, and how was he supposed to treat Hugh as a de facto second in command when he skipped the less glamorous parts of police work.

He skidded around the corner, hoping to make an unobtrusive entrance, when he heard the chief's booming voice. "Finally, Detective McElroy's decided to grace us with his presence. Speaking of presents . . ."

The whole of the force began to sing "Happy Birthday." His secretary, Paula, held out a platter of donuts arranged into the numbers 4-0. One had a candle stuck in it.

Hugh blushed. He *hated* being the center of attention. He hated *birthdays*. They were basically markers in the calendar year to renew his license and his registration, and to have an annual checkup.

Paula walked toward him and set the platter down on the table, so he could blow out his candle. "Make a wish," she said, standing at his shoulder.

"Who told you it was my birthday?" he said through a rigid smile.

"Facebook," Paula murmured. "Never should have friended me."

Hugh closed his eyes and made a wish, blew out the candle. "We all chipped in," one of the junior detectives said, "and we bought you this." He held up a cane, decorated with a bright red bow.

Everyone laughed, including Hugh. "Thanks. That'll come in handy when I want to beat the crap out of you later."

"Paula," the chief said, "don't forget to make a prostate exam appointment for our boy." He clapped Hugh on the shoulder. "All right, grab your donut and let's get back to work. It's not like it's Jesus's birthday. Just Hugh's."

Hugh accepted the good wishes of everyone in the department, until he was left alone with Paula in the staff room.

"You don't look so happy for a birthday boy," she said.

"I'm not a big fan of surprises."

She shrugged. "You know what my husband got me for *my* forti-eth?" she said. "Knocked up."

Hugh laughed. "I don't think that's in the cards for me."

"What did you wish?"

He opened his mouth, but Paula waved her hand. "No, no, that was a trick question. You can't tell me, because it won't come true. Honestly, Hugh. Have you never had a birthday before?" She handed him a plate with three donuts on it. "You get the extra, be-cause you're special. But only for today. Don't go letting this get to your head." She grinned and left him alone in the staff room.

He took the candle from the donut on the top. What he'd wished for was, quite simply, the one thing he couldn't have. He wished that everything could stay the way it was, right now—with Wren making him eggs for breakfast, and people who cared enough about him at work to throw him a silly party, and his health intact. He wished that he could keep getting up morning after morning, with the world remaining unchanged. That was the thing about feeling like life was good. Even when it was—*especially* when it was—you knew you had something to lose.

MY GOD, COULD THIS BE any more embarrassing? Izzy had barely approached the reception desk before a wave of nausea rolled over her. She'd bolted for the door marked BATHROOM, and had gotten profoundly sick. She wiped her mouth and then took a stack of pa-per towels, wet them down in the sink, and rubbed them over the clammy skin of her face and neck.

There was a knock on the door, and Izzy opened it a crack. "You all right?" said the woman who had been sitting at the front desk.

"I am so sorry, Miz—"

"Vonita," she supplied.

"I am not usually quite so rude," Izzy said.

Vonita passed her a small tin of ginger mints. "These help," she said, matter-of-fact. "When you're ready, come on out and we'll get acquainted."

Izzy closed the door and sat down on the closed toilet seat. She found herself thinking of the time she was in third grade and she didn't have a winter coat. She had gone to the school secretary and told her she needed to check the lost and found, and then she had picked out a coat that didn't belong to her. The worst part was that the school secretary had known damn well it wasn't Izzy's coat, but she didn't say anything.

Vonita was being nothing but kind, but there was something in her eyes that made Izzy feel like the other woman already knew all her secrets.

Well. Izzy was a nurse. This was not the first time she had faced something new and overwhelming, and it was not the first time she'd had to bluff her way through a situation until confidence caught up to her.

She might be in an abortion clinic, but she had been and always would be a survivor.

As SOON AS SHE HAD seen the blood, she knew it couldn't be good. Women Olive's age didn't have spotting, especially when they weren't heterosexually active. Add to that the pain she'd had urinating and the odd numb tingles in her leg, and it was enough for her to go to the Center. For years, that was where she had gone for her gynecological checkups. Harriet, the nurse practitioner, had done an exam and then had turned to her. "When was the last time you had a Pap smear?" she had asked.

Well. Long enough that Olive couldn't remember.

"Olive," Harriet had said. "I think you should see an oncologist."

That had been two weeks ago. In the aftermath, she'd had a chest X-ray, an abdominopelvic MRI, a CBC, and an electrolyte and liver series. She had heard what the oncologist said, but maybe she didn't really believe him. Or maybe she needed to hear it from someone she knew and trusted.

She sat now in the examination room, waiting for Harriet to come in. The medical file from the gynecological oncologist's office was in her hands. It might as well have been Greek:

Fungating mass, exophytic, with obstruction of the right pelvic sidewall.

Moderate right hydronephrosis; posterior involvement through the rectosigmoid serosal and muscularis . . . pelvic and paraaortic lymphadenopathy . . . no evidence of ascites.

Creatinine: 2.4 mg/dL; hematocrit: 28%

Hell, Greek would have made *more* sense to her.

The door opened. "Olive," Harriet said. "How are you feeling? What did the oncologist say?"

Olive handed her the file. "I should have brought a translator along."

Harriet scanned the papers inside. "Neuroendocrine carcinoma of the cervix," she read. "Oh, Olive."

"Carcinoma," Olive repeated. "That was the one word I *did* understand." She shook her head. "The doctor talked to me. Well, he talked *at* me. I just . . . stopped hearing him after a few minutes."

"You have cervical cancer," Harriet said gently. "I'm so sorry."

"Are you sure it's not a mistake? How *could* I? I'm a lesbian."

"Lesbians actually have higher rates of cervical cancer," Harriet said. "They don't get monitored because they aren't having penetrative intercourse. There's a certain type that nuns get—not the kind that's squamous cell cancer, which is associated with HPV—but one even virgins can contract."

"Well, thankfully," Olive said, "I'm not one of *those*." She looked at the nurse. "How bad?"

"It's stage four, metastatic. Do you know what that means?"

"It's like winning the lottery," Olive replied. "But Shirley Jackson's kind."

Harriet stared at her blankly.

"Never mind."

The nurse looked down at the numbers again. "It's in your lungs; possibly in your liver. It's blocking your right kidney." She looked Olive in the eye. "I'm going to level with you. It's unlikely that someone whose cancer has spread this far can be cured. I'm sure there are things the oncologist can do to help you have a good quality of life, but . . . you should get your affairs in order."

Olive felt her mouth go dry as dust. She, who always had a witty retort, had nothing to say. "How long?" she finally managed.

"Six to eight months, I'm guessing. I hate to say that, Olive. And I hope to hell I'm wrong. But if I were you, I'd want someone to tell me the truth."

Olive sat in the stew of that information, sinking in her own sudden, inevitable mortality. She felt Harriet's arms come around her, hold her tightly.

This. This was why she had come to the Center. She knew already what was hiding inside that medical folder. She had just not wanted to face it alone.

There was a sharp rap on the door, and then Dr. Ward stuck his head inside. "Harriet? It's go time." He smiled at Olive and closed the door again.

Olive had so many questions: Was it her fault—some deficiency in diet or some promiscuity in college that had led to this? How would she tell Peg? Would it happen fast, or would it be a slow decline? Would it hurt? Would she still be herself, at the end?

Harriet stepped back, still holding Olive's hands. She gave them a final squeeze. "I need to go assist. You going to be all right?"

She left without hearing Olive's response. But they both knew the answer, anyway.

WHEN WREN HAD STARTED HIGH school, two months ago, she suffered the usual freshman pranks: being told there was a pool in the basement when there wasn't, finding shaving cream in her locker, being squirted with water guns as she walked down the foreign language hallway. She learned pretty fast which routes through the school were safe and which ones weren't. The place she hated the most, however, was the Pit, which was an outside corridor connecting two arms of the building, where the smokers hung out between classes. She'd run the gauntlet, knowing these kids smelled her fear and her naïveté, and were making up their minds about her without knowing her at all.

That's what it felt like now, walking past the line of protesters. Some of them smiled at her, even as they waved posters of bloody babies in her face. Some chanted Dr. Seuss: *A person's a person, no matter how small.* "Can you come here for a sec?" one woman said, with the kind of apologetic smile you use when you are truly sorry about asking for help, because your car has broken down on the side of the road or your phone is dead and you need to call home or you are juggling too many groceries in your arms and wishing you'd been smart enough to take a basket. Instinct tugged her in that direction, because Wren had always been a good girl. The woman had red hair and funky purple glasses and looked incredibly familiar, but Wren couldn't place her. Still, she didn't want to run the risk that the woman might recognize her, too—what if she worked at the police department or something, and spilled this secret to her dad? So she ducked her head as the woman stuffed a little goodie bag in her hand, like the kind you got at a kid's birthday party.

Just then her aunt was glued to her side. "You're not going in there alone," Bex said, and Wren wrapped her arms around her aunt's neck and hugged her tight.

Wren knew it made her sound like a total bitch, but she didn't really pine for her mom. Part of it was because her mother had left when Wren was little; part of it was because of her aunt, who filled in any empty spaces.

Aunt Bex had sewed her a colonial dress for the American Revolution unit they'd done in second grade. (Well, she'd hot-glued it—she wasn't particularly good with a needle.) She had never missed a T-ball game and brought sweet tea for all the other parents. She even hung Wren's lame watercolors on her wall; she, who was an artist and knew damn well they were terrible. It seemed to Wren that having a mother had a lot less to do with a few sweaty hours of labor and delivery and a lot more to do with whose face you always looked for in a crowd.

As if she needed any more proof, here was Bex beside her, even though Wren knew how much it cost her. She knew Aunt Bex had never had children and that fact maybe even had something to do with her aversion to the Center. But in a way, Wren was secretly glad Bex belonged only to her.

By the time they were buzzed inside, sweat had broken out between Wren's shoulder blades. "You sit down," Wren told her aunt. "I can check myself in."

There were a few people in the waiting room, and a television was on, with the sound muted. At the reception desk sat a woman with the most stunning tower of braids Wren had ever seen—thick red and black snakes twined around each other. She wore a name tag that read VONITA, and she was on the telephone. She smiled at Wren and held up a finger, suggesting she'd only be another moment. "In the state of Mississippi it's a two-day process. That's right. So Thursday would be your counseling session, your lab work, and a sonogram. The next day, when you have your procedure, you'll be here from an hour and a half to three hours. If you want to schedule an appointment I can help you with that now." She paused, then picked up a pen. "Name? Age? Date of last period? Good contact phone number? So you're scheduled for Thursday at nine A.M. Now, write down your appointment date and time because we can't verify if you call back and ask when it is, for confidentiality reasons. You have to bring a hundred and fifty dollars and your photo ID. Cash or card. No large bags, no purses, no kids. All right, then. You're welcome." She hung up the phone and smiled at Wren. "Sorry about that. How can I help you?"

"I'm here for an appointment," Wren said, and then hastily, "But not . . . not like the kind you just scheduled. My name's Wren McElroy."

"Ren . . . Ren . . ." The woman scanned a list.

"With a *W*."

"Ah. Here you are." Vonita checked her in and handed her a clipboard. "Just fill out this form for me, and we'll get you in as soon as possible."

Wren sat across from the television. She scribbled down her information—the usual stuff—name, address, age, allergies.

Beside her, Aunt Bex was going through the little goodie bag Wren had been handed by the protester. Smarties. ChapStick. A pair of tiny blue knit booties. "Well, those are sweet," Bex said.

She dug out hand sanitizer, breath mints, and two small soaps.

"Maybe they think we're all dirty," Wren said. She plucked the flyer from the little bag and began to read: *Please don't rush into this decision. Abortion is FOREVER.*

If you are in an abortion center right now, you can just leave. You don't have to tell anyone. If you've already paid, we can help you get your money back.

Wren opened the pamphlet. There were pictures of gummy, bright-eyed babies.

Before I formed you in the womb, I knew you. — *God*

"You think that's a direct quote?" Bex asked, reading over her shoulder.

Wren stifled a laugh. "My history teacher would not accept that citation."

On the back panel was a list of the alleged consequences of chemical and surgical abortion:

Perforated uterus, chronic and acute infections, intense pain, excessive bleeding requiring transfusion, risk of future miscarriages, infertility, cancer, death.

Feelings of guilt, anger, helplessness. Mental breakdown. Depression, nightmares, and flashbacks. Inability to feel joy about life. Feeling of separation from God. Fear of not being forgiven. Alienation from family and friends. Loss of relationship with boyfriend or spouse. Promiscuity. Drug abuse. Suicide.

It reminded Wren of those ads on television for antidepressants. *Yeah, we'll stop those mood troughs, but you might wind up incontinent, with high blood pressure, with increased suicidal tendencies, or, hey, dead.*

Wren looked at the bold type at the bottom. *YOU ARE NOT ALONE. WE CARE ABOUT YOU!*

Suddenly she remembered where she had seen that redheaded woman. She was the parent of a ninth grader, and she had raised holy hell over a unit in health class where they studied contraceptive options. The day Wren had to roll a condom onto a banana, the woman had barged into the room, spewing craziness about impressionable minds and God and the rhythm method. Wren had felt bad for her son, who was moved to the library during health from then on.

Wren shook her head, now that she realized that this woman who was anti-contraception was also anti-abortion. Wasn't that counterintuitive? If you didn't want abortions, shouldn't you at least be throwing free condoms and birth control pills out to anyone who would take them? Shouldn't that woman have been *cheering* for Wren to come to the Center and get the Pill, instead of berating her?

Wren looked down at the pamphlet again. *WE CARE ABOUT YOU!*

Or not.

She walked across the room and tossed it into the trash.

"DADDY," BETH CRIED. "*DADDY?*"

Frustration foamed in her father's wake, but he didn't look back as he left. He nearly mowed down the nurse, hurrying to get away from her.

Away from what she had done.

Jayla peered at her. "You okay?" she asked gently.

Beth shook her head, unable to speak.

The nurse sat down on the edge of Beth's bed. "I didn't mean to eavesdrop," she said, "but it's pretty hard when the door's wide open." She hesitated. "The ER isn't my usual rotation, you know. I work on the ortho floor, but I'm covering for a colleague who needed a personal day. So I'm not sure what the protocol is here."

Beth wiped her eyes. "What do you mean?"

"Well, in ortho, if I found out my patient is an intravenous drug user or has some other history she didn't disclose to the doctors, I'd tell my supervisor. It could be a matter of life or death. What I'm trying to say is that you really do need to tell me the truth." She looked at Beth. "So," she said, "which is it?"

Beth blinked at her. She felt the walls pressing in.

"You told *me* you didn't know you were pregnant. But I just heard you tell your father you went to an abortion clinic."

Beth flushed. "I want my father . . ."

"If you had a surgical abortion and it didn't go right and *that's* what's caused the bleeding, your health could be in danger. Beth, you could die."

Beth wiped her eyes with the corner of the hospital johnny. "I *did* go to the clinic," she admitted. "But they said they couldn't help me unless I went to a judge. So I filled out all the forms and got a hearing scheduled and then I got a call saying the judge couldn't see me for two weeks." She looked up at Jayla. "I couldn't wait that long and then go back to the clinic. It would be too late."

Beth started to cry so hard she couldn't catch her breath. "I didn't have a choice," she sobbed, curling into herself, making a shell of her own body. "You get that, right?"

Jayla stroked her back. "Okay," she said. "Okay. Deep breaths."

If only they had used a condom.

If only she wasn't under eighteen.

If only the judge had shown up when he was supposed to.

If only she had lived in Boston or New York, where there wasn't just one clinic, but many.

If only it hadn't been so damn hard to fix this on her own.

If only she'd kept the baby.

The thought crawled into her mind like a spider. She would still have faced her father's anger. She would still have been a whore, in his eyes. For all she knew, he would have thrown her out.

For all she knew, he still might.

That made her cry even harder, which was why she did not hear Jayla slip into the hallway, take out her cellphone, and call her husband. "Nathan," the nurse said, "I need your help."

JANINE SAT ON THE EXAMINATION table, panicking. It was one thing to come into the Center using a fake ID, register for an abortion, and sit through a counseling session. But it was another thing entirely to dodge the state-mandated ultrasound. Somehow, she needed to get the evidence she had come here for. Just last month in another state, a pro-life girl had gone into a clinic undercover, like Janine, and had told a counselor that she was thirteen and her boyfriend was twenty-five and she wanted an abortion. The counselor had said, on tape, *I didn't hear that.* The damning audio had made the rounds of the Internet, and had even aired on *Hannity*.

Janine heard the quick knock and slipped her phone into her

dress pocket, hitting the record button on the voice memo just as the door swung open. The social worker smiled. "Hello there," she said. "I'm Graciela. So we're going to do your ultrasound, right?"

Janine felt herself break into a sweat. She needed to get this woman talking. "Wait!" she blurted out. "I have allergies!"

"To latex?"

Janine swallowed. "To, like, everything. I forgot to write it down."

Graciela made a note in her file and then turned on the ultrasound machine. It hummed alive, as if they were all an orchestra and this was the note they must become attuned to. "What if I don't want an ultrasound?" Janine asked.

"I'm afraid you don't have a choice. The state says I have to do one today, and ask you if you'd like to see it. You can say no, if you want." Graciela paused, her hand holding the wand. "You seem a little nervous."

In any other situation, Janine would have thought, *This woman is kind.* But although Graciela might still be a lovely human being, it didn't change the fact that she had made the choice to work at an abortion factory. It wasn't like you could get prenatal care here, if you wanted it. The last undercover spy that Allen had sent into the clinic had worn glasses with a tiny camera in the bridge of the nose, and she had video of this very woman saying no, they did not offer pregnancy care, but could refer her to a place that did. They really shouldn't call themselves a reproductive healthcare center if they weren't willing to help women reproduce.

Once, she had been in a clinic like this, not as a spy but as a patient. Did she have an ultrasound there? Why couldn't she remember?

It was not until Graciela handed her a Kleenex that she realized she was crying. "Are you nervous? *That* I can fix," the social worker said. "But if you're crying because you don't know if you've made the right decision . . . that I *can't* help you with."

Janine thought of the voice recording in her pocket, closed her eyes, and prayed for something to happen—*anything*—that might incriminate Graciela, before Janine was incriminated herself.

FIFTEEN WEEKS WAS THE TRICKIEST. When Louie had a patient come in fifteen weeks pregnant, he knew he was in for a challenge. The fetus's bones would have just started to calcify, so it would have to be disarticulated. The way Louie explained it was that the uterus was like an ice cream cone. Imagine you had an Oreo at the top and needed to get it through the bottom of the cone; of course you had to break it into parts. In Mississippi, there was an additional wrinkle: by law, you could not use forceps while a fetus still had a heartbeat. This law was passed by nonscientists who believed that fetuses at six-teen weeks could feel pain—which they could not. But as a result of political posturing, Louie had to amend his procedure, adding extra steps that might cause more risk to the patient, instead of doing what was best for her.

That meant Louie would start with an ultrasound. Cytotec caused sustained uterine contractions, which meant that most of the fetuses would be asystolic due to the constant squeezing. But if that wasn't the case—if there still was a heartbeat visible on the ultrasound—it was up to Louie to use suction to bring the umbilical cord down and transect it to end cardiac activity.

Louie told the patient none of this.

He looked at Joy Perry, who was his primary concern for the next quarter of an hour. Like all his fifteen- and sixteen-week patients, she was the first and last procedure of the day. She had come early for the Cytotec—eight hundred micrograms in pill form—which were inserted by him, vaginally, to make the cervix pliable.

Now she was lying back, her pale hair in a ponytail that spilled over the edge of the procedure table, like the tassels on his grand-mama's brocade curtains. He met her gaze through the valley of her bent knees. "This is going to take about seven minutes," Louie said. "We're gonna get you through."

He glanced at Harriet, his nurse du jour. He'd worked with Harriet long enough to have a shorthand with her, but truth be told, Louie flew to seven different clinics throughout the South and Plains states and he was used to working with a rotating panel of RNs and nurse practitioners. They were all exceptional, standing by the side of the women on his procedure table; providing him with a syringe of lidocaine when he needed it and a gentle whisper of support when his patient did. A flick of Louie's eyes to the right, and Harriet took Joy's hand in her own and squeezed.

He touched her knee.

"Wait!" Joy cried, and Louie lifted his hand immediately, five fingers outstretched. "I . . . I didn't shave . . ." she murmured.

Louie stifled a grin. If he had a dime for every time he'd heard that. He knew what it was like to be in the dentist's chair and wonder if you had a booger in your nose; he understood what it was to be a patient, and vulnerable. Time to administer some vocal local. In Mississippi, he wasn't allowed to give any narcotics—not even Xanax—to relax a patient.

"Now, Miz Harriet," he said, in an exaggerated tone. "Didn't I tell you not to bring me any more ladies who didn't get a Brazilian before coming here?"

He saw it—the tiny crack of a grin on Joy's face.

"You're going to feel a little pressure." Louie pressed the inside of the patient's thigh. "Just like that. I'm gonna put the speculum inside now; you relax that muscle. There you go. Where you from?"

"Pearl."

"Right next door." When Louie chatted through the procedure, he wasn't trivializing. He was normalizing the moment, putting it into context. He wanted the woman to know this abortion was a sliver of her life, and not the benchmark upon which she should judge herself.

As he yammered about the traffic in Jackson, Louie wrapped a ball of gauze on the tenaculum and swabbed Joy's cervix with Betadine. Harriet, his partner in this dance, smoothly held up the lidocaine vial while he filled the syringe. "Little pinch coming. Give me a cough now." As Joy coughed, Louie grabbed the edge of the cervix with the tenaculum and injected the lidocaine at several spots around the ring of tissue. He felt the muscles of her thighs tense. "You know people who can cough on demand can also fake things? Did you used to fake tears to get your mama not to spank you?" Louie asked.

Joy shook her head.

"Well, I used to do that. Worked every time." He reached to his left for one of the metal dilation rods, and inserted it into the cervix and then out. Then a slightly larger one, and another after that, all the way up to 15 millimeters, as the cervix opened like the shutter of a camera. "So were you born in Pearl?"

"No, Yazoo."

"Yazoo," Louie said. "That's the place with the witch." Sometimes he thought he knew more about the states where he performed abortions than their own residents did. He had to, for moments like this.

"The what?" She flinched.

"You're doing great, Joy. There was some swamp witch who lived in Yazoo during the eighteen hundreds. You really never heard about her?" Louie asked. "You're gonna feel fluid now; that's normal." He ruptured her membranes and leaned back as a gush of blood and amniotic fluid spilled between her legs into the tray beneath. Some splattered on his sneaker. "She died in quicksand, I guess, when the police were after her? Just before she passed, she vowed she'd come back in twenty years to haunt the town and burn it to the ground." Louie glanced up. "A little pulling now. Just breathe. All I'm doing is maneuvering around inside your uterus, and using the ultrasound to guide me."

From the corner of his eye, he watched Joy's fingers grasp Har-

riet's more firmly. He bent his head, intent on his work, taking the
fetus out with forceps. He pulled out clots of pink tissue, some recognizable, some not. At this stage of pregnancy, the calvarium was
just solid enough to not collapse with suction. If it got up into the
high corner of the uterus, it had a tendency to roll around like a
beach ball. In with the forceps, out again. A miniature hand. A knee.
In and out; in and out. The G clef of a spine. The squash-blossom
calvarium.

"Anyway, twenty years later, in 1900, there was a freak fire in the
town that burned a hundred buildings and two hundred homes. The
townspeople went to the grave of the swamp witch, and sure enough,
the tombstone was broken and the chain around her grave was all
torn up. Spooky as hell, right? Now, just another minute . . ."

Louie knew *exactly* what it meant to disrupt a life process. At five
weeks, he'd see nothing but a tiny sac. At six weeks, a fetal pole with
cardiac activity—but no limb buds, no thorax, no calvarium. By nine
weeks, there were differentiated body parts: tiny arms, tiny hands,
the black spot of an emerging eye. At the fifteen-week mark, like
today's procedure, the calvarium had to be crushed to fit through a
15-millimeter cannula. As a provider, you could not unfeel that moment. And yet. Was it a person? No. It was a piece of life, but so was
a sperm, an egg. If life began at conception, what about all those eggs
and sperm that didn't become babies? What about the fertilized eggs
that didn't implant? Or the ones that did, ectopically? What about
the zygote that failed to thrive when implanted and was sloughed off
with the uterine lining? Was that a death?

Up till twenty-two weeks of pregnancy a fetus wouldn't survive
without a host, even on a respirator. Between twenty-two and twenty-
five weeks, a fetus might live briefly, with severe brain and organ
damage. The American Congress of Obstetricians and Gynecologists did not recommend resuscitating babies born at twenty-three
weeks. At twenty-four weeks, it was up to the parents and doctors
to decide together. At twenty-five weeks, the American Medical

Association suggested resuscitation, but also said that the ability to survive was not a sure thing. There were plenty of babies diagnosed late in the second trimester with anomalies that were incompatible with life. If those babies were born past twenty-nine weeks, they would feel pain when they died. In those cases, was abortion murder, or mercy? If you decided this was an exceptional case, what about if the mother was a heroin addict? What if her husband beat her so bad she broke bones several times a year? Was it ethical for that woman to carry a baby to term?

He got it, he really did. In that boggy mess of blood and tissue were recognizable parts. They were familiar enough to be upsetting. The bottom line was this: a zygote, an embryo, a fetus, a baby—they were all human. But at what point did that human deserve legal protection?

"We're in the homestretch now." Louie turned on the suction and swept the cannula along the uterus. "You never heard that story about the witch?"

She shook her head.

"And you call yourself a Yazooite!" Louie joked. "What *do* people from Yazoo call themselves?"

"Cursed," Joy said.

He laughed. "I knew I liked you." Louie felt for the familiar grittiness of the uterine wall that let him know he was done.

Whether or not you believed a fetus was a human being, there was no question in anyone's mind that a grown woman *was* one. Even if you placed moral value on that fetus, you couldn't give it rights unless they were stripped away from the woman carrying it. Perhaps the question wasn't *When does a fetus become a person?* but *When does a woman* stop *being one?*

Louie glanced down at the tissue in the tray between his patient's legs. The contents of the tray were swirled and amorphous, like a galaxy without stars. It was part of his job as a physician—if all the products of conception couldn't be accounted for, then there would be infection later. It was also philosophically important to him as an abortion provider to recognize the procedure for what it was, instead of using euphemisms. He finished his silent count of limbs and landmarks. He could feel Joy's womb starting to shrink back down.

He stood so that he could look his patient in the eye, so she would know he had *seen* her—not just as a patient, but as the woman she was and would be when she walked out that door. "You," he told Joy, "are no longer pregnant."

The woman closed her eyes. "Thank you," she murmured.

Louie gently patted her knee. "Miz Joy," he said simply, "you don't have to be grateful for something that's your right."

How was it, Joy wondered, that she was ending a pregnancy and talking about ghosts? Maybe it wasn't all that far off the mark. She knew there were all sorts of things that could come back to haunt you.

She felt cramping, and she winced. She could still hear the whir of the machine that did the suction. It seemed like an oversight; surely they could have given her headphones, like the kind they had on planes that canceled out all the noise? Or piped in heavy metal music, so that you wouldn't have to lie here and listen to the sound of your pregnancy ending?

Maybe that was the point—they didn't *want* to make it easy. They wanted you doing this with your eyes (and your legs) wide open.

Joy stared at the ceiling at a Where's Waldo? poster, where there were a thousand penguins wearing red-and-white scarves and one lone guy in a striped hat. Why would you try to find Waldo? Let the poor guy stay lost.

The suction was a choke, a throttle, a throat clearing. Little vacuum, Joy thought. Cleaning up her mess.

Nine a.m.

HUGH WAS PAINTING WITH WATER. THAT'S WHAT HE CALLED POLICE work that was not only painfully boring but ultimately a complete waste of time. Today, it was processing a 2010 Toyota RAV4 that had been taken for a joyride after its owner, a college kid, left the keys in the ignition. It had been found off the side of the road, dented and reeking of pot. Christ, you didn't have to be a detective to figure out what had happened here; or to realize that the amount of time that Hugh spent processing the car and the scene—a dusty ditch off the side of the highway—was going to exceed the value of the check the insurance company would eventually send the owner for repairs. Who wanted to spend his fortieth birthday getting the fingerprints off a stolen vehicle? He sighed as he attempted to dust the interior. It never worked, because of the texture of the dashboard, but if he didn't do it, he'd be told he had overlooked evidence. He'd already photographed the vehicle 360 degrees and also taken pictures of the tracks in the grass made by the tires. He had noted how far back the seat was reclined, what station the radio was tuned to, what detritus lived in the console. Later today, he would have the dubious honor of contacting the car's owner and giving him this list—gum, KIND bar, water bottle, key chain, baseball cap, receipts from a Piggly Wiggly, junk mail—and then ask the guy what was missing. Hugh would bet his house that the owner wouldn't be able to answer. There wasn't a person on earth who could accurately catalog the contents of their console and glove compartment.

He stood up, feeling himself sweat beneath the collar of his shirt. He was supposed to canvass the area to see who might have heard or seen something, but he was literally six miles from the nearest exit, and the only visible evidence of humanity was a giant Confederate flag that snapped in the wind across the highway, towering over the tree line as a reminder or a threat, depending on your politics. Hugh set his hands on his hips and jutted his chin toward the flag. "Well?" he demanded out loud. "Would you like to give an eyewitness report?"

Deciding that he'd done due diligence, Hugh started back to his own car. He had to burn all these stupid photos to disk and do a shit ton of paperwork now. True, nothing was going to come of this case—they'd never find the thieves—but even if it sucked, he was going to do the right thing. This mantra was as much a part of Hugh as his height or his hair color or his lineage. True, this had not been his intended career path, but then he'd met Annabelle and they'd gotten pregnant. Somehow instead of tracking the movements of the stars at NASA, he had wound up tracking the movements of the residents of Jackson, Mississippi. He had watched *Columbo*, like every other kid in the eighties, and detective work had seemed an exciting backup plan. Well, the joke was on Hugh—he wasn't thwarting jewel heists, he was dusting for fingerprints on a gas cap.

His cellphone buzzed in his pocket, and he answered, thinking it might be the owner of the vehicle. He'd left a message that morning for the kid. "McElroy," he said.

"Hugh."

His eyes closed. He'd conjured Annabelle, just by thinking of her. "You weren't who I was expecting," he said, and in the silence that followed, he turned over the implications of that sentence.

Her voice sounded like filigree, delicate and irreplicable, with a hint of a French accent that he supposed was cultivated after years of living in a foreign country. "I wasn't going to forget your fortieth," Annabelle said. "How are you?"

He looked around at his surroundings—the looming Confederate flag, the trampled knee-high grass, the scraped and dented car. Instead of giving an answer even *he* wouldn't want to hear, he turned his back away from the highway. "What time is it there?" he asked, squinting into the sun.

She laughed. God, he'd loved that sound. He remembered playing the fool, sometimes—leaving a shaving cream mustache intentionally on his upper lip when he came downstairs in the morning—just to hear it. When had he stopped making her smile? "It's quitting time," Annabelle said.

"Lucky you." There was a bubble of silence. Amazing, to think that she was so far away, and he could still hear the hesitation in her voice.

"How is she?"

Hugh exhaled. "She's good."

Annabelle had agreed to give him custody of Wren because, she said, that way Wren could be as comfortable as possible. If her parents were splitting up, at least she got to stay at home with her friends and her father. Hugh had always believed that her magnanimous gesture was a result of guilt: she knew she had cheated; as a consolation prize, she left Hugh the best part of their marriage.

"Are you happy, Hugh?" Annabelle asked.

He forced a laugh. "What kind of question is that?"

"I don't know. A Parisian one. An existential one."

He imagined her with her long red hair, a waterfall that used to slip through his hands. He could still see her face when he closed his eyes—the pale eyebrows she had darkened with a pencil, the way her eyes darted left when she lied; how she bit her lower lip when he made love to her. When you lost someone, how much time had to pass before the details began to fade? Or at least the feeling that you had an unfinished edge that might unravel at any moment, until you were nothing more than a tangle of the person you used to be? "You don't have to worry about me," Hugh said.

"Of course I do," Annabelle replied, "because you're too busy worrying about everyone else."

There were seventy-five hundred miles between them and Hugh felt claustrophobic. "I gotta go."

"Oh. Of course," Annabelle said quickly. "It's good to hear your voice, Hugh."

"You, too. I'll tell Wren you called," he promised, although they both knew he wouldn't. The relationship between Wren and her mother was more complicated than the one between him and Annabelle. He felt the way he did when he misplaced something important—a little angry at himself, a little frustrated. Wren felt like she'd been the important thing that was misplaced.

"Take care of yourself," Hugh said, his subtle way of acknowledging that her new lover couldn't do a good job of that and she was on her own.

He hung up, savoring his small and lovely victory of a sentence.

AT PRECISELY 9:01 A.M. WREN popped out of her chair and walked up to Ms. Beckett, the health teacher. Everyone was taking a test that involved labeling the parts of the male and female reproductive systems—with points taken off if you spelled *fallopian* or *vas deferens* wrong. Ms. Beckett was pretty cool, as teachers went. She was young and had married the hot gym teacher, Mr. Hanlon, last year. Although Ms. Beckett hadn't officially told anyone yet, it was clear from her ever-loosening wardrobe of jumpers and caftans that she was going to need a long-term sub in a few months while she was on maternity leave. There was a poetic justice to that, Wren thought—a sex ed teacher who had gotten pregnant.

It was also why she knew that if she walked up to Ms. Beckett's desk and told her the truth—she needed to leave school to get the Pill—the teacher would probably have covered Wren's tracks for her. But it wasn't like contraception was a valid excuse for getting out of class, so she did the next best thing when Ms. Beckett looked up from her computer. She screwed her face into a grimace of abject pain and whispered, "Cramps."

The magic word. Thirty seconds later, she was walking through the school with a pass to the nurse. Except instead of turning right to go to the nurse's office she made an abrupt left and walked out the door near the foreign language wing, letting the hot sun scald her. She reached for her phone and texted, and ten seconds later, Aunt Bex's car pulled up to the curb. Wren yanked open the door and slipped into the passenger seat just as one of the school safety officers rounded the corner of the building. "Go," she urged. "Go, go!"

Aunt Bex screamed away from the curb. "Lord," she said, as her tires squealed. "I feel like Thelma and Louise."

Wren turned to her blankly. "Who?"

"My God, you make me feel like a dinosaur." Aunt Bex laughed. She reached behind her, fumbling around the backseat until she grabbed a paper bag, which she dropped into Wren's lap. Wren didn't even have to open it to know it was donuts.

She supposed that it was moments like this when it paid to have a mother around. But to be honest, her mom was so *extra*, living in an artists' commune or something in the Marais and getting piercings in places where not even Wren would want them. Aunt Bex wasn't the next best thing. She was better.

Wren slouched in the seat and put her feet on the dashboard.

"Don't do that," Aunt Bex said automatically, although it was hard to imagine how this old beater of a car could be damaged in any way by the footprint of Wren's shoe. There were paint rags on the backseat and empty buckets and dust from stretched canvases and everything smelled a little like turpentine.

"Go ahead," Wren said.

"Go ahead?"

"Give me the lecture. What is it you always say? A free lunch isn't ever really free."

Aunt Bex shook her head. "Nope. This lunch has no strings attached."

Wren sat up, tilting her head. "Really?" Her aunt was the only person who seemed to understand you couldn't schedule when you fell in love, like it was a doctor's appointment. "Aunt Bex," Wren blurted, "how come you never got married?"

Her aunt shrugged. "I'm sure the story you're hoping for is much more romantic than the truth. I just didn't, that's all." She glanced in her niece's direction. "I'm not taking you here today because of some unrequited love of my own," Bex said. "I'm taking you because I'd rather you have the Pill than an abortion."

Wren reached into the paper bag and took a bite of her donut. "Have I told you I love you?"

Her aunt raised a brow. "Because I'm taking you to the Center, or because I got you chocolate crème?"

Wren grinned. "Can it be both?" she asked.

When Olive went to kiss Peg goodbye, she found her wife underneath the sink trying to fix the trash disposal. She took in the sight for a moment, admiring the wriggle of Peg's hips and the swell of her breasts as she reached up to do something to a pipe. Hell, Olive might be old, but she wasn't dead. Yet.

"How did I get so lucky?" she mused out loud. "Marrying a plumber. And a hot one at that."

"You married an engineer with plumbing skills." Peg slipped out from the cabinet. "And a hot one, at that."

Peg smiled up at her. Olive wanted to memorize every detail of their life together: the chip in Peg's front tooth, the lip of pink sock peeking out from her tennis shoe. The orange juice sweating on the counter, and the newel post of the banister that fell off its perch weekly no matter how much wood glue they used. The scatter of pens near the phone, tossed like runes, that were all out of ink. There was such art in the ordinary, it could leave you in tears.

"Where are you off to today so early, anyway?" Peg asked, sticking her head back underneath the sink.

Olive hadn't told Peg about going to the oncologist's office last week; she had hid the file with the confusion of numbers and tests underneath the mattress, where Peg wouldn't find it. It was tucked inside her purse now, for the nurse at the Center to interpret. But did Olive really need the translation? She knew, even if she needed someone else to say it to make it true. "A checkup. No big deal."

Olive heard the throaty growl of the disposal, and Peg's arpeggio of laughter. God, she had danced to the music of that laugh for a decade now. She felt like an explorer moving through a world she had always known, charged with cataloging the minutiae of the common, the grooves of the routine, just in case a thousand years from now someone else wanted to see things exactly as they had looked through her eyes. The way her hand slipped seamlessly into Peg's in the dark of a movie theater when they didn't have to worry if anyone might be shocked by two old women in love; the long silver hair, coiled into the shape of infinity in the shower drain; the cool, possessive stamp of her kiss.

What she would miss were these details. She wondered if, when you left this world, you got to take a certain number of them deep in your pockets, clenched in your fists, or tucked high on the roof of your mouth, with you forever.

* * *

WHEN LOUIE WASN'T PERFORMING ABORTIONS, he was teaching new doctors how to do them. He was an associate professor at the University of Hawaii and Boston University. He started his semesters the same way, telling the students that over five thousand years ago, in ancient China, mercury was used to induce abortions (although it most likely also killed the women). The Ebers Papyrus from 1500 B.C. mentioned abortions. He showed a slide of a bas relief from the year 1150 decorating the temple of Angkor Wat in Cambodia, where a woman in the underworld was getting an abortion at the hands of a demon.

He told his medical students that Aristophanes mentioned pennyroyal tea as an abortifacient—just five grams of it could be toxic. That Pliny the Elder said if a woman didn't want a pregnancy, she could step over a viper or ingest rue. Hippocrates suggested that a woman who wanted to miscarry jump and hit herself on the bottom with her heels until the embryo released and fell out; if that didn't work, there was always a mixture of mouse dung, honey, Egyptian salt, resin, and wild colocynth that you could insert into the uterus. A Sanskrit manuscript from the eighth century recommended sitting over a pot of boiling water or steaming onions. Scribonius Largus, the court doctor for Emperor Claudius, had a recipe that included mandrake root, opium, Queen Anne's lace, opopanax, and peppers. Tertullian, the Christian theologian, described instruments that match the ones used today for a D & E and said Hippocrates, Asclepiades, Erasistratus, Herophilus, and Soranus all employed them.

Abortion had been around, Louie told them, since the beginning of time.

"I got a new one for you, Dr. Ward," Vonita said as he wandered into the reception area during a five-minute break. "Tansy."

"She a patient?"

Vonita laughed. "No, it's an herb. Or a flower or something. It was used in the Middle Ages to abort."

He grinned. "Where'd you learn that?"

"Reading one of my romance novels," she said.

"I didn't think romance novels covered that topic."

"Well, what else you think is gonna happen with all that sex?"

He laughed. Vonita was one of his favorite people in the world. She had run the clinic since 1989, when the previous owner had retired. She painted it orange because she wanted it to stand out proud, like it had on its best Sunday clothes. Vonita had grown up in Silver Grove, cinched tight in the Bible Belt, and her mama was a devout Baptist. When Vonita opened the clinic, the church here had contacted her mama to let her know what her wayward daughter was doing. *Vonita Jean*, her mother had said on the telephone, *don't tell me you're opening an abortion clinic.*

Then, Mama, don't ask me, Vonita had replied.

"How busy am I gonna be today?" Louie asked.

"Do I look like a crystal ball?"

"You look like the person who does the scheduling."

She grunted. "Well. I hope you ate a big breakfast today, 'cause it may also be your lunch."

Louie grinned. It would be busy; it was *always* busy. He'd already started his first case, in fact, a woman in her second trimester who needed her cervix softened before the procedure. She'd be the first and the last patient he saw that morning. The waiting room already had women in it who were here for their counseling sessions, who would come back tomorrow for their procedures. They came from Natchez and Tupelo and from around the corner. They came from Alligator and Satartia and Starkville and Wiggins. There were 48,000 square miles of Mississippi and this was the only clinic at which you could get an abortion. You might have to drive five hours to get there, and of course, you had to wait twenty-four hours between counseling and the procedure, which meant more travel expenses that many desperate women couldn't afford. Vonita had on speed dial the names of benefactors and organizations she could call when a woman showed up who didn't have money for lunch or bus fare home, much less enough for a procedure. And then there were the women who had to be referred to other states, because the Center only performed abortions up to sixteen weeks.

Vonita was emptying one of the blessing bags that the protesters handed out to the patients, who often—bewildered—turned them in at the reception desk. "I've got three sets of booties," she said, "but I'm holding out for a little hat." She glanced up. "You do the Cytotec?"

"I did indeed," Louie replied.

Vonita held up a little hand-printed card from the blessing bag. "Defund Planned Parenthood," she read. "You think they know we're not a Planned Parenthood?"

It was like using the word *Xerox* instead of *copy machine*. Plus, federal funds already were legally prohibited from being used for abortions. They covered gynecological care; abortions were self-funding. In fact, they were the only procedure reproductive health services clinics offered that didn't operate at a loss.

If Planned Parenthood *was* defunded, it wouldn't stop abortions. Abortions would literally be the only things they could afford to do.

Sometimes Louie felt like they only existed in relation to the antis. If they all disappeared, would he go up in a puff of smoke? Could you stand for something if there wasn't an opposition?

He watched Vonita sweep the contents of the blessing bag into a trash can. "Ladies, who's waiting on labs?" A peppering of hands went up. Vonita pressed a button on her phone and summoned Harriet to come get the next wave of patients for their blood tests. She did this fluidly and seamlessly; it was like watching a conductor raise beauty from the discord of an orchestra.

"Hey, Vonita," Louie said, "you ever think about taking a vacation?"

She didn't even spare him a glance. "I'll take one when you do, Dr. Ward." The phone rang, and she answered it, already dismissing him. "Yes, honey," Vonita said. "You've got the right place."

IN A SMALL BANK OF chairs beside the lab, Joy sat with her earbuds firmly jammed into her ears, listening to her Disney playlist while the Cytotec did its work inside her. It would take a few hours before her cervix was soft enough to be dilated, which meant that she would be in the Center for a while, while other women came and went.

She shifted, slipping a crumpled picture out of her pocket. Yesterday, she had been one of a dozen women here for counseling, getting labs done and listening to Vonita walk through the forms required by the state and hearing Dr. Ward talk about the procedure. She had also been asked to give a urine sample, and had an ultrasound. A woman named Graciela had been the one who performed it; she had hair that reached past her hips, and even though her voice was soft, she was speaking by rote. "We are obligated to offer you the opportunity to listen to the fetal heartbeat and to see the sonogram," Graciela told her, and to Joy's surprise, she heard herself say yes. Then she started to sob. She cried for her own dumb luck, for her loneliness. She cried because even though she had taken every precaution possible, she had wound up—like her mother—boxed into bad choices because of a man.

Graciela had handed her a tissue and then squeezed her hands. "Are you sure you want to do this?" she asked, breaking from the script. Although she wasn't talking about the ultrasound, she put the wand back in its cradle.

"I'm sure," Joy said. But she didn't know if she believed it. Peeing on a stick was not seeing a fetus on a sonogram. "I want to see it," she told Graciela.

So Graciela squirted gel onto her swollen belly and ran the wand over her skin, and abracadabra, a silver fish swam onto the little screen. It morphed into a circle, a curve, then a fetal shape.

"Can I . . ." Joy said, and then she swallowed. "Can I have a picture?"

"You bet," Graciela replied. She pushed a button, and a little printout curled from the machine. Black-and-white, in profile. She handed it to Joy.

"You must think I'm crazy," Joy murmured.

Graciela shook her head. "You'd be surprised how many women want one."

Joy had not known what to do with the ultrasound picture. She only knew she could not leave without it. She didn't want to fold it into her tiny wallet, and yesterday she had been wearing pants without pockets. So she had slipped it into her bra, over her heart. She told herself that when she got home later, she would crumple it up and throw it away.

She still had it with her today.

BETH FELT LIKE SHE WAS swimming up from the bottom of a deep pool, and every time she tried to see the runny yolk of the sun, it seemed to get farther away. Then suddenly she surfaced in a rush of noise and activity. She was dizzy and dry-mouthed when her eyes popped open. Where the hell was she?

She slipped a hand underneath the blanket that was covering her and touched her belly, then lower, to the bulk of a pad in her underwear. Awareness struck her, one drop at a time, until suddenly she was soaked in the truth: they had asked her if she was pregnant and she'd said no, and it didn't squeeze her heart to say it because it wasn't a lie. But still, they had done a urine test and a blood test and had rubbed an ultrasound wand over her belly, as if they didn't believe her. The last thing Beth remembered was looking up at the ugly fluorescent lights on the ceiling, and then she didn't remember anything at all.

She tried to speak, but she had to dig deeper to find her voice, and when it came out it didn't sound like hers at all. "Daddy?" she rasped.

Then he was leaning over her, his warm hands on her shoulder, her arm. "Hi, baby girl," he said. He smiled down at her, and she noticed the deep lines that bracketed his mouth, like a parenthetical statement of fear. His temples had brown age spots she had never seen before. When had he gotten old, and why hadn't she noticed?

"Where am I?"

He smoothed her hair away from her face. "You're at the hospital. You're going to be fine, honey. You just rest."

"What happened?"

He looked down at the floor. "You were . . . losing a lot of blood. You needed a transfusion. Whatever it is, baby, we're going to get through this together."

Beth wished that could be true. She wished, in a crazy way, that the doctor would come back and tell her she had a rare and terrible cancer, because that would almost be easier to hear than the fact that she had disappointed her father.

He reached over, averting his eyes, tugging her hospital johnny more firmly behind her to tuck it in. "Don't need to give a free show," he murmured.

She had read somewhere that the victims of the Inquisition had been made to pay for their own punishments, their own imprisonment. To escape death, they had to offer up the names of others who did not believe Jesus Christ was God. Whether or not they were actually innocent had nothing to do with the process. Beth took a deep breath. "Daddy," she began, and just then the nurse came into the room.

She was round everywhere—cheeks, butt, boobs, belly—and she

smelled like cinnamon. Beth remembered, hazily, that face leaning down over her own. *I'm Jayla, I'm your nurse, and I'm going to take care of you, understand?* "It's about time," her father said. "It can't be normal, that much blood, from . . . there. Is my daughter going to be all right?"

Jayla looked from Beth to her father. "Maybe I could talk to Beth privately?"

That was the instant that Beth understood her Day of Judgment had come, her moment before the Grand Inquisitor. But her father didn't know this, and so he interpreted her sudden stiffness as fear instead of fatalism. "You can talk to us both. She's only seventeen." Her father gripped her hand, as if he could be the strength for whatever bad news was about to be delivered.

Was it Beth's imagination, or did Jayla's eyes soften as they met hers, as if she could couch the impact of her words? "Beth, your tests came back. Did you know you were pregnant?"

"No," she whispered—a syllable that was maybe a lie and maybe a denial of what was surely about to happen.

Beth could not look her father in the eye. He lifted her hand, and for a breathless moment she thought that she had been wrong about him, that he would stand by her or forgive her or both. But instead he tugged until she could feel his thumb rubbing over the thin ridge of the silver promise ring he had bought her for her fourteenth birthday, the one that was supposed to signify that she'd stay pure until her wedding night. "Are you . . . did you . . . ?"

The nurse murmured something and slipped out through the curtains of the cubicle. Beth hardly even noticed. She was somewhere else—behind a playing field, under the bleachers, with stars overhead that spelled out the answers to questions she was afraid to ask out loud: *Should I . . . ? What if he . . . ? Could this be . . . ?*

Yes. Yes. Yes.

For one night, she had been worshipped. A boy had lit fires inside her in places she had not known could burn. He had prayed with his hands and his mouth and his promises, and she had made a single mistake: she had put her faith in him. Even after everything he had done, she had turned the memory of that night over and over in her mind until it was so smooth and polished it was no longer an irritating grain of sand, but a pearl.

She *had* to see it that way, because if it wasn't rare and special, then she was an even greater fool.

But her father wouldn't think that. She had believed that nothing could ever hurt more than the moment she realized John Smith was not a real name, that she had willingly given away something she could never get back—not just her virginity, but her pride. But this, this cut more deeply—the look on her father's face when he realized Beth was damaged goods. "Please, Daddy," she begged. "It wasn't my fault—"

He seized on that escape hatch. "Then who did this to you? Who hurt you?"

She pictured John's lips grazing the inside of her thigh, his mouth closing over her. "No one," she said softly.

Her father clenched his fists. "I'll kill him. I will *kill* him for laying a hand on you." His words were full of angles and edges. "Who. Is. He."

For a moment, Beth almost laughed. *Good luck finding him*, she thought. But instead of directing her fury at whoever John Smith was, she turned the full force of her blaze on her father instead. "This is why I couldn't tell you." Her own voice scared her with its true and perfect aim. "It's why I went to the clinic in the first place. Because I *knew* you'd be like this."

Her anger shook the curtains. Her fingernails bit into her own palms. She was a hydra. Her father had cut her down, and something twice as strong had grown in its place.

Somewhere, distantly, Beth realized that it had not been sleeping with a boy that had made her a woman. It was not even the pregnancy, or trying to remove it. It was this: being forcibly treated like a child, when she wasn't one.

Her father stared at her. "I don't even know who you are," he said softly, and then he turned on his heel and left.

JANINE KNEW PART OF THE disguise of being a woman who wanted an abortion involved fooling her own tribe. She and Allen had talked about this, how it was safer, how it was almost a quality control checkpoint before she entered the Center. If she could get by the other pro-life activists with her blond wig and her hoodie pulled up to shadow her face, then she could likely convince the employees inside. Plus, if she walked past everyone and they didn't call out to her the way they would any other woman, it might look suspicious.

So the only person who knew who she was, as she walked for the first time on the other side of the fence, was Allen. He met her gaze and then turned away to talk to another activist. Meanwhile, the others began trying to get her attention. She knew that the Center considered this harassment, but honestly, it was good citizenship—if you saw a murder in progress, wouldn't you stop it?

"Good morning," Ethel said, stretching her hand over the fence with a little pink bag dangling from her fingers. "Can I offer you a gift?"

Janine felt her heart pound. She couldn't speak; what if Ethel recognized her voice? Instead she reached out and snatched the blessing bag. "You don't have to go through with this," Ethel said triumphantly. Janine knew why—if you could actually get one of the women to *take* a bag, you had already gotten into her head. "We can help!"

Turning away, Janine rang the buzzer at the Center's front door, and two seconds later she heard the buzz that would let her enter. There were maybe ten other women sitting in the waiting room—

young and old, calm and jittery, Black and white. The woman at the reception desk had a name tag, VONITA. Janine gave her alias—Fiona—and watched Vonita highlight her name on a list. Then she checked her watch. "You're the last one," she said. "Let's get you in for a quick lab test and you can do the ultrasound after counseling, so we don't hold up the process. It means you'll have to stay afterward, but only for a few minutes. Sound good?"

But Janine said nothing. She had expected the nerves that would make it difficult to be a spy. She had not expected the PTSD, the sudden wave that knocked her off her feet and made her see not this clinic owner and this reception desk, but one she'd visited long ago in a different state.

"I'm gonna take that as a yes," Vonita said, smiling. She patted Janine's hand. "I know you're nervous, but I promise you, we'll get you through."

Janine was whisked into the back to have her blood tested for her Rh type, and to give a urine sample. Janine's was in her purse in a little baby food jar. Allen had gotten it from someone who knew someone who was pregnant, and she hadn't asked any questions. In the bathroom, she poured it from the jar into the specimen cup.

When she entered the waiting room, Vonita was just starting the counseling session. She sat down between a woman whose eyes were so heavy-lidded she might have been asleep, and a woman who was taking notes diligently in a spiral notebook. "I run this clinic," Vonita was saying, "and I am glad you've found your way to us. Now, we're gonna spend a few moments together, and then the doctor is going to come talk to you as a group, and then you're going to have a chance to meet one-on-one with him."

As she spoke, she walked around the semicircle of seating, handing out clipboards with paperwork. "All of you have a file, yes? On the top is a prescription for azithromycin, which is given to you prophylactically so you don't get any type of infection. I need you to get that filled and bring it with you when you return for your procedure." She looked around, making eye contact with each woman to make sure they understood.

"The sheet underneath that prescription is what we're going to work on first. It's your twenty-four-hour informed consent. Mississippi law says that you can have an abortion twenty-four hours after completing this counseling session. This form signifies that you have made two visits, the first one being today. We're going to fill out the areas marked with X's to document that you're here for your first visit. So. Take your pencils, and let's all do this together."

Janine blindly followed the instructions, making up a fake address for her fake persona, and scribbling the date and a signature. The woman beside Janine who was taking notes held up her hand. "What about the time?"

"Dr. Ward will fill that part out for you when you meet with him." Vonita held up a fan made of brightly colored pamphlets. "These are booklets that the Department of Health requires us to give to our patients. This first one gives alternatives to abortion, like programs for unwed mothers and licensed maternity homes and adoption information, and it tells you where the health departments are located all over the state. The second booklet shows you how a fetus develops from beginning to end of a pregnancy. The third booklet tells you what your risks are when you have an abortion, as well as when you have a baby. And the last one is my favorite. It's about contraception." Everyone but Janine laughed. "Today is the day you need to decide what kind of contraception you'd like to have when you leave here."

This surprised Janine; she had known that the Center was a murder factory, but not that they also tried to *prevent* pregnancies. She pressed down so hard on her mechanical pencil that the lead broke.

"Now, please sign and date the form to acknowledge you were given these materials." There was a tired thread in Vonita's voice, as if this were a script she had memorized long ago. "The second portion of this page will be filled out when you come back. You'll have to reaffirm your decision by signing again. Any questions yet?"

A few women shook their heads. The others just sat in silence.

"We do two types of abortions here at the Center," Vonita said, and Janine leaned forward on the edge of her chair. "There's the surgical abortion, which the doctor performs; and there is the pill—the medical abortion—which is an option if you are ten weeks pregnant or less."

"Which one's the fastest?" a woman blurted out.

"Girl," Vonita chided gently, "I'm getting to that! If you decide to have a surgical abortion, you'll be here for three to four hours, although the surgery itself is less than five minutes from the time you go into the operating room till the time you come out. You recover for about a half hour and then our nurse will give you discharge information—both verbally and in writing—about how to take care of yourself, along with a phone number to call for emergencies, and a date to return for a checkup. Surgery patients, if you return for a checkup, it's fifteen dollars for the pregnancy test, and thirty dollars if you see the doctor. What I suggest you consider is you give yourself three weeks, then go to your regular physician for a checkup; and you get a pregnancy test from the pharmacy and do it yourself. You should have a light line or a clear result, and if you do, you can go on your birth control method."

A young woman with beads in her hair that sang asked, "Does it . . . hurt?" Everyone perked up, listening carefully for the answer.

Yes, Janine thought. She felt herself sinking backward into the darkest corner of her mind, the vault where she kept the memory of her own procedure. It hurt in all sorts of places, when you least expected it.

"There is some discomfort," Vonita answered. "We suggest that you take deep breaths, in and out. There will be a nurse in the room to help you get through the process. It's doable, that's what I can tell you, but it's also not a garden party." She surveyed the group. "Now, pill patients, when *you* come in you will be here for an hour and a half. You'll be in a room like this, a few of you at a time. The doctor will give you the first pill, which stops your pregnancy from growing and tells your body and your brain that you're about to abort. Then he will send you home with four pills in a little package. Twenty-four hours after you've taken the first pill here at the Center, you are eligible to take those other four pills. There's a window, so if you're at work at noon the next day, stay at work and then take the pills when you get home. You'll bleed for about three weeks; it takes that long for your hormone level to go back to its natural state, and after that you come for your checkup."

"Which one do you recommend?"

"Only you can decide," Vonita said. "If you are ten weeks along or less and are eligible for the pills, you get to avoid surgery. But surgery is over and done with more quickly than the pill procedure. So really, it is up to you."

Janine found herself thinking of her brother, Ben. He lived in a group home now, and he bagged groceries for a living. He had a Down syndrome girlfriend he took out to dinner and a movie every Friday night. He was obsessed with *Stranger Things*. He had the same Sara Lee pound cake every night for his dessert. He was happy. On the other hand, was she? She had devoted her livelihood to saving innocent babies, but was that out of faith or guilt? She glanced around the room and wondered how many of these women would have their abortions and feel like a burden had been lifted; and how many, like her, would let it govern the rest of their lives. But she said none of this.

She forced her attention to Vonita again. "Now, after I finish up talking, the doctor is going to come out here and talk to you as a group. He's going to explain exactly what he does in the surgery and exactly how he administers the pill. If you have any questions, you can ask him at that time. If you have any private questions, you can ask him after that, during the individual session he has with you.

During that time, he will say what the law requires him to say to you. He'll review your ultrasound and your medical history and he'll sign off on your paperwork. Then you'll go to the reception desk, and schedule when you're coming back. I'll tell you how much you owe and who your doctor is going to be the day you return." She tidied the stack of paperwork on her lap. "Questions?"

How do you do it? Janine thought. *How do you counsel this, when you know they will leave here completely different women than when they arrived?*

She looked around at the other women. *How can I save all their babies?*

How can I tell them that the decision they make today might not feel right tomorrow?

But she said none of this.

"Can I work the next day?" someone asked.

"Yes," Vonita assured her. "Do you need a doctor's note for an absence today?"

"No, ma'am."

Vonita nodded. She looked around the room. "We hope you are not here because anyone has forced you to come. We are required to tell you that you do not have to go through with this procedure if you don't want to."

From beneath lowered lashes, Janine held her breath.

What if she stood up now, and said she was making a mistake? What if she blew her cover and told these women that they needed to think of their unborn children? What if she became their voice?

But she did not, and no woman wavered.

IZZY WAS STUCK IN TRAFFIC at a construction zone, so by the time she got to the Center, the trip had taken a half hour longer than it should have. She parked lopsided and grabbed her purse and locked the doors to the car as she was running up the path that led to the

Center's front door. She didn't even hear the protesters, that's how *frazzled* she was.

When she was buzzed inside, a man in scrubs was just settling down in a cluster of women, starting to speak. The woman at the front desk took one look at Izzy and started to laugh. "Sugar," she said, "take a deep breath. What can I do for you?"

Izzy did. "I am so sorry I'm late," she began, and she realized that could be interpreted in so many different ways, and that they would all be right.

LOUIE CALLED IT THE LAW of Three. Most of what he told these ladies had also been said by Miz Vonita, and he would repeat it to them yet again in the individual doctor-patient sessions that followed. But he also knew that these women were too shell-shocked to be absorbing even a fraction of the information, which is why, by the third time, he hoped that it had sunk in.

There were eleven women in front of him: seven Black, two white, two brown. He paid attention to the race of those who came to the Center because for him, the politics of abortion had so much in common with the politics of racism. As an African American male, he could imagine quite easily what it was like to not have jurisdiction over your body. White men had once owned Black men's bodies. Now, white men wanted to own women's bodies.

"I am obligated by the state to tell you some things that are not medically true," Louie said. "I am obligated to tell you that having an abortion increases your risk for breast cancer, even though there is no evidence to support that." He thought back, as he always did, to the patient he had treated once who had breast cancer, and who had terminated her pregnancy so that she could pursue treatment. *My risk of getting breast cancer is zero*, she had said flatly, *since I already have it*.

"I am obligated by the state," he continued, "to tell you that with abortion, there are risks of injury to your bowel, bladder, uterus, fallopian tubes, and ovaries; and that if you have injury to your uterus that's severe enough, we might have to remove your uterus, which is called a hysterectomy. But guess what? Those are the exact same risks that you'll have if you give birth to a baby. In fact, you're more likely to have those risks giving birth to a child than having an abortion. Now. Y'all got questions for me?"

A woman's hand crept up tentatively. "I heard you use knives and scissors to cut up the babies."

Louie heard this at least every other counseling session. One of the things he wished he could tell women who wanted abortions was to never, ever google the word. He shook his head. "There are no knives, no scissors, no scalpels." He made sure to correct her use of the term *babies* as gently as possible. "If patients wish to see the *tissue* after it's removed, they can. And it is disposed of with respect, in an appropriate legal way."

She nodded, satisfied. Not for the first time, Louie was amazed that a woman who believed nonsense like this would still be brave enough to schedule an appointment.

He looked into the eyes of each of the women. Warriors, every one of them. Every day, he was reminded of their grit, their courage in the face of obstacles, the quiet grace with which they shouldered their troubles. They were stronger than any men he'd ever known. For sure, they were stronger than the male politicians who were so terrified of them that they designed laws specifically to keep women down. Louie shook his head. As if that could ever be done. If he had learned anything during his years as an abortion doctor, it was this: there was nothing on God's green earth that would stop a woman who didn't want to be pregnant.

THERE WAS A STUFFED LOBSTER on George's daughter's bed. It was red and wore a little white hat like a Victorian baby, and he had won it for Lil at a church fair. He sat in her room, the way he used to every night when he tucked her in, before she told him she could read her *own* books, thank you very much. She had been seven at the time. He remembered laughing about it with Pastor Mike. He didn't find it funny now. In retrospect, it seemed like the first step on a path that would ultimately take her so far away from him he couldn't even see her in the distance.

She had wanted that lobster so bad that he'd paid more than thirty dollars to a huckster to get three baseballs he could pitch into rusty milk cans. The first time he won, he was handed a little stuffed snake the size of a pencil. Damn bait and switch. But Lil had been next to him, clapping every time he got one in, and so he'd traded up until he got to the stuffed animal of her choice. The fact that she still had it after all these years was a testament, he supposed, to what it meant to her.

Or maybe she hadn't wanted to let go of her childhood any more than he did.

When she was little, every Saturday morning in the summertime they'd drive out in his truck to get crawfish. Lil would curl up next to him on the bench seat, her legs dangling and kicking because her feet were nowhere close to hitting the floor—happy feet, he'd call them. There was a creek that was shallow enough even for a five-year-old, and he and Lil would grab a bucket from the backseat, take off their shoes and socks, and wade in. He taught her how to find the rocks that would make good hiding spots. If you lifted the stones too fast, you would startle the crawfish and stir up the mud so they scurried away. If you lifted the stones slow, you would be able to surprise the crawfish. You could pick it up with your hands then, minding the pincers. If they had a good day hunting, Lil would help him boil them in a broth made of onions, lemon, and garlic. They'd eat them with potatoes and corn on the cob, until they fell asleep in the lazy slant of the afternoon, bellies full and fingers still slick with butter.

Once, Lil had lifted one of the crawfish to find rows of little red eggs stuck underneath her tail. *Daddy,* she had asked, *what's wrong with her?*

She's gonna have babies, George had explained. *So we have to put her back, and let her do just that. You don't mess with a mama, Lil. She belongs with her babies.*

Lil had been quiet for a moment. *Daddy,* she'd asked. *Who messed with my mama?*

He had scooped his girl up and out of the water. *Let's get home before the crawdads get out of that pail,* he'd said. Because he couldn't very well tell her, *I did.*

Now, he lifted the pistol that was cradled in his lap and stood. As he did, the paper he had found on her bedside table fluttered to the floor. He stepped on it as he left the room, his heel landing square across the heading at the top. *Medication Abortion Authorization and Informed Consent,* it read. *The Center for Women's Health, Jackson.*

Eight a.m.

With a flourish, Wren set the plate down in front of her father: a fried egg, and a drippy candle stuck into a smile of melon. "Happy birthday to you," she finished singing. "By the way, that would have been way better if I had a sibling. Harmony sucks when you're an only."

"You're overestimating your singing ability," her dad grunted.

She laughed. "*Someone's* feeling grumpy."

"Someone's feeling old as Hell."

She sat down across from him. "Forty is the new twenty," she told him.

"Says who?"

"Me," she sighed. "I *told* you you never listen."

He smirked and took a bite of his egg. She didn't have to look at his face to know that it was perfectly cooked. Her dad had been the one to teach her to fry one correctly. The way to ruin an egg was to not be patient, and to heat the pan too fast, which would make the egg stick to it. You had to be slow, methodical, deliberate. Wren had lost track of how many times her father had come into the kitchen when she was making breakfast and would automatically turn the flame down. But, as much as it pained her to admit it, he knew his shit. The eggs she cooked were works of art.

She folded her arms and rested her chin on them. "So I've been saving this one for today," she said, and immediately he perked up. For as long as she could remember, they traded facts, mostly about astronomy—which her father had introduced her to so long ago she couldn't remember not being able to pick out constellations like Andromeda and Cassiopeia and Perseus and Pegasus. "Astronomers found a massive star that exploded in 1954 . . . and again in 2014."

Her father's eyebrows shot up. "Twice?"

She nodded. "It's a supernova that refuses to die. It's five hundred million light-years away, near Big Bear. Usually supernovas fade over a hundred days, right? This one is still going strong after a *thousand*."

Her dad had taught her that stars needed fuel, like anything else that burned. When they started to run out of hydrogen, they cooled, changing color to become red giants, like Betelgeuse. But *this* star had defied the odds.

"That is an excellent birthday fact." He grinned. "What's on the agenda today?"

She shrugged. "I'm going to check on my meth lab, wire a million to my offshore account, and have lunch with Michelle Obama."

"Give her my best," her father said. He ate his last bite of the egg. "Do you know how few people can cook a perfect egg?"

"Yes, because you tell me at least twice a week. I have to go or I'll miss the bus." She circled the table and leaned down to kiss his cheek, breathing in the familiar smell of starch from his uniform shirt and bay rum from his aftershave. Wren thought that if she ever wound up in a coma, all the doctors would have to do was wave that combination of scents under her nose, and surely she would wake. She stood up and reached for her knapsack on the counter, but before she could get it, her father grabbed her arm.

"What aren't you telling me?" he asked, narrowing his eyes.

She forced herself to meet his eyes. "What?"

"Come on. I'm a detective."

Wren danced away from him. "I have no idea what you're talking about," she said.

Her father shook his head, smiling. "Never let it be said I spoiled a birthday surprise."

Wren walked halfway to the bus stop at the end of the street before she let out the breath she was holding. How had he known?

She wasn't hiding a birthday surprise. She was going to get birth control today, at the Center. She was cutting health class to do it, which felt somehow karmic. Wren thought of how she and Ryan had talked about this: whether it made sense to use condoms, if their safety rate was good enough, how if Wren got contraception, she would do it without having to tell her father. That much she and Ryan agreed upon. Ryan didn't relish the thought of her detective father, with his standard-issue Glock, finding out that his daughter was sleeping with him.

Wren knew there were girls who were so unromantic they had sex because they wanted to get it over with. There were others who were so starry-eyed they truly believed that the guy they had sex with the first time would be their one and only. Wren was caught somewhere on the spectrum between the two. She wanted to have sex for the first time with someone she could laugh with, if things got weird or didn't work. But she also knew there was more to it than that. She knew your first time could only happen once. There were so many memories that you *didn't* get to pick—like being the only kid in her class who wrote a Mother's Day card to her aunt, or turning seventy shades of red when she had to explain to her father that the reason she'd called him from the nurse's office wasn't that she had the flu, but that she had gotten her period. Given that, shouldn't you get to choose *this* memory, and make it perfect?

The bus pulled up to the curb, exhaling heavily as its doors swung open. She picked her way through the rows, past the jocks and the brains and the theater nerds, and slid into a blessedly empty row. She pressed her cheek to the cool glass. The next time she rode this bus, she would be taking the Pill. She wondered how many other girls on the bus were. She wondered who was having sex, if they all felt as swollen with that secret as she did.

One day she would tell her father that she wasn't a virgin. Like, when she was married and thirty and having a baby.

As the bus chugged toward the school, Wren thought maybe this was a birthday gift to her father, after all. He got to think she belonged only to him, for a little while longer.

Hugh was forty, and he felt every fucking minute of it. He flattened his hands on the table, bracketing the plate of breakfast Wren had made him, which he had scraped clean. You'd think that things would be different, that there would be an invisible line between yesterday and today to mark the fact that he was this old, but no. He was still headed to the same precinct he'd been at since he became a cop. He was still a single parent. The table still had one wobbly leg that he hadn't managed to fix. The only new thing was silver in his beard stubble, which frankly he could have lived without.

He supposed that this was the age that men began to wonder if they were doing anything that would leave a mark on the world. If he died today, what would be said at his funeral? Sure, he had made a difference in the lives of individuals, given his career. And he would not have traded a moment of his time with Wren. But he wasn't a genius. He wouldn't invent something that eliminated fossil fuels or allowed for time travel. He'd never negotiate world peace. He supposed if every individual man did his best, then the greater balance tipped toward good rather than evil, but that didn't keep the individual daily chain of one's life from feeling, well, mundane.

Plus, dammit, his back hurt after he'd been on his feet all day in a way it never used to.

He feared—although he would never admit it to anyone—that this was the crest, the pinnacle. That the rest of his life would be a slow march down the hill; that he had already experienced the best of what was coming to him. What was getting old, anyway, except dragging your feet toward the inevitable?

He was saved from skating further down this morbid path of thought by the buzzing of his cellphone. Bex's face popped onto the screen, and he smiled, shaking his head. "Happy birthday to you," she sang, as soon as he answered. "Happy birthday to you!"

He let her finish her off-key rendition. "I think I know who Wren gets her dubious singing ability from," he said.

"*Because* it's your birthday," his sister said, "I'm going to let that slide."

Hugh scratched his neck. "Tell me, does it go away?"

"What?"

"This feeling that it's the beginning of the end."

She laughed. "Hugh, I'd give anything to be forty again. You must think I have one foot in the grave."

She was fourteen years his senior, but he never thought of her that way. "You're not old."

"Then neither are you," she said. "What are you doing to mark this festive occasion?"

"Protecting and serving."

"Well, that's depressing. You should be doing something extraordinary. Like taking a salsa lesson. Or going skydiving."

"Yeah," Hugh said. "I don't think so."

"Where's your sense of adventure?"

"Tied to a paycheck," Hugh said. "Today's just like any other day."

"Maybe you'll be wrong," Bex replied. "Maybe today will be unforgettable."

He carried his empty plate to the sink, ran water over it, like he did every morning. He grabbed his badge and his car keys. "Maybe," Hugh said.

* * *

EVERY MORNING JANINE WOKE UP and said a prayer for the child she didn't have. She knew that there were plenty of people who wouldn't understand, or who would call her a hypocrite. Maybe she was. But to her, that just meant she had something to make up for, and this was how she was going to do it.

She padded into the bathroom and brushed her teeth. There were anti-lifers who would rather cut off their arms than change their opinions. But she *could* try to make people like that understand how she felt:

Start with the sentence *The unborn baby is a person*. Replace the words *unborn baby* with the words *immigrant. African American. Trans woman. Jew. Muslim.*

That visceral *yes* that swelled through them when they said that sentence out loud? That was exactly how Janine felt about being pro-life. There were so many organizations set up to combat racism, sexism, homelessness, mental illness, homophobia. Why shouldn't there be one to fight for the tiniest humans, who were the most in need of protection?

Janine knew she would never be able to convince everyone to believe what she did. But if she changed the mind of even one pregnant woman—well, wasn't that a start?

She reached for the wig that she had propped over the neck of a shampoo bottle last night. Inclining her head, she slipped it on, fitting it tightly against her scalp. Then she looked in the mirror.

Janine grinned. She didn't look half bad as a blonde.

OLIVE LAY ON HER SIDE, watching Peg sleep. There was so much she did for her wife that Peg did not acknowledge. The first cup of coffee that was always too bitter? Olive took it. The floor was a mess? Olive vacuumed while Peg went for her morning run. The sheets on the bed that were fresh every Sunday? Didn't change themselves. Olive had done these things because she loved Peg. But now, she could see into the future. A year from now, Peg would spit out her coffee, wade through tufts of dust bunnies, sleep in sheets that were never washed.

Maybe they would smell faintly of Olive.

The truth was, for years now, Olive had been unable to imagine a world without Peg in it. Peg was about to have to imagine a world without her.

Peg's eyes opened. She saw Olive staring and snuggled closer into her arms. "What are you thinking about?" she murmured.

Olive felt her throat tightening in the grip of the secret she held, and it felt wrong, unnatural. "I'm thinking," she said finally, honestly, "about how much I'll miss you."

Peg smiled, closing her eyes. "And where exactly are you going?"

Olive opened her mouth and then hesitated. She might have to count time, but she didn't need to start the clock yet. She pulled Peg into her arms. "Absolutely nowhere," she said.

JOY DID NOT REMEMBER HER dreams, as a rule. This came, she was certain, from sleeping with one eye open at foster homes, to make sure that another kid wasn't stealing something that belonged to her—a book, a candy bar, her body. Yet months ago, the night before Joy had taken a pregnancy test, she'd imagined that she had a baby, wrapped in a blue blanket.

She'd had the same dream last night.

Her alarm had awakened her—another anomaly; normally she woke up at least five minutes before it went off. But she couldn't be late today. So she had showered quickly, only to realize that her razor was broken. She did not eat—she'd been told not to—and since she was not supposed to drive herself home, she called for an Uber.

Her driver had pictures of his children stuck to the dashboard of his Kia. "Going to be a hot one today," he said as they pulled away from the curb, and she silently cursed. She didn't want a chatty driver. She wanted one who was mute, preferably.

"I guess," she said.

He glanced into the rearview mirror. "You in town for the convention?"

She imagined this. What if there was a convention of unhappily pregnant women? What if they filled an entire conference hall? What if there were breakout sessions for Self-Doubt and Stupid Choices? Or a sitting area where you could cry, and a soundproof room where you could curse as loud as you wanted at a man, at your rotten luck, at God?

What if there was a keynote, with a motivational speaker who could truly convince you that tomorrow was going to be better than yesterday?

Scratch that. It wasn't the pregnant women who needed a convention to educate them. It was the people who were rushing the gates, telling women like Joy she was going to Hell.

"So you're not a dentist?" the driver said.

"What?"

"The convention."

"Oh," Joy said. "No."

She had entered the Center's address into her Uber app but now she wanted to get out of the car. She wanted to walk. She needed to be alone.

"Can you pull over here?" she asked.

"Everything okay?" The driver slowed and put on his blinker, rolling to a stop.

"Yeah. I just need to . . . This is great. I got the address wrong," she lied. Never mind that they were literally beside a parking lot with a defunct video store that was boarded up. "It's just around the corner."

"Okay, then," the driver said.

Joy started walking. She felt the sun on the crown of her head; it might have been a blessing. She could hear the car rolling along behind her, slowly crunching the gravel on the side of the road. *Pass me*, she thought. *Jesus Christ, leave already.*

The Kia pulled up beside her, and the driver rolled down the window. Joy felt like crying. Why today, of all days, did she have to get the Uber guy with a conscience? "Ma'am," he said, "you forgot this."

She came closer and saw that he was holding up the blue blanket that had been in two of her dreams. It had not been in the backseat with her.

Joy blinked at it. "That doesn't belong to me," she said, and she kept going.

IZZY WAS YAWNING AS SHE drove. She hated night shifts, and she had worked long enough as a nurse in the ER at Baptist Memorial to be able to avoid them. But she had willingly swapped with a colleague, Jayla, because she had to take the next two days off.

She had already been on the road an hour and a half, and she had another hour left, and she knew this because she had googled it multiple times, as if the answer might change. But still, rather than leaving Oxford at six A.M. as she had intended, when her shift ended she had taken the elevator up to the birthing pavilion.

Nobody had stopped her from going into the nursery; she had her ID clipped right to her scrubs. To her surprise, though, there had been only a single baby. It was a little boy, swaddled in a blue blanket. He had a name card: LEVON MONELLE. One tiny fist had punched the air, and his mouth had been wide open. Izzy had watched him cry and flail around a little bit, and then through some miracle of guidance, his hand had landed on his lips and he'd started to suckle.

You were never too young to learn to be self-sufficient.

She had stroked a finger down the tight mummied wrap of his

little body. Was it dishonest to not tell Parker she was pregnant? Or would it be worse to tell him, and then break up with him?

Izzy had grown up with her face pressed so hard against reality that it was impossible for her to believe in mythical creatures: fairies and unicorns and men who cared more about Izzy's future with them than about her past. She had tried to picture herself in Parker's world, learning how to ski and spending fifty bucks at a movie on seats and popcorn and sodas without feeling guilty. But if she became that woman, she wouldn't be Izzy anymore. And wasn't that who he had fallen in love with?

It was better this way. Parker would never know. He wouldn't be forced to stay with her out of some misguided sense of honor or chivalry. Once he had space and time to think it over, once he settled down with someone more *like* him, he would realize she had done him a favor. Someone who had grown up getting by day to day just didn't have the resources to dream about the future.

When Izzy had left the little room, she'd stopped at the nurses' desk. "How come there aren't more babies?"

The nurse had looked at her like she was crazy. "They're in the rooms with their mamas."

Izzy had felt like an idiot. Of course they were. Even now as she drove she wondered about Levon's mother. Had she needed to get a good night's sleep? Was she sick? Was *he*?

Izzy was afraid the answer was also something any vaguely maternal female knew, which was why she hadn't asked the L & D nurse. If she needed confirmation that she was making the right choice, she'd received it.

The GPS on her phone told her that in two miles, she would be turning right. She put on her signal, following the directions carefully because she was not familiar with the roads in Jackson, Mississippi. But even with her detour to the nursery, Izzy knew she would be fine. Barring unforeseen traffic, she would reach the Center in plenty of time for the first appointment of her abortion.

* * *

You HAD TO GET UP ridiculously early in Atlanta to get to Mississippi by eight A.M., but Louie preferred sleeping in his own bed to sleeping in a hotel. He spent so many days of the month jetting to Kentucky and Alabama and Texas and Mississippi and other states where abortion clinics were being shut down left and right, that when he could pull up his own covers and rest his head on his own pillow, he moved heaven and earth to make it happen.

He was in Mississippi four times a month to provide abortion services, as were three other colleagues who rotated coverage, flying in from Chicago and Washington, D.C. Louie had known that working in the Deep South as an abortion provider was more challenging, say, than working on the East Coast. The biggest difference between the North and the South was not the weather or the food or even the people—it was religion. Here, religion was as much of the atmosphere as carbon dioxide. You had to offer folks a chance to be pro-choice not in spite of their faith, but because of it.

Louie liked routine, and he adhered to it whenever possible. He knew the flight attendants by name, and always reserved his favorite seat (6B). He drank coffee, black, and he ate a KIND bar and a yogurt that he packed from home. He used the time on the plane to catch up on medical journal articles.

Today he was reading the research of a team from Northwestern University, who had recorded a zinc flash at the precise instant a sperm fertilized an egg. A rush of calcium at that moment caused zinc to be released from the egg. As the zinc burst out, it attached itself to small, fluorescent molecules: the spark that was picked up by camera microscopes.

Although this had been seen before in mice, it was the first time in humans. More important, certain eggs glowed a little brighter than others at the moment of conception—the same ones that went on to become healthy embryos. Given that 50 percent of eggs fertilized in vitro weren't viable, and that often it came down to a clinician guessing which one *looked* the healthiest—the implications of the study were significant. The correct embryo to transfer was the one that had burned the brightest at the moment of fertilization.

"*Then God said, Let there be light*," Louie murmured to himself. He shook his head in wonder. Those infinitesimal bits of zinc determined whether an egg would become a completely new genetic entity. Science never failed to humble him, just as much as his faith, and he unequivocally believed that the two could exist side by side.

As a resident, he'd sat with his share of terminal patients, and what you heard was true: people who were dying talked of a tunnel, with a warm glow at the end.

It stood to reason that both life and death began with a spark of light.

Louie was so absorbed in the article that the jolt of the plane hitting the runway startled him. He gathered up his reading material and waited for the seatbelt sign to go off. Then he stood up and pulled his suitcase down from the overhead bin. He traveled only with a carry-on, preferring to keep extra clothes in Vonita's office just in case.

He said goodbye to Courtney, the flight attendant, and turned left when he entered the terminal. He knew this airport by rote: when TSA PreCheck got busy, at which gate he could find Starbucks, where the men's rooms were. He knew exactly how long it would take for him to get his rental car and drive to the Center.

And as always, because he was on such a predictable schedule, his welcome committee was waiting for him when he arrived.

One of the regular protesters at the clinic met Louie at the airport without fail, waiting at the base of the stairs near baggage claim, which was the only route to the rental car agencies. Louie liked to think of the dude as Allen the Anti. He held a hand-lettered sign that said LOUIS WARD MURDERS BABIES. Louie didn't know what pissed him off more: that the man was as regular as clockwork, or that he misspelled Louie's name.

Allen was standing, as usual, with his sign. Louie never engaged. He knew better. But this time, the sign was spelled right. It was enough to cause Louie to slow his gait. "Dr. Ward," Allen said, smiling. "Good flight?"

He stopped. "It's Allen, right?"

"Yes, sir," the man said.

Louie glanced at his watch. "What do you say we grab a bite to eat?"

He had fifteen minutes of slush time because his flight had come in a touch early. And he felt safe in the airport, surrounded by people. Maybe it was possible to walk in another person's shoes, without trampling his steps.

Allen tucked his sign beneath his arm and they walked back up the stairs to McDonald's, where Louie treated the protester to a Big Breakfast and coffee and then sat down across from him at a table in full view of anyone passing by to get to the ticket counter. "Can I ask you why you meet me here?" he asked.

Allen swallowed and smiled. "I want to shut down that murder factory you work in," he said, as easily as he might say, *It's been a really warm October*.

"Murder factory," Louie repeated, turning the phrase over in his mouth. "How long should the women in my care go to jail for their offense?"

"Hate the sin, not the sinner," Allen said.

"Unless the sinner is me, right?" Louie clarified. "So if you could, you'd ban all abortions?"

"Ideally."

"Even in cases of rape and incest?"

Allen shrugged. "Really, how big a percentage is that?"

"You didn't answer my question," Louie pressed.

"You didn't answer mine," Allen countered. "And even if it's one of those rare circumstances, that doesn't mean you're not committing homicide."

Louie thought of the sac he removed during an early abortion. It was tissue that didn't feel pain or have thought or sensation. To him it was potential. To Allen, it was a person. And yet who would argue that there was no difference in the moral implication of chopping down a hundred-year-old oak tree versus stepping on an acorn?

Allen took a mouthful of eggs. Yet another life potential squandered, Louie thought. "You know, I consider myself pro-life," he said. "I just happen to be pro-the-life-of-the-woman. I'd call you pro-birth."

"I could call you pro-abortion," Allen said.

"No one is forcing women to have abortions if they don't ask for them. It's the difference between supporting free will and negating free will."

Allen leaned back in his chair. "I don't think you and I are ever going to be on the same page on that."

"Probably not. But maybe we can agree to neutralize the public space around policy making. We're all entitled to our religious beliefs, right?"

Warily, Allen nodded.

"But we can't make policies based on religion when religion means different things to different people. Which leaves science. The science of reproduction is what it is. Conception is conception. You can decide the ethical value that has for you, based on your own relationship with God . . . but the *policies* around basic human rights with regard to reproduction shouldn't be up for interpretation."

Louie watched Allen's eyes glaze with confusion. "Do you have a daughter, Allen?"

"I do."

"How old?"

"Twelve."

"What would you do if she got pregnant now?"

Allen's face flushed. "Your side always tries to do that—"

"I'm not *trying* to do anything. I'm asking you to apply your dogma personally."

"I would counsel her. I would take her to our pastor. And I would be confident," Allen said, "that she would make the right choice."

"I don't disagree with you," Louie said.

Allen blinked. "You don't?"

"No. Your religion *should* help you make the decision if you find yourself in that situation. But the policy should exist for you to have the right to make it in the first place. When you say you can't do something because your religion forbids it, that's a good thing. When you say *I* can't do something because *your* religion forbids it, that's a problem." Louie glanced at his watch. "Duty calls."

"You know, it's always funny to me how pro-choice folks were all actually *born*," Allen said.

Louie grinned, gathering their trash. "Thank you for the company. And the dialogue."

Allen picked up his sign. "You make it very hard to hate you, Dr. Ward."

"That's the point, brother," Louie said. "That's the point."

BETH HAD TRIED TO DO it the right way. She had gone to the Center, which might as well have been on Mars, given the distance and the cost of the bus ticket. She had filled out the parental consent waiver and had it filed back in her own county. It wasn't *her* fault that the judge whiffed out on her to go on a *vacation* with his wife. Judges shouldn't be allowed to take them, not when other people's lives were hanging on their verdicts.

In the end, she had run out of time. The pills had come from overseas, and the instructions were in Chinese, but she still had the paperwork from the counseling session she had attended at the

Center, including the instructions for those getting a medication abortion. She remembered the lady at the clinic who'd talked to the group, saying that there was a time cutoff for the people who took the abortion pill. She couldn't remember what that magic number of weeks was, but Beth was sure she was beyond it now.

She was in the bathroom, doubled over with cramps. At first she was sure she had done something wrong, because there hadn't been any blood at all. Now, it wouldn't stop. And it wasn't just blood, it was clots, great dark, thick masses that terrified her. That was why she had come to sit on the toilet. She could reach behind her and flush. She was terrified of looking down between her legs and seeing tiny arms and legs; a sad, minuscule face.

She felt her insides twist again, as if someone had attached a thousand strings to the inside of her belly and groin and yanked them. Beth drew her knees up even higher to her chin, the only thing that brought relief, but to do that she couldn't sit. She got off the toilet and rolled to her side, sweating, groaning. Her breath shortened, stuttered links on a chain.

The thing that slipped between her legs was the size of a clenched fist. Beth cried out, seeing it on the linoleum, pink and unfinished, its translucent skin showing dark patches of future eyes and organs. Between its legs was a question mark of umbilical cord.

Shaking, she grabbed a hand towel and wrapped the thing up (*it wasn't a baby, it wasn't a baby, it wasn't a baby*) and stuffed it into the bottom of the trash, arranging tissues and makeup wipes and wrappers on top of it, as if out of sight would be out of mind.

She was starting to see stars, and she thought maybe she was dying, but that didn't make sense because there was no way she was going to Heaven anymore. Maybe she could just close her eyes for a minute, and when she woke up, this would never have happened.

She heard a pounding, and for one terrified moment she thought it was coming from the trash can. But then it got louder, and she realized someone was calling her name.

Beth wanted to answer, she did. But she was so, so tired.

When the door broke open, the lock shattered by her father, she used all the energy she had left to speak. "Don't get mad, Daddy," she whispered, and then everything went black.

GEORGE LEFT THE TRUCK RUNNING, parked illegally in a fire zone. He dashed to the passenger side and lifted his unconscious daughter into his arms, carrying her through the automatic doors of the emergency room. She was bleeding through the blanket he had wrapped around her. "Please help my daughter," he cried, and he was surrounded immediately.

They took her away, setting her on a gurney and rushing her into the back as he followed. A nurse put her hand on his arm. "Mr. . . . ?"

"Goddard," he said. "That's my girl."

"What happened to her?" she asked.

"I don't know. I don't know." He gulped. "I found her like this in the bathroom. She's bleeding from . . . from down there . . ."

"Vaginally?"

He nodded. He tried to see what the doctors were doing, but there were so many of them, and they moved around her, blocking his view.

"What's your daughter's name?" the nurse asked.

When she was little, and couldn't pronounce her name, she called herself Lil Bit. That stuck for the longest time. As she grew up, he had dropped the second half of that term of endearment. But he was the only one to call her Lil; everyone else used a different nickname.

"Elizabeth Goddard," George said. "She goes by Beth."

LAST NIGHT, BEX HAD DREAMED of a piece of art that was still inside her mind. It was a pixilated fetus curled on its side. In the white space, though, carved out by the absence of arms and legs and umbilicus, you would see the optical illusion of a profile. And if you looked closely, you'd know it was hers.

She was not surprised that today, of all days, she would find inspiration. Just yesterday she had finished her last commission. It was time to start fresh.

She had already called Hugh to wish him a happy birthday and she had finished a cup of tea. Her body was humming with anticipation, like a child waiting for the sun to rise on Christmas. She was going to savor every second of this morning, pluck it like a violin string, let it sing through her.

In the closet of her studio where she kept her paints and her turpentine and her brushes there was a tiny panel that, with the press of a finger, would bounce free to reveal a hiding spot. It had come with the house. She had no idea what it had been used for by the previous owners—a safe, maybe, or hidden love letters. Bex kept a shoe box inside, one that she pulled out now and set on her workbench.

Inside was an impossibly small blue cotton hat, and a hospital bracelet: BABY BOY MCELROY. And then, best of all, the photograph—fading now, into rusts and yellows and greens that she associated with the seventies. It was 1978, and there was Bex in the hospital bed, fourteen years old and holding a newborn Hugh.

Bex could have gotten an abortion—it was legal—but her mother, a devout Catholic, talked her out of it. She came up instead with the solution that became a secret. From the moment Bex left the hospital, she was no longer Hugh's mother, but his sister. Her father got a job in a different state and they moved there, plastering over the subterfuge until sometimes Bex even forgot the reality. There had been a point when her mother died that Bex had considered telling Hugh, but she was afraid he might be so angry that he'd hate her. This she couldn't risk.

Bex still got to watch Hugh grow up, have a baby of his own. So did the labels really matter?

It had taken her forty years of careful practice, but she allowed herself regrets only one day a year—this one, Hugh's birthday. She took out this shoe box, and she pictured the parallel universes of her life. In one, she was Hugh's mother, Wren's grandmother. In another, she had fallen in love again, married, and had a child she could gather into her arms anytime she wished. In a third, she went to art school and moved to Florence and became a sculptor, instead of staying in Mississippi to watch over Hugh after her father had died and her mom became an alcoholic.

Bex, who had *not* terminated her pregnancy, had still lost a potential life that day—her own. But when she started to grieve for what she had missed, she redirected her attention to the lives that had been saved, literally, by her son—the battered wives, the suicide jumpers. The teenager Hugh had pulled from the freezing river last year. Wren.

No. She would not have changed a thing. Or this is what she told herself, anyway, when she let the question rise high in her throat, when she felt like she was choking.

Bex carefully put the photo in the bottom of the shoe box and placed the bracelet and the hat inside. She carried it back to the closet and slipped it into its hiding place. Then she pulled the trapdoor into place again, sealing the crypt of this memory.

Occasionally she wondered if, after she died, someone would find the shoe box. Maybe whoever bought her house. She wondered if they would create a mythology around the artifacts, if it would be a tragedy or a love story. It could, Bex knew, be both at once.

She shut the closet and then opened the curtains in her studio. Sunshine spilled onto the wooden floor, like golden grain from a silo. The sky was clear, as blue as her son's eyes. It was why she had named him as she did—her only hint. Even at fourteen, Bex had already pictured the world as an artist did, cast in shadows and light. Even then, what mattered most was hue.

Hugh.

Bex smiled, reaching for the stretcher bars and unprimed canvas. *Today*, she thought, *is a good day to be born*.

Six p.m.

NONE OF US CHOOSE OUR PARENTS. BUT SOME OF US GET LUCKY.

For one perfect moment Wren felt her father's arm close around her. She could smell him—bay rum aftershave and starch. "It's okay," he whispered, his breath moving the hair at her temple. "Everything is okay now."

She believed him. She always had. She believed him when he swore to her that there was no reason to be afraid of the dark, and taught her how to read the stars, so she would never feel lost in it. She believed him when he printed out articles about Internet predators and catfishing and left them taped to her bathroom mirror. She believed him when he ate a spider to prove that it wasn't so scary after all.

He gently pushed her back, his eyes catching on their clasped hands. "Wren, go on now," he said.

She couldn't make herself step away. Wren, who had gotten herself into this mess because she couldn't wait to grow up, wanted nothing more than for her father to rock her on his lap and never let her go.

"Let me finish this," he murmured.

She took an unsteady step toward the white canopy of the tent. There were cops there, motioning to her, but no one came forward to grab her.

Once, there had been a tornado in Jackson. Wren remembered how the sky turned the yellow of a jaundiced eye, and how the atmosphere felt pregnant. The moments before the wind slammed into the city, the air had gone so still that Wren thought the world had stopped spinning, that time had started to move backward. That's how it felt just then, and it was why Wren turned around halfway to the command tent.

She heard her father's voice, as he spoke to George Goddard. "Think of your daughter."

"She'll never look at me the same after this. You don't get it."

"Then make me understand."

Wren was staring at the shooter when he pulled the trigger.

WREN'S FATHER USED TO TELL her a story about how he'd been her hero from the moment she was born. She was in the hospital, and the nurses were doing whatever tests they had to do before a baby could be discharged. One of them was called the Guthrie test, which required the newborn's foot to be pricked and several drops of blood to be dripped onto a diagnostic card. It was sent to the lab to test for PKU.

The nurse that day was inexperienced, and when she pricked Wren's foot, the baby started to wail. It didn't bleed enough, so she had to prick Wren a second time. She squeezed the baby's foot, trying to manually extract blood. By now, Wren was howling.

Her father stood up and grabbed his daughter away from the nurse. He wrapped Wren in a blanket and announced that they were going home. The nurse said this wasn't possible, that she had to finish the test by law.

I am *the fucking law,* her father said.

He still wasn't allowed in that hospital.

HEROES, WREN KNEW, DID NOT always swoop in to rescue. They made questionable calls. They lived with doubts. They replayed and edited and imagined different outcomes. They killed, sometimes, to save.

Wren was wrapped in a space blanket, shivering, even though it was still hot outside. Her ribs hurt from where she had been tackled by a member of the SWAT team. Would the gunman actually have shot Wren? No one knew, because instead her father had scooped up his weapon and fired three shots into George Goddard.

On live television.

There had been a lot of activity—her father being pulled away by the SWAT team; paramedics loading the body into an ambulance, because a doctor had to pronounce the shooter dead.

The shooter.

Wren realized, with a little start, that title applied to both men.

She was sitting on the flatbed of a police truck when her father approached. His arm had gauze wrapped around it. Goddard's wayward shot, the one meant for her, had struck him.

She had come to the clinic because she didn't want to be a little girl anymore. But it wasn't having sex that made you a woman. It was having to make decisions, sometimes terrible ones. Children were told what to do. Adults made up their own minds, even when the options tore them apart.

Her father followed her gaze to the Center. Bathed in the last throes of sunset, the orange walls looked like they were on fire. "What's going to happen to it?" Wren asked.

"I don't know."

She found herself thinking about Dr. Ward and Izzy and Joy and Janine. About poor Vonita. About the nameless women who had been in the Center before Wren got there, and the women who would show up tomorrow for an appointment and trample over the police tape if they had to.

"Aunt Bex is waiting for us," her father said. He held out his arms, as if Wren were still little, and swung her down from the flatbed. Wren saw him wince because of his injury.

When she was tiny, she used to play a game with him by tightening her arms and legs and straightening her backbone to be as rigid as possible. *I'm making myself extra heavy*, she would tell him, and he would laugh.

I'll always be able to carry you.

The night sky rippled, blue stars rising and red ones fading. They were surrounded by life and death. They moved past the chain-link fence that ran along the perimeter of the Center. On it, the protesters had hung a long curl of butcher paper: IT'S A CHILD NOT A CHOICE. Wren had walked past the sign this morning, and remarkably, it was still intact.

A few feet past the Center, Wren stopped. "You all right?" her father asked.

"Just a second."

Wren ran back to the fence. She ripped the banner off, crumpled a long piece, and threw it on the ground. What remained she speared on the top of the chain link to secure it.

CHOICE.

She surveyed her work. *There*, Wren thought.

Many years later, when Wren told this story, she didn't remember amending the sign. She didn't remember whether the fence outside the Center was plaster or metal, how small the closet had been, or if her aunt's blood had spilled on tile or carpet. What she remembered was that, as she left with her father, it was the first time she held *his* hand, instead of the other way around.

AUTHOR'S NOTE

The National Abortion Federation compiles statistics on violence committed by anti-abortion protesters in the United States and Canada. Since 1977, there have been 17 attempted murders, 383 death threats, 153 instances of assault and battery, 13 individuals wounded, 100 stink bombs, 373 break-ins, 42 bombings, 173 arsons, 91 attempted bombings or arsons, 619 bomb threats, 1630 incidents of trespassing, 1264 incidents of vandalism, 655 anthrax threats, 3 kidnappings.

Eleven people have been killed as a result of violence targeted at abortion providers: four doctors, two clinic employees, a security guard, a police officer, a clinic escort, and two others.

Anti-abortion extremists are considered a domestic terrorist threat by the U.S. Department of Justice.

Yet violence is not the only threat to abortion clinics. In the past five years, politicians have passed more than 280 laws restricting access to abortion. In 2016, the Supreme Court struck down a Texas law that would have required every abortion clinic to have a surgical suite, and doctors to have admitting privileges at a local hospital in case of complications. For many clinics, these requirements were cost prohibitive and would have forced them to close. Also, since many abortion doctors fly in to do their work, they aren't able to get admitting privileges at local hospitals. It is worth noting that less than 0.3 percent of women who have an abortion require hospitalization due to complications. In fact colonoscopies, liposuction, vasectomies . . . and childbirth—all of which are performed outside of surgical suites—have higher risks of death.

In Indiana in 2016, Mike Pence signed a law to ban abortion based on fetal disability and required providers to give information about perinatal hospice—keeping the fetus in utero until it dies of natural causes. This same law required aborted fetuses to be cremated or given a formal burial even if the mother did not wish this to happen. The law was blocked by a judge in 2017.

In Alabama, a 2014 law required a minor to get a judicial waiver for abortion from a court, where a guardian ad litem would be provided as a lawyer for the fetus. In this same law, a parent or legal guardian had the right to appeal the bypass, delaying it until the girl was past the point where she could legally abort. A federal judge struck down this law in 2017.

In Arkansas, women must be informed that it is possible to reverse the effects of the medication abortion with progesterone. Similar bills have been introduced in Arizona, Colorado, California, Indiana, Idaho, North Carolina, and Georgia. Americans United for Life, a powerful lobbyist group, made abortion pill reversal part of its model legislation for 2017. However, there are no formal studies that support the claim that a medication abortion can, indeed, be reversed.

On March 19, 2018, after this book was submitted to the publisher, Governor Phil Bryant of Mississippi signed into law the Gestational Age Act, banning abortions in Mississippi after 15 weeks of pregnancy, making it the state with the earliest abortion ban in the United States. He tweeted, "I am committed to making Mississippi the safest place in America for an unborn child." The law makes exceptions for severe fetal abnormality, but not rape or incest. Doctors who perform abortions after 15 weeks must file reports explaining why, and if they violate the law their medical licenses will be endangered. The Jackson Women's Health Organization—the "Pink House"—is the only abortion provider in Mississippi, and already cuts off abortions at 16 weeks. There is no medical or scientific reason for the change.

There's a mistaken belief that legislating barriers to pregnancy termination, or overturning *Roe v. Wade*, will end abortions. Precedent doesn't suggest this—in the 1950s up to 1.2 million unsafe abortions were performed annually. According to the Guttmacher Institute, the rate of abortions declined from 2000 through 2008, in spite of their legality. But breaking down the numbers is important. For women in poverty, abortion rates increased 18 percent. For wealthy women, abortion declined by 24 percent. That means poor women are getting pregnant when they don't want to. In fact seven out of ten women who terminated a pregnancy made less than $22,000 a year. In 2004, three-quarters of women surveyed said they had an abortion because they couldn't financially care for a child. No study to date has asked if improving socioeconomic conditions for these women would decrease the number of abortions.

For this book, I interviewed pro-life advocates. They were not religious zealots; they were men and women whose conversation I enjoyed and who were speaking from a place of deep personal conviction. All of them were appalled by acts of violence committed in the name of unborn children. They told me they wished that pro-choice advocates knew that they weren't trying to circumvent women's rights or tell women what to do with their bodies. They just wanted the women who made that legal choice to realize that life was precious, and that their decision would affect an innocent.

I also interviewed 151 women who had terminated a pregnancy. Of those women, only one regretted her decision. The majority thought about the abortion daily. When I asked them what they

wished pro-life advocates knew about them, the responses were
heartfelt. Many wanted to convey that a woman who makes this decision is not a bad person. As one woman said, "I don't need people
shaming me because of a choice that already hurt my heart to have
to make."

I met with the staff at the Pink House. I also had the privilege
to shadow Dr. Willie Parker as he performed abortions at the West
Alabama Women's Center in Tuscaloosa, Alabama (and yes, the fictional Dr. Ward bears a close resemblance to Willie). Dr. Parker is
one of the fiercest champions of women I have ever met, and he is
a devout Christian. He chose this work because of his faith—not in
spite of it. He feels that the compassion in his religion means he has
to act on behalf of others instead of judging them. It is Dr. Parker
who invented what he calls verbicaine—the conversation meant to
relax a patient during the procedure. It is not intended to trivialize
what is happening. It is meant to put the event into context. An abortion, he feels, should not be the benchmark by which a woman will
measure her entire life. I urge you to read his book, *Life's Work: A
Moral Argument for Choice*, to learn more about his journey.

In Birmingham, thanks to the generosity and grace of three patients, I observed a five-week abortion, an eight-week abortion, and
a fifteen-week abortion. The first two procedures took less than five
minutes each, and yes, I saw the products of conception, and there
was nothing that would suggest, to the naked eye, a dead baby. The
fifteen-week procedure was more complicated, and took a few minutes longer. Mixed amid the blood and tissue were tiny, recognizable
body parts.

Dr. Parker believes in transparency in his work. He understands
that a fetus is a life. He does not believe it's a person. His question comes down to the moral responsibilities we have to each other.
While pro-life protesters are protecting the rights of the fetus, who
is protecting the rights of women?

The woman who had come in to have that abortion at fifteen

weeks had three other children under the age of four. She could not afford another child without compromising the care of the ones she already had. Did coming to the clinic make her a terrible mother, or a responsible one?

I myself have not had an abortion. I always believed myself to be pro-choice. Then I got pregnant with my third child, and at seven weeks began spotting heavily. The thought of losing that pregnancy was devastating to me at that time; in my mind this was already a baby. However, had I been a college sophomore with a seven-week pregnancy, I would have sought out an abortion. Where we draw the line shifts—not just between those who are pro-life and pro-choice, but in each individual woman, depending on her current circumstances.

Laws are black and white. The lives of women are a thousand shades of gray.

So can we solve the abortion debate without legislation? Let's begin with the principle that nobody *wants* to have an abortion; that it's a last resort. If we assume that the pro-life camp wants to reduce or eliminate procedures, and that the pro-choice camp wants women to be able to make decisions about their own reproductive health, perhaps the place to start is before the pregnancy—with contraception. In the United States, in 2015 there were 57 teenage births per 1000. In Canada it was 28 per 1000. In France, 25. In Switzerland, 8. The difference is that those other countries actively promote contraception without judgment. This isn't the case in the United States, because of religious beliefs that favor procreation; however, if the endgame is to reduce abortions, promoting contraception would be the easiest solution.

If the greatest number of women choosing abortions do so because of economic issues, then this, too, is an area to consider. If pro-life advocates could prevent abortions by raising taxes and volunteering to adopt, would they? If pro-choice advocates believe women should be able to make a decision without external pressure, would they give up some of their income so that women who are financially strapped but want to continue their pregnancies can?

To that end, it's worth asking what would happen if we made social services more readily available to pregnant women. Increasing the minimum wage would give women the financial security to raise a baby, if they so choose. Government-funded daycare would eliminate the threat of losing their jobs. Universal healthcare would allow women to believe they could financially afford not just the birth of a child, but its continued existence.

There are other avenues to explore, too, that might reduce the number of women who end up having to terminate. Employers who drive away pregnant women should be penalized. Guaranteed prenatal care at no charge might encourage women to carry to term, and could be set up through a network of adoptive parents who foot the bill in return.

Honestly, I do not believe we, as a society, will ever agree on this issue. The stakes are too high, and both sides operate from places of unshakable belief. But I do think that the first step is to talk to each other—and more important, to listen. We may not see eye to eye, but we can respect each other's opinions and find the truth in them. Perhaps in those honest conversations, instead of demonizing each other, we might see each other as imperfect humans, doing our best.

—*Jodi Picoult*, March 2018

ACKNOWLEDGMENTS

There were multiple professionals in women's reproductive health and medicine who shared their expertise with me: Linda Griebsch; Julie Johnston, MD; Liz Janiak; Souci Rollins; Susan Yannow; Rebecca Thompson, MD; Margot Cullen, MD. David Toub, MD, gets a special shout-out because he was willing to Skype with me while he was ironing pants on a Saturday night, when I had a question that couldn't wait.

For showing me the other side: Paul and Erin Manghera.

For their legal brilliance: Maureen McBrien-Benjamin and Jennifer Sargent.

For helping me understand the role of the hostage negotiator: John Grassel and Frank Moran.

For teaching me how to tie a tourniquet and put in a chest tube, just in case this current career doesn't work out: Shannon Whyte, RN; Sam Provenza; Josh Mancini, MD.

Thanks to Candy Chang, who—like Bex—creates art installations themed "before I Die."

For spirited discussion, and/or for allowing me to steal pieces of their lives: Samantha van Leer, Kyle Tramonte, Abigail Baird,

Frankie Ramos, Chelsea Boyd, Steve Alspach, Ellen Sands, Barb Kline-Schoder.

For reading early drafts, back when there were still sixteen main characters: Laura Gross, Jane Picoult, Elyssa Samsel.

For the sensitivity read, spot-on suggestions, and for just being an awesome writer who lets me gripe via text about how hard this job is: Nic Stone.

For being the best in the business: Gina Centrello, Kara Welsh, Kim Hovey, Debbie Aroff, Sanyu Dillon, Rachel Kind, Denise Cronin, Scott Shannon, Matthew Schwartz, Erin Kane, Theresa Zoro, Paolo Pepe, Christine Mykityshyn, Stephanie Reddaway, Susan Corcoran, and Jennifer Hershey. I would not be nearly as willing to walk through fire if you all weren't at my side.

To the employees of the West Alabama Women's Center in Tuscaloosa, Alabama, and the Jackson Women's Health Organization in Jackson, Mississippi, and others who walk the walk: Gloria Gray, Diane Dervis, "Miss Betty," and Tara; Alesia, Mamie, Renetah, Francia, Tina, Chad, Alfreda, and Jessica.

A giant thank-you to Willie Parker, MD, who educates, inspires, and ministers to those who need it the most. I'm honored to call you a friend, and I'm awfully glad women have you in their corner.

Finally, I am grateful to the 151 women who were willing to tell me about their abortions: Joan Mogul Garrity, Jolene Stark, E. Johnson, "M," Christine Benjamin, Megan Tilley, Susan (UK), Laura Kelley, Sarah S., Leanne Garifales, Dena, Natasha Sinel, Emma, Jennifer Felix, JLR, Roberta Wasmer, Nina, Eileen, Nancy Emerson, Laura Rooney, Heather C., Jennifer Klemmetson, Alie, Amanda Clark, Heidi, Lorraine Dudley, Brooke, Shirley Vasta, Lisa Larson, Cynthia Brooks, Melissa M., Tori, Kara Clark, Sonia Sharma, Andrea Lutz, Claire, Alison M., Rae S., Megan, Melissa Stander, and the dozens who did not want to be named. It is my hope that as more stories like this are told, fewer women will have to remain anonymous.

BIBLIOGRAPHY

The following materials were useful to me in the writing of this novel:

Baird, Abigail, Christy Barrow, and Molly Richard. "Juvenile NeuroLaw: When It's Good It Is Very Good Indeed, and When It's Bad It's Horrid." *Journal of Health Care Law and Policy* 15 (2012).

Camosy, Charles C. *Beyond the Abortion Wars: A Way Forward for a New Generation*. Wm. B. Eerdmans, 2015.

Cohen, David S., and Krysten Connon. *Living in the Crosshairs: The Untold Stories of Anti-Abortion Terrorism*. Oxford University Press, 2015.

Eichenwald, Kurt. "America's Abortion Wars (and How to End Them)." *Newsweek*, December 25, 2015.

Fernbach, Philip, and Steven Sloman. "Why We Believe Obvious Untruths." Sunday Review, *New York Times*, March 3, 2017. https://www.nytimes.com/2017/03/03/opinion/sunday/why-we-believe-obvious-untruths.html.

Gilligan, Carol, and Mary Field Belenky. "A Naturalistic Study of Abortion Decisions." *New Directions for Child Development* 7 (1980).

Graham, Ruth. "A New Front in the War over Reproductive Rights: 'Abortion-Pill Reversal.' " *New York Times Magazine*, July 18, 2017. https://www.nytimes.com/2017/07/18/magazine/a-new -front-in-the-war-over-reproductive-rights.html.

Johnson, Abby. *Unplanned: The Dramatic True Story of a Former Planned Parenthood Leader's Eye-Opening Journey Across the Life Line.* Tyndale, 2010.

Knapton, Sarah. "Bright Flash of Light Marks Incredible Moment Life Begins When Sperm Meets Egg." *Telegraph*, April 26, 2016. https://www.telegraph.co.uk/science/2016/04/26/bright-flash-of -light-marks-incredible-moment-life-begins-when-s/.

Kowalski, Gary. "The Founding Fathers and Abortion in Colonial America." *American Creation* (blog), April 6, 2012. http://american creation.blogspot.com/2012/04/founding-fathers-and-abortion-in .html.

Miller, Monica Migliorino. *Abandoned: The Untold Story of the Abortion Wars.* St. Benedict Press, 2012.

Oakes, Kelly. "51 Mind-Blowing Facts About Life, the Universe, and Everything." https://www.buzzfeed.com/kellyoakes/mind -blowing-facts-about-life-the-universe-and-everything?utm_term =.om3qZdoZjz#.eb2M06802R.

Parker, Willie. *Life's Work: A Moral Argument for Choice.* Atria Books, 2017.

Paul, Maureen, et al. *Management of Unintended and Abnormal Pregnancy: Comprehensive Abortion Care.* Wiley-Blackwell, 2009.

Perrucci, Alissa C. *Decision Assessment and Counseling in Abortion Care: Philosophy and Practice*. Rowman & Littlefield, 2012.

Pollitt, Katha. "Abortion in American History." *Atlantic*, May 1997. https://www.theatlantic.com/magazine/archive/1997/05/abortion -in-american-history/376851/.

Pollitt, Katha. *Pro: Reclaiming Abortion Rights*. Picador, 2014.

Saxon, Lyle, Robert Tallant, and Edward Dreyer. *Gumbo Ya-Ya: A Collection of Louisiana Folk Tales*. Bonanza Books, 1984.

Thomson, Judith Jarvis. "A Defense of Abortion." *Philosophy and Public Affairs* 1, no. 1 (1971). http://spot.colorado.edu/~heathwoo/ Phil160,Fall02/thomson.htm.

Wicklund, Susan. *This Common Secret: My Journey as an Abortion Doctor*. PublicAffairs, 2008.

a
spark
of
light

Jodi
Picoult

A Reader's Guide

A Conversation with Jodi Picoult

Random House Reader's Circle: Your books are always very well researched. What was involved in that process for the writing of *A Spark of Light*?

Jodi Picoult: There was a lot to learn. I spoke to hostage negotiators, lawyers, ob-gyns who perform terminations, and had the opportunity to shadow an abortion provider who flies to underserved communities—like the "Pink House" in Jackson, Mississippi, and Birmingham, Alabama. I learned how to put a chest tube into a patient in an emergency-field situation and practiced in a hospital lab. I interviewed clinic owners, multiple people who are pro-life, and 151 women who had terminated pregnancies. I learned a great deal about the history of abortion in the United States, and how it was not always considered a question of morality. I also studied statistics and patterns in those who terminate. Although the number of abortions has declined overall in the United States, that's a flawed statistic. Abortion has actually declined for wealthy women, but has increased for poor women. Seven out of ten women who choose abortion make less than $22,000 per year, and 75 percent said the reason they wanted to terminate a pregnancy was because they could not financially afford to have a child. I also learned that since 2012 politicians have passed over 280 laws restricting access to abortion at the state level.

RHRC: Did your feelings about the issue of abortion evolve during the research and writing of the novel, and if so, how?

JP: To be honest, I consider myself pro-choice and always have—but had I found myself with an unwanted pregnancy, whether or not I terminated would have depended on my circumstances at the time. It's that which troubles me the most—given that an individual woman's decision about abortion may evolve in her own lifetime, depending on whether she is employed, married, in school, was raped, et cetera—how can we legislate abortion as black or white? I did come away with two revelations during my research and writing that really shook me, however. The first was in speaking to pro-life individuals, who were not the fervent religious radicals I expected, but ordinary, thoughtful folks. They wanted to impress upon me that they do not want to tell women what to do with their bodies—they simply want them to realize that in their having a choice, there is "someone else" who doesn't. The second revelation was that of the 151 women who had terminated pregnancies and spoke with me, only one had regrets . . . and yet fewer than 20 wished to be acknowledged by name in the book. They preferred to be anonymous because they were afraid of being shamed by others, or because they did not want people to know they'd had an abortion. One out of four women will have an abortion in her lifetime—yet society still makes women feel ashamed to speak their own stories out loud.

RHRC: This novel has a very unusual structure, proceeding backward through a single day. Was it simply an interesting creative challenge? Or did you choose that structure for a specific reason related to the subject matter?

JP: Since I read Charles Baxter's *First Light*, years ago, I've wanted to write a story backward. I was just looking for the right story with which to do it. A book about where life begins, and about how we conceive the ideas and beliefs we have, seemed perfect. I wanted the big reveal in *A Spark of Light* to not be what happens with the gunman, really, but what brought all these people together in the first place. I will also confess that although I was the one who willingly chose this structure, it nearly killed me. It's the hardest thing I've ever written, technically.

RHRC: You often tell your stories from multiple points of view, but the ten POVs in this one might be a record even for you! Why did you undertake that kind of challenge? And do you have a favorite among these characters?

JP: Ironically, there were about eighteen POVs initially, but my editor wanted me to winnow them down! I knew there were going to be a lot of different head spaces to inhabit in this book, and I also knew that I would be playing around with time—so I didn't want to do multiple first-person voices. Instead I chose a subjective third person, because I thought it would be easier to keep straight for both reader and writer. I loved writing Wren, and I loved writing Olive—but I have to admit, Dr. Ward is my favorite.

RHRC: No matter what their feelings on the issue of abortion, many of the characters are preoccupied with being a good parent. What do *you* think it means to be a good parent?

JP: I think a good parent is a guardian, a warrior, a comforter, a sounding board, a teacher, a learner, and a soft place to land whenever necessary. I also think a good parent is anyone who questions whether he or she is a good parent.

RHRC: Are certain books harder to write than others? How did the writing of this novel affect you?

JP: The hardest books to write are the ones that challenge me on a personal level. *Small Great Things* takes the cake for that, because it opened my eyes to my own role in racism in the United States and made me realize I had to do a better job working to dismantle it. This one gave me pause in a different way. Philosophically I believe in a woman's right to choose and make decisions over her own body. I thought I'd have to work hard to keep the balance from shifting in that direction when I was writing, so that I gave both sides equal play. But there were many times I wondered if the narrative tipped too far in the *other* direction. It took me a while to realize the reason it felt that way was because even if you believe in a woman's right to choose, there is no woman who does so lightly, or without realizing the *potential* of a human life. The gravity of the decision, and, yes, the grief of loss are too often mistaken as proof that abortion is morally wrong—when in fact they are only proof of the complex humanity of the women who have to make that decision.

RHRC: You use a Martin Luther King, Jr., quote as the epigraph for the novel. What does this quote mean to you?

JP: This book starts and ends with a gunman who, ironically, comes to murder people because (in his opinion) they murder babies. Dr. King's quote reminds us that the same extreme passion that can lead to single-minded violence might just as easily be expended in the pursuit of empathy and understanding for those who might hold beliefs different from ours.

RHRC: You've been very involved in the production of a musical called *Between the Lines*, based on a book you and your daughter,

Samantha van Leer, wrote. What was different between the artistic process behind the creation of a story in the musical-theater medium and creating a story in novel form?

JP: Imagine that you are a runner, and one day you decide you want to swim a mile every day instead. You're still getting lots of exercise, but new muscles will be sore at the end of the day. That's the difference between writing a novel and writing a libretto. You have only about 110 pages in a musical, so every word counts. Also, instead of using only dialogue and narrative to move the story forward, you often use music instead. I can't tell you how many times something we've written into the libretto of the show has been co-opted by our songwriters to use as lyrics—-and it's *so cool* when that happens, because it's a reminder that writing a show is a joint pursuit. The hardest thing about working on the musical is that when I go to write a novel, it's incredibly lonely! But I think bouncing between different types of writing is good for me and strengthens me as a writer overall. And I must like it, because now in addition to my work on *Between the Lines*, I'm co-writing the libretto of Markus Zusak's incredible novel *The Book Thief*!

Questions and Topics for Discussion

1. This novel is told in reverse, counting back in time the hours of the hostage standoff. Why do you think the author chose to structure the book this way? How does this unique structure affect your reading experience? How would your reading experience be altered if the book had been told in a more traditional chronological format?

2. The story is narrated from the points of view of ten different characters: Wren, Hugh, Bex, George, Beth, Olive, Joy, Janine, Louie, and Izzy. Why do you think the author chose to include so many different perspectives? Was there a voice that you connected to most strongly? Why? Was there any character that you had difficulty connecting to? Why do you think that was?

3. Hugh discovers that his daughter is one of the hostages in the Center after he has already begun negotiating with George. What do you think of Hugh's decision to remain on the case when he has a personal stake in it? Do you think he has a stronger ethical responsibility to his police force and the community at large, or to his family?

4. As Bex reveals to Hugh that she—behind his back—took Wren to the Center to get birth control, she wonders, "Were some betrayals kinder than others?" Discuss the different types of betrayals that appear in the book. How would you answer Bex's question? How do you define "betrayal"? Is there ever a time when betraying someone is the right thing to do?

5. Financial security is one of the issues identified as a reason why some women choose to have abortions, and it is certainly a factor in Joy's and Izzy's decisions. How have their experiences with poverty affected each of their choices? Do you think financial security should be a factor when considering abortion, and if so, how big a role should it play in one's decision?

6. We learn that Janine, a pro-life protester, has had an abortion herself. What do you think of her decision to have an abortion despite her pro-life beliefs? What do you think of her choice to commit her life to pro-life protests even after securing an abortion for herself? Do you find this behavior hypocritical or understandable?

7. Joy and Janine are often framed in parallel to each other within the book. Initially, they seem to stand on opposite sides of the pro-life/pro-choice debate. By the end, do you think they have found common ground? Do you understand where each one's beliefs are founded? Is it possible to form a connection with someone "opposite" you and still maintain a commitment to one's beliefs?

8. At one point, Rachel, the employee who escaped from the Center, accuses Allen and his fellow protesters of being responsible for the hostage-crisis situation, saying, "If people like you didn't spout the bullshit you do, people like *him* wouldn't exist." Is this a fair accusation? Is there a point at which one does *not* have the right to voice one's beliefs? If so, where should that line be drawn?

9. Louie Ward states that, as someone pro-choice, he has no problem with wanting to give rights to an unborn child, as long as it can be done without taking away the rights of the pregnant woman. Is this a viable position? Is it possible to reach common ground with this condition?

10. Much is made of the fact that current laws governing abortion rights wind up inadvertently hurting women because of the variations in the circumstances that brought them to choose termination. If one starts with the basic belief that no one wants to get an abortion, are there ways to decrease the number of terminated pregnancies that do *not* involve legislation?

11. Beth finds herself in a devastating situation in the hospital after performing her own abortion when she could not secure it by legal means, nearly dying and now facing arrest for her actions. Do you think the Mississippi abortion laws are applied fairly to Beth? Do you think her situation is unique? Could Beth have taken another course of action? Why or why not?

12. Dr. Ward questions whether there is a moral distinction between chopping down a hundred-year-old tree and stepping on an acorn. In what ways do you agree or disagree? How does this comparison inform the question of reproductive rights?

13. George thinks that he has to make Hugh understand his actions and says, "Sometimes doing the right thing . . . means doing something bad." In order to accomplish this, George shoots at Wren as he releases her, and Hugh immediately returns fire at George. Do you think Hugh's act of violence and rage toward George can be equated with George's act of violence and rage toward the Center? Why or why not? How are these actions similar? How are they different?

14. Throughout the novel, each character grapples with her or his actions and weighs them as right versus wrong. For instance, Wren goes back and forth between thinking that she is doing the right thing by seeking birth control in the way she feels most comfortable and worrying that she has actually done something wrong by deceiving her father and putting her aunt in danger. Discuss the other moral battles each character faces internally. What do they think they have done right, and what do they think they have done wrong? Do you agree with their assessments of their actions? Why or why not?

15. By the end of the book, we discover that these characters' lives are interwoven in more ways than one and that each individual has much more to his or her story than what we first see on the surface. Were you surprised by any of the interconnections that were revealed? Which twist struck you the most strongly?